THE SONGE OF IF
(THE GIFT)

THE SONGE OF IF (THE GIFT)

Pierrick Euston

M.P. Hash Publishing Company

First published 2018 by M.P. Hash Publishing Company

ISBN-13: 978-1-7328259-6-3

Library of Congress Control Number: 2018960657

Copyright © M.P. Hash Publishing Company 2018

Note to cover, title page, and quotation:
The Fell Types are digitally reproduced by Igino Marini.
www.iginomarini.com.

With love, this story is for my children and their children
and their children and their children and their children,
without whom this tale would have no meaning.

With devotion, this book is for Mihaela,
without whom these words would not exist.

With appreciation to Alexandra,
who shared her family and her chickens
with a lost and searching traveler.

With gratitude to Ioana for her generosity and care.

With memories of Holly and her poetry.

And with a feathery fancy that
Sally Hawkins will enjoy this.

Table of Contents

"Nature is afraid, when the wind rumbles,
lest the silence may leave her and something else take its place.

"The silence is gathered together tightly in the storm,
but darts up in the lightning,
flashing without thunder through the forest.

"There is a fear in the bending of the trees. It is the fear of the
creature faced with change and transformation."

Max Picard

Prologue

A Tale

There was a tale told for generations. It was a tale filled with the blue of the skies and the green of sweet buds, of the buzz of small insects and the smell of spring flowers, of the ripple of streams and the white eye of the moon as it looked from the sky with the glow of the sun. From the drying lives of elders to the blossoming spirits of children, the words were passed down like cherished, carved heirlooms hewn from a timeless slice of nature.

But that is long past. Although the story remains known by some in this village, the words rustle as brittle as a bouquet of dead leaves and emit all the fragrance of a corsage of dried flowers. For in the story now told, time hides the true message and blocks the sun's light behind too many trees in our forest of years.

Yet the message, as all messages, cannot fully forsake its tale. It lingers. It hides in the trees; it waits to be sought. Or it comes as is needed, say to children and old men and innocent creatures looking, searching, maybe not for the tale but for that something it gives. So it still comes to this peaceful village of marigolds and worry when the wind blows just so, and a lone rooster crows, and the golden sun sets through a burnt orange sky, and a full moon glows grey through a blanket of churned clouds. It arrives in the sleep then flees with the light, and though hidden from thought, it hovers in dreams.

When the tale was first told, it was a time (so it began) when a young, single tree stood by a small, simple church near a gentle, slow stream. The church, made of limestone from the ground where it stood, was but the simplest of rooms off a single-lane road. It had been built by a priest who had made this his home and had come to this spot no differently than we when we find a new home, through escape and adventure, then sorrow and chance.

By the time he arrived, the priest was tall, bent, and thin with soft cheeks, halfway through a weary, long life. Once, he had been a fine scholar, a brilliant young man, the last of a family from holy Avignon. He had travelled and learned all that was needed, philosophy and Greek, medicine and law, theology, the arts. In Rome, he found love, and he brought home his bride to live fully and warm. But that life was illusion, a future not to be. As often occurs in fantastic tales of this type, God failed in His promise (or perhaps changed His mind) and the man's life filled with promise was nothing of the sort, to be altered with the ease of a shifting soft breeze.

Taken by sickness, his young beauty died.

They say anger, then hatred, overflowed his blue eyes. He cursed the high heavens and the broken man, distraught, sank deep in despair. Then one night with a madness brought by echoes of silence, he fled from his home; with nothing and no one, except for his demons. Out in the world, he sought out his sins, his will for destruction, the end to ravage his mind and empty his soul.

For years, he did wander, from village to town to underground grotto before being left as a beggar in Toulouse where everyone knew him as the man no one knew.

Then came the nights of the ravaging storms. So fierce and relentless, that night was remembered by all who survived. The frenzy of nature questioning all. That night drove the man mad. He raised his fists to the lightning and cursed the deep thunder and marched at the wind that whipped the cold rain. Dazed and half-dead, he was found the next day, purely by chance, at the gate to a monastery beside a stone arch.

The monks took him in. They kept him alive in an old, empty smokehouse, away from the others, where in fevered, frightened rêverie he lay for anguished weeks with crazed visions and ghosts. And when he finally awoke, the brothers would say, when he opened his eyes, they pierced with belief and his innocent smile brought tears to the monks who stood and bore witness.

The man, supplicant, distraught, begged the brothers to remain. And after a decade of study, he was sent to this village, where Gascony and Languedoc merge one with the other, to spread the Lord's message and guide a new flock.

Several years passed while he built the small church. He felled every tree. He cut every stone, meticulously, they say, carving the initials of one gone on each of the blocks before he laid them in place. When the church bell was hung, the two doors were opened. Then, with shovel in hand, the priest marked a large plot with long steps to the south and then to the west. It was there he would lay his brethren to rest and, in the center, with prayer, he planted a tree.

Many years traveled past, then as occurs with all life, one day his time came and his soul was set free. And as he saw the end coming, he carved one final message for the tree to teach on. Three simple letters he cut deep to remain, and he laid there before it a stone block to explain. It was the last thing he did before his eyes slowly shut. Then, he peacefully left and was placed in the ground by the tree that he loved and left as his gift.

* * *

Yet, here, the tale does not end. It has reached no conclusion, because like all of our stories, they but serve to prelude what follows where we turn.

Yes, what a fine tree it was. Generous and sturdy, it freely shared all – its shade and its beauty – with comers and goers, either amorous or grieving. It welcomed the farmers, their wives, and the children who visited, at least, each Sunday for prayer. So, there the tree thrived, for centuries more. Through battles and wars, and marriage and death, it remained as intended by the priest for believers who relied on its strength.

But this land was not peaceful, nor was it calm. Celts, Romans, and Franks had all come. They came for its pastures, for plentiful forests, to slaughter its animals, to reap its ripe fruits, and to love its fine women. And as wave after wave of new conquerors came through, they would take or destroy whatever they chose.

The tree, in its youth, was noted for strength and thought to have powers to enchant and control. Men slashed its long limbs to fashion long bows. Its branches were snapped for magical wands. Its berries were plucked for poisons and potions. So much of its force was used for dark ways, the tree became bitter and drained by despair. It hardened to life. Its sap slowly thickened. Its needles went dry and its berries soon vanished. The strong bark, once supple, shredded and peeled. Its plentiful branches were chopped down to three. The tree, with no tears, let go of the present, dried memories and no future were all that remained.

And there the tree sat, there it did linger. For centuries more. Forgotten. Unneeded. Lifeless and useless to all who might visit. It questioned its fate and doubted its gift. It cursed its long life and its roots in the ground. It looked to the sky. It watched the moon float, the sun run its course. It saw clouds floating by and the cycle of seasons repeat evermore. It saw everything move. All creation slid by. Even the stars beyond reach, eternal and still, reawakened each night and followed their dark stellar path through an endless full void. The tree asked why life was never the same, yet here it remained. The world never was what it was, or what it became. And thus the tree wondered, if it's true that all life must changes, then why should its place remain singly the same? Why alone in the world must it always not change?

The tree remembered the priest. It cried a last tear. Then it closed itself down, in the way that trees have, and it entered a slumber where it embraced a long dream.

Still, this was no common tree. It was so filled with the ghosts of those buried beneath, they who followed its roots to find the small branches that reached up to the sky, that the tree's spirit grew strong as it slept through the years. In fact, it was said, that the tree became stronger and more resolute in dreams than its thick hardened roots could hold to the ground.

Then one day it happened. At the start of a year, back at the time when the world starts to blossom, there came a shattering storm and the tree awoke with a start. Its resolve had returned. A strength resolved to break free. The winds howled in its face and screamed at its skin and with a sudden, fierce gust, there came a crack and a shatter, and the tree was torn loose. It was no longer bound. Change returned to its nature. And it started to walk, to leave its old home, to escape its hard past, and to wander the world. It would seek a new future. It would discover its place.

With no destination, it chose to head south, toward the arc of the sun, which had given it strength through all its dark years. It crept slowly at first, as slow, they say, as a snail walking backwards, so that no one alive could see its advance.

Slowly, so slowly, it pushed its way forth. For centuries more. One blade of grass at a time, one crumble of soil. Stealthily and quiet, not a pebble was shifted as it imperceptibly moved forth. Through generations it slid from the graveyard's dead center. At last to the gate, then through two hundred full moons, it cleared the old fence. Once in the clear, it was free to move faster. Then, through patches of nettles and across a ravine, around rocks and dead stumps, it climbed up through a friendly, dense thicket, saying hellos and goodbyes to the oaks and the beech, the walnut, an ash, and it gave a special adieu to the juniper, its cousin.

For several hundred more years, it kept climbing and pushing. It was determined to break free, free of the shadows, to find a new place, to create a new home. And there at the top came the day of arrival. That indefatigable tree finally found a small spot – a spot where the sun shone all day and stars played during night. It was in a yard by a house made of stone like the church. A shed to the right and a barn straight ahead. Small voices of children, small chickens, small dogs. Small ducks, small plants, and even small cats. And there in a house, a small family of worries. The whole world was small; the tree knew it was home.

Through the lives of a dozen or so farmers, it placed itself center, as it lived long before, with other souls near. To the south, one limb faced. Its two longer arms reached back north to its home, to its birthplace, where his old priest remained.

There the tree stayed. No one knew where it started. Everyone thought it was born just right where it was.

Everyone, it's said, except for those who can see when the moon glows just so, or if the light of the sun finds a spirit of sorts, when the delicate carvings under each of its limbs willingly shows their fine letters and its message of home.

Yet that rarely happens. Few people can see. And to most who will hear it, this tale's but bare words.

Still, the tree does not mind. Disbelief cannot alter the truth that is there. This tree, you will know, shall remain as it is as much of this world as we on the ground are one with the sky. For we are of the sky when time floats in our dreams. And we live in our dreams, die with them as well, and so must this tree with its story to tell.

Chapter 1

Morning Shadows and Dawning Sun

Solitary was the moment. There was no breeze. There was no movement. The air was musty and thick as it absorbed the yellow light that snuck around the thin wooden slats of the ramshackle wall. There was only calm and peace, tranquility itself distilled to a substance that overwhelmed and protected. Marie was, she supposed, the only one to feel it. She was, to be sure, alone there to know it.

Lying still, Marie heard a grasshopper move. She recognized the clumsy, yet gentle, movements below. The sound was delicate, not a rustle precisely, more like a finger ticking, pricking, clicking the bristles of a broom, a gentle snapping of straw, a scratch of pebbles shifting. Birds called from outside. The farmer's door opened. Water dripped gently from the wall of the barn. Two cows lowed. A child called from far off.

Marie welcomed the sounds. They added to her calm and completed the sensation of place. They were familiar, comfortable, confirming. She did not know if other movements came from inside or out; she only cared that she felt safe and hidden, her head loosely swaddled within a blanket of feathers. Her breath, in smooth rhythm, spread the cloak of a warmth that came from her body and with each shallow exhale, the dampness and sweetness built, then dissipated, around her.

The sensation at that moment was not the absence of something; there was indeed an unexpected presence of nothing. Tangible and oppressive but like an unwanted friend, it insisted to be welcomed as a surprise companion. And still the warm solitude hung, hung there inside her, and when she reached to hold tight, it refused to last longer than that ungrabbable instant when the cushion of sleep yields silently and heavily to the weight of awake. Her mind reached out with a grasp, yet the dreams slipped and withdrew, as all our dreams will, faster than thoughts race, farther than wings reach. Indeed, as we all know too well, the more insistent our attempt, the more urgent do dreams ever strive to depart.

Except for the faint sound of the bell from a small village church, there was no rhythm to be marked on this early spring day, no succession of minutes to be counted out like the rows in a field of well-sown wheat. In southwestern France, on this farm, on this morning, it was but two stretches of arms and one blurry blink after an uninterrupted sleep. It was that extended span of time between the lowing of cows and a begrudged ruffle of feathers. It was, more precisely, the moment when the sun begins renewing the soft dry warmth of the rock-speckled earth.

Marie refused to move. Enrapt and alone, in her solitude she was the whole world. She was everyone. The only one. In the single place that existed. And she loved this feeling. She curled in her bed, pulled her feet in more firmly, and turned her head gently to rest her neck. Aware of her body, she ignored it, focusing instead on the pictures that remained in her head. Although her dreams were now gone, random impressions remained, echoes of lost sounds, floating memories of friends, swaths of vague colors, undulations of clouds, affirming smiles of loved family, chirpy shrieks of quick laughter – each warm image overlapping the next, yet set on a vague landscape of a melancholy darkness that permeated all. Without consciousness' grasp, these emotions and sights flowed, wildly mingled into a swirling knot that twisted and reshaped themselves by tumbling about and melding together.

But it did not last long. It would never last long.

Is it fair to curse interruption when it shatters our solitude from the world outside? When it rudely intrudes on the stillness within? When it sends our calm fleeing? Or does solitude surrender when the mind wanders too far, and the outside world is beckoned? Whether it was the soft movements of creatures awakening, or the snaps and popping of wooden slats expanding in the light and the warmth of a rising new sun, Marie's meandering journey abruptly reached an end, her distant thoughts broken as she was returned to the present. Why, she wondered, could she not make these moments last longer? Why, she lamented, must they end always too soon? Yes, that's the sneaky thing about interruptions, she decided. They never exist until we notice them.

With eyes still ablurry and a mind still awander, Marie saw a distorted, faint shadow across the far wall suddenly move. It caught her, startled. She stared at it. She lifted her head. "Oh," she thought, and she shrank deeper in her nest. Somehow the light grey form seemed more real than the body lying with her. She raised her head slightly and saw the patch of blocked light again move. "I'm over there," she reflected. "Yet, here I am still."

Marie felt cheated that her day on the farm had returned. It was not welcome. It was not flowing. It did not have the colors she wanted. She tried to recapture her slumber and demand the return of her dreams, at once so shuddersome yet so sweetly alluring. But dreams cannot be ordered to return after they tuck themselves away. They must come on their own and in their own way.

She again heard the church bell ring from somewhere down the hill and she wondered how long she had been lying there, living in her head, in her "thinking box," as she called it. She was thankful for that box – to whomever, to whatever – as it was the only vibrant path she traversed in her day.

Marie raised her head fully, arched her back, and leaned to her side. It was time to rise, to flutter, to give a little stretch, and to leap from her bed. Yet her weariness was awake and, as occurred every morning, it turned her weightless drifting heavy from the feathery floating of memories to the familiar burden of now. But the farmer had come out, so she must hurry to the yard before the other birds swooped from the sky or flitted from rafters to peck at her food

Chapter 2

Marie Meets Day and Says Bonjour

Outside her coop, shadows shared the yard with the sunlight warming the ground. The two, the radiant sun and the chalky earth, were so different, Marie thought, so opposite in their place. Yet she marveled at how they could not resist each other. These two, pressing for attention in such competing ways, could not live apart, could not thrive alone, and would be without purpose if they had not each other to touch on this farm.

Walking across the yard, Marie blinked twice and sneezed once as she glanced up at the rising sun just under the arch. Her food was by the stairs. The farmer liked it this way. It was his routine. To avoid the damp grass and assorted sharp rocks, he fed Marie from a flat, green plastic bucket just outside his front door, down the front steps to his right. It was not a typical way for farmers to feed chickens, but he found no reason for shoes or to take the few steps out into the yard when the cat and the dog were fed precisely the same way at precisely the same time on the opposite side of the very same steps.

Finished with breakfast, as much from routine as from interest, Marie wandered back toward her house, past the old tree that languished in the center of the yard. She stretched her wings in the damp morning air. Nothing had changed. She saw the tall wire fence off to her right, the trees still without leaves and the down-slope beyond. She looked at the small stone shed to the right of her house and turning to her left, followed her gaze along her front door until it reached the giant barn that lurked overhead. Behind her was the driveway on which stood the lopsided car, near the skeletal tractor, and behind them the archway through which one could walk out into an ocean of fields.

This was her view every morning. Indeed, her days, like those of most lonely chickens, varied only, if at all, by the fleeting mood of the weather. It might rain overnight. Then the mornings provided a welcome display of puddles around which she might dance and discover some momentary joy in a playfulness she worked somewhat hard to create. She might splash the edge with one foot and jump backward from the spray. She might pick up a small pebble and toss it to the brown center to see it hit and force ripples in all directions. She might coax an ant toward the water by flicking it gently, but repeatedly, and then kick a little splash in its general direction – not with spiteful or aggression, but in the fun naughty manner of a laughing older sister.

Her favorite, of course, was to wait for the cat. Fun with ants was a solitary fun. It's hard to get much reaction. But with the cat, that was a shared type of fun, even if Marie was alone in being the one who enjoyed it. Besides, the cat was too old and disinterested to chase Marie, so what was the harm in attempting to engage him? "Now I splash, and you get wet, how's that for a little tete-a-tete?" She knew the rhyme was not very clever, but she enjoyed it, and she called it out each time the cat walked on after shaking its head. And let's not forget, if it rained hard enough at night, then worms would appear and how Marie "played" with worms, well, we need not describe. After all, this was a French farm where all manner of creatures is inspected, dissected, prepared and devoured. And while we have no need for the details, be assured the worms did not like this, and though Marie would apologize, she found it too hard to resist.

But most days were dry and sometimes they were hot. Then, Marie found shuddering patches of shade and sat among the clumps of green and brown grass with the speckles around her of white chipped stones. She would find whatever place she preferred and, after scratching the ground for the coolness beneath, she would sit for a moment and scrape her wings left and then right, sensing the wordless connection that can exist even between a lonesome small hen and the dry dusty earth. It seemed to her at those moments that the ground, in fact, was not as foreign or as different as it might appear to most others but was simply another type of friend to be acknowledged and welcomed and invited to sit down. These specks of clay and rock, she concluded, were no different than her except they didn't run, didn't shout, and didn't open their eyes. They didn't laugh, or dance, or eat, or cry, or even splash in puddles. And they didn't have feathers. That, of course, was too obvious to mention. But except for those few things, she reasoned, they were rather similar to chickens and she liked that. She liked the ground and believed that it, too, probably had a story to tell and a past to forget.

Mostly, then, Marie enjoyed the variety and the excitement when she might wake up to find the day was not like the last. Although she had no favorite, cold and windy were never welcome. But there was no worry of that today. Today was bright and sunny, clear and warm, with not the slightest of breezes falling on her feathers. It was a day almost without description – no clouds, no wind, no ominous pressure, no scent, no noise, nothing but what's common on an early spring day.

She sat down and stared at the farmer's huge house, its western-most wall directly opposite her own. With the sun's rays beginning to climb, the white carved stones looked yellow and grey at this time of day. They were beautiful, Marie thought, like the rind of old cheese that is caked with lines and pockmarked with age. It was a perfect surface because it was a wall that looked as walls were meant to look. She thought now how her mind played sometimes and imagined the walls were watching her, too. Some days, she thanked them for their silent protection. Other times, they only stared, mocking her for a puniness and insignificance that she herself could feel. Or sometimes she would walk near them and imagine her terror if they began to lean over and start to fall down. She would hurriedly stop and force a new thought, switching the roles that played in the scene. She would let out a laugh and tease them by running and jumping far out of reach.

"See?" She would smile and then giggle back at them. "I am too fast, and I can just run, and you must just sit there, and watch me have fun."

Marie enjoyed making herself laugh. She enjoyed talking to the walls. Even cold hard things have a spirit, she thought, like the dried twigs that were a tree and the bits of small string that moved with the wind. Now, don't jump to conclusions. Marie was not silly, no sillier than most. She had merely discovered, like us, the more burdensome the thoughts, the more we cling to illusion. When lost in the woods, we imagine mystery and courage. When stuck in routine, we conjure adventure. We all, in our way, seek a playground for refuge, construct meaning from pattern, and though a simple, young hen, Marie was no different.

At this moment, however, Marie stopped her games. Seated on a dry mound of dirt, she wiggled her bottom to smooth out the surface and leaned to one side as she scratched out a pebble from under her right tail feathers. She sat there for a time. For a long time, it seemed. In fact, a very long time. Just how long is that? Well, it is said, as we know, that dogs live a full year for each of our seven. If that is true, then chickens, we suspect, repose for a minute for each of our thirty. And after what seemed to be hours, Marie finally stood up.

Without destination, Marie walked the inside edge of the yard. The grass grew to the stones of the farmer's old house where it always stood tall and seeded in summer. Now the drooping grey and brown remnants were knotted and wet and had that putrid sweat of decay as its tops merged and fell over. She nodded as she passed. Then at the house's far end, away from the driveway, she came to what little remained of an old wire fence that ran the width of the yard and halted its progress at the side of the shed. While fence was its name, it clearly no longer had a mission. There were sections collapsed. There were holes at its base. It fenced neither anything in nor kept anything out. Marie did not like that it no longer tried, and she turned left at its end, back toward her coop, along the front wall of the shed where the flowers and weeds fought for their small patch of the sun. As she walked farther on with the tree asleep to her left, she finally came to the door of her coop, which was nestled between the short walls of the shed and the soaring stones of the barn that towered above. She looked at the coop. The weathered white paint peeled in long thin strips off the weather-worn wall and around her front door, which was riddled with scratches and a random pattern of dents.

She continued her walk to the barn. Milk cows stood lowing, eating, and doing other things that cows do while they stand. As a child, Marie would wander in and visit. But she had stopped long ago. It was a sad barn really, with the cows struggling to stretch their necks farther than the chains would allow. Marie understood the cows had to eat and the farmer's son needed their milk. She knew the son was busy and could not chase the cows every day through the fields. The old farmer was not spry enough to help his son with the business. But still, Marie did not like the look on the cows' faces, or their tone of voice, as they were shackled indoors. She did not like to think that other animals, however unpleasant they might be, should live in such ways. She might walk past the open doors, but she never went in. Besides, the cows were not friendly as most unhappy things are not. So she preferred to avoid them and turned back to her yard.

That was the extent of Marie's daylong ventures. These were the boundaries of her making. The farmer had no gates. He built no restrictions. But for Marie it did not matter. She had no desire to explore. Knowing she could wander, for her, was enough. She did not have desire to walk out some unplanned distance or pass through the arched entrance out toward the fields, or even hop through the fence, to find some new freedom beyond. Her thinking box assured it. Walking thirty-eight steps beyond the edge of the yard would not change how she lived; walking thirty-eight thousand would change it too much. No, Marie was content to find her own small adventures through her own small steps in her own small yard and to create her own broad journeys without ever slipping out much past the long shadows of the walls.

Now, pacing slowly from the barn to the center of the yard, Marie neared the old tree and suddenly stopped. She spun herself around, leapt forward, and dashed to her left. With no warning, she charged at the crocus and daffodils struggling to thrive at the base of the shed. Reaching the edge of the grass in seven quick steps (she always counted), she stopped and pushed her beak within an inch of their leaves. "En garde!" she shouted, and she tilted her head. "You weren't expecting me, were you? Ha! I could have eaten you if I wanted!" she barked in her most menacing voice. She gave them a stare and kept her eyes wide open. Certainly, there's no doubt, that if plants had eyes, or ears, or arms, these poor little things would have jumped from the ground, thrown back their branches, and shrieked with surprise. "Parbleu!" they would have cried, and Marie would have won. But none of that happened except in Marie's imagination. She would now wait a few more days before she did this again. She knew if she did it too soon, they might be expecting it.

Marie continued her walk and felt a little bit lighter. She lifted her head and bowed it forward as she stepped. At that moment, she was regal, commanding the yard as lady of the coop. Playing the queen always made her feel pretty. Indeed, for Marie, feeling pretty was a game. It was as good as any other. It had nothing to do with how she appeared. The fact was, she did not know her appearance. Few chickens do. Marie tried only rarely to catch a glimpse of herself. At best, she saw a distorted blur and a jumble of pale colors in a shimmering puddle, or an odd reflection in a car's rusty hubcap, or a translucent round figure in front of a window that the farmer had removed and placed temporarily on the ground leaning back. Mostly, however, she gave it no thought and did not much care, because, it is true, we can covet from afar, but not truly miss, what we never possessed.

It was, in fact, a shame at this moment that more chickens don't have mirrors. With her sense of heaviness gone, and with a day warm and bright, Marie did indeed look radiant in this afternoon light. She was a thin hen, to be sure, not plump nor made round like the others you see. What few curves and small bumps she had were defined by her frame, not by the grain and the scraps that the farmer dished out. Yes, her legs were too thin, and her wings half the right breadth. But her body was perfectly proportioned for a hen who was skinny.

Despite her striking appearance, few people noticed. Hens rarely get studied the way they deserve. It takes more than a lover of beauty to notice all things beautiful, and if one had bothered to stop, they might have noticed that Marie had a face that was classic and strangely fluid in proportion. She possessed the bold and supple curve of a wildly strong nose, and a noble softness in her cheeks that sat in perfect symmetry. Her bearing recalled centuries of France as if she were descended from hens who sat gently on the lap of an old peasant woman shrouded in long woolen shawl, both hen and the shrew staring ahead as a Renaissance master painted his canvas. Like any good model, Marie's gentle mouth and unpresumptuous gaze could indeed be beguiling. A tilt of her head could bring a slight smile. Her quick eyes, bright and lively, could bewitch the right viewer with a spirit and playfulness that shared itself unselfishly. Yet, if captured in a moment of quietude and reflection, Marie's look was a vulnerable one, unwittingly displaying a depth of sadness and doubt that was irresistible to a gentle heart, revealed in its silence as if echoed from darkness and bounced back from a dry well.

But of course, there are so few admirers who see such things in this world. Marie was just a chicken, and who has the sight to notice the laughs, games, and tears of a small farmyard hen?

* * *

Never too early, evening arrived. The days, drenched with time, continued to drip forward. Marie had managed to pass through more lonely hours. She had sat in the sun and had lain in the shade and had drunk from the bucket and had scratched at the ground. She had scampered around the limping black dog and had chased yellow butterflies and had played all her games. She had spent untallied hours rummaging in her thinking box visiting some chickens she knew in her past, talking and laughing in ways that never happened. And for no reason at all, she had looked off to her left then to her right and then up and then down and had repeated this over and over as quickly as possible.

She also had spun herself around as she did as a child playing dervish with her friends to get dizzy and tumble. She had rubbed her wings and had shaken her head and then she ran and hopped and paced and walked in circles very slowly. She had sat for hours, on and off, under the quiet, old tree and looking up, had imagined herself jumping among the three branches. And every once in a while, but not very often, she had remembered the faces of those she still loved and had wished they were here to kiss her once more.

Now shadow was flowing out over the yard and darkness was flooding high up the stone walls, slowly rising to the top where rotting wood joists held up the thin clay bricks of the house's red roof. Marie stood and walked toward her coop. As she neared the entrance, the same emotions swam through her that were there each night. It was shelter, her home, but also a closet of memories she wished would stay shut.

She climbed up to her nest, her body heavy and slow. These were the most difficult moments – moments of tiredness when her thoughts would wind slowly along the way of their choosing and seek out places she did not want to go. Old friends or lost family would appear uninvited and let themselves in. She welcomed them with a smile but with the heavy black knowledge that they were not truly there and no matter if they were, they would leave again soon, certainly by sunrise.

Going to bed alone, then, was what she knew every night. Her head, filled with the pleasant sounds and games of the day, helped ease the battle of missing friends and other longings she did not want to accept. She curled herself in, pushed from side to side to smooth out the straw, and rested her head on her upper right wing. That is how she slept. She avoided perching up high, instead preferring a nest, a nest like the one where her mother would be.

With the slight rustle of movement outside and the ting and cling of the farmer eating in his kitchen, she let the visions of the day cascade and romp through diminishing flashes of her hours all alone. She closed her eyes and searched through her past. She tried to envision a few happy moments, perhaps walking the warm yard, and imagine her movements in time that was real. She wondered if she could see herself move at the very same pace, across an identical span, in both space and duration, as actually took place earlier that day. Had she scampered through the grass at the same speed that occurred now in her mind? Or had she slowed her imagination too far and it was taking too long? Of course, memory condenses to make room for the now. And if we slow it too much, we can never move forward. To untangle and repeat it, true moment by moment, is the challenge that confronts us as we struggle with days gone. Would she ever know again the precise speed of past times? Oh how, she wondered, to put back together the duration of her life so that its moments played like a tune with the discordant notes all removed. And with her last thought of the day, as with all her long days, she wished once again not to dream of the past. To wake clear and light without the repeated morning sadness of vanishing friends, quieted laughs, lost hazy days, and the missing warmth of boisterous joys. That was her wish.

And just so, or thereabouts, Marie existed in her daily life. It was her silent time of hours, she would later reflect. A time that both concluded and ended after one more long day. It would be a day like none other. A day to be welcomed. A day to be feared. A day in her future she would never regret.

Chapter 3

Clock and Chores Greet the Old Farmer

The old farmer awoke with the sun before six. He lifted his head slightly and looked at the grandfather clock standing firm along the wall past the foot of the bed. Its face stared with a ticking, matter-of-fact, bloodless gaze. Like a sentinel it watched, presenting through the gloaming the passage of time, its one arm swinging left then right, left then right, left then right, then left once again. The farmer's body lay straight. Face up, he had disturbed the blanket not a bit. He barely moved when he slept. His arms by his side, his head on the mattress, he had snored and coughed his way through another night with a light but uninterrupted sleep.

The windows bedroom looking south, over the driveway between the arch and the barn, were his daily alerts that morning had come. As he glanced outside, he could, if he chose, recollect the day that was yet to begin as if he had lived it already. His routine was the same, not out of choice, but because there was no choosing. He would rise, dress, breakfast, walk, direct himself to some created task and glide himself through many isolated hours. He had lived this for years. Nothing was new. And the windows staring brightly and the ticking in the silence reminded him each morning he lived there alone.

Slowly, the old farmer leaned onto his left side and crawled his legs off the bed. Sitting, he stopped for a moment and looked back again out the window behind him. The cows lowed, birds chirped, and, being as it was, on or about Easter, church bell rang not far off. The clouds were still, and the air was heavy. The calm of the morning carried no message of change or alarm.

The farmer rose with the unsteady balance of lingering sleep, dressed mechanically, made his toilet satisfactorily, and walked to the kitchen. As he entered, he turned to his right, scooped a bowlful of food, a cupful of feed, and lifted the bucket of yesterday's leftovers and carried them carefully out to the front. Each was set down in its place by the steps and the first chore was done. Animals were fed.

In the kitchen, the farmer pulled opened a deep, heavy drawer from under the head of a large, brown, flat wooden table. With three strong strokes, he cut the bread against the top of the drawer, adding to decades of scars from this everyday sawing. Within a cupboard of abundance, he pulled down a jarred preserve, left by his wife, into which he scooped a small spoon then roughly scraped the contents onto the bread. A glass of cold water, several red grapes, a large wedge of cheese and an overripe plum concluded his breakfast.

With the plate in the sink and his glass on the counter, he looked to his right and through the closed window. The northern sky had yet to lose the azure of night. The trees started to show the beginnings of leaves and the creek down below could be seen running full. That was a good sign as water for the well was often valued as more precious than time.

The old village church, seated down the small hill, rang its bell once again. It was unusual to hear. The church, sparsely used if not nearly forgotten, had little occasion to celebrate its presence when not the final day of the week, and it not being Sunday, the bell sang in a way that sounded out of practice. But such things happen when Easter arrives, and the priest is new. A call to his flock, like a rooster to sheep.

The day was awake. Dew still clung, birds finished their song and shadows warmed. By the door, the farmer found his boots and tugged them on. He turned left down the stairs, headed out through the arch, along the stone driveway then into the grass, out toward the field. He would inspect any damage the sanglier might have caused to the new, planted corn.

The daily routine seldom changed. There was little reason for that. The cows were there, the dog was there, the fields were there, the birds, rabbits, ducks and skinny hen were there. If needs existed beyond the farm, he would consider them later. Besides, there were few challenges he desired nor many new jobs he could endure, not out of weakness, just an indifference.

Frailty, he was grateful, continued to spare him a visit. His health was as strong as might be expected at his advanced years with the toil, weather and hardship he endured. A man does not farm for his life, stay in reasonable health, and maintain his wits without accruing a storehouse of strength that pays its dividends well beyond those of a comparable man who sits in the city. His neighbors, however, such as there were, could be forgiven to underestimate this fact.

The farmer appeared more brittle than he was – both in physical as well as social demeanor. His thin, lanky body, medium height, slightly stooped, with shoulders slanted to one side, gave the suggestion of feebleness, as if he might unexpectedly toddle over. Looking more closely, or rather, more astutely, an observer found less reason for concern. Although tottering slightly, he never lost his balance. His gait was sure, if slow, and his arms had a strength and a will as deeply set as his eyes. Most undeniable, though, was what one could see in his hands, for some people's lives are disclosed nowhere as clearly as there. His fingers retained the confidence that the rest of his body seemed to lack, as if his whole of self-worth had migrated to his hands which achieved, which had made, through a tireless pursuit, the breadth of his life. It is said that eyes are the window to the soul. If true, then hands are surely the gates to how the soul lives.

Then again, with the farmer, those gates were usually tucked into pants pockets, so others, no matter how artistically minded, were forced to revert their gaze straight back to his face. And it was there an observer might find a long story.

With soft grey eyes and a strong crooked nose, in his avian glance there was the history of France. He had a smile of ailing teeth, high pronounced cheekbones, hollow cheeks beneath, and a narrow jaw that still delicately pointed. His thinning grey hair, always slightly disheveled, swept straight back over old lengthened ears. Tanned skin on his face, his neck and his hands contrasted with the white with blue streaks that defined the rest of his body, like grass under cover when it loses its green. Indeed, so much did this man look part of his landscape that he could walk through a crowd and be noticed as little as a stalk in his field. The one single impression, if in fact one was left, was that here was a man who belonged where he was.

To those relatively few who had made his acquaintance, it must be said, there was one other thing that was unmistakably true. It defined him to others and it never failed to impress. The farmer was quiet. Not that he whispered in hushed tones. No. The farmer was quiet in a manner few people are. The farmer rarely spoke. Not to his neighbors, not to those strangers, not even to family. He would spend hours, in fact days, not saying a word. On the farm, it was true, there was no one to talk to. But in a welcoming crowd, he would smile his response with a nod of his head. If forced to emit some kind of sound, he could muster a "yes" or just as often a "no," or find the briefest three words to supply a full answer. "It seemed best," he would say as to why he chose one thing. "It will rain." "This will pass." "Yes, it's hot." These were his opinions no matter the weather. "How are you?" "I am well." "If you please" Those were his answers. The collection seemed endless of three-word expressions.

Of course, it goes without saying, a man who speaks little shows just as much in expression. No arms raised in excitement. No hands sweeping the air. No clenched fist and a jab. No taps on the head or slaps on the knee. A handshake was fine but not a squeeze of the arm. And if kissed on both cheeks, he stood harmlessly still.

So little did he offer, in word or in look, it was a puzzle to say if he was shy or only quiet, like deciding if the night sky is full black or just a deep, dark blue with all color removed. The answer to both mattered the same. Then again, shy people often belie their smile with a glint of fear when presented with another. That was not the case with the farmer. No. He was but silentious, reserved, unaccustomed and unwilling to show emotion to the point of absolute avoidance, even in accepting an embrace or an unstoppable touch, not just from neighbors, but also from family. He was not unkind. He could even be charming when, or if, he desired. And generous. Yes, let it be clear. He was abundantly generous, offering his reticence to everyone he met. He was decidedly unselfish in this one regard. The farmer was, in fact, a man who shared with everyone his essential desire to remain in himself.

Chapter 4

Farm of Fields, Sanglier, and Remnants of Family

C hallenged with direction, thoughts tend to flow straight. But define a path well and the more a mind wanders. So it was that on this morning the farmer strolled at a steady pace and followed the path that wound around the edge of the neatly sown field and separated the ordered rows from the irredeemable rocks, spiky bushes, dead trees, and a ditch.

The timeless path was plotted as most paths are plotted, without forethought, through nature, created by man circumventing the fertile while avoiding the thorns. Shorn from wilderness by centuries of feet, hooves and carts, it maintained its presence by maintaining utility. There had been no plan for its creation; it was necessarily there. A few hundred yards on, the trail led to the right, all the way snaking between the now ankle-high corn and a gaping wall of trees down the hill to the left. Soft green tops of the new spring grass bounced from his shins and hindered the glide of his steps. It already needed cutting. He must tell his son it was a chore worth completing.

The old farmer's goal was that of most days. The destination did not matter. There was no true aim, just the pursuit to go someplace, anyplace, as something to do. He had chosen today to inspect if sanglier trampled through the southern field overnight. Sometime earlier, between his breakfast and his boots, this question was important. There was little, if anything, he might do in response. They could destroy the whole field overnight or carve out giant boar silhouettes. They were too difficult to find when searched for during day and he had no intention of hunting by night. But the walk awarded the morning a goal until lunch.

Following the southern edge of the field, he continued his clockwise walk along the bordering trees. The thick, pleasant smell of rotting old pine and decaying, fallen leaves mingled with the sweet, heavy scent of a vigorous new grass and damp, warm buds. Explain it as geosmin, petrichor, low molecular weight volatile compounds, the name is unimportant. It's the result that's unmistakable. It is grass, earth, flowers, rain. It is life, death, decay, birth. It is the world. And it is the aroma of time. Along this path, the fragrance to the left and the scent to the right let one indulge alternately in the luscious interplay between the neglected and the wild and the cultivation of the fresh. It changed every day and had been the same forever.

Halfway around the field and two steps to his right, there were the tracks: foot-wide paths where the nocturnal boars had romped through the night and entered the forest. He kneeled to inspect. There were about nine of them, he concluded, most of them small. He wondered if the brood's father remained with them. It was early in the year, about the time when the male leaves the group and heads out alone. That is the way nature works, with some, he knew, if nature's whispers and sighs were overly strong. The farmer shrugged, whether or not the boar father was there was information that had little use, the answer to a question that sprouts from nothing and withers, once answered, back to its home. He took in a deep breath and looked to his left, his eyes following the trampled path deep into the forest. He had played there as a boy, not often as there were too many chores, but enough to have had dreams of forested adventure. Forging new paths among the juniper, walnut, wild cherry and beech. Aiming sticks at invisible invaders. Hunting girolles as if mining for gold.

The farmer paused for a moment. It all had happened faster than expected. He had found the tracks with no trouble and with that hollow twinge of success that accompanies achievements with no second purpose, he began walking again. Everywhere he looked was the oppressive, but welcome, presence of all that he was. The land. His land. And more important always, the land of his parents, and the many parents before. So many parents. There was no record of the land before their arrival. For all that was known, they had been there forever. And in that presence, they forged an alloy of flesh and of soil, a mixture that lived in a slow state of decay yet embraced the renewing and dying each year. To move is illusion, all the years seemed to say. Yet the moments this day, with its green buds showing and spring flowers abloom, again gave hope and shouted how nothing stays firm.

The old farmer reached the far turn at the end of this field and looked up to his right, onto a small rocky rise. An expanse with small trees and flat, hardscrabble land. It was his daughter's field, the one he bequeathed her after she left. It was but a small piece of farm, with too many rocks and not enough soil. It could not be tilled, but like land anywhere, it too had its value. While it did not seek to give birth, life sought to find it. Breaking through were persimmon and fig. Watercress in spring. Dandelions. Purslain. The occasional black truffle. Wild asparagus at the edges where it twirled around bushes. The land existed, and like all land, he thought, that was enough to be precious. The invisible steps of uncountable forefathers were what then, for him, raised it up near the sacred.

This joy he felt for the land that he owned could not, however, overcome the fact that his daughter's land was a field of silent sadness. The old farmer stood and again saw her before him, standing in the field, rising like a stray sunflower whose seed was delivered by a purposeful wind. He saw his girl as a child. Her saw her fully grown, standing and smiling, the sun's yellow glow surrounding her delicate straight frame. His vision of her fluctuated between the small girl she was and the grown girl of now. She had moved years ago, overcome, he knew, by the incessant pace of too-static days and the singular horizon of its slow-motion life. She left to absolve herself of what the haunting needs of unhappiness told her would disappear if only she left. Whether it's borne of the rolling fields around us or the waves of discontent within us, we are enticed from hollow boredom by the alluring narcotic of escape. How easy it would be if only we could travel without ourselves as companion.

The farmer had once lived the same struggle. But with each season passing, his internal landscape, his fields of the future, grew more and more barren. There is no rotation of crops when we are both the seed and the field. New plantings still come but the harvest grows small. It happens to all. The daughter must learn. She was seeking her place; she was cutting her way. And like any father (no matter how close, they all watch from afar), he worried where it led her and when she would stop.

It was different for his other children. They were now men with separate lessons to learn. They had children and they struggled with the pressure of wives and the questions of family that invariably come. Charged by society to force a path forward, they pretended, of course, they had not become lost. Where they were headed, they could not have said. But they were convinced, at least, they went the right way. The old farmer had no favorites so to each had been promised his own plot of land by which they equally shared what he had of the past.

His daughter, however, was the youngest and so, it is never fair but most often true, she had the gentlest and most special place in his heart. He thought she was strong like her mother, yet open to the damage life invariably brings. With vulnerability comes radiance and his daughter, he believed, was made a beautiful woman as much by weakness as by strength. The way her hands turned upward whenever she smiled, and her voice would lower just after her eyes. How quickly tears came whether in joy or in sadness. These, to him, were traits of his wife, and reflexively caused him to worry and doubt. It was true that his daughter shared much with his wife. But it was his own reflection that he most failed to see. We are but a canvas half-hidden when we are the portrait, preferring to study the part that we know, avoiding the unknown of ourselves we do not. Yet under any distortion remains the true object. So the old farmer's deepest worries arose from those loves his daughter shared with him well.

With the call of a crow, the old farmer's attention came back to this field of untillable land. The land was not created to be worked. But no matter. It was given as reminder that no matter her rejection, a part of her remained, irrevocably, irredeemably, here, wherever she went. This land, which fed her and generations before, provided the grace that made her life possible. We create for children only their bodies, he considered, but eternal land will forever feed souls. Someday she will see. She might walk through the field and see the strangest of clouds float by. Or sit in her bed and hear a lonely crow caw. Or be stuck by spring nettles and be stung for a moment all the way back. At some time in the future, he knew she would know. He was pleased with his gift. To those who had heard, it appeared she was punished. Land of no value was the dessert she deserved. But just the opposite was true. It was all that he had he knew never would change. It was born to be fallow and would always lie fallow. That was the gift he hoped she might open.

The old farmer looked up the rise to his right. With hands in his pockets and an upraised chin, he moved his head slowly and looked from his left to his right. The sun climbed high and he stood nearly an hour, seeing the birds and watching the land. The plants were healthy and the white limestone rocks were sprinkled about and shone across the hill. The air was still, and the smell was strong. He loved this land, the land of his family, the land of his ancestors, the land of past kings and the grave of past battles. He saw as a child the way he imagined the prehistoric caves, the bison, the reindeer, the grottos that are carved by underwater rivers, the great oak forests home to sanglier, the waves of visitors and conquerors – Iberians, Celts, Romans, Arabs, Franks, Normans. Christians, Charlemagne. All the names, their presence, the battles, the bloodshed, the armies, the peaceful lives of those who farmed, those who gave birth, all those who engendered generations to come, the rapid succession of centuries measured no more than by grandfather to grandson, repeated over and over, and it all added up, one after another, and it all led to him – and he to his children. Here he was, an intermediary between all that had passed and all who would come, all who would move this great continuum on, into the future with an eternity of harvests.

At the top of the hill, an old gristmill still sat. He saw the small valley fall down to the left, the woods, the fields, the fences, and the house of a neighbor. He shifted his weight and pulled his hands from his pockets. Men who are wealthy in years recount their life as a rich man his money. So as the old farmer collected his days, the thousands melted to one and the singles were either forgotten or lost. From his first decade of life he saw himself running free as a boy, the next decades or so came his father in his hat and soldiers walking past, then the rust-red tractors, the contrast of winter, a partnership of sons, then babies, their cries, and the kitchen with family. He saw his mother, his father. He saw them as they looked when he was a boy and he saw them as they looked before they had died. They looked old in each image, yet they were younger than he as he was standing there now.

All it came and disappeared in rapid succession. The images were familiar, recalled and presented as if selected repeatedly from a small photo album. With straight arms dangling and his hands loosely clasped, his left thumb rubbed against the right. Over and over, without knowing or thinking, he marked a rhythm with each stroke. His left thumb, then right. Left thumb, then right. Left thumb, then right. He remembered himself, traced his sequence of years, and wondered how he came here, standing by himself, facing the world as he was as a child.

A tractor started and interrupted his trance. He had had no intention of moving and would have stayed there visiting had his concentration not been broken. The outside world, and with it the present, returned with a sad smile. He turned to walk home.

He chose the field's northern edge. It was the shortest way home and he approached the stone arch in less than an hour. There stood the box tree and linden tree, framing the arch. The box tree sat left, a great beast of wood, indeterminably old, rose and dominated its stretch of stone wall. A statement of nature, full of old life and wise vigor. And there was the linden. Ah, the linden was there. Planted

decades before, it caused windows to open for the true scent of home.
A gentle yellow in spring and green until fall, its dried flowers warmed
the year round and soothed late at night. Resolute in their place in
front of the wall, the two guarded and spoke of the life in the yard.

The farmer walked between them and through the front arch. As
he neared the house's front steps, he saw something move quickly to
his left. A flash, a blur of color and motion. He stepped past the stairs
and continued straight on. At the side of the house, he peered to his
right. Marie was standing at the edge of the grass, staring closely at the
young marigolds that grew with the weeds along the base of the shed.
She did not move. Her head tilted an inch left, she moved her beak
and clucked a few times, and walked slowly away. Marie turned around
again, looked back at the flowers, held still, and clucked some more.
Then, she slowly walked over and sat with her back to the motionless
tree. She flapped her right wing and sat stiffly and still against the bare
wood.

The farmer watched a moment. "That's an odd one," he thought,
before turning back to the stairs. Inside the front door, he pulled off
his boots, went to the kitchen for lunch, then headed to his room for
his two-hour nap.

* * *

That afternoon was typical. The old farmer walked the barn, fed
his animals, checked their water, waited for mail, rummaged through
piles, sought out more tasks, and rearranged objects that had nothing
in common. Then just so with chickens, and sooner than for children,
evening came for the farmer as well. The sky began to darken and
cradled the sun just above the horizon.

The farmer pulled down a heavy iron skillet and placed it on the
stove to reheat his dinner from the previous night. He stepped to the
sink and found a small water glass from among the clean dishes. The
wine was on the table and he filled his glass two-thirds of the way.
After cutting the bread and filling his plate, he sat down to eat. All was
quiet but for the crying of cows and the thrumming of crickets. The

dog was heard circling then lying in the driveway beyond the front door. The farmer felt the air turning heavy. He thought of his walk. He thought of the farm. He thought of his daughter.

With dinner finished, the church bell again rang. He saw the old petre, the one who said mass at the end of the war. He saw the candles, the robe, and smelled frankincense burning. He stretched out his legs and the old farmer was there, as much if not more, than those seated within the candle-lit chamber.

He had filled in his life with events that gave purpose, events that wove threads between a succession of days, when repetition begets habit and a solid life forms. He had raised children correctly, with admonishments for blasphemy, for sin, and for doubt. Sunday mass came each week, holiday dinners, bedtime prayers and thanks for their blessings. His wife saw to that. He provided the judgment and guidance that comes from a father. Then eventually, as happens, there is no one who follows. And there the steps end. The waiting sets in. Just so it was with the farmer, his crumbling foundations still firmly set, that he rarely bothered with church, the one down the hill, along the path of the driveway, then left down the road. He again heard the bell. Again, he heard thoughts. He would speak the words silently, if he chose to speak words, at home, outside, where he knew he was heard as well as anyone sitting, then kneeling, then standing among the small pews. He was not reticent with god, just sparing in attention. They remembered each other and, from time to time, he supposed it mattered to both.

Other diversions had gone along the same path. They were no longer missed. Just reading, he thought, he would enjoy that once more. A passion from childhood, as an adult, an escape. The world of words he had read, they remained real but were scattered, while the images lingered, though they lessened each year. Flaubert, Gautier, Hugo, Colette, Proust, even Camus, were still scattered among forgotten and now-brittle yellow books that filled lower shelves, with his children's Hector Malot, Enyd Blyton and Comtesse de Ségur. A collection of Dumas, bound as part of a publisher's cheap tribute to the height of easy commerce and the strength of French tradition, still sat on the top shelf of the bookcase for adults. The green clothed volumes, dulled with sticky dust, were souvenirs of good intentions. They were no longer of use. The old farmer's glasses cold bring focus to his eyes, but nothing could be worn that would focus his mind. He could see each letter and how they created each word and each word had a meaning. But meaning demands context, and context, it seems, requires someone to remember. Despite a firm binding, separated by chapters, printed black on white background, with letter next to letter, a book is just words. And words, like a life, have no meaning alone. So the farmer did not read.

Instead, he sat quietly, beside the kitchen table, in a high-backed wooden chair, waiting for sleep. He thought briefly of his walk and again of his daughter. How different she was. So much like her mother, he thought. Independent and headstrong, stubborn yet gentle, spiritual and mild. He remembered her last letter and went to the cupboard for a pen and some paper.

"Dear Charisse," he wrote. "I received your last letter. The farm is doing well. Pepin bought two cows and now has 15 and the crops have been planted. Mostly corn this year. We are all hoping to get more rain. The land and our well need it. There is nothing we can do without rain and last year was too dry to get a good crop. There is not much new here. The neighbors are the same. Crazy old Cecile (you remember him?) waved his gun again at a tourist who stopped at his house. They were taking pictures of his sunflowers. No jail, just another warning. Myra still lives and helps out sometimes when I ask. And sometimes when I don't. She asked about you. I have not talked to your brothers. Harietta still comes. She's the same but older. She gets more tired easily now. We are all getting older as the past piles up. But that's how it is. I was interested about the class you are taking. Do you find it easy to understand? Is this something you plan to do a long time? Is this like the class you took last year? Are you planning to visit soon?

As always,

Your father

Another day finished, he stood and sensed the air turning strange, an unexpected turn but there was nothing to do. For most of us, little unnerves as a fickle companion in whom you must trust, but nature had exhausted all its tricks to the farmer. He no longer worried about what it might bring.

Lying in bed, he shut his eyes and saw the day just past in disappearing snippets. Mostly, he saw his family as they were. The children were small, and his wife was smiling. He held these images, but given the years and a full attic of memories, the carelessness of sleep opened indiscriminating gates. All manner of clouds flooded his mind as it carried him off into night.

Chapter 5

Marie and the Old Farmer
Sit in Repose

The next morning, Marie and the farmer awoke as usual, attended to their morning activities as described, and spent their early hours as if flipping the pages of a book well-read. They each had their breakfast. They each had their walks. They each went the circuitous routes of their individual choosing – Marie in the yard, the farmer in the field. Each found, however, that this day, for some reason, they walked a bit slower and looked up more often.

The sky was overcast and the air a trifle too warm and a bit too dry for an early spring day. Silver white clouds hung low and churned slowly, disclosing light grey ruffles that would appear and be gone as the blanket moved north. The dissipated light cast the flat glow of dusk despite the early hour. The sky's monochrome hue drained any distinct measure of distance. All was painted on a flat canvas held out just beyond reach. The green of the grass slept dull and frozen and melded with the brown soil and white stones, all woven together into a bulky spotted carpet that rolled out in all directions. Trees stood in the distance but had no depth. Hills rose as a theatre's backdrop and the scenery stood silent. Sounds normally heard from afar as thin vibrations, had a resonance that both permeated and emanated, it seemed, from all directions with no source.

This was a day when clarity never comes. It was a day when all passes as a dream. The mind never fully awakens yet is too rested to sleep. The eyes lose focus and the thoughts follow suit. It was a day when one stares to the distance and thoughts wander unyoked.

This, then, might help explain how the two of them, the old farmer and the hen, found themselves that afternoon languidly sitting oddly together. It was quite a sight had anyone seen. They were almost as twins, paternal to be sure, one small with hanging feathers, one long with drooping clothes. Each had thin legs, jauntily poking forward and heads on long necks, casually leaning back.

Had they been sitting on a bench, or lounging on chairs, the sight would have been striking. But seated as they were, at the base of the tree, it seemed expected and right. With backs sharing the trunk, a unity took form, and what was now three in repose (including the tree) appeared as but one in perfect alignment.

Marie and the farmer had discovered with some effort crevices in the trunk that neither poked nor pushed. It was not an easy task. Among the sharp streaks of ridges and the many swirling gnarled knobs that jutted from its side, the tree demanded much searching to settle one's back against its rough surface.

Marie, on this day, had come first to find rest. Bored by her walk and weighed down by that sodden sense of a goalless direction, she had given up the thought of any games for the day. She considered her nest but disdained the idea of spending a day, then a night, then awakening the next day, in the same place as always. An empty house is oppressive with no contrast of thought.

"Bonjour, old tree," she said, as usual, when she approached the massive trunk. "Are you feeling rested? Would you like to talk? Or do you prefer to sit quietly for a while. Yes? Well, I'll join you if you don't mind."

With that, Marie moved a stick out of her way, turned around, and with her back to the tree, leaned against it slowly and sat on the ground. A couple wiggles to her left, a shift to her right, then a small slouch, she found the right spot. As she raised her right knee and pulled her foot toward her, she looked around the yard and out through the fence.

The thicket of trees that ran down to the ravine was dense with undergrowth and bushes and dead leaves and large branches. There were several old trees that had begun to fall over but were caught by their neighbors and held at odd angles. Those trees, Marie supposed, had acquiesced over years to the punishments of life – to the winds, to the ice, to the heat, or perhaps, more brutally, to the drought of despair. Those trees, those former trees, were either too young or too frail or too weak to withstand the realities of this world, she supposed. It was perhaps not their fault. Sometimes living things are just not born with the spirit for life. They prefer to uproot and merely to lie down, to be carried asleep than to face the pain that existence can bring. When this happens, as everyone knows, the ritual for trees is to cremate their corpses. This is what trees believe and what man does in their honor. Marie had seen this occur many times.

So why, Marie wondered, did this tree persist? Why did it bother? This tree at her back. In many ways, it was mistaken for not a tree at all. It was better a monument – a monument to trees, a statue of wood, or a petrified figure of misplaced stone. Or perhaps it was sculpture, a solitary reminder that this once was a land of fairies and giants. Marie enjoyed this last thought most during her fantasies as a child. A ridiculous thought, of course, but there was something lyrical in the tree's curves, dominant in its insistence, and mystical in its silence. Even the cat thought so.

To most, however, who had grown used to its presence, it was just an odd, old tree. In the center of the yard. Rising no more than the height of the house, its base the diameter of a fallen tractor wheel. Its gnarled, sturdy trunk was virtually naked with some carbuncular growths that pushed out from its sides. What little bark remained was in two long meandering patches from the base near its roots to no more than half-again the height of Marie. It had one gaping hole that ran all the way through and crevices that gnawed from the sheer exhaustion it felt by holding itself together.

The tree had none of the life-giving branches that covered others of its kind with small, green needles that sometimes exploded with deep-red berries. It consisted only of three enormous and impossibly wrinkled – well, Marie did not know what to call them. They were not branches exactly. They were not trunks. They were probably once limbs, but now they were more like arms, yes, that's it, like thick stubby arms, slightly curved and covered with coarse wooden veins that spiraled around their arched, knotty reach.

Those three arms pointed upward and outward, each in a different direction, like a three-pointed star. Two of them, sloping back, tapered from their shoulder to what Marie called their fingers, were equal in length, extending from the trunk about two-thirds up and projecting as far as the trunk was high. Both pointed northward, while one veered east and the other preferred west, upraised and outstretched, pointing out over the valley, holding, as it were, the church between its imagined hard grasp.

Their opposite triplet faced straight south, like the head of a statue with its face to the wind. Thicker and shorter than the others by half, it had a more upward tilt and tapered not so gently. Although not much more than a stump of a limb, this southern sister had a bearing that suggested it held dominance. It sat on the top of the trunk and had a somewhat snooty pose, Marie thought, the way the ducks walked past her with their beaks toward the sky and their eyes decidedly taking no notice.

Even from a distance, the tree's wrinkles, knobs and curves were impressive to see. Up close, its deeply weathered surface had wondrously delicate grooves that swam upward and around in perfect alignment. It was as if something had torn away an ancient skin to expose a grey-brown body that, in its refusal to surrender, had hardened its resolution, as well as its fibers, even more powerfully and determinedly than the limestone that shared the ground with its roots.

Given this texture, it was no surprise that finding a spot to welcome a back could be challenging. Marie, however, knew from practice almost precisely where to sit.

For the farmer, it was a bit more difficult. He arrived later in a somewhat unexpected manner, the result of a chore he discovered while rummaging the cellar the previous day. Decades before, a spring had dislodged from inside a lock and though it was no longer needed (having been replaced by a hook soon after it broke), today was the day he had chosen to fix it. Out the front door and down to his left, he walked to the heavy wooden door of the cavernous basement. Just three steps down, he entered a tomb of large stone walls that had ravenously swallowed discarded or lost pieces of the house's long history.

Another bedroom to the right and one to the left, there was much to be rediscovered in the rooms in between: the remnants of a kitchen, a store of jams and empty jars, shelves of forgotten pots and utensils, and a room of discarded pumps and machines and broken engine pieces. It was there he found the object of his search and he carried up the lock, a screwdriver, and a small pair of pliers. Returning outside, he sat on the stairs facing west toward the yard.

As he examined the lock, he looked up and noticed Marie walking slowly. She approached the tree and kicked at the ground. Her mouth picked up a stick and shook it away. She looked up and then down and over to her left. With several small steps, she turned around and rubbed her back against the tree. Then with unexpected ease, she pushed her legs out and slid her bottom to the ground, flapping a wing and bobbing her head.

The farmer thought she had slipped. Then he saw her look up. She did not move but fixed her eyes straight ahead and pushed her legs out, before sliding her right foot back in toward the tree.

With his elbows on his knees, he studied her a moment. Looking down, he shook his head slightly and then looked back up. Marie was seated as if resting on a lounge chair next to a pool.

The lock in his hand, he regained his focus. With the removal of screws, he took off the top of the long black box that housed its internal workings. As he began resetting the pivot and placing the spring to the latch, he realized that he had forgotten the oil, which was kept in the shed. Now, with the screwdriver and pliers in his left hand, he grabbed the lock with this right and walked across the yard and into the small stone building. It was on his way back, just by the tree, that the cover of the lock slipped out of his grasp. He bent down on one knee. The cover was found and after combing the grass, he found the small spring. Two screws had landed on a patch of clear ground but two more were missing. For the next few minutes, he continued his search. Then he placed the tools to his left and the small pieces of lock on the bare ground to his right. After carefully studying a square of brown earth and white rocks, he sat down on the spot, his back to the tree, and he pushed his legs out. Leaning forward, he scanned each clump of the grass until he found the two missing screws. Then, he pulled his right foot in towards him and lifted his knee. With the spring back in place and after a few drops of oil, he replaced the cover and tightened the screws.

The farmer looked straight ahead, across the stones of the driveway and through the edge of the arch. He looked down at the lock. There before him was the day years ago when it broke. Amid some typical boisterous struggling, his children had twisted the bathroom door knob, slammed the door hard and dislodged the spring. He wished now he had not scolded them. It was just childhood exuberance. He could hear his children playing, their laughter, their silence, his steps, their punishment. It had taken twenty or so years to fix the lock in ten minutes.

It must be true for any parent that there are moments and places we remember children best. The moments will be different, but the places are likely common. A child's empty room, the remaining cold bed, a silent playground with no movement, even a tub dry and clear. Whatever location our children gathered for playing, for shrieking, for laughing, or making a mess. For the farmer, the old tree was indeed such a place, an enduring center of much past commotion. He had not found himself under it since he was a child. It was not an object of memory, but a focal point of sorts, around which the playing, the shouts, the stories, the battles, and so many conquests occurred through those years. His back too now searched for a spot on the trunk where his bones were not poked, and he stretched both his legs and they crossed at the ankles.

With his mind now drifting, he thought of the years when his children were small. They played in the yard and shouted and cried as they ran fast in circles and argued and laughed. To an adult, their games had no meaning, concocted and made real alone by their hidden and shared imagination. The yard in those years was forever full, his children and chickens swarming and skittering, each sharing the space as they crisscrossed and scattered amid gallops and yelps and clucks of bright youth. The images were inseparable. Children and chickens. Chickens and children. And as the boys had grown, his young daughter remained. There, in his mind he saw her alone, sitting and talking and holding a hen. The farmer's eyes were now closed. His breathing was steady. His head was bent forward.

Whether it was unity of moment or a gracious alignment, there the two were, Marie and the farmer. The old farmer and Marie. One near the other, neither aware, neither thinking to yield, neither holding a clue what the other was thinking.

The tree for Marie was still a good friend, a bit boring it was true, but reliable and there. It was her chair when she sat. It was her shade from the sun. It was her scratcher when she rubbed her backside against it.

Marie also found the tree a location of soft memories. All she need do was sit and think back to so many days. She shut her eyes. Just being near would beckon lost dreams, console recurring sadness, and help mourn many losses. She remembered as a child how it was her enemy when she charged, or her fellow Musketeer, steady and trusted, when a cardinal approached. She remembered her days there as a feathered Joan of Arc, bound at the stake, or Vercingetorix pushing back Romans, or Clovis, Charlemagne, Napoleon, de Gaulle – names she had heard though not the stories behind them. She recalled being there with others. She thought of the times her mother would talk to her as they hugged its cool shade. She pictured the days during which she linked wings with other children and played around the tree as it stood and watched.

Smiling, she thought how it was also, at times, a menacing fiend. Sometimes an ogre. Her smile broadened as she remembered she convinced herself it was sometimes a monster – a looming, threatening, devouring Huguenot that threw evil spells and cast menacing shadows in the yard late at night. She shuddered as she thought how she once saw it moving – yes, slowly moving – its arms fully outstretched, its trunk leaning forward. She has seen this one night, in the moon's silver shadows, from the corner of her eye.

Marie took a deep breath and felt a breeze had begun. It had a light touch and she caught a small whiff of a distant strange fragrance. She saw herself again and she continued the feelings she had when very young, romping with playmates while she still enjoyed some. She was happy, giddy, shrieking with joy at the scampering and chasing, at being young, fresh and strong. She felt herself smile and wondered for a moment if her mouth had just moved. She caught sight of her mother. She heard her faint voice. She saw her calm smile. All became real, yet she knew it was not.

Marie opened her eyes. A pounding in her had grown more pronounced. The air had become warmer though the sun had set lower and the wind was bringing an odd sort of smell. She looked behind to her right. The farmer was gone.

Marie suddenly realized the wind had strengthened as it pushed at the trees with a rustling sound. It was odd to have the wind pick up with such force, especially this warm and in the late afternoon. The sensation was strange. A breeze, then a gust, forced their way through. They came from the south, from the field through the arch and straight up the driveway to her yard and the coop. Usually the winds came down from the north and were slowed by the trees. She did not mind some wind or some rain, but this felt too different. It was warm, not crisp. It had a taunting insistence and it blew the wrong way.

Marie grew increasingly anxious. There was something about this. It had happened before, but the memory was vague, and the thoughts were unclear. The cows lowed oddly, and the birds were aflutter. The crickets chirped in such a strange manner and the mice scurried about as if in a panic.

Marie tried to ignore an ominous dread that was building within her and, instead, to calm herself by playing a game. This wind promised surprises, she thought, like others before. After each storm, countless bits of exotic objects had floated to her yard. Marie thrilled at discovering small lengths of string or torn scraps of paper. Her favorite, when they came, were specks of bright fabric. She kept as her treasure odd remnants of various cloth, some with tasseled red and green thread poking out the worn edges. After each wind, she hunted for the new. She did not know where these fragments originated. They just appeared. They were magical and mysterious, and she convinced herself they were filled with tales beyond her imagination. She created pictures built from small memories of unknown objects in her past.

Each small piece of cloth that she found was taken back to her nest and gently preserved. She spent hours and hours smoothing them down, over and over, again and again, first the center, then the corners, the center, the corners, again and again. She only had three that were large enough to smooth. Most were tiny scraps of no more than four or five threads. There was too little fabric to cover her nest, but she loved looking and stroking them and knowing they were hers. Many days when it rained, and she would stay in her coop, she would dream of wearing a dress made of these threads, like the dresses of girls who would visit the farm. She had seen simple ones on the old farmer's daughter-in-law or ugly large ones on the old neighbor who stopped by. She had seen long flower dresses when the farmer's daughter would visit. And twice she remembered frilly white ones on a girl who came rarely. She could hear the girl now, shrieking that way that little girls do just to hear themselves playing when involved in a chase.

Those pleasant thoughts, however, were soon interrupted. Brought to the present by dust blown in her eyes, something compelled her to go in for the night. And as she began to stand up, she heard the farmer closing shutters. That was not a good sign. Marie's head was aching. Her body was tired.

Inside the house, the farmer's temples were now pounding. He knew what to expect. Both he and Marie suspected a bad night. Yet

neither the old man nor the hen could have possibly suspected the
interruption that would come.

Chapter 6

A Storm of Remembrances, or How the World Does Change

The uninvited wind came fiercely from the south. It gave no reason for arrival and sought no permission for its presence.

A fast-moving tempest, it coursed over land with anger and vengeance. And it arrived on schedule. Its schedule. Skimming and sliding its way over the sea, it pierced a welcoming entrance at the Roussillon plain. It flew north, then east, confronting all with its message. It battered whatever it found, and when that was depleted, it sought out more – because as wise men know, unless winds confront dense wood, they lose their force and are disappear, distended. This wind would not permit that. It was not failing into the emptiness of space. Its gusts, in syncopated rhythm, appeared and withdrew, lined up together as an unseen army of enormous proportion, following a path cut by nature, dipping through valleys and curling past hills, screaming and roaring along rivers and fields, approaching in waves, pushing and pushing. Its deception was to still for long pauses, then suddenly appear and ferociously hit before pulling back again in false retreat. As if testing and teasing, its vanguard leaned at the world's barriers. The first volley fired, the full army came. The clouds giving witness, they were at the horizon.

The sensation at first was of a typical spring storm when it delivers a wind, an onslaught of thick clouds, a promise of rain. But this was different. An eerie warmth increased, and the air was uncomfortably light. Overcast all day, the sky now thickened and grew more grey, an odd hint of brown woven into its hanging fabric. That sense of impending rain, indescribable but unmistakable, was replaced by hot dust.

The sky's swirling, moments ago a pleasant motion of rolling clouds, was ominous now, tumultuous and violent. Precisely what moment the soft rustling of trees mutated to a low sound of hushes and repeated weak moans could not be remembered. Now listen. There are higher-pitched whistles and more incessant low howls.

Yes, an urgency was felt throughout the farm. The swallows gathered up under the barn's roof and noisily chirped to each other in warning. Insects jumped or crawled more directly on their way from the grass. The gnats and the flies disappeared from the yard and the cows lowed at a serious, disturbing and consistent pace. A cacophonous alert with creatures flying and leaping was sounded in the yard.

The farmer hurriedly finished his tasks. He had foreseen the coming wind with the barometer plummet and was taking precautions to the extent they were possible. Not all could be protected, and so he collected loose items and anything that might give way to the winds. Plastic bins and a bucket, a rusted shovel and a blue, worn tarp were placed in the barn. Two window frames with the glass missing and three broken screens, leaning along the wall of the house, were carried to the cellar, followed by a single folding chair and two torn yellow plastic cushions he kept out front for afternoon rests.

He walked along the driveway, with the house to his right, then he turned left at the barn, past the double doors that led to the cows, past the next entrance on the right where the straw was piled loosely, then turned left again past the tractors that sat under an expansive metal roof. From here he hastened back along the mostly empty stone building that sat opposite the barn, of which the outer wall created the all-stone perimeter that faced east to the field. That building connected to a long-abandoned smokehouse, which doubled as the southern support for the arch, which led to the wall that attached to the house. As he walked his counter-clockwise route, he latched each door or pulled them as tightly as their sagging hinges allowed. He saw the dog enter the barn. He knew the cat would find its own shelter. He looked up at the house and at the rust-red clay tiles that overhung the stone walls, and at the two thin black wires that extended to a floodlight that shone over the driveway. But there was nothing he could do to keep them secure and with the taste of grit in his teeth and his eyes hit by sand, he headed inside to wait out the winds.

Like an angry tide rising and threatening with an uncertain crest, these winds now arriving were a cruel tease of nature that never gives in. With each surge of wind, we hope it's the last. Short pauses of calm tempt us to believe the anger is abating. Then another crashing wave, larger than the last, and fear grows again that the end is retreating and moving farther away.

With sand in her eyes, Marie scurried back to her coop. She hurriedly jumped to her nest and settled in low with her shoulders slouched forward. She listened as her house began to vibrate and shake. For Marie, all that nature offered was here in her yard. The arrival of forces that came from afar, that knocked at her door, that swarmed outside, were like unseen beasts riding in on the back of a gale. She did not understand where this anger was born, this wind that arrived and tormented, wave after wave and pushed at her door. She tried to imagine its face and, to understand better, the land it was from. But all she heard was its voice, its moaning and knocks. It must come from a world beyond what she knew, from somewhere, she thought, with no farms and no chickens.

As its strength built, the wind pulled the sky darker. After momentary pauses, during which Marie thought the quiet might come, she was again jolted and startled by a fresh onslaught of howling and rattling. She heard the trees groaning and swaying, popping and snapping as they strained to hang on. The various pitches of rustling were growing, loud chorus: small leaves pelting the walls mimicking the sound of a fine, hard rain; clumps of large dead leaves on thin, brittle branches thrashed at each other like wicked cat o'nine tails; dust and sand pummeled the walls in a demonic hissing spray. Small branches ripped as they broke from their spines and were picked up and hurled with clicks and flat thuds.

Marie began shaking as the thin walls of her house trembled and cracked. The door fought against the latch. The roof of her house shifted, then lifted, then crackled back in place during short periods of calm. Dust blew and swirled from gaps in the floor and bits of straw soared like small missiles in the air.

What was it about this that terrified so? The howling? The shaking? The growling? The desire? Terror, when new, could never reach so deeply, so deeply to touch a hidden memory that lived. That was it, she remembered. This was how it started that night. With the emptiness of dread that something was out there fighting to get in. The realization shot through her. And her shaking turned violent and she rocked back and forth. "Go away," she said quickly. "Oh, please, go away." And yet this time there was more. Marie shuddered from the smell. The smell made it worse, especially the smell. It was dry and sandy with a brutal, awful scent. A scent of no life. She had never known it before. Yet it told her what it was. It was the dry smell of desert, the scent of earth deserted, the reek of parched life. And the unnatural warmth. Out of place. Out of time. Yes, the wind was the same, calling and pushing. But it was different this time. It made all feel more desolate. It was worse. Yet how could it be worse than that terrible night? How could anything be worse than the horror that night?

"Oh," she cried. "No, no please," she whispered. Her tears started flowing, involuntarily, one then another; before she was aware, they spread down her cheeks and ran into her nest, where her face pressed against the thick straw. "Oh no," she again whimpered. Her mind flashed like shattered lightning. "Like this. It was . . ." she stopped. "It was . . ." and her breath caught hard. "It was," she repeated, "it was just like this."

Marie shut her eyes and folded herself in more tightly, as tightly as possible. There was nothing to do but wait out her fear. And terrifying it was. She tried not to move. She kept her breath shallow. Her chest barely moved. Even the slightest shift made her more vulnerable. She tried again to squeeze lower. She pushed to sink farther and deeper down in her nest. Small puffs of struck at her back, lifting her feathers in menacing fashion, like fingers of a demon teasing and threatening. The wind was inside, and its touch made her shiver.

She opened her eyes. She was overwhelmed by the grey. Only small and sharp shards of dead yellow shown from the driveway through her wall's cracks and under her door. She raised her head, unable to resist, to look at the door, waiting in horror for the latch to succumb and the door to fly open. But her eyes stung each time she tried to peek out and she caught only a glimpse of the dust swirling crazily in her dark, shaking room.

As relentless as the wind, so was Marie's fear. Cowering now with her head beneath a wing and her body pressed low, the images of a child were all she could see. She had been so young, barely old enough to run, and too young to understand the reality of fear.

Marie could not stop shaking. Her body trembled in uncontrollable spasms. The pictures were flooding her, overwhelming her small life. She saw the others around her. The nests were all full and the faces were dark, but enough light remained to see a reflection in their eyes. She could not remember how long they had waited. Through these noises. The same. The very same noises. Metal bending. Wood cracking. At the time, at her age, she thought it was thought a giant was picking up the coop and throwing it down. Its corners had bent, and the walls started slanting. Sudden jerks and vibrations. Whimpers and sobs.

She had huddled with her mother, asking what was the matter. The cries became muffled as her mother placed a wing over her head. She told Marie not to worry, that nothing would happen. It was just the wind, that was all, and it would soon go away.

But it did not go away. How long did that take? How long did that last?

And then the worst came. A deafening crack. A terrifying crash. The rip of wood splintering. Thunderous and paralyzing, the sound filled the coop. It pierced, then exploded, in the breast, down the spine. The cruel thuds of falling planks and the snaps of dry boards. Huge branches that ripped loose then crashed through the roof. The ceiling hung in pieces and hung mangled above. Two walls disappeared. The others had gashes torn through. Small branches with dead leaves and shards of thin slats filled the straw floor as screams filled the night.

Oh, how Marie still knew those screams. The shrieks filled her ears. Some pleaded for help. Some weakly sobbed. Moans and aching cries intertwined with one another. Agonizing wails continued. But the childlike whimpers were the worst.

For hours it seemed, everything froze. Just the sounds of the carnage, the horror, the pain. Then the sun came to mock. The light and warmth did nothing but set snapshots in the mind of a child. Marie would never lose those pictures though they were thinned and hollowed by the distance of time. But the eyes of the dead would forever hold onto their depth. The eyes of her friends lying lifeless in blood-soaked straw. Others alive but crushed under branches. A few wandered aimlessly in hope but in vain. Most stared with eyes wide, made unable to move by a terror within. Heads rocked deep in grief, soothed with a motion that helped ease the fear. Scattered nests on the ground, all had been toppled. All the smashed eggs and an abundance of feathers like multicolored snowflakes, dripping with red, clung everywhere.

Either the storm ended or Marie's ability to bear further witness. Her next memory was silence. There was a commotion of men through the wood and the feathers and the corpses and blood. The chickens who were able were pushed out of doors. The rest were carted, away from the yard. Her mother was hurt, but she was trying her best to keep that fact hidden. She stayed with Marie and the two moved away and sat by the tree. She remembered them sitting, the soft calming voice of her mother who soothed.

That was the night Marie's childhood ended though her age remained young. The coop, emptied, was completely torn down. Marie's mother fell ill. Within days, she, too, was taken away. The farmer's son, as with the others he collected that night, tossed her into a red wheelbarrow, and carried her off, turning left at the shed and past the decrepit, wire fence. The red wagon with flaking paint, with rust holes through the bottom. So much depended on that one wheel of death. Marie could see the cart clearly, with its sides hiding the corpses, as it rattled and bounced over the brutal, white-speckled ground. The others who survived were eerily quiet, placed into cages, piled on a truck and driven away.

Marie was now huddled, thinking, shivering, shaking, remembering the others, remembering those days. The regrets piled up as quickly as faces. The pain of hollow words that were so clever at the time, those said and unsaid, came rushing back with the smiles of the others long forgotten. Their colors. Their eyes. The way they had stood. Their bothersome chatter.

Through a greying, heavy veil of unforgiving self-reproach, Marie saw her regret standing before her, pointing to the others she wished at the time would leave her alone. Or, as her memory now insisted, with a slow push of tears that were filling her eyes, she had hoped they would somehow vanish and forever go away. She had not liked them. She made it known and they knew it. She wanted the peace she found only with her mother.

Oh, how they forever droned on, with cackles and cracks, with chitters and chatters. With talk of the coop, complaints about food, and all the inanity of "rooster gossips" – that's what they called them – comparing their crows, comparing their toes. Then they would talk of their eggs and the fluff of their feathers and silly little things, the ugly shape of hens' tails, the crooked curve of their wings. They were pointlessly dreaming and squawking of chicks and guessing whose baby would have the most feathers.

Yes, hens can be cruel. But of course. Why not? There was no place to go. What else could they do? They found great sport in teasing. Bickering, harassing, they delighted in spotting and announcing some fault, whether imagined or real, in one in the group. Each had her turn, as day in and day out it was not much fun to turn only one of them ugly. Boredom set in when the victim frowned, finally cried, and slowly turned away. Then the group would rejoice with that hollow feel of fullness that comes for a while after crushing a spirit. Then the next day again, another target was found. And so it went every day. So it went every night. What else could they do?

Then came "that day" (as Marie later called it) when her cruel christening began. She tried to structure her face and smile like the others who had been the target before. But the smile would not come. And the more she fought to control each small muscle, the more the battle was lost, and her face fully froze, and her eyes opened wide. In the end, her mind went all scattered and she could think of no words, which of course did not matter, because her mouth would not move. Her silence and her stare provoked the jeers and names all the more. She was all bones, they said, and she sat like a frog. Yes, "frogbones," they called her. Her feathers, too long, dragged at her feet. "Featherfootfoot" someone said. Her eyes were too round, and her face was too pointed. Only some of this was true, much of it not. But it did not matter. These things could not be changed so the names pierced with precision and left poisoned tips deep inside.

Although the older hens moved on to spread rumors about each other, the young ones kept their focus on Marie. It was mindlessly easy. Marie routinely lost herself in play as an innocence and joy overtook her small frame. She couldn't help it. Self-consciousness left as excitement arrived and she held nothing back and she forgot where she was. She jumped with abandon and spun without end. She rolled like a ball and splashed, yes, like a frog. She laughed 'til it hurt. She talked to the plants. She ran with sheer freedom, overjoyed and alone. And this was her downfall as a solitary figure is the readiest of targets. "Marie runs like a duck!" the young chorus began, while each glanced at the others for smiles and approval. "Hey, flap your wings more!" someone else then screamed out. "And give us a quack!" And that's all it took. Marie suddenly stopped running. She walked to the tree, sat down, and she cried.

It was on that day, that one cheery day, they had ruined her fun. They taught her embarrassment and to be self-conscious among others. How could she be blamed if she disliked them all? The whispers and gestures and giggles and glances. They continued to hurt.

But she was determined not to show it or let it be felt. And she thought she succeeded. Yet, from that day forward, she never ran again. Not when someone watched.

So, there it was. Marie grew up avoiding the others. She was lost in their world and despite attempts at friendship and sometimes kind words, conversations were forced and made her heavy and tense. There was nothing to discuss. Thoughts have a line, no matter how short, and the lines of others shared something, drawn as they were with the same hand and same pen. But the lines Marie drew were different somehow and did not intersect those made by the others. Marie had no complaints about the food or the coop. She rarely even thought about eating or sleeping. Roosters did not intrigue, and she avoided discussing feathers and weight. And she was certainly not interested in all that talk about chicks. They're annoying and noisy and take too much time. Besides, look around, there were others for that. No, the lines of her thoughts spiraled and floated, not on a plane but in their own special sphere. They meandered about and intertwined and got tangled. Like a cushion of straw, they were made of long strands, and they were jumbled and woven into strange fabrics with colors.

Except in her sleep, Marie rarely thought of the others. But tonight it was different. Tonight there were howls and banging and cracking and for the first time since those days, she was wishing deeply, frantically, that they could all be here once more. Oh, to see their faces, hear their laughs, really hear, really hear, even in taunting – their silly, sweet laughs. Their sounds and their bickers were innocent enough. What harm was it really? Why did I ever stay apart? It wasn't their fault. They didn't know better.

Yes, Marie's loneliness now was different than the past. Surrounded by others, loneliness creates its own dwelling place. Despite all the others, that was still loneliness, sure, with the pointing and teasing, but the solitude stood in warm contrast to others. It was a strange warmth borne of choice, of resolve, of her strength. But this present real loneliness was but naked and cold. It existed with no witness, with no one to watch. It had only itself as companion and it was the emptiness of mirrors held in front of each other, the fading reflections receding to nothing.

Suddenly she saw that strange nothing that comes from knowing what's missing, when the nothing becomes real, and the nothing is something. A palpable absence made her life feel yet more thin and more weak. What was life really? Just a series of days for a hen left alone. If she were killed, she was nothing. All was the same and Marie never was. A small chicken is gone, and no one remembers. Death was abstract, even after that night, and it had left her alone. But now here she shook, imagining the others who were taken that night, and she knew death had not gone, it had just not yet found her.

Marie's sobs would not stop, but they were not for herself. Oh, the terror they felt. What a nightmare it was. How wrenching their fear. Their horror was real and then it was gone. Why did she remain? Her tears pouring out, her remnants of pride, were nothing compared to the small lives that they lived. Why was she here, a shivering bundle of feathers with heart pounding beneath? Meaningless tears meant for others who could no longer see. A penitence said in silence for no one to hear.

But ask yourself this: Does not a flutter recall the breath of lost days? Can not a storm bring remembrance of the meaning of wishes, whether whispered by priests or innocent creatures? The scene of a dream is as real as the past. We distinguish the two as between a cloud and the fog. If nothing happens in nature that can go wholly unnoticed, can the tears of a hen be said to cause not a ripple? A ripple of sound? A ripple of memory? A ripple among the infinite ripples outside a coop in a storm? If the past makes the present, then is anything gone? The overtaking we allow. We permit the illusion. We find a thin comfort in creating a new. But the ripples remain. All around us to hear. All before us to see. All upon us to smell. Like the linden delivers when its blossoms bring promise of tears filled with love. These are not cherished because they appear to us now. They are cherished because they existed before. They all were, and still are, in everything here. Our memory ensures it. The ones we are born with and those we collect. Through all generations. We can sleep, we can dream, but we can never escape. Like the wind, they compel us, unrelenting and swift. Like this wind from the south that blows with insistence, these memories compel that all in its path recall once again. And like memory, this wind, too, showed no forgiveness. No hint of kind sternness. No sign of harsh lesson. No whisper of tone. Perhaps it was there. Unintended. With the message. The judgment it gives. For punishment often comes with a reason, contained in the giving or learned through the suffering. But all is remembering. And in remembering is pain.

The tree stood silent witness. The wind, the sand, sweeping in harsh gusts tore at its skinless trunk. It was a different wind, a different air, a different scent. It held nothing within it, but it was strong and in strength is recalled many others. For all strengths are but cousins. Strength of power, of emotion, of neglected resolve. Strength of doubts, doubts of source and doubts of the present. Strength of truth, of what is, and what never will be. Strength of all that persists behind all that remains. For it is nature's strength that insists and reawakens our past. It turns us with force to confront where we are. And tonight came this gift, this gift of pure nature, the remembrance that lives until all breath is gone.

"Oh, mama," Marie sobbed as she rocked forward and back. "Why did you go? Oh, why did you leave?"

Marie's shoulders heaved uncontrollably. She tried in vain to push herself lower, to hug, to feel something firm underneath. Yet she felt nothing, just a bottomless pit she was falling within. The wind was so close, just inches away through the clattering wall. It could shatter with ease. It was attacking just here. It wanted her now. It was determined to find her and take her away. She saw the wall exploding, the roof collapsing and crashing, the wooden slivers slicing, the barn's stone walls crushing – the scenes would not stop. Her body shook hard and her breath would not come.

"Why didn't they like me?" She continued to cry. "Why didn't I try? Someone come back. please someone. Someone. Please mama come back."

Then, out of the howls, Marie heard a crack. Deafening. Like thunder when lightning hits by your side. Outside. A piercing, splintering sound. A ripping, snapping crunch with the explosive popping of pulp and living fiber torn apart. Then came a shatter, immediately, a crackling, a splitting of wood. Then a smashing of branches. And through the grey dusted light, Marie's eyes flashed open and she saw a hundred shadows jumping outside. Just then, a thousand shattering glasses came splattering on her roof and the hard, heavy bangs of a hundred or more hammers. Her breath caught in her throat. Marie jumped and inhaled. The ground shook with a shudder. Like the night she remembered. Her body tensed as she screamed. She stared at the door. She dared not look up. She waited for the cries. The whimpers and wails. But then nothing. There was nothing. Just came the old silence. The silence brought on by the whistles and howls from her only companion that was cursing outside.

With the crash, Marie stopped thinking. Past images were gone. Words were abandoned. Her fear melted to numbness. Just her shivering remained, and penitential tears dropped again down her face to her nest. Eventually, and graciously, she grew exhausted from crying. The wind's howls and its moans began to blur and to mix with the rattle and rustle of small objects inside. She was too tired to remember having fallen asleep, but later, she was sure that her mother had been near.

* * *

At the sound of the crash, the farmer awoke. He had left the hall light on in anticipation of damage. He looked quickly around and saw all undisturbed. Not frightened, just cautious, he lived through too many storms to have exaggerated worries. He knew a second crash would have come if a window had been broken or a tree breached the roof. No second sound arrived.

Sitting up slowly, his feet fumbled to find his brown leather slippers, the ones that were worn through to the matted white gauze under his heels, the only ones he had. It was too warm for a robe. The rattling of shudders and an unsteady moan accompanied the whistles heard outside. It was the height of the storm and he was tempted to peer out his two-bedroom windows. But the windows faced the south and were taking the brunt. To open is to welcome and a bedroom is a sanctuary, especially at night.

Wearing only a pair of light blue boxers with a small piece of hem in the back hanging down, the farmer walked to the kitchen, past the front door. He smelled sand in the air and could feel the warm puffs that forced their way in. Under shiny grey hair which was still asleep standing up, his temples throbbed deeply as he looked through the panes that framed the door on both sides. The floodlight shone, and he saw the two wires flapping in the violent clouds of straw that appeared trapped in a vortex of battling currents.

As he entered the kitchen, the old farmer turned on the light that hung above the large table. The two bulbs sat hidden behind a streaked-yellow glass lamp shaped like a bowl, and the light pierced his eyes with a painful brightness. He was suddenly confronted by a crowded room of still objects. The shelves of jams, pots and plates stared at him. The table lay sleeping in the center of the room, which was inhaling and exhaling, its walls pulsing slowly in then out. The closet doors to his right were silent and closed. The fireplace on his left sat lurking and waiting. This room was alive during day. Now, all sat passively, with eyes slightly opened, like a sleeping dog awakened in the middle of night, knowing it was not yet time for his walk. There was a hovering presence, but it was not the objects that haunted. It was the manifest emptiness from those who were not.

Leaning over the sink at the far side of the room, the farmer raised the bottom pane, its white-painted frame decaying nonchalantly with age, and he opened the shutter, gripping it tightly. A small spider in the window's upper right corner scurried to the top of its web. From this angle, the farmer could see all the tall trees that might threaten the house. Of course, he saw little in the darkness, mostly grey shadows and shapes, flailing and bending before returning upright, but he saw enough to know that nothing had fallen too near to this side.

He carefully closed the shutters and window and glanced to his right where two empty rooms looked out on the fields past nothing but a dark void and a turn in the driveway. Also out front were the box tree and linden, but they were too far from his room to make such a crash.

The farmer switched off the kitchen light and walked toward his room. The hallway's bare bulb hung suspended by wires through a small metal plate where a large moth lay still. The floor creaked under his feet. The shuffle of his slippers hissed from his steps. As he passed under the light, his shadow swept beneath him, from the back to the front, and quickly lengthened to his knees along the side wall and then slid and grew past his room to the right. As he stopped at his door, there, for a moment, he saw himself standing. His shadow cast grey, laying still from his feet, stretched out before him and then bent up a door. It was the door to a bedroom where his children had slept. It was years since he entered. There was nothing in there. Nothing he needed, so it sat patiently alone. But now there it was, beckoning sternly in silence, calling an old man to open once more.

Approaching the room, his shadow shrank before him. Then the room welcomed him with a breath of its still, cool air, and as he stepped slowly inside, the coldest of chills clenched the top half of his spine. He paused for the shudder. Then he turned toward the windows to the left facing west and leaned his right knee on a child's empty bed. His slipper fell slowly off his foot to the floor. As he had in the kitchen, he held tightly the shutter and pushed it open just an inch. There it was outside, a tree or a branch, leaning low through the yard, its leaves tossing furiously, battered by the wind. The top branches waved and lay beating on the coop. But the trunk was held in an odd sort of way, as if suspended by something before hitting the ground. The farmer was relieved. He remembered the destruction from the previous storm when the oak branches fell and he rebuilt the small coop.

Shutting the window, the old farmer turned back towards the door. The light from the hallway projected a straight path of light, framed and long, illuminating a large bed that lay sleeping in the center of the room. He stopped. Assorted fabrics languished on the bare mattress. In the shadows, books lined up expectantly and boxes in no order lay cluttering the floor. There was a doll on one shelf. A pencil. A ball. On the walls, aging posters. That nighttime phenomenon when objects lose all color yet are more alive and more real when the eyes are averted, kept the farmer looking about. Remnants with no depth. Keepsakes with no content. Souvenirs with no history. At least, not for him. They were discarded or forgotten bits of his children's lives. They were familiar by extension, not as details of their years, but reminders of their passing. With a second and a third turn of his head, he abandoned the room and went back to bed.

As he lay on his back, the farmer took in a long, deep breath. He would need his son tomorrow to clear the fallen tree. It was odd, though, he thought, how anything had fallen from that side toward the barn. It was a southerly wind and the trees stood to the north.

With the wind's steady low moan and recurring howl nestled back in his ears, the farmer's drifting thoughts took him back to the earlier storm. The destruction it caused, not just to the coop, but all over the farm. Trees were uprooted and large sections of the roofs of the barn, of the house, were ripped off and scattered. It took weeks to recover, but all had been fixed. All was repaired. All was the same.

Except for the chickens. Many were crushed. The others were sold. With the coop fully gone, it gave him good reason to lessen his chores. Besides, caring for chickens was meant for the women. His mother had done it when he was a boy and then his wife later on when he worked in the fields. The coop, near the house, was part of their chores. Then later, of course, his daughter took over. For the first several months, it made her feel grown, before responsibility and routine stripped the chore of enjoyment. Still, she quickly grew to love them (as edible pets), to be talked to and held during long idle hours, knowing full well in that simple, farm-child wisdom, that none of her friends would see her grow old. When the coop had been crushed, a strange sadness plagued the farmer. Not for the chickens for death comes to all. But for the threat of negation of those others he loved. They were not there to care. They were not there to help. And it was their absence that led him to rebuild the coop. One hen he kept, too thin to be sold, but enough for some eggs. Besides, just one hen, what harm could that bring?

The old farmer shrugged his left shoulder and rolled slightly to his right. His eyes made slow small movements under their lids, and his thoughts turned hazy, uneasy perhaps, brought on by the storm. He heard creaks in the hall and he remembered his children at various ages coming into his room while the wind hollered outside, or maybe lightning or thunder scared them awake. They would come to his room, seeking his bed, and he now saw the looks on their faces as they stood by the door. His wife always got up to comfort them back.

He rolled further to one side and saw the bright, empty kitchen as it was earlier that night. Then appeared the rooms of his house, one by one, in no particular order. The bedrooms. Two off the kitchen. Two in the basement. The one next door and the one he was in. There was a living room, of sorts, that had three wooden chairs and a table, piano, and shelves full of books. The hallway with one hanging light. The attic, a storehouse of discarded, old lives. The bathroom, a toilet, racks to dry clothes, a sink but no tub, a free-standing shower with a drain in the back. The dank rooms downstairs filled with the dying debris of the farm's passing years. And the kitchen once more, its grey-yellow walls and the rust-colored linoleum. He saw the rooms all in color, but they were all indistinct, with the hues muted and flat.

A loud rattling of shutters interrupted these pictures and the images faded out and he sank quickly inward toward the open space of sleep. It is impossible to say where in the sequence of thoughts are the beginnings of dreams. Our memories are blind guides on that forever unplanned journey. The farmer suddenly found himself walking through a field of fine growth with the path he was on leading into a large forest to his left. The wind pushed at the trees, and the tops, all vibrant green, swayed with the rustles and hushes of spring warmth.

Stepping over small twigs and large sticks, he saw thick trunks on all sides standing straight and close in. The ground cover was green, and millions of small branches, like stiff ragged brown veins, cloaked him and angled in all directions above his head. He recognized it all. It was the forest of trees he had known all his life. He was in a world of detritus, walking past stones and half-rotten logs. At his feet was a thick cushion of dead leaves, yellowing juniper needles, delicate ferns with brown withered tips, the burnt yellow flesh of wild girolles, and bouquets of long tufts of supple, green grass. He stepped lightly and walked – a confident hunter who knows the terrain.

As he looked out ahead, the fractal nature of life all split in two, again and again, left and then right, up and then down, again and again, nearer and nearer, farther and farther. The path he walked along suddenly divided. The way to the left ran deeper and down into an unfocussed, thick forest. Giant black boulders, glistening and wet, appeared to breathe and grow larger the longer he looked, and an underbrush of twigs grew thicker and confused as the path stretched out farther and curved down to the left. Covering the path were the decaying skeletons of trees with branches that crisscrossed and meshed into each other. And the more that he watched, the more the trees grew thick until the path disappeared. He could not see if the path came to an end or if the end was only hidden. Either way, the path seemed to lead nowhere. It dissolved as it expanded into random fragments of direction, none clearly marked, each impossibly obscured. Perhaps in that direction, one created a path and merely placed it in woods. Or was it a path in the forest that led to the forest itself? Or to a woodsman perhaps who always stayed beyond view, the woodsman of all woodsmen, who brought us the same and the simple at once? It was impossible to tell. There was no one in sight. And beyond all he saw, there was an illusion of clearing, bathed in yellow-green light, but it was too far and too vague to measure the distance. He felt compelled to keep walking. So he chose to the right and walked with the left path receding and blurring the farther he went.

With each new step, he now felt the suction of mud pulling at his feet. A glistening black tar of muck before him formed a ribbon of decay that led out of the woods. It was well-marked and well-tramped. Branches were cleared. Weeds pitched inward along the trained sides. The mud, frozen in time, showed lingering footprints that would never wash away. With each season that passed, he knew the mud became deeper in the constant shadow of trees, and no number of travelers could stomp the path smooth.

Then a new clearing appeared. The sun shone on a field just paces away, past the edge of the woods, beyond the trees and the brush. He saw near before him a familiar large hill with small yellow flowers and delicate plants. Large white rocks stood dry and sparkling in the field. The sky was an unfocussed light blue, as in summer middays when, without clouds, there's no depth. He stepped from the woods and was hit by a wind. Then everything before him turned a sepia hue as if thrown into a photo by Blanquart-Evrard. A dry heat with fine sand pummeled his face. The warm sun was now gone, just a withering light that came from no source. The fields laid out before him all looked the same but with color removed and a tan dust blowing past. He lost all direction. Any paths that existed were hidden behind or beneath a deep haze. He was only feet beyond the edge of the woods and he had no place to go. He'd never seen this before. It was all drained of life. It was arid and hollow and ghastly in barrenness and ghostly in presence. The sweet smell of grass was replaced by stinging hot sand. Plants and trees were standing but without color or life. Even the stones looked dead, more lifeless than usual, their white sheen despoiled and made dirty by time. The farmer's dream was overtaken by a surge of confusion. What had happened so suddenly? Or had this always been true? Had he not noticed? Then from somewhere behind, he heard a small cry, then a whisper, a flutter. The wind spun him around. He had never been here before. Yet there was his farm. But the direction was new. That must explain it. How else could this happen? Look at the landscape, the hills, the woods, and the paths. A warm rush pushed up from his chest all the way to his head. This was all here before. But the colors. The brightness. The effusion of life, of gaiety, of joy. It wasn't his farm. He knew every inch, every rock, every weed. He knew where he stood. But the scene was all new. How could this be? Which way did he face? Blue butterflies with red, white butterflies with yellow, yellow ones with black, thousands of them, flitted and circled in a weightless dance. Grasshoppers bounded among the strong yellow stalks that waved and swayed as they held and released one jumping, then the next came along. Brilliant colored petals of glorious shapes sang out their beauty atop the green, delicate stems. Birds floated above as if sent down to watch from slow-moving, white clouds, which nodded and smiled as they glided away. Millions of white stones sat glistening and perfect, sprinkled on the ground like grains of sugar on a cake. All was alive. Everything vibrant. Trees, tall and thick, with deep brown on bottom, bright green above, standing resolutely and proud in an aura of yellow. And in the midst of it all, standing before him, the most majestic tree posed. As if at salute, it soared upward and out. Its three aging, large branches filled with a gauze of tiny green needles, red berries abounded, dotting the surface like a huge speckled egg. Its trunk, enormous, a full wagon wheel around, was covered in bark, unblemished and patterned, unrivalled in nature.

And there standing beneath, he saw his young wife, looking as she had the first time they had met. She wore a blue dress with her hair pulled straight back and they smiled to each other and nodded hello and then walked side by side, very slowly, and silent.

Just then, there was a touch of soft rain and the wind began to blow clear. He opened his eyes. The empty right side of his bed slept before him. The hall light crept in through the cracks at his door. The large clock clicked slowly beyond the reach of his bed. Trees rustled outside, and the sound of light fingers tapped at his roof. The worst was now over. The wind would soon stop. The air would turn cool. The farmer pulled at a pillow, pushed it next to his head, rolled flat on his back and fell back to sleep.

Chapter 7

Winds of Freedom and Fear

Caged and cramped in a small wooden crate, placed high in the back of a dilapidated, black truck, Aramis huddled low to shield himself from the threatening wind. Tired from a long day of travel, he was unable to sleep, made anxious by the journey and what promised to come. Now, when sleep would normally take over, the ceaseless blowing and violent bangs made it impossible to rest.

The fierce wind, rising over the valley and up the abrupt hills of the town, concentrated its way through the narrow, curving streets. Its anger, increased by the obstructions it found in this ancient Roman French town, tore at ill-fitted wooden shutters, dangling striped awnings, and hanging painted placards. Road signs twisted and bent before returning upright like small metal catapults. Sheets of used paper and curled wads of dirty plastic leapt from trash cans and were hurled through the air with an erratic arching and diving like the flight of adolescent bats. The clanging and rattling of lampposts and chains could be heard from all corners. Angry howling and hooing sang the dominant message and whistling and hissing provided harmony strains.

Aramis sat tense. His black feathers twisted and pulled by the penetrating wind, he fought hard not to move. His crate perched high, on top of the boxes of fat, glossy aubergines and light green courgettes from the greenhouse of the driver's small farm. Arriving early for the next morning's market, the farmer had parked near his stand and retired for the night after a bottle of wine in a small hotellerie that was resided down the street. He did this each week. The market was small but so were his dreams. The little money he made selling whatever ripened that week gave him enough for the trip – and perhaps a bit more.

But this week was unusual because an old priest had died. Now, his dying was not unusual; even old priests don't stay long. What was different for the farmer was that the pastor, a now-deceased neighbor, had offered him his chickens as they would need someplace to stay. The farmer solemnly obliged – and now had too many roosters. "Thank god," he thought later, "I know just how to put him to good use." He brought him to market to find him a probably short-term new home.

And there crouched Aramis, covered in his cage by a blue plastic tarp that was thick and heavy with rips at its edges. All he could see was a dim night hue as the streetlights shone through. He could not seek the sky. That bothered him the most. What light shone through would brighten and darken as the tarp flapped up in waves.

Thinking it might rain, the farmer had placed Aramis' crate in the center of the back, in pyramid style, so the rain, if it came, would course over the sides and not collect in the back. But this old tattered sheet was quickly overmatched. With the strongest of gusts, it started to shred. The edges flapped wildly, whipping and pulling violently from its ropes. With each resurgent blow, the wind found its way in and pushed up at the tarp like a horizontal sail in a midst of a squall. Lifted repeatedly from below, the plastic tore at the edges and inched its way from the truck. The wind whistled in ridicule. Then, with a single swift snap, an unseen hand snapped the tarp up, pulling out one corner and peeling it back. With the added weight and the pull of the free flapping side, the other corners were forced to join in and they all were insisting to tug free. And as the flailing tarp smacked down on the boxes and leapt up like a kite, it doubled itself under and miraculously hoisted Aramis' cage up and over the side.

A true miracle? Likely not. But to Aramis, at that moment, it was convincingly divine. He was flipping through the night air inside a cage built from a few slim wooden slats which were wired to brittle boards which was hurtling to the sidewalk which now unexpected awaited his imminent arrival. Stunned by the impact, Aramis lay on his side. A wheel of the truck hulked directly before him. He was dizzy and did not move. He was still in the box, except now it felt as if it were lying on top of him. He leaned to his left, then rocked to his right. His feet fought to find ground as he pushed on the slats. His left wing was stuck, and his feathers were lodged between the overturned crate and the curb of the street. He took some deep breaths. He could not stay where he was. Without a cover or protection, he would be exposed to the storm, all night, all morning, until the farmer returned. He struggled to pull in his wing. Rocking forward then back, forward then back, he finally pushed the cage over and it fell off the curb. Four or five large feathers, he did not stop to count, were left on the sidewalk, then teasingly vanished, swallowed by the wind, and flew down the street.

Aramis sat up. He looked straight ahead and pressed his face near the slats. The sand and the dust formed a sheer, dry mist before the streetlights that shone up at the top of the hill. The wind pushed at the cage, then pushed it again. Aramis lost his balance and fell backward, forcing the crate onto its other side. He looked down again and saw a jagged shadow sticking out toward the truck. He pushed at it with a foot and a thin wooden slat bent outward. He tried it again, then tested them all. They had been dislodged by the fall. The chill of panic ran through him. He felt his heart pound.

As he readied himself, turning slightly to one side, an excitement turned to fear. Although no one was near, and it was middle of night, he felt a surge of worry that someone would come to scoop up the cage and lock him back in. He quickly turned and poked his head through the break and scrambled roughly from the box. The thin twisted wires scratched deep through his feathers and tore at his skin. He felt his knee twist and go numb for a moment.

Suddenly, freedom. Aramis stood on the curb. He expanded his chest and began a deep inhale, but the wind came at him with repeated hard gusts and cut his breath short. Which way to run? Follow the wind and scamper up the hill? Or struggle against it and run down out of town? The streetlight, which minutes before had been a life-saving help, transformed to a searchlight, menacing and fierce. He could not stay there and wait out the wind. He needed to run, to get away from the light, away from the truck, away from the buildings while everyone slept. Again, the weight of panic hit him. Someone was watching. He flapped his wings and tried to fight his way down, down narrow streets, down the steep hill, away from the market and the people who would come.

Into the face of the wind, however, Aramis could barely move. He struggled step by step, trying to stay hidden. But he was no match for the wind's fury. He planted his feet, flapped furiously his wings, and pressed his body forward, but he was repeatedly tossed back and sent tumbling to the ground. The more his wings insisted, the more they betrayed and displayed their true purpose, one of nature's perfectly tuned instruments to be played by the wind.

Slowly then, and carefully, Aramis pressed his way forward. Past café chairs that were chained to thick trees, he scrambled behind cars, crouched under bushes, anything he could find to help block the wind. He found momentary refuge down stairs to locked doors and tried to keep his eyes lowered to protect them from the sand. He tasted the grit in his mouth and felt the sting in his nose. One by one, he passed streetlights that showed him a path but also stood silent as jailers alert for escape, ready to shout at the first sign of a guard. The effort seemed endless, dragging out time with each small advance, distending the night which he feared might soon end.

Midway through escape, Aramis found refuge. Protected in a corner of a massive stone building and its long set of front steps, he was able to rest and recover his strength. Looking up, he saw what he thought was a castle leaning over and he felt the vertigo brought on by the swirling sand and exhaustion. He saw the building's faint lights glowing from candles through its many-colored windows and the urgency of the moment fell from his mind. In its place came a mixture of a thousand brilliant memories of his recent, lost past. It must be a church, he thought, the largest he had seen. The warm flickering light, windows that glowed a dim purple and red. He saw a woman holding flowers, and blue faces of men, each frozen in place, telling their story from their place in the glass. For an instant, Aramis felt a secure sense of comfort as he had long ago when he would wait near a window to hear the music within. For that briefest of moments, he saw himself hiding between the long pews, out of the dark and safe from the wind. He wished now he could enter. But for a rooster, he knew, the doors would not open. It was time to push on; the sun might soon rise.

By the time Aramis reached the final edge of the town, his body felt twice its weight from the long night of exhaustion. His heart pounded, his mouth swelled from the brutal dry air and he struggled for breath as each inhale bit at his lungs and tore through his throat. The wind started to calm as he neared level ground. He slowed to a walk as he met with plowed ground and tripped through a field while he widened his distance from the one road that led out. His challenge now was not pushing forward, but in finding his way amid deep ruts in the ground and past high clumps of grass. He tried to focus his eyes, but they teared from the sand and all was a blur.

Aramis looked back periodically and saw the town on the hill behind him and its sparkling lights. The small stone buildings glowed tan in the haze of the thick, brown air, which was beginning to cool. Aramis felt an increasing weight to the air that made it easier to breathe and he hoped it would rain. He stopped for a moment, his shoulders slumped low with his wings hanging down, and he turned in all directions to decide where to go. But little could be seen out off in the distance. Just a scatter of lights and blackness between. No landmarks. No paths. He had walked away from the road and away from the town. He now needed the sun to show him a path, to give him a plan, though what it could be, only morning would know.

Aramis finally allowed his body to sit. He found a small clump of spring growth next to a rut cut deep enough in which he could hide. And he lay there, collapsed, the fear of discovery replaced by the smell of soil and soft rain. His thoughts floated back to what he wished in the crate. Before the wind came. Before his escape. He was precisely in that place of where he dreamed, no place in particular, but in a field, free and clear, with no sounds and alone. He knew this would end, but he breathed easily now, an ease born of success carried on the wings of exhaustion and the realization that he again was facing an unknown, free future. So many times, this was what kept him alive, invigorated by the rhythms in the crackle of time, especially those moments when the unimaginable end closed in then but missed him, and as if for an instant, he did not exist. The end will still come, he yawned, but the future lives on, and with it, I go. Tomorrow, I'll look . . . tomorrow, I'll find . . . tomorrow I'll be . . . and with those unfinished thoughts, Aramis plunged steeply into a deep, empty sleep.

Chapter 8

A Day of Pleasantries, Introductions, and Dinner with Family

T he first light of day cast long, dingy shadows down the streets
of the town.

The slight wind turned cool and a brief rain stopped,
leaving all things with clear glistening streaks of rinsed lines, cleansed
of the fresh, tan patina that clung in between. The brown-yellow
mixture of distant sands, delivered overnight from a guest now
departed, was a tacit reminder, though the marauders are different,
invasions still come. Indeed, this town had seen its fortunes change
with every new language of those who controlled it. Yet here it still
was. Today, strictly French, modern invaders were mostly English and
others who passed through on tours, the foie gras and the wine its
industrial riches.

The market on Sundays was of particular appeal. With no
traditional town square onto which the church's front doors flung
open with a plaza and fountain, the streets of this town flowed down
all sides of the hill like a woman's loose braids fall from the nape of
her neck. One has a sense it was planned, but at some point in time, it
appears random nature took over. So the vendors each week would
take their positions and sprout down the streets from the top of the

hill along the curves and the twists, going this way and that, filling whatever open pleasant space they could find.

As with most worthy markets, the attractions were local. Vegetables and meats harvested from nearby farms. Wines, dark and full-bodied, spoke of the valleys and their role in French history. Jarred jams and preserves, smoked meats and small fish, pungent soft cheese, nuts and dried fruits, candies and cakes were offered up streets and down. Everywhere was nature frozen in time. That was its treasure, jellied in jars, hidden in cans, wrapped in brown paper, soaked in thick oil, floating in water, immersed in sea brine, protected in plastic, splayed out on tables, staring through glass, stacked in wood crates, waiting in boxes, all had been growing, or breathing, or ripening, or beating, or eating, or yawning, or smiling, or playing, or sleeping, or blossoming, not oh-so-many days before. They had been picked, or plucked, or harvested, or killed, or stripped, or boiled, or baked, or dried, or shelled, or pickled, or sliced, or smoked and they were all presented like a timeless display of the world's life on a plate. Then come hurry over here to the stands of made products. Random fabrics and poufy towels, plush coats and stone carvings, orange blankets and straight candles, petite figures and round plates, brittle vases and, yes, even cup-shaped cups, and don't forget those sets of fondue, ready for purchase and useful at home to clutter the shelves. In the center of all, at the crossroads of merchants, sat cafes and tables, serene this morning with chairs chained, leaning in, umbrellas removed, and the sidewalks dutifully prepared for a sweep. Shop owners sat. A few lights were on. Early helpers rushed in, setting out breads and preparing the coffees and cheese and meats especially for tourists who would come bounding in soon for a full Sunday ritual.

Yes, streets, blocked to traffic, were soon to be covered by hundreds of shoppers, onlookers, inlookers, outlookers, and downlookers, who would sprout from small cars parked at odd angles with their wheels turned hard to face the stone curbs. Then would begin a cacophony of language, a living bustle of humans, the burst of ill tempers, entreaties and questions, indecisions and shrugs. It was repeated each week. Waiting two and three deep, clumps of families and strangers who clustered for goods, would compete for the attention of distracted vendors who, more often than not, were contentedly talking, discussing weather and children with some disinterested friend who stopped by unannounced. Sharp words could be heard between shoppers in no hurry. With no place to go, merely here for enjoyment, they were impatient and cross because someone stepped absentmindedly before them in line. Scowls were adorned more often than smiles.

Down the streets, the broken formations of trundling shoppers were forced to stop and crowd to the left, around human barriers, to infiltrate through the slow-moving swarms. With the jostling of children, the bags bumping and swooshing as they rubbed one another, exasperated sounds replaced kinder words of amends. Then, the groups that descended, reversed their path at the end. Climbing slowly back up, they would stay to the center, veer left or spin right as their attention was captured by an overlooked item. Many just stood, reconsidering a purchase they previously declined. Rebukes rang out as children shoved through. Retail greetings were said, every so often, but none diminished the looks and expressions that held a dare to anyone buying. Mostly, wheeling and dealing, and hurling and burling, and hawking and trawling and cawing was heard. The meek met the unctuous and the bold persevered. In other words, yes, it was a lovely French market.

Willing to forego this warm abundance of humanity, the farmer always sought to come early. He rarely bothered to visit the market. It was not a far drive, but there was little he needed his son would not bring and he could always ask a neighbor to pick up supplies. But he promised a friend, whom he had not seen for months, to come to the stand where the man's family sold wine.

The old farmer was two hours late and disappointed to see crowds. Oversleeping is not a problem unless no one else does. Remember, he did not dislike people; he simply preferred them as a group to be somewhere else. They had little to offer and he even less. No, the farmer's qualities, though admirable in their honesty, were not widely endearing. But they were his and, offering no apology nor any hint of discomfort, he implicitly forced others to accept Indeed, this apparent diffidence, so stout to be regal, presented itself as something almost spiritual, so complete it was now a part of his being. The truth is, of course, whether he was indeed a spiritual man, it cannot be said. No one can truly judge that for another, nor, perhaps, especially in ourselves.

Now, as with many ennobling qualities, the farmer's reserve placed him in a vulnerable position. To those he encountered, he was not taciturn, but dour. His silence was deemed stern. His reticence, haughty. When considered by others, he was not often defined by what he did say (for not saying was what he did very well), but rather by the mood his interlocutor was in. The suspicious were suspicious. The simple remained simple. The clever were more clever. Yes, in silence we send any message they want – especially when delivered to someone we don't know. And that, for him, was most of the world. Because for the old farmer, nowadays, there were two types of people: those he had known and those he would not. On any given day, he met – or rather, saw – solely the latter.

With neighbors, it is true, the reception was different. The old farmer had spent his life on the farm as they had on theirs. He was considered quiet. Polite. He was never social. But they knew he would welcome and offer "bonjour" to anyone who happened to stop for a moment. But best just a moment. He was not in the habit of inviting them over. Why would he? But he never bristled at the thought that someone might visit. Amiable and polite, with a smileless mien, he had in fact a few qualities, even many perhaps, that his neighbors could tolerate. And he offered little to be caricatured. His slightly balding head offered no special topic. His downcast gaze provided no threat. His slow, weathered gait, his unpresumptuous presence, none of it showed an abundance of pride. Still, it was true, he was never convivial. But that was ok. Neither were his neighbors.

"Ah, there you are!" shouted Jacques, his friend, as he saw the old farmer come down the hill.

The old farmer looked up and caught his friend's eye. He made no expression, except to raise his eyebrows slightly, as he hunched his shoulders inward and stepped lightly and unnoticed through the swelling crowd of others.

"Bonjour, my friend Mortimer," said the vendor with his smile unabashedly displaying three randomly missing teeth. Jacques, as rotund as a king and as tanned as his leather vest, wore an old blue beret as if to prove he was French. In all the town, it was likely the only beret that was not on a table or already tucked on the head of a tourist.

"Bonjour," said the farmer with a passive, pleasant grin. His lips stayed together while the corners of his mouth rose a sufficient distance to indicate pleasure. He approached with his hands in the front pockets of his old brown cotton trousers. His head stayed partly down and his eyes, always passive, kept a steady soft gaze. "How are you?"

"I am well, my friend. Merci, merci. And you? You look fit as ever not an ounce of warm fat." And with that last statement, Jacques, the king, rubbed his own belly, which sat comfortably protruding in his red knit shirt that pushed aside and opened his deep brown vestments like two swinging doors. A friend since childhood, when he and the farmer attended the same school, Jacques rarely waited for answers, especially from the farmer. What was the point? When sitting on a see-saw and the other person refuses, one accepts to do both the seeing and the sawing.

In response to the last comment, the farmer peered down at Jacques' stomach, keeping a polite, nonjudgmental, gaze. Jacques turned to look at the crowd, standing, as always, with his mouth slightly open. His small, childlike nose, dwarfed by his brown flecked cheeks that sat in layered jowls down to a blazing present from Civatte, was apparently incapable of inhaling enough wind. So his mouth stayed ajar, noisily hissing and wheezing, that is, when it was not smoking a cigar or munching on any food that came near. Yes, Jacques, as they might say, cut an interesting figure. He was not wholly unattractive. He had an infectiously jovial quality that led others to a quick, unconscious smile regardless how much he might be overcharging them. And with his ears and eyes as miniature as his nose, he could appear downright elf-like thanks to the leftover tissue that settled near his jaw.

"Wellwellwell. It is good to see you. How are you? How about that storm?" this happy elf king asked. It was clear it was not the first time that morning he had asked that same question. In fact, he appeared downright happy the storm's arrival brought a topic. "So, it hit you too did it?"

"Yes, we felt it," the farmer said softly. "It was bad. But no damage." The two stopped for a pause, one to look down, the other to wheeze. "How about you?" the old farmer finally inquired.

"Oh we only suffered a lost shutter and some tiles on the roof. And a fence was knocked over. That's all that I saw but I had to leave early. I'll probably find more trouble when I get home." He said this with a shake of his head and a breath of resignation that told of a history of punishment from nature. That can't be all the damage, he seemed to be saying, not on my farm. Jacques paused. Down the street, a woman was shouting, and a child was wailing. Scores of people were meandering within inches of his table, staring at the bottles, a few looking up at the two men as they passed. "Those winds are from Africa," he said.

"Yes, maybe," the old farmer said softly, slightly raising his left shoulder in half a shrug. "Things like that happen. It could have been worse."

With the niceties done and the topic of storm too quickly exhausted, the two friends stood and talked, in a mostly one-sided conversation, about the winter, their farms and still more of the weather. The church bells would ring and Jacques would keep talking. He told of his sister's illness of the joints, and how his brother visited from his house near Toulouse. His wife was at home with her cousin and niece. No, they had not travelled as they found it more difficult in winter to leave. Yes, it was too bad about Martin, but he'd been sick a long time. Still, the funeral was short, and his family looked well.

Jacques also told how his son had moved to Marseilles. His other two children were well with their problems. "But that's what life brings," he said, extending his arms and raising his hands. "The storm and the droughts are all we remember. The peaceful days are the ones we forget."

The old farmer listed his children as he did each time. He described where they lived and what jobs they had taken. He talked of the farm and what summer crops had been planted, that one of the cows died in the winter, but his son bought two more, and milk prices were steady so the farm did its job. Yes, they still have dinner on the last Sunday of each month, and his grandchildren were strong. One boy was six, the other was eight, and yes, why not? Of course, they're in school.

"Ah children are wonderful," said the smiling elf-king gourmand, his lips smacking on grapes preceding the crunching of the pits. "But grandchildren are sacred. Our new seeds in the ground. You can't have too many."

The farmer looked at his friend.

"But you already know that," he continued. "You have – how many? – eight, nine of your own? No matter how old, they never grow up. Not for us. They will always be babies. Even the oldest. She's at university. Still a baby to me. It's not the same for us old friend. Sure we get older. A full head from our life. A full belly from god. That's the way it should be. Then the time comes and up we die. But in the meantime we stay as young as our thoughts and as happy as our playful parts will allow." And here the jolly Jacques stopped for a laugh, his second and third chins dangling and swaying with the two platysma bands flapping to and fro. "What I don't understand is why getting old is unfair. It's not that age is not fair. That's nature am I right? Nothing fair about nature. But getting old. For example why am I still so young yet my wife got so old?" And once again, it was time for a laugh, and another handful of grapes. "That's why god gives us children old friend. It's his reward for being husbands. I mean if we can't kiss our children and give them a hug what good is it all? What else have we done?" And with that, Jacques reached out and squeezed his old friend's arm and gave him a questioning look, not expecting an answer. No answer came. He returned his gaze to his table to straighten the bottles and try to lure in more tourists.

The farmer stood watching. An accordion player, as colorfully ragged as his scratched, sparkle-red instrument, strolled past and stopped near. The whining of Rondeau de St. Justin lay a piercing din over the market. The two friends kept silent. No need to shout while they tried not to listen. Incessant refrains, played over and over. Four times, repeat. Four times, repeat. Four times, repeat. Four times, repeat. Jacques grumbled loudly, wishing the maestro would refrain someplace else. Then he opened a new bottle to use for free samples in small plastic glasses. The tortured tune ended, the two men resumed with topics that glanced briefly toward politics and then bounced off some war and they shook their heads slowly and shrugged both their shoulders and shifted their feet, the farmer's hands in his pockets, his friend's waving wildly. Jacques stopped frequently to answer strangers who asked if he made the wine himself and what were the grapes. The men noted accents. To one English-speaking woman, the answer was no, you do not drink it cold. It is not for sangria, Jacques said with disdain, and the round friend rolled his eyes while glancing at the farmer. American, he thought; even Canadians know better.

At the end of two hours, the farmer said goodbye and stopped to buy bread and beef sausage for dinner. He nodded and half-smiled to two women he knew, or maybe he didn't, but it's polite to be safe after they nodded to him. If he had known them, he had forgotten their names and whether, in fact, he'd ever known them at all.

The old farmer found his car, an old blue sedan with flaking rust near the wheels and more scratches and dents than places unblemished. He placed the bags in the back, tugged twice at his door and slowly slid in, positioning and fidgeting into a well-worn spot. He inched the car down the street in the lowest of gears with his foot on the brake, waiting patiently and repeatedly for other drivers to park.

The road curved down steeply to the right in an elongated half-circle. He had driven this path since he was a boy and except for car fashions, little had changed along this road out of town. Well, more precisely, it was a road that one took either up to enter or down to leave, as none of the roads came directly in or out. They just wound around the sides until they got where they were going. It was not important which one took. The roads eventually crossed, as most roads do, if you go far enough.

At the bottom, the farmer turned left and headed for home. At the next intersection, he stopped, turned right, then drove past the open flat fields that showed early spring growth. The ankle-high plants all leaned to one side as if sown at an angle or combed into place. Wherever you looked was the dark, rich soil that gave this land life. The old farmer slowed to turn left when he noticed a blurred movement of something dark in the field. It was a large, black rooster limping slowly away.

* * *

Aramis awoke with a start. A black-feathered ort on a great French brown table.

The ruts and the bushes helped protect him at night, keeping his face from the wind and hiding his feathers that waved in the breeze. But when the first light of sun sliced through the cool morning air, warming him back into a deep, second sleep, he became a shiny black morsel and he panicked to see he sat alone in a field. His eyes opened before his brain could keep pace and he closed his throat tight to stop it from crowing (which, you must believe, is a thousand times harder than stifling a yawn). He sat for a moment, looking down, looking up, looking left, looking right. He saw the town on the hill and remembered the terror. And he knew he was not safe. Solitary roosters don't sit in a field, not if they plan to live very long.

His first thought was to run. To where and which way? He had been spun around and twisted and faced a strange landscape. He poked his head up, just over the plants and turned around slowly. A clump of trees was the closest but that was near town. For miles, it seemed, were flat fields with small growth. Too soon in the season. There was no corn, wheat, or sunflowers to pass safely through. The only refuge he saw was a tree-covered hill far away to the west. He stood very slowly and started to run. But after that extraordinary night and the tumbling he took, his feet barely moved. He felt the sting from torn feathers and the scratches he suffered scrambling out of the cage. There was the wind, then the rain, then the cool of the night. His body was heavy, and his muscles rebelled.

For nearly an hour, Aramis struggled to cross the field. He waited, carefully, before crossing a road, and was nearing the hill when he heard a car stop. He looked back quickly. An old blue car had pulled off the road. An old man in brown pants began walking toward him. Aramis kept his eyes down and ran, feebly, hoping to escape. But it was too late. The man did not stop, but approached him directly, his eyes fixed forward. Aramis saw himself running and flapping his wings, but his limbs refused, and he stumbled and fell. His mind was soaring; his body was failing.

The farmer, walking carefully, lacked the speed and the litheness of youth. But his coordination remained as did the quickness of his hands. He hunched over slightly and took small steps toward Aramis. His experience with birds had taught him how to approach. With caution and ease, he squatted on one leg and leaned slightly ahead. His left arm extended, he swung it slowly from his side, ready to grab with his right straight ahead. He expected to lurch forward and even fall if he needed. But the rooster barely budged. "Strange," the old farmer thought as held the two legs of the limply flapping rooster. "Might be sick. Could be hurt." The farmer walked back to the car and opened the trunk. He placed Aramis in and shut the hood. Now, this is not the way a farmer would normally transport a rooster. But the farmer had no cage, and no one wants a scared sick bird sitting loose on the back seat. They have, it's been noticed, a desire not to stay.

As the farmer drove slowly along the dirt road, watching as he did for large rocks and larger holes, he began to wonder where to put his unexpected guest. If it was sick, it needed to be kept apart from the hen, a few weeks or a month depending how it looked. Then suddenly, he asked himself, what was he doing? There had been roosters for sale at the market. They crowed several times, but he never thought to buy one. Roosters are cheap. He doesn't have one because he doesn't need on. Now, here he was, a child with a sidewalk coin tucked neatly in his pocket, not kept because it's needed, grabbed solely because it's free.

And as with that coin we initially planned to take home, more than once the farmer thought to reconsider, reach in and toss it back down. After all, it was nearly worthless and certainly dirty. Just let it go. But let it go where? Into the woods? Out in a field? It would not survive. Besides, a rooster might be useful. The hen might have been killed. Perhaps we let them make a few spares. There's room, after all. The new coop is large. And if he changed his mind later, the rooster has other uses.

Turning left, over the creek and past the stone church, he continued up and around to the top of the hill. As he spun the wheel right, he decided where the rooster would go. At least a few weeks. It'll either die or get healthy. And in the meantime, he thought, some neighbors will be called. The guilt of keeping another's rooster is never worth the soup.

The farmer drove through the arch of the yard's entrance between the box tree and linden. Light brown sand could be seen everywhere. The small stones on the ground, normally white and reflecting, looked tired and dull seated on the forgotten earth of the yard. The red tile roofs were mostly cleaned by the rain and the walls were streaked as if a million long tears had washed the apathetic dust of time from its face. The old black dog stood slowly and hobbled forward as the car pulled in. The farmer slowly got out and delivered the bread and sausage into the kitchen then came back out to care for the rooster.

He had decided the old smokehouse was best. The other buildings were used for storage or tools. If released into there, the rooster would surely escape through doors when they opened or else die somewhere it would be difficult to find. The smokehouse, unused, was the sensible place. It was built generations ago and formed the southern base of the arch that began at the house. Circular and pointed at top with red clay tiles at odd angles, the building had long been empty. It was built to cure meats and for all sorts of drying before the protective duration of freezing and cooling had been moved to the kitchen and other devices. Now it was left there to hold up a wall.

* * *

In early afternoon, the old farmer's daughter-in-law arrived. Dark-haired and pretty, with heart-shaped lines that would frame the gentlest of smiles, Dorothee had dark eyes and skin that was light by nature but ruddy and rough from long days outside. In her strong hands, she carried a large pot with a freshly killed rabbit and packs of herbs and vegetables still in their bags. Dorothee had the step of an athlete and the confidence and competence of a contented farm wife, still showing a coquettish smile and the ripeness of youth, which combined with a motherly shape, made her a beauty in nature not found in the city. Still young, she already had the look found in old photos of farm women, their long hair plaited on top or pulled back in a simple ponytail. Her low-waisted dress and her shoes, a worn leather variety of no particular style, made one feel she could be relied upon for any challenge, particularly one brought on by the weather. She was sensitive and kind and, because she loved animals – three cats and a rabbit for petting, not eating – she stayed away from her husband's cows.

It was Dorothee's habit to begin the dinner early the last Sunday of each month and cook it in the large farmhouse where the family would gather later that evening. Her husband was still attending the herd and cleaning the shed and his two milking machines. Their two young children were playing in the long expanse of grass between the two houses, which sat no more than a few hundred yards.

The kitchen was large with a hulking gas stove set next to a white, roughly plastered hearth. Inside, hanging between the blackened, square chimney stones, were the heavy black metal hooks, which held the pots and utensils used until the old farmer's wife died. Countertops were sparse but the large wooden table in the center of the room was heavy and broad and could easily accommodate a dozen for dinner so that is where Dorothee always spread out her cooking.

Washing and scraping vegetables, she looked out of the window and heard the children playing. They were chasing something, she knew, by the way they were running and shouting "Got you!" one instant and then "Watch it!" the next. Then, not inevitably but certainly predictably, a shriek was heard. And no less than distinguishing the call of two crows, it took the ears of a mother to know who it was. "Neville, be nice," Dorothee shouted out the window. "Be nice to your brother! Remember what I told you!" The boys resumed, pretending they were adventurers on horses and dreaming of the grand things that all grown-ups can do. Between the shouts and the running, while their imaginations recovered, they pictured themselves as tall as their parents and travelling to far places that looked remarkably like the farm.

Their father and grandfather passed to check for damage from the night before. The boys ran up to the men and asked them to play. Their father carried a ladder on his left shoulder and placed a gentle hand on their heads, one at a time, as he walked by, giving them a pat and their hair a quick twirl. "Not right now," he said, and he returned his gaze up to the roof. His father walked behind him, hands in his pockets, watching the ground.

Inside the kitchen, the blackened iron pot performed its resuscitating miracle, exhaling its steam, bringing to life its moribund surroundings. Each object in the room, the static herbs, the waiting jams, the expectant jars, the lingering plant, the sleeping cold pans, and the ripening, sweetening, decaying fruit, was given back color and reminded once more why it was there. Even the clock ticked and counted each passing moment with a bit more enthusiasm. And now the fragrance builds slowly, roots from the ground, savory plants, an animal stewing, the windows frosting with dew from the soup and the kitchen becomes what it is, at least for a day, one Sunday a month, for just a few hours. The mushrooms, and shallots, and tarragon, and parsley, the final, strong pinches of quatre épices, each joined the song that was hummed in the hissing. No other room comes alive like a kitchen when even one single pot is on the stove, exuberantly steaming. Like clothes hung day-after-day from a nail on the wall, when they are plucked and worn, what just moments before was some dead shapeless fabric, they come to life in a way that shouts: "Allô, here I am." So with this kitchen, at last being worn by a vibrant young woman, it was finally animated, dancing and alive.

At just after four, the children were called, and the men began to take off their boots. Her husband, Pepin, brought the wine to the table while Dorothee sliced the bread on the top edge of the drawer. Glasses were filled two-thirds of the way and a pitcher of water was placed in the center. Dorothee delivered each a bowl of fresh soup.

"Happy Easter," Dorothee said to her father-in-law as he leaned well over the table to lift and draw in each spoonful.

"Is it?" he said, in a tone that was as much a statement as a question.

"Yes, of course," she replied, forcing a smile. Sometimes, for Dorothee, dinner once a month felt a little too frequent.

"I didn't know," he said. "It came so soon."

"Yes, it's today," she said. "We took the boys this morning. You didn't go?"

"No. I heard the bell, but I went to the market. I promised Jacques I would be there."

"The service was pretty," Dorothee continued. Her voice, which at home would stay so pure and direct, tended toward that special soft lilt we often slip into when at these types of social, Sunday dinners. She also had the habit of wearing that same sort of smile with raised brows usually reserved for the old or infirmed, whether we know them or not. It was similar to the way we might regard small children except the play of brightness in our eyes is belied by a weariness that weighs down the mouth. "It was longer than usual. The young petre is maybe a bit too enthusiastic. You should have gone, though. You would have liked it."

"Maybe," he said. "Church is for youngsters. At my age, God knows where to find me."

"Yes," she said, as she saw her two little boys, sitting on either side of her, looking up at her in question. Then she guided her spoon back into her bowl. "I suppose He does." She looked at her sons and at the table before them. This was not the time to argue the importance of church. Her own religious activities, and so that of her family, were limited to but a few days now and then, and did not even include a holiday dinner this year.

As the farmer and Dorothee, who were seated facing each other, resumed their attention to the soup, the two boys and their father were nearing completion. The clanging of spoons on the sides of bowls grew louder. Each reached for a large piece of bread. After the comment that church was for youngsters, neither sons nor the father had lifted their eyes. The two boys were lost on adventure. Their father, as usual, was lost to his cows. The conversation meant to them as much as Esenç and Dumézil. No one had listened. They had not heard a word.

No, as the three of them sat there, mechanically lifting, leaning, slurping, swallowing and repeating, they formed a triumvirate of brothers. No matter that one of them was tall, had a two-day brown stubble, a much deeper voice and only half the smallers' gene pool, each had hair with just a hint of past combing, each rested a left elbow at the mammoth table's edge, each had a streak of warm soup on their chin, and each fixed furtive eyes downward with voices, when heard, were kept still lower.

All that differentiated the three was under the table where Bellamy, the youngest, swung his two feet, first the left then the right, then the left then the right, beneath his, the highest one of the eight mismatched chairs. But assuming one did not see, these were triplets to be sure: the six hazel eyes, the three long straight noses, the narrow soft cheekbones, the three high foreheads and the small, pointed chins. Only the middle child, Neville, was blessed with the lips of his mother, full and curved and placed there like an invitation to be kissed.

As the unheralded, and reluctant, autocrat of the table, Dorothee ate quietly until the farmer was finished. "How was the market?" she asked, her tacit role again fulfilled, that of showing interest in her father-in-law.

"It was fine," the old man said, looking up briefly before reaching for bread. "I saw Jacques. We talked."

"And how is he?" She reached to her right as she stood, wiping soup from her small son's chin before he quickly turned away. "Was his wife there also?"

"No," said the farmer, with a single shake of the head. "We were spared at least that. Enough wind last night to do us both for a while."

With looking up, Pepin gave a hushed burst of a laugh, and tore his bread in half.

"Was there any news in the town? Any damage from last night?" Dorothee asked, her back to the table as she lifted the rabbit from the stove.

"Not that I saw. A few things knocked over. Nothing serious. Pepin says your house came through," the old farmer said.

"Yes, thankfully, the storm was not too bad."

"A tree fell down!" blurted Neville, excited, his enthusiasm slightly muffled by a large wad of bread tucked in his right cheek. At eight, the boy was glad that he thought of something, anything, to say to be part of the grown-up conversation. It was particularly satisfying when the subject he picked was met with some interest. He stopped and looked expectantly at his grandfather, his round eyes wide below brown bangs that feathered in all directions.

Yes, his grandfather said, it was unusual to fall in that direction. But it was one of the trees uprooted last year and was leaning toward the yard. The swaying trees must have dislodged it and it fell toward the barn. It was lucky that it did not hit anything, he said. Still, it should have been taken down and cut up last year. Pepin, who had his eyes lowered as he reached for his wine, glanced up at his father, who was seated to his right. He knew he was referring to him, that he should have taken care of it a long time ago. Then Pepin looked at his wife. Neither said a word.

As the sun outside pulled back its light and began to cool the room in a serious yellow, the buzzing of two flies was heard, and ignored, as they attempted to escape through the kitchen's window screen, the incessant fan of their wings tapping a tinny ting on the metal threads. An assortment of birds announced themselves repeatedly on the trees not far. Their young would soon fly. And then came a rustling through the grass. Perhaps it was the cat. Readying to pounce. Yes, the day was turning on its way to completion. Those in the world who still survived might wake up tomorrow. Those who did would see the sun arc high. For others, their last dawn was gone. Some on the farm ate. Some had been eaten. Nature's evident cycle, inside many others, and the one that defined, had begun its descent.

The meal inside moved from the soup made from stew to the pieces of rabbit placed into flat bowls, each made clean by the mopping of bread. The boys mostly fidgeted and both swung their legs while they asked their mother for pieces with bones. Next on to the salad and to cheese and some fruit and then to a cake with some tea for the grownups.

The conversation surfaced intermittently, the sounds of voices breaking through the loud chewing of children. The farmer mentioned he saw two older women whose names he did not remember and described them by listing the friends of their friends. Pepin identified them as classmates of his mother from a neighboring town. The children's old teacher, who had also been seen, was then discussed as someone they liked.

After another long pause, the farmer looked up while he lowered his fork. Peering at Dorothee, he said matter-of-factly: "I picked up a rooster."

Dorothee looked at her husband who had not stopped eating. The children looked at their mother, awaiting a signal to see how to react. Dorothee smiled.

"A rooster!?" cried Bellamy still looking at his mother.

"He was out in a field. I found him on my way home."

"Can I play with him?" asked Bellamy, the smallest, hoping to chase someone new. "Can we keep him with the chicken?"

"He's in the smokehouse," the old farmer said. "He needs to stay there. At least a few weeks."

"We'll see," Dorothee said, explaining to her son in a way he would best understand. She looked at the old farmer. "Do you want to keep him? It might be good for the hen. The coop has plenty of room."

"Maybe," the old man replied with a shrug. "I need to ask if anyone has lost a rooster, so I don't know if we will keep him. Besides he might die. We'll know soon enough."

"A month!" Bellamy complained. "That's forever. Can I play with him tonight?"

Dorothee raised her right hand and held its palm facing the boy. A universal sign to stop. "We'll wait until the rooster is let out. You just need to wait," she said, pushing his hair back off his forehead and removing a crumb from the left side of his mouth with her thumb.

"Grand-pere! Grand-pere!" Neville shouted to make sure he was heard. It was his turn to talk since his brother had just spoken. His mother gave him a small sign to lower his voice. "Did you see the tree in the yard?" he asked.

Yes, said the old farmer, repeating his answer about the tree that had fallen. "I've seen it. Your father and I will clear it this week."

"The tree looked funny," continued the boy. "I think it got hurt. It seemed to be twisted in a funny new way."

"Yes, yes, yes," said the boy's father. "Grand-pere said he saw the tree that fell. We'll clear it away soon."

"No, not that tree," the boy said. "The old dead tree. The one in the yard. It didn't fall down. But it's different. It's strange."

* * *

It was early that morning when the bell of the church had startled Marie. Exhausted by the tension of the previous night, she remained shaky and weak, unnerved by waking to the terrible memories that had left a carpet of small pieces scattered behind. She had slept badly but her slumber, when it did finally come, was so deep that no dream could once again surface. With her head slowly clearing, images from the storm began to reinvade her thoughts. She did not want to move. She did not want to eat. She was thirsty and sore, but she did not want to leave. She wanted to stay still and to lose those haunting and violent pictures that are never erased, only hidden, only covered by distraction and painted over by dreams.

All of the day, she remained huddled in her bed. She heard the farmer leave then return. Doors unlatched and then shut. The trunk of the car was opened then slammed. The children played and then ran through the yard, shouting, stopping, talking, laughing. She liked them both, the younger one the most. Although they chased her sometimes, they were never hurtful or cruel. They never did catch her, but she enjoyed their attention and the sounds of their voices as they giggled and ran. They would burst into her coop and she did not like that. But that was better, she thought, than for them not to come at all. Marie particularly liked Dorothee. It was her long hair and her dresses. Marie thought what she wore was like feathers, but more flowing and soft, when tossed by the wind. Marie envied her the flowered fabric that she wrapped herself in. It made her arms look like undulating branches from a graceful, thin tree that was made of bright cloth.

It was not until dusk that Marie left her coop. She heard the children leaving with their mother after dinner. She wanted to see them to feel less alone and remind herself that others lived on this farm. She saw them walk past and caught only a glimpse of Dorothee's yellow cotton dress covered with light blue flowers and green leaves. Marie ran to her door to see them before they turned left at the side of the shed. The cool air felt good and had a crispness that was lacking for the past two days. She felt safer now with the familiar spring smell and she noticed the fine sand that sat like a defeated mist on the grass and the bushes.

But as she stepped out her door, Marie's wings began shaking. There it was. Straight ahead. Looming above her like a fallen dead giant. A monstrous, toppled black column of wood, arms held out, as in a desperate attempt to reach out forward, grabbing at whatever lay beyond and beneath. Marie jumped to her right, out from under its threat. The tree's lifeless cold branches covered her coop and, broken and shattered, littered the yard. Marie started to tremble. Lying there still, yet ominous in death, the trunk had leapt past the fence, had lunged straight for her and had plunged itself down in one final attempt to crush her small life. It almost succeeded. But somehow it stopped. Look. There it was. It hit the old tree in the center of the yard and was held up, firmly, as if cradled in death.

"I could have been killed," Marie thought as her stomach quickly tightened and she felt the need to sit down. "It was just like before. That tree would have crushed me. Just like before." Her stare continued as she surveyed the massive cold tree from the branches on her coop down the long lifeless trunk that reached far off to her right. Its base disappeared outside the fence, showing only the short thick roots that protruded on top like mortified fingers. Its black skin, already flaking and peeling along the lower thick half, showed assorted new tears where the impact occurred. Even the freshly exposed flesh under the rips from last night was flat, lifeless, and was laying there cold. Marie shivered as she looked at the way the tree rested. There was something strangely wrong with how it was balanced, a strangeness that added to the mystery and her fear. It looked almost suspended from an invisible line. She wandered from a distance around to the side. She stared, then looked up, and walked more to her left, never taking her eyes off the spot where it stopped.

Then suddenly, she saw. She saw what had happened. And a chill ran deep through her and her eyes would not move. That cannot be right. That's not possible, she thought. Marie looked down. She remembered. Then she looked up again. How did this happen? My god, that can't be. It's not real. But it is. She had been moments from death. Fewer than she knew. Yet something stopped the destruction. Her death. Annihilation. And there, what saved her was before her. It was undeniably clear. It was impossibly true. The old dead tree that sat silent in the center of the yard, the one with two massive branches that had always faced north, the two very same branches that now reached to the south, had spun halfway around and had caught and was cradling its fallen dead brethren to halt its plunge to the ground.

Chapter 9

Aramis at Home in His Own Bastille

Aramis' future, never more than distant orange flames flickering in a cold black void, disappeared from his thoughts. He did not know, he could not know, what was to come. His fortune had changed too rapidly. Freedom. Capture. Cage. Freedom. Capture. Cage. Freedom. Capture. Cage. Was the cruel teasing pattern bound to continue? How many times had it happened before? Or was the pattern imagined, as one conjures a fate, but only in hindsight and then used only to dream of a never-ending future? If life was over, Aramis thought, let the end come quickly, but with just enough time to think through all that has happened. Any conclusion brings relief, whether a play's rhyming couplet, the last drop of rain, or the ultimate page. Will this be any different? Will the moment that annihilates bring final revelation? Or is that indefinable last instant the first and last breath, with all that came united as one and erased with no meaning? These were the questions and the questions never left. They could only be ignored. How else to get through? How else to find sleep, to wake up the next morning, to breathe once again the sinister air?

So here they were still. The questions. No answers. Only the repetition of words. The more often spoken, the less meaning they retained. His mind raced back over the past two days, at all the events, unforeseen. His memories out of sequence, he tried to line them up and stretch them out to imagine them at their full temporal span. Where was the clue that might connect a past to a future? The cages and capture offered nothing to examine. It was his escape and his hopes that dominated his thoughts. He had unexpectedly snatched control of his life, and the air he inhaled during that short breath of freedom would not leave his lungs. But his freedom was past. Like now-lost companions, he and his freedom had travelled together and were then torn apart. Only he made this journey. His twin remained out there. Only he was tossed into a dark, stone smokehouse. His other half was running and breathing in a flat brown field.

After finding his footing in his new dark, musty cell, Aramis stared into the gloaming where the roof met the walls. He spent several minutes standing and turning his head, straining to focus on the thin shards of light that illumined themselves but too little else. Like spotlights through a smoke-filled room, narrow beacons cut through a haze of swirling, flying dust and settled in the middle of a barren stone wall to his right. The door behind him shone in places with an indirect light as the sun teased the edges. The room suggested a cellar, the top half lighted while the bottom receded outward into thick darkness. It was an illusion, he knew, as he had not fallen below ground level and there were no steps leading up to a door. Slowly, his large, dark eyes adjusted to the shadow, to the light, and to the distances they defined around him.

With the patches of light slowly seeping together, Aramis studied the cut stones that formed the foundation. They were large and stacked carefully with little room in between. He thought of the hands and the planning that went into its construction and tried to picture the men working to find the right stones. He looked up toward the top. These were not the same men. This was replaced sometime later. See how the mortar is missing and light from all sides come pouring through the gaps. Only balance and gravity hold it together. Look how the roof mindlessly rests on the random-stacked stones, the warped and water-rotting beams lifting and sloping the tiles at precarious angles. There might be a way out, Aramis thought. If he could reach the top stone and carefully perch, perhaps he could contort and twist his body through. But from his perspective on the floor, it was impossible to gauge if enough room existed through any of the obscured, sun-breathing holes.

Aramis hoped there would be time to check later. He was too sore now to attempt the delicate flights and he needed sleep for his spirit – the spirit that remained walking alone in the field. He began to pace slowly, his anxiety denying him the ability to rest. Step by step, he discovered the floor was too crowded with the scraggly remnants of hard and soft objects, poking up and out in every direction. He walked slowly, carefully, banging his legs now and again into some shadow that proved a low-lying obstacle. His feathers brushed against something and he recoiled, edging to one side and stepping gently around it. Finally, he found a small clearing and sat down. From there, he kept his gaze low, away from the glare, to let his eyes adjust to the darkness. He began to recognize objects. It was a mausoleum of debris, of discarded bits of farmyard, objects frozen in place, thrown or laid there as if buried with the dead or to adorn a room that was forever to be sealed. A thought shuddered through him. Was this his new home? Was he being prepared? Or was the door never to open, and he was never to leave? Buried alive. Shut in this smokehouse forever. It brightened him momentarily to have such dramatic, even playful, ridiculous thoughts. But what else could he do? To dwell on the real was to riddle through a maze that has neither beginning nor end, to wrestle oneself to a known conclusion of despair. They were all foolish games with no satisfaction. They were all ponderable questions with no answer, no end. He shook his head and stood up. His eyes, more adjusted, found the now semi-darkness disclosing more shapes at uncertain distance. He needed distraction. He saw no place to perch so he carefully stepped forward, and he started to collect whatever soft objects he found. Small clumps of straw were scattered about and the brittle remains of a decaying newspaper were stacked on one side. He pulled at each slowly, creating a nest as well as he could to give him both warmth and a semblance of a place to belong.

Aramis involuntarily began to relax. His reservoir of tingling energy that had his muscles twitching uncontrollably began to deplete. His unfocussed thoughts slowed, and the presence of his body returned in painful force. He found his way slowly toward the front door for a drink of water, not to sate a thirst as much as to ease a soreness in his throat that continued to sting from the previous night. His eyesight adjusted as the sun crossed overhead, removing the glare of bright streaks through the pool of floating dust, and he returned to his place and curled his long frame tightly in the center. It was not as comfortable as he hoped, but it was better than a crate or his night in the wind. His right side pressed firmly against an old metal bucket and his back pushed against the stone wall, his shoulders hunched forward as he stretched his neck down slowly. He rested his face against his chest, relieved to let go of the growing heaviness of his mind.

Various waves of rolling images arrived, accompanied by scenarios of what might yet come, from those he considered likely to others more fanciful, all unrealistically too well-defined. These scenes appeared one by one, little snatches of pictures, little snippets, quick flashes as if he were tumbling downhill. The images were not his. They were presented to him. He was running through fields. He was inside a car. Behind four stone steps. Hiding behind an old tree. He was tossed upward and back, he fell into a ditch. He drank water from a stream. He was back in a crate. Then he felt himself hanging upside down, the farmer holding his feet. Aramis opened his eyes. He heard cows lowing. No, the farmer had not placed him in this stone cell with food and water only to kill him that evening. It might happen yet. But not until tomorrow. Then again, maybe he would stay there, to live among others. He had done that before. Or maybe he'd be caged and taken back to a market. He dreaded this most. The long hours of doubt that could not be ignored. He felt his mind pace, and he hoped by not moving, he could force it to calm.

The fact is, in that morass of emotions where paradox reigns and with which we all live, there was much in Aramis that was relieved to be locked in the smokehouse. The certitude of incarceration, exclaimed by a heavy, latched door, freed him of any immediate thought of escape. It removed a temptation to take flight once again and wander down an avenue of certain, dead-end fantasy. No, for now, Aramis was oddly contented to be kept back, contained in a large stone room with limited light, small puffs of air, a serving of food and a long reservoir of stale water. He became resigned to this night, and with that he found an absolution from worry, the type of removal that lightens the thinking. In a familiar way, Aramis felt he was free and he shifted his thoughts, expelled all the present, and set himself a course into a new, imagined future, to an indeterminate time, in which he would be tempted to run to an undiscovered place. And with one final sigh as his head sunk still lower and his neck stretched still more, he gave into his body's demand to let go. His mind followed gratefully, and gentle slumber took firm hold.

There are welcome occasions when the gates of sleep quickly open. At once, Aramis found himself embraced by an overgrown field, thick and plush, green on bottom, the top yellow-tan bristles waving and swaying as if teasing the air. There was sunshine and flowers, morning rising beyond hills, a great lightness and light, vibrant pollens and seeds, the weeds and the insects, leaves sweet and minty or dense and pungent, a perfect carpet of life, which if not for nature's grand humor, with its rapacious fine insects and disguised nettles and thorns, who among us would not flop on our pure, naked backs and lie there all day? It was selfless nature at its purest and Aramis was floating down a trail of uncertain duration.

Within moments, with a violent, fearful start, Aramis awoke abruptly and half-consciously grabbed to save those images, that pasture, that path. With a fleeting glimpse of sunflowers and grass, his eyes blinked open suddenly to a sliver and they saw blurred, dancing spots of hazy silver light, like tiny candles that shown without a small flicker. He recognized the small gaps in the walls and knew it was sunlight, that it was not yet night. The snapshots of his dream had faded. He could not hold on. Was that trail he was on flowing smoothly as one, like connected patches of a quilt, fluttering in the wind? Or were the pictures broken sequences, sporadic images, a montage?

Aramis shut his eyes. The green fields slipped away. Aramis' bright dreams lost their color. He heard noises now. Outside the smokehouse. Or were they imagined? He sat without expression. He was at his past home. He was again in the yard of the small, quiet pastor who sat on his terrace and watched his chickens at dusk. There the man was, so pale, seated at his table on one of four chairs, tea set before him, hat on his head and pen in his hand. With an absent look, without blinking, he stared straight ahead. He rarely took note of the stack of white paper inside a red leather cover always placed on the table. He looked off to the distance and glanced down at the chickens, cocking his head and smiling as they ran. Soft demeanor and clean-shaven, with a round face and small eyes, the pastor raised, then lowered, his bushy dark eyebrows for what seemed like no reason. He smiled and showed his teeth that protruded at angles and jumped sideways and out through his thin lips. And then he looked at Aramis before returning his gaze back up to the sun and raised his white tea cup up to his lips.

Slowly, the pastor stood up as the sun began to set and he turned to walk into his small white stone house. Glancing over his shoulder, he held out his right hand and signaled to Aramis to join him inside. Aramis stood still, uncertain the sign was directed at him. But the pastor repeated his gesture, signaling with his hand, with a wave to come forward. It was clear he beckoned for Aramis to follow, and the pastor turned again and entered his house.

Curious but wary, Aramis felt his legs step forward though his head did not move. It was if only his feet and his eyes were floating to the man. Across the hard, grey stones set in the path, he saw at his feet pieces of crumbled, brown bread sprinkled before him and Aramis lowered his gaze briefly and felt a sudden urge to eat. But he stopped himself, ashamed, and continued to walk, embarrassed by his desire. He hoped the pastor had not noticed.

Before Aramis realized it, he stepped into the man's house, between large wooden doors that curved inward as they rose and formed a point at the top. Indistinct carvings protruded on the front. The pastor had turned right, but when Aramis entered, he was suddenly aware the pastor was gone. Aramis stopped and looked up. He was not in a house. He was standing inside the heavy wooden doors of the pastor's small village church. They were the same carved doors where the man had presided. He recognized them, the carvings of symbols brought to life in relief. How could have he not noticed? A chill ran right through him. He saw the glow of the windows, purple and red, with blue pictures of men, a woman holding some flowers. Now, he was standing to the side of the pews, two-thirds toward the back, against the right wall. He did not turn around. The door was no longer there. He knew without looking. He was inside the church and with each forceful inhale, his panic increased. He was forbidden from church. He was in the wrong place. He was not allowed here. He had to leave quickly, before he was caught. But he could not turn around and retreat back outside. He had to run somewhere. But where was escape?

Aramis' first thought was to run left, then down the aisle toward the back. But he stopped himself, worried the loud clicks of his footsteps on the polished wood floor would attract attention from someone who was near, though there was no one to see. He glanced up to his right and saw two great candles burning in the glistening silver stands at the front of the room. Transfixed and in awe, his mouth fell open and his face lifted higher.

The moment did not last long. With a sharp inhale, his awareness returned, and he walked quickly ahead between the dark oak pews that spread out before him. He felt the warm pressure of blood rushing to his head. His heart raced, and his legs felt weak and he crouched low as he carefully moved forward without making a sound. All he heard was his breathing. In slow, halting steps, he gently placed one foot down, then lowered the next, supporting his balance with his right wing pressed against the back of a pew. He held his head down. Step after step, he saw the floor before him. Suddenly, he stopped. He had reached the center aisle. Like an impassable border, it extended to the left and the right, the far side farther than anything he imagined, a perilous chasm without any cover. Yet it dared to be crossed. There was no place else that Aramis could go. Again, he stopped and stared for an instant. Here was the path leading up to the altar, traversed for generations through christenings and death. An exhilaration swept through him. He was inside a mystery he had never understood, kneeling at the crossroads of worshipper and worshipped. Aramis fought a sudden temptation to make his way up to where others knelt down in supplication each Sunday. Just once to walk up and gaze at the cross and the pictures that adorned either side of the sacred. To stand at the pulpit with crucifix before him and the table and chalice and candles and fabric. To see, to make sense of that which he lacked, of what was denied. He wanted the answers that were sure to float there. Without learning these secrets, he was lost to the heavens and all that was needed was contained in this room. Somewhere here must be the ephemeral keys that were granted each church from the hands of St. Peter. That's what he wanted. The keys to the door.

Why couldn't he find them? He was inside a church. He was finally here. It was home to the truth, invisible but near; the whispers of angels, silent but real. They must have all fled when they saw him walk in. The room was now cold, empty of memories but for those who were gone. Aramis was terrified. He stared at the pews across the wide aisle. They dared him to cross, to risk in a leap and trust he'd be safe. But his legs now felt numb, his heart pounded his chest. He held his breath for a moment and tried to will himself gone, to disappear from the spot and return to the yard.

Just then, Aramis heard a loud thump from somewhere. Without stopping to think, he panicked and ran out and turned to his left, hoping to find a door straight ahead. His wings flapped wildly, and his feet slipped uncontrollably along the smooth floor. He expected any instant an unseen hand to grab him from above as he flew past the last row and looked up at the door. The massive cracked wood extended up beyond sight. The carvings of saints jutted into the room and two handles with locks shone the dark color of brass. The door was locked with no key. Aramis was trapped and, without taking a breath, he spun to his right and sprinted along the left wall. A rush of blurred stones and countless pews flew by. Windows, with a bright light shining, passed high overhead as he ran far up the path. His eyes watched the ground, then up at the front, there was again no place to go. White walls all around him, he collapsed to the ground and curled himself tightly, waiting for judgment, waiting with terror.

Aramis heard another large bang and his body jumped hard with a furious start. His breathing was rapid. He opened his eyes. The sound, to his left, was the farmer pouring in food. Where he sat was still dark, though the gaps in the stone facing out to a field shone with a peaceful calm with a dim bluish light. He saw vague shadows outside and he heard receding footsteps along the gravel of the driveway as the farmer walked away. The dream suddenly flashed back in pieces through his mind. Had the dream fully ended or did the farmer interrupt? He was not caught in church. The terror was gone. It never had happened. None of it was real. But the dream would not leave him. He could still feel the fear. He stared down at the floor. Oh, so small he had felt, so helpless, so guilty. The dream was condensed as if it happened at once. He could still see the pews and the two burning candles.

Aramis, sore and still shaking, stood painfully slowly and straightened his body with a few deep groans. Stretching with care, he lifted his wings and raised on his toes and bent over slightly, twisting left and then right. As he pushed his wings down, he shut his eyes tightly, then rolled them inside, left to right, then again. He could still feel the sting of the dryness and sand.

With the sun waking to his right, Aramis began to feel the first signs of warmth. Soft beams of yellow sat up near the ceiling. He walked to his food, and thought he heard movement, a scratching, a flutter, then scratching again. He heard the cows low and heavy steps from the dog as it slowly limped past. A cat gently meowed, stretched, then softly walked by. He pressed his face to a gap between two large stones at the base. He could see with one eye the front of the house, but just a few stairs and a slice of green yard that sat out behind. He thought he saw movement behind the front steps, a quick bobbing, small head and a slight shadow behind. But the movement disappeared, and he turned back to his food.

* * *

Aramis finished eating and sat by the door, where the space at the bottom allowed for a hint of fresh air. The room continued to warm while the patches of visiting light brightened and slid at an angle down the top of the wall. As he leaned back to relax, random scenes devoid of emotion unexpectedly surfaced from the terrible dream. Aramis thought of the pastor who kept him and remembered with sadness the pain and surprise that everyone felt as his fresh, young replacement removed them all from the coop. It was every man's right to rule over chickens, but he did not understand why they were taken so quickly.

He missed the old man, with his large smile and white hands. Those times had been pleasant and, thinking of them, brought a melancholic smile. Aramis wondered why his smile waited until now rather than appearing during those days. His memory now was filled by the sun and green fields and the seeds of plowed land and the taste of small insects and the smell of bright flowers and the touch of a breeze. He could see his past yard and hear the pastor talking. He enjoyed listening to sermons as the pastor practiced to himself. And he remembered how the man would often come to visit the hens in the yard and how he would stop and bend over and smile at a few. Then why was Aramis so restless in the midst of that life? A life that was civil, and tranquil, and safe.

Because it was not! How hated memory plays tricks! There was nothing safe, or tranquil, or civil at all. The longer something lasts – does that make it safe? That's what others believed. But life taught him more. The illusion of the stable. We float down a river and look only at the water. How smooth it all looks. There's barely a ripple. But look up. Trees passing. There are rocks all around. You got here, that's true, but there's no promise of there. You probably won't make it. He had warned others so often. Then he fell for the trick. How peaceful it seemed. The pastor, the yard, and sun. Aramis knew it was not real. Each would come to an end.

* * *

For days, then, Aramis fought with an overwhelming ennui, an ennui of the place, a place, he would think, from which no afterward exists. Through exhaustion, and fear, and agitation, and dread, through the oppressive ubiquitousness of himself in that room, drowning in thoughts, too close, too bare, too direct, he sat for long periods, most of the night, or slowly wandered in circles with little rest during hours when the light, free outside, was shimmering and dancing just beyond the silent, heavy walls. A growing darkness was the norm, whether real or imagined, and, with what little light languidly dripped in through the gaps, he was able to see most of the room, except the bottom-most section of the walls near the ground. He learned which of the stones protruded into his path and he stepped lightly to one side as he passed between the wall and the various scattered objects that jutted up and out. In his mind's lighter moments, a discarded bucket, old cans and a bottle became inanimate companions to which he would nod. To a mangled stove pipe and a long twisted axle, he would bow and duck under as he made his way past.

Over seven long days, his strength slowly returned as the soreness abated from the night of the storm. In its place came impatience and that energy, both restless and unfocused, that inevitably follows. He tried several flights to the ceiling to peer out the gaps. It was dangerous because of the objects below, and after squinting in the light, the bottom seemed blacker as he fell back to earth. His forays, however, confirmed no openings through which to escape.

Most of his hours, for lack of distraction, he spent thinking of elsewhere and teasing out pieces. The present held nothing but the limits around him. The future existed as a shadowy hope. He picked at the past, recalling his owners and a succession of chickens, a few friends, none close, some acquaintances, and many strangers. He played with these faces and the names he remembered. Was he seeing them all or only a few? Certainly, not all, that was not possible. But how many were missing? He never would know. The beauty of memory can be how it forgets. Although we know that it is there, we're never tortured by the lost, those elements of past in which all is forgotten. With faces appearing, one by one, some with names, some without, Aramis came to realize there was no one he missed. That was odd, he thought. And probably sad. Sure, there were many he liked, two or three even fondly, and he had had fun with the others, laughing and playing, and at various times, a friendship would grow. He enjoyed some of their friendship, and even small aspects of many, but their closeness was by chance, a combination of place, a coincidence of age, and a shared need to try. Now, as he saw them, he felt neither ache nor a longing to return to those days.

That had not always been true. It was after he was a child. Oh, he hated these pictures that his memory would not shed. When he was a child, his mother would cry. It seemed now that all through his childhood, his mother would cry. She never spoke of the reason. She just held him and told him to enjoy a long life, then with tears on her cheeks, her eyes closed to the present, she would rock back and forth, her red and black feathers curling in tight. That's all he remembered. He never heard her laugh, at least not that he knew. Days upon days, he remembered his mother, so tired, alone sitting and rocking and sobbing. It was a long time before he learned the full reason. Later, he discovered that his mother would weep when her friends disappeared. Tired hens and old roosters. They were suddenly gone. Then she told him that someday she would go. He shouldn't worry. He'd be fine. He should smile and play and enjoy a long life. And for a while, he still enjoyed living, with his sisters and friends, in the yard, in the coop. But, as he got older, as we all do, friends began to go missing. It all seemed strange at that age, with no reason nor warning. Yet it occurred so often, and no one discussed it. Life would go on with or without any of their friends. Then came a day he will never forget. Where were his sisters? All but one disappeared. Three in one week. He demanded to know from his mother, from others, where they were going and why he remained here. His mother fell ill. Yet no one would tell him, until his anger and his curses grew too strong to ignore. So, one awful day, the coop's oldest rooster stopped and pulled him aside. He explained about life, about their eggs and their owner. He told in detail why they lived and how it would end. He said it was the same for them all, just the timing was different. That's where the others had gone, including his sisters, and yes, it was true, they would never come back. With that, his world ended. It was a devastating story. Impossible. Brutal. Aramis was numb. Then life was not life. Life was a trick. It was not even theirs but the one who showed care. How evil. Meaningless. An invisible terror, a terror that ended . . . that only would end . . . when the hands of that terror would appear with a face. . . . And with that one simple story, echoes began to appear and all that came after came after he was a child.

For the next three days, Aramis did not move. He had been thrown into a pit. Silence, and stillness, and night were the universe. Those words were familiar. He wondered from where. "That the result would be death. I knew too well to doubt." Yes, it was the old priest reading. "The mode and the hour were all that occupied or distracted me." The priest was reading aloud. Aramis' crow refused to come. All life was betrayal; all that he'd lived turned worse than foolish. It was hollow. Unthinkable. He looked at the sun and scoffed at its shine. How could it shine when all was so black? Why did it mock by giving him warmth? And the earth and the plants and the water and all – all was a hoax. It was a conspiracy to hide the full emptiness within, the sheer foolishness of all, and the thud of all dreams. Only the clouds showed an attitude that they, alone, understood. Dispassionately floating, not caring, not playing, stopping for nothing, they stayed aloof and above with no regard for us here. Aramis wished to be inside them and hidden, carried away, to where no one would find him. But cruelty compounded, with his wings he could not fly. He was bound to the earth, which he had thought gave him life, but now was a tether with his mind at the end. He had no place to go. He knew nothing of the world. He was told to accept, acquiesce and forget, to live as if each day was a lifetime, to welcome the night as the end of a journey. Use his crow, he was told, to exclaim his survival and assert through its strength that his energy still flowed. Do not blame the old farmer. He was not the source of the terror. The terror just is. It would come for him, too.

Aramis tried to accept. But then the inevitable came. On an overcast morning with the mist hanging low, he saw the farmer approach, then came screams and commotion from inside the coop. His mother was chosen and taken away. There was nothing to do. Aramis stood frozen and watched, unable to move as they carried her past the side of the house. It was the last time he saw her, tucked under an arm, her face hidden to him with her feet kicking wildly. His legs crumbled beneath him and he sat where he was and stayed there all night. No more, he concluded, would he take a cowardly path, sitting and waiting, letting others, so ignorant, determine his end. As dawn approached the next morning, Aramis stood, looked up, and followed the clouds.

Seated now, in the smokehouse, the tale belonged to someone else. It was too long ago. More imagined than remembered. Unreal in its distance and more an echo than thought. But, oh, his sweet sister. She was still there. He never returned. Why did he leave her? How could he leave? That pain would not stop. What must have she thought? How was he that cruel? By now, she was gone. No more doubts, no more fear. We should be thankful, he thought, if thankful we can be, to both be alive and then reach our end.

Aramis took a long, deep breath and leaned back with his legs crossed before him. He had three worlds before him: the outside in light, invisible but heard; the cage he was in, too close and too silent; and the parade in his mind, too loud and too real. Six days had passed. He had not made a sound, and though the echoes were growing, he managed to keep them at bay. Instead, he sat with eyes closed, hearing the three worlds collide, alternating their presence in uncertain order.

Suddenly, footsteps approached. It was late afternoon, and something was different. The farmer came only once in the morning to fill up the water and pour the feed in. Now, the sun was set low, its light, yellow and warm, high up the right wall. No, something was wrong. Aramis stood up with a start. He opened his eyes and prepared to take flight.

The slow steps came near, and the door handle moved. The rusted, black latch jumped with a dull, heavy scrape. All of a sudden, a blinding wall of bright light leapt into the room, overwhelming everything inside. Aramis' heart jumped violently, and his knees began shaking. He averted his eyes and stood perfectly still, except his wings start to tremble. He waited, not moving, expecting the farmer. But the farmer did not enter. Instead, he was leaving, slowly crunching across the driveway's small stones.

And the door was still open. A wall of fresh cool air took over the small room. Aramis squinted and blinked several times. It was too bright to look, with piercing glints of white, then of yellow, then of blue as he tried. Instead, he looked down, and saw for the first time the full expanse of his cell. The objects around him looked smaller and lifeless. They were pieces of metal, of no use and discarded. The dark corners at bottom that had receded to nothing, were quiet and harmless, nothing but dirty white stones set deep into the earth, not dismal grey and dim yellow as he thought they must be.

Aramis looked up and shielded his eyes with one wing. He inhaled, then exhaled, two or three times, and walked out of the smokehouse, his lungs full of air. The sun low to his left, a slight breeze swept his back and under his feathers. A chill down his spine, he stretched out his wings. And Aramis, in what felt the first time in his life, let out a long and clear crow, proclaiming his presence, announcing survival. There was no mistaking its message. It was an exceptional crow, extraordinary and good.

Chapter 10

A Very Strange Day When the Door Opens

The farmer spent a puzzling week. He felt ill at ease. He felt disrupted. His typically calm and routine days were disturbed. Physically, he was healthy, as healthy as, well, as a healthy old man can be. Without getting too personal, let's say only that his joints ached no more than usual. His breathing was clear, inadequate to his desires, but sufficient for his efforts. His hearing and eyesight were no more attenuated than they had progressively become over the decades, whisked clean, as it were, of the distracting perspicacity of youth. His digestion, though lagging, was still chugging along. And his voice remained strong, even if seldom proof was given.

No, his physical attributes passed the week in equanimity. It was his inward constancy that faltered, his quotidian balance, that compass for life's landscape that subtly, but resolutely, tells us which way we walk. And the calibration of time, or, more precisely, the span of time between his non-events, was out of kilter. Too much time piled up here. Not enough over there. He was aware of something, like a vague sensation that someone, perhaps, was playing an April Fool's trick with his clock, or was resetting the sun. By the time he noticed, his pattern had unraveled – not just one, but indeed his pattern of patterns. How many we all have, like a stack of maps with one road, absentmindedly followed with good reason and no thought. But reverse the cold and hot faucets, move the front door to back, or throw away the hat stand, and you might as well spin a man around and camouflage his way. And with just that one road wiped clean from the cartographer's tool, a man is forced to remember how he got where he is as he searches for an exit.

Yes, suddenly for the farmer, the way had disappeared. Of course, as will happen, the signs began small as insignificant missteps that don't mean a thing, or at least one supposes, until it's too late. So, one morning after Sunday with the kitchen light on, the farmer peered down, then returned to his bedroom to put on his clothes. The next day, he awoke, ate a normal breakfast and went back for a nap. That morning, Marie and the dog, and yes, it was so, that even the cat, paced and wondered and waited for their food. And one evening at dinner, he sat down with his plate, then was back up for a fork, and then again for a glass, then again for the water, then again for the bread. And here's the cabinet – what did I come for? He had his shoes, but where were his socks? And so on it went. Where are the gloves? His hat? The broom? He turned on the hall light as he went out the door. Had he not brushed his teeth, or was this the second time?

Although he did not notice, his dusty path was becoming a jungle. Everything seemed foreign, overgrown and covered yet, at the same time, it was if it all was revealed. Every step forgotten, then every step rethought. He walked out his front door. Does he go left or the right? Stand up or sit down? Raise this hand or that? All the moves we take for granted, each decision that we make, when considered one by one sets that paradox in motion when each minute lasts forever as the hours overlap and time does not allow for anything to be done. No reason today to walk in the fields. Next week will come to traipse through the woods. It was more important to stay home. Look at the chores that need to be done. The welcome mat insists to be shaken. The steps to the cellar call to be swept. The firewood in front cry out for restacking. How had he not noticed? Too much to do. When unexpectedly illumined, even the most mundane takes on brilliance.

And in truth, the chores were warranted, like making the bed or cleaning a soap dish. Whether there were, more objectively speaking, tasks with greater importance could not be said. Was raking small stones that were the sparse driveway more in keeping with the cosmos than moving a box from the shed to the barn? Perhaps to the box, but not to the stones. They didn't care. And it didn't matter. The farmer did not wander more than twenty feet from his house, so he noticed at random and rejiggered the import of whatever he chose. Look over there. Sacks of feed out of place. The store room's a mess. Small branches are scattered all over the yard. It was time for a bundling. No need to leave the clutter.

Now, one might have considered his activities (if one was observing) little more than a typical spring cleaning since it was that time of year. The sky was clear blue with pervasive qualities of renewal. Nature's green force was sprouting its head. The crocus was gone. Daffodils still showed. Trees burst with the droplets of life at the tip of each branch. The birds and the insects seemed more intent and vivacious. Flocks of clouds, when they came, steadfastly migrated and, it would seem, with a pre-defined route to an important destination. With the air's crispness and clarity, inhaling gave a sharp cool tinge to the nose and there was a clean chill to the hands and the back of the neck. It had all the qualities of days meant for straightening and opening and airing out big empty rooms. All that was true. But here the windows stayed shut with the carpets inside. The farmer never ventured inside during daylight all week.

There was no need. Beginning with a sweater and a jacket over an old long-sleeved shirt, the farmer removed each layer in succession during the first languorous hours as the sun rose up high. Through lunchtime, during which it had not yet occurred to him to eat, his small activities and the ground generated a heat that lasted until dusk, which then reminded him once again of the need to eat supper. And then into the house, where the kitchen sat, expecting, with the welcoming shelves at attention and the appliances ready. They were poised to speak, to offer assistance and to ask, "how might we help?" Although the farmer heard nothing, he noticed with detail how comfortable they looked. The hearth, the oldest, was the commander of sorts. The three buckets in front: for whatever will burn; for what animals will eat; and the last, a collection of what little was left. Then sat the stove, then the counter, then cabinets. Then more to the right, to the turn of the wall, sat the sink and the drain board and a shelf to the door, then across to the refrigerator, more shelves and more drawers and then still more cupboards and a stuffy closet stuffed full of other stuff never used. In fact, everywhere he looked, was something that belonged, holding and storing and offering to give. A room flavored by time, perfumed by the spices of all who ate there. Perhaps it was the surfeit of that which remained of the thick weighty presence of those now departed. But increasingly these days, the farmer lingered at the table, staring across, and more slowly than normal tore at his bread. He chewed the warmed food, drank his red wine, and sometimes ate a soft pear with three slices of cheese. And with the last sip of wine, sleep distantly called, and serenely whispered that the day was at end. With his dish in the sink, he stepped lightly to bed.

Because changes, we all know, have a way of arriving when we're not at home, it was Friday before he noticed five days had slipped past. He felt well-rested and stronger, strangely clear-minded, as he pursued his distractions. It was not until breakfast one morning, the thought first arose. He had not left the yard. A week had flown by. His mind had been wandering and he had lost his routine. He saw himself now, sitting there, unusually extending the length of his small meal as he stared at the bread, then the knife, then the glass, and he picked up his fork. Look at the tines. The two on the inside have both sides tapered in. The two outer ones are straight, only their inner edge is angled to a point. Were they always this way? He had grown up with these forks since before he could talk. Nothing was new, and nothing had changed. So why the past week? Why these strange thoughts? The rooster's so silent. It had not made a sound, or had he not noticed? And then there's that hen. He had been staring at her, even seeking her out. Why had he done that? Why does he care? The two are just chickens. They're for food when alive and especially when dead. Several times, in fact, he found the hen in the coop, acting listless and bored, as much as he could impute the sense of boredom to hens. When not in her house, she was under the tree, not pecking, not running, not walking, not playing. That's no way for a chicken to sit, back to the tree, legs straight forward, for hours on end.

Then there's that tree. The farmer thought of the tree. How could he not? His grandsons had come to watch him and their father cut, and split, and cart away logs from the tree that had fallen. The boys kept running, with all four arms and twenty little fingers, pointing and waving, insisting to both men that the old tree had moved. "See there, this goes that way," called the two taking turns. "And then this is there and that one's like this. Don't you remember? This had been more there before that one fell." The farmer and his son nodded without looking. Yes, yes, they both said. Watch out for the saw.

By Tuesday, the fallen tree had been cleared. The next day, the old farmer ventured into the shed for the rake. He saw the branches and twigs and fetched the tool from the shed. He stood by the house with his back to the sun and felt the warmth on his neck while he pulled the rake toward him in slow and long motions, over and over, a hundred times more, the rake scratched at the ground. Suddenly, though, the farmer stopped and looked up. There, cast on white stones of the shed's long front wall, were two silent pillars, projections of shadow, his and the tree's, as they stood side by side. Up to his left, the old tree's massive two limbs extended as two fat grey bars on the coop's outer wall, raised and thrust back. On the red roof of the shed was the old tree's third branch reaching off to the right, stretched back as it climbed the slant of the tiles. The farmer held his rake midway through a stroke. There was something different. There was. But what? Had he seen this before? He had no memory of these shadows. He had certainly stood here, so why did this scene look suddenly new? The farmer shrugged and continued his chore, but he kept glancing up, as if the answer was written and might be announced any moment.

But no answer came. And each day that went by, the question resurfaced. He would walk past the tree and look up and then down. The wood was not torn. The ground had not shifted. How could he not know? It was here his whole life. But he couldn't remember. Had the tree looked this way or was his mind playing tricks? Did it move? Even slightly? Or was it always this way? He had sat there last week, fixing the lock. He had walked through this yard for more than seventy years. He had played on this tree and then watched his children there, too. How could he not know which way it had faced?

From that day on, he discovered surprising new reasons to walk through the yard, none of them pressing but each with a purpose that suddenly occurred. He thought to check the small flowers planted near to the shed, though there was nothing to do but clear off some leaves. Then later he went to prune back a bush. Then out with the snippers to cut down the grass that eternally hugged and wilted yellow by the house. With both knees on the ground, his head hunched over, it took only minutes to finish each job. From there, he would sit, his arms round his knees and let hours pass as he let his mind wander. So, it was, on a Thursday, he never moved from the yard, but sat there all day, and watched the shadows cross slowly. He kept watching the tree. It was becoming more difficult to deny what was slowly revealed. But it could not be true. It would have made as much sense to have the farm spin around. Or the house, or the stars, or for cows to start flying. Trees cannot spin without being pulled from the ground. Even if hit with a terrible force. Yet something has happened. But this makes no sense. I'm sure that it was. My memory is wrong.

The week, then, in short, was lived in a haze, the way many of us see things when perception recedes, as if we'd spent the day with a fever while reading a book and then quickly looked up. No matter the reason, a distance widens between our world and theirs. A synaptic delay separates thoughts from perception. Words, when they come, are someone's creation. Whether cause or effect, revelation and loss are always companions.

It was for that reason, it was met with rare relief when the postman stopped by. Rare, because the postman never brought the mail up the long drive unless he had a package that would not fit in the box. Relief, because the man, even more than his delivery, was a distraction so complete that it usually meant the day was disrupted, that plans were abandoned. But being this day, when one more disruption gave soothing continuity, the farmer welcomed the postman with an unexpected acceptance. Standing with aged effort, the farmer walked around the corner of his house and met the postman out front.

"Bonjour" they each said.

"How are you?" asked the farmer.

"Just checking for damage," the postman explained quickly. "I feel it's my duty, you understand, as a government official."

The farmer knew what this meant. He had no special package. He was picking up, not dropping off, embracing his own nature and searching for gossip. Everyone knew the postman delivered more tales than he ever did letters.

The farmer nodded his head and proceeded to disappoint. None of his answers were worth repeating. The farm had survived and, too bad for the postman, no one was hurt. There'd be no report, official or not.

"Ah, very good, very good," the postman remarked. "Count yourself lucky. Not everyone can say the same. Just down in . . . " and the postman launched into his one true vocation, delivering the news, nevermind the mail. The farmer stood silently, while listening to stories of the damage at neighbors, of fallen trees on a road, and of the son of a friend (of the postman, not the farmer), who had just joined the army. "He should have stayed home where he'd be of some use," the government official and former Aspirant said with unhidden disdain.

The farmer was enjoying this, like having a stranger arrive and describe a visit to Mars. And it was not just the words. It's never just words. The story from one man can bring you to tears, while the same from another makes you laugh 'til you fall. The ones from the postman always held your attention, whether or not you heard what he said. It was the man himself that had you in awe. He was a curious fellow, about as tall and cozy as a dried stalk of corn, who had such a rare knack for grooming that the farmer, and everyone, could not help but marvel. What he said never mattered. Just watching him speak was well worth the visit. It was like god's little joke, the kind he plays on us all in one way or another. And here was the postman, teasing right back.

It was the only explanation that made any sense. Having been granted early in life an exceedingly, and impressively, bald patch of head, the postman concluded, at some point in time, to shave the rest of his pate, possibly for consistency's sake. But evidently, his head had objected, and diverted the hair, in adamant protest, straight down the sides and not just onto, but into his ears. And there it took root, sprouting and flowing like silk from a corn, a glorious display of man's ubiquitous ability to regard, or to not, whatever he wants. It was a mystery to all that he never considered, neither apparently did his Amazonian wife, that his ears (at least) were past time to harvest. No wonder the neighbors gave him a nickname, Poilu la Poste, but not to be cruel, so never to his face.

Now the postman was talking. "But that was not all," he said, and the farmer attempted to follow the plot. There was the one-eyed dog that was found in the river. Lost by a tourist from England, they say. Yes, from England. Oh, the Germans are better. Remember the time . . . ? And several more stories about no one they knew. And you hear about Martin? Oh, yes, you know. Then how about that fire? No, that's not my route. But the others in the office say it was no accident that it happened on Monday. Supposed to rain next week. That'd be good. Ah, look at the time. At least thirty minutes are lost. Where does time go when there's so much to say? Ok, time to rush off. Done for the day. Hope you stay well. Good evening to you. The postman began to walk back to his car in that springy lope of his, as if his shins were too long and his feet made of planks. The farmer turned and saw his old smokehouse. "Oh, Mr. Ricoeur," the farmer quickly called out. "Could you please check if someone lost a rooster in the storm?" No, not killed, the farmer explained. Lost in the wind, in the field, by the road.

Both men nodded, and the old farmer walked back toward the house. He looked down and examined the mail in his hand. The electric company – a bill. A colorful card – sheets and towels are on sale. A catalogue of tractors – all lined up on parade. A letter from his daughter. He knew by the handwriting without checking the stamp. He sat down on the steps and placed the other mail to his side. Leaning back and pushing out his right leg, he reached into his pocket and pulled out a penknife to open the envelope. He took his glasses from his jacket's breast pocket and opened the pages, more than usual, he thought, and he began to read.

Dear Papa,

I hope you are still well. I received your letter and you said you felt fine. I worry, though, because you are alone, and I know that sometimes you try to do too much.

Aunt Harietta tells me you had a storm down there yesterday. I hope nothing was damaged, but that is why, I suppose, I was thinking about you and worrying. Pepin is next door so please ask him for help if you have any problems or damage to the house. I know he is busy but I'm certain he will do whatever needs doing. I know Dorothee would do anything for you. So just let her know what needs to be done. She'll get her husband to be a good son – wives are good at that, aren't they?

By the way, you were right about Harietta. I talked with her a few days ago and she did sound tired. But she told me she won't have to move. That's good for her since she doesn't like to go anywhere. It's good for you too. She can keep coming to have supper with you every now and then. Frederic and Oliver sound happy also. I have not spoken with them in a month maybe, but they are busy with their lives, their children, their funny wives and their work. Charmaine and Bernadina really are different. I know they are kind and they love their husbands and children, but I do wonder how my brothers survive. Remember the time Bernadina threw away all the dishes because they were old? I thought of that a few days ago as I needed to clear out some space from my cabinets. I think she should live with you for a month. I can't imagine what she would do to your kitchen. And Charmaine. Have you seen her recently? I spoke to Neville a month ago. Is she feeling better? I can't imagine having five children. It would be funny to see you and Bernadina try to live together, but I don't think the same with Charmaine and her five little ones. For your own sake and safety, I hope they never come and stay with you. I wish them all peace if you speak with them.

Papa, thank you for your letter. Yes, I will visit soon, but I have not made reservations yet. I have been very busy. But I will make plans and let you know.

You asked about my house. You should visit. It's lovely and there is room for you if you come. I can get you a ticket and pick you up. Pepin can take you to the airport. I'd love to have you here for as long as you can stay. I have many friends you would enjoy meeting. They are smart and kind and they are interesting people, from all over the world with many different jobs. You might enjoy the city also. It's been so many years since you visited, right after mother died, and we did enjoy going into shops and walking through the parks. We could do that again.

My work is going well. I'm taking more classes, but I'll have to wait to see if they are truly teaching what I want to know, or what I need to know. I don't know if I will go until the end.

I've read a few books recently and I will bring you one that I think you would enjoy. It's about a man who travels to different places all over the world. He writes about how the geography and the history and the food and the animals have made these people who they are and how it all fits together with their religious beliefs and how society is trying to crush their beliefs and change who they are. He writes that they don't understand. They have known for centuries who they are and they don't need to go looking but then others come to their villages and farms and country and tell them they're wrong and there is too much they don't know and they should learn about it and go other places to understand the world better. I'm not sure if those people should be left alone or whether the plan in the world is for everyone eventually to know everyone else and everyone should all leave and travel and meet each other. (Maybe the computer is god's first step in the plan.) But people tell them that they need to become aware of the world and many of these people respond by asking why? But one man leaves and travels and comes home. He then tries to explain what he saw. The book's not really about him, but somehow he's the one you remember when you're finished.

It's an interesting book and for some reason it made me think about mother and how she used to say that you have to wake up, not just in the morning, but all day also. You have to stay awake and see the world and yourself. You cannot daydream through life. Remember when she'd walk through the house and call out "time to wake up" when she saw us just sitting, or reading, or playing a game? She used to say that we had to do what we were placed here to do. I wish I had paid more attention to her. Maybe I could remember more.

I think of that because sometimes I wonder if I'm just daydreaming. How do we know? How do we know if we're dreaming of our home or if we've found it already? Is there always a new destination even if we sit still? Is there such a thing? Do we ever find anything or anyplace while we're searching for it? Maybe our destination hides until we stop looking. Maybe I've already found it and I don't even know. Maybe that's why I don't know where to look. But aren't we forced to look? We must have goals and our job is to find them. I achieved some, I suppose, but mostly they keep changing. I get near one and then realize I was wrong. I feel sometimes like I'm always wrong. I get near the end and see that it's not what I thought it was. It's not the end at all. The people or the place or the job is not right. I don't know how to explain it. But we must have goals, we must seek something, even if it changes. Isn't that right? If we don't, then either we don't grow or we don't know ourselves well enough to know where to seek. And then our goal is to know ourselves better.

Well, I don't expect you to answer these questions. I'm just chatting a bit with you about what's on my mind. So nevermind the questions. Just write back and tell me how you are and what's new on the farm. I enjoy your letters more than trying to talk on the phone. I can reread them if I want. So tell me, do you have any new plantings this year? How are the animals? And how are my nephews? Have they broken any arms yet climbing those trees? Are they still bigger than the chicken or are they shrinking as you told them they would if they did not eat their supper? Maybe they are now smaller than the chicken. If that's so, they should be kept indoors. By the way, how is that hen? Is she still putting up with you?

I hope you are well and all your dreams come true.

Love,

Charisse

The farmer stared at the white space under the last page. His right hand, holding the three sheets gently, with his thumb on the top and his four fingers beneath, curled the bottom corner to keep the top from drooping. He was looking not at the paper, but at his daughter's fine face as he thought it must have looked when she was writing these words. Charisse had ended the letter the way she ended all her letters. It was almost childlike, that wish, and he liked the fact she never changed it. His gaze rose an inch and he studied her script. Her letters flowed with ease and seemed bold and melodic in their rhythm of curves.

"She's a fine girl," he thought. He sat there staring and picturing her, his grown-up girl, like a sunflower stem, strong and straight, standing up tall, yet vulnerable and in a field all alone. She was now a grown woman, headstrong and clever, but what he saw was a little girl with skinny white legs and long brown hair, shy and insecure, laughing with her chickens. How she loved those chickens, he said to himself, without forming any words.

The farmer's eyes began to fill. "I must be sick," he thought, and with a hard, conscious breath, he exhaled with deep force through his avian nose and lowered the papers and leaned his head back while he stared straight ahead under partly closed lids. The farmer sat for several minutes. Roaming images of the past flowed through his mind. It was a distraction too strong and complete to be noticed.

The afternoon was passing. The sun was setting, casting the barn's cool shadow to the base of the steps. The farmer's trance was broken by a cool chill that swept between his shoulders. Rising slowly, he folded the letter four times before placing it into his front right pocket. As he stood, the site of a door caught his attention and he walked straight ahead, across the driveway to the side of the arch. There, without turning his head, he reached out with his right arm, swung the smokehouse door open, turned around, and went into his house.

A few minutes later, standing in his kitchen, the farmer heard a strong, deep, and resounding crow.

Chapter 11

Dreading the Unmet Other

The farm stopped. There were no moos. No singing birds. No jumping grasshoppers. No twittering butterflies. No rustling wind. No barking dog. No stirring grass. No movement. No sound. For a prolonged second, the world held its breath.

It had been more than a year since a rooster's crow had been heard in this yard, heard on this farm, or heard with such force. The sound was forgotten. Now, here it was. Although memory is a deceiving partner, even in all its years, never was heard a crow such as this. Overwhelming and powerful, it was a crow that hushed all else in shame, directed other sounds to kneel, and challenged any noise in the yard to compete in vain. Heard in the stillness of a placid warm day, a rooster's crow is one of nature's great exclamations. Its unmistakable clarity, its piercing call, its absolute insistence is equal only to the roar of a lion. Both animals, barely related, yet gloriously maned, asserting, announcing, and commanding their world. All the rooster lacks is the thunder and ferocity, and perhaps the chill of death, the other delivers. But it is no less wondrous and pure for the lacking.

Marie, lying in her nest, sat up suddenly, her head snapping to attention, her eyes flashing open, and the feathers on her back bristling instinctively for flight. It was such a singular and unexpected crow, so near but impossible, she thought, that she was half-certain she was dreaming. She waited, without moving, for a second crow to confirm. All was silent.

One at a time, sounds returned to the yard. The cows lowed. Then, a grasshopper jumped. A breeze rustled leaves. The cat walked by. It meowed. A tractor started from over the hills. Buzzing resumed. Scratching was heard. Birds called as they alighted. Marie became certain that she had been mistaken. All had returned. It was a dream to be sure.

The sound of the crow, however, stirred Marie from her boredom. She arose slowly and fluttered to the ground, looking for a bit of food and wanting a long drink. She stretched slightly and wandered to her door, poking her head out to test the air and adjust her eyes from the denuded light of the coop to the dusky brightness outside.

She looked at the tree, then calmly moved right. There, across the drive, a black figure stood against the white stones of the smokehouse. Like a statue. A specter. Or worse still, an invader.

Marie's wings fell slack while her head rose slightly, and her mouth slowly fell open. She did not know what to do, and more pressingly, she did not know what to think. Her reaction was not of pleasure or displeasure. It was a stunned awareness that another chicken, like her but not like her, was present. She could feel the blood rush to her head. She was flooded by panic, not from fear but confusion.

She broke her gaze quickly and turned, stumbling, back inside. "What is this?" she thought. "What is this? Who is this? Why is he here?" Then in rapid succession: "Where did he come from? I should not have run in. I should go back out. I bet I looked scared. I should go back out. Oh, is he alone? How many more? Oh, why is this happening? And why now? What is this?

Marie quickly convinced herself not to go out. It would look awkward and planned. She would stay in her coop. But she would stay out of her nest. She could never sit still, and if he, and the others, of course there were others, oh, how many others, would come into the house, there must be many others, he would not come alone, she did not want to be caught sitting alone in her nest. If she was lying in bed, she would feel more exposed when they suddenly burst in.

Oh, why are they here? She asked herself again. And who was that one? He saw me for sure. Now they know I'm in here. Marie's shoulders slouched forward. She stared at the ground. Why can't they leave? The storm was enough. The tree almost killed me. Now this? Now this? New housemates to deal with.

Marie walked over to the far, left corner of her coop, put her back to the wall, sat down and waited.

Aramis had also seen Marie. He had come outside to take his first glimpse of where he was, where he had been for almost a week, where he was captive and where he might live. He saw the open field to his right, through the archway, past the linden and the box tree, and his first thought was to run. But wait, he thought. Best to consider. That will come later. There's time for that still. First, see the surroundings and search out who else, what else, where else was around him. As he looked left to the yard, into the afternoon sun that shone too brightly in his unacclimated eyes, there, unexpectedly, was a small bright head, bathed in light yellow, the red top and white feathers glowing forth like a beacon. Unlike Marie, Aramis was not startled, but he was surprised. He had been there a week and he had heard no crow nor incessant clucking that inevitably comes with a coopful of hens.

Now she was gone, having vanished inside before he had time to react. He had stared without flinching, not with intent, but as his mind emptied and gaped. Then she turned around so quickly. He could barely remember now what he saw. And she had certainly seen him. But she had not spoken, made a greeting, or waved. Or had she? Perhaps. But not that he noticed. He could not remember. He only recalled his surprise and impression of a light yellow and red – and very pretty – blur.

For several minutes, Aramis stood in precisely the same position. He looked slightly to his right and slightly to his left, but his eyes continued to dart back to the coop.

No one appeared. Aramis waited. There was no movement. Aramis waited. He kicked the ground with his right foot and turned his head slowly as his eyes looked about. Then, as always occurs when we stand for too long, our survey of landscape turns its eye back on ourselves. And at that moment, Aramis caught himself looking. He did not want it obvious he was waiting for her should she suddenly decide to poke her head out. So, he quickly turned around, stepped inside the smokehouse, seated himself strategically by the far side of his door, which he carefully kept open, so that he might see, at an angle, if she were to exit the coop.

"Oh, I hadn't thought of this," he muttered to himself. "How could I have been wrong? Of course, I'm not alone. It's a farm. There are probably dozens in that house. There always are. But they're so quiet. Oh, I never thought of this. How stupid of me. This is going to be hard."

Aramis was not upset to live with others. He knew well how to keep himself apart. It was mostly that he dreaded the routine of meeting them. Forcing a smile, being oh-so-polite, hearing (then forgetting) all of their names, feigning an interest, pretending to care, hoisting up that friendly persona. Then they would stare from the top of his disfigured comb to the bottom of his feet, repeatedly glancing at his legs, in a way they hoped he might not notice, as they tried to guess his age. And then he would answer all of their questions for the next week or so. That's what he dreaded. The questions. The questions they'd have. Would he lie? Omit? Or tell them the truth? No, not that. A portion perhaps. But never tell all. That gives them too much and hens can't be trusted.

Well, I'm too tired now, he thought. The sun is setting. I can meet them tomorrow. I can always leave later. Here's the arch. There's the field. It was this thought that had consoled him many times before, in too many coops, helping him survive through tumultuous nights. It was the one thought he relied on. What fate has in store, we never would guess. Yet, after it comes, it might not be expected, but it's never surprising.

Aramis yawned. Again, a new future. What is it with hens? I'll wait until morning. It's too late tonight. He looked at the field. I'll decide all that later. I can leave when I'm ready. And I can always leave. I can always be ready.

With that last thought tucked in tight, he stood up, walked to his pile of paper and straw, moved himself about, and bedded down for the night.

* * *

Marie, in the coop, still had not moved. She remained seated in the corner, waiting for the impending intrusion. Another change to her life. Another altered path she could neither plan nor avoid. She tried to stay focused on the door, though her mind wandered back as time slowly passed.

She sat, in disbelief, that this was how the long week would end. Not since that night, and during what came soon after, had she felt so alone and so lost in the present. She had succeeded long ago in stopping her future.

"Now this," she thought. "Others are here. Why is my life full of sudden interruptions?" She shook her head at the thought that she preferred to be alone, to be by herself, in her unwanted loneliness.

She raised her head to the door. She waited and listened for the unwelcome guests.

She saw Aramis again. Who was he? she wondered. Where did he come from? Where would he sleep? And where are the others? Oh, why don't they come!? This last question screamed in her head. "If they're going to come in, just please get it over!" She tried to relax. "Maybe, they won't. Maybe they're gone. Maybe they went back to wherever they're from."

Marie knew that was not likely. Chickens do not show up from no place and just as soon disappear. So, Marie stayed where she was. She did not want to spend the night in the corner, but she would not go to her nest. What if, in fact, he was all alone? Somehow, she knew she could not decide whether she wanted him here or hoped he would leave. She did not want either. Or more likely, both.

Chapter 12

An Overdue Acquaintance and More

Marie awoke in the corner in the same uncomfortable place, in the same uncomfortable position, she had fallen asleep the night before. As she opened her eyes, she recalled immediately what had transpired, that prolonged wait with an ominous sense of impending intrusion, the doubts and fears that had plagued her sleep with the questions of what her life would become smothered again by the presence of others.

So, Marie was pleased, relieved, but mostly perplexed, that no one came in during the night. She had prepared herself for the arrival of others, even practicing in her mind how she would greet them and what words were best to explain who she was, and which was her nest. She expected, or hoped, they would be polite, as they themselves would be dreading what they might find, and she planned to act as hostess, inviting them politely to enjoy their new home.

Living with a new group of strangers, however, brought back the painful memories of before. And here, this new group would be coming as one. They would be friends. There would be cliques, there would be leaders, there would be patterns, and they would outnumber and outwit her, and speak behind her back. It would not matter that she was here first. That they were the new ones. That this was her home.

But they had not come. She heard nothing all evening and she slept through the night. "Maybe I'm wrong. They all went away." And as that thought drifted and she along with it, the spell suddenly broke with a mocking first crow. Marie kept her head down. "No, there they were. That rooster's still here. The others are with him. Oh, now here's another." She lowered her head slowly and remembered a saying she had made up when young. "Some hens are born to roost; some have roosters thrust upon them." There was nothing funny about it now, to her, at that moment, and she cringed after being hit by a third, deafening crow.

Whereas Marie felt enslaved to host a detestable, yet unavoidable, party, imagine how Aramis felt. He woke up thinking himself the lone uninvited guest at a houseful of friends. He arose and cleared his lungs three powerful times. The crows made him feel stronger and, with the soreness of muscles gone, he arched his back and felt more sure and clear-headed than he had in weeks. He imagined the coop and saw the face of Marie as he had glimpsed her before. He would look for her among the others, he decided. It was best in a crowd always to move, and as she was the only one he had seen, seeking her out would at least give him direction.

The time had come. Aramis stretched and took in a deep breath, filling himself, steeling himself with strength and resolve. He reached his front door. He stopped. Was there no way to avoid this? Put off the encounter? He tried to convince himself to go back and sit down. But what good would that do? They were here whether he liked it or not. The farmer would not let him stay in the smokehouse forever. Eventually, if he stayed, if he lived, he would be taken to the coop. Aramis recited simple phrases from the pastor. "Anticipation is more stressful than any act we perform." "New chapters must begin with the first page being turned." There were those and many others. I'm tired of hearing that, Aramis thought. He peered out his door and looked to the left. There was no one outside.

"They might still be sleeping," he thought, hesitating again. He took a deep breath. "It is better now when they are all inside."

Slowly and lightly, he walked toward the coop in what he hoped, if someone was watching, appeared a casual, confident, nonchalant manner. He pulled in several more, deep breaths and kept himself standing up straight. With a gentle couple pecks, he tapped on the sash of the white wooden door. He took two steps back and waited. There was no answer. They must not have heard, he thought. That was odd. Coops are never quiet at this time of morning. Yes, this place is strange. Stepping forward, he knocked again a bit harder.

"Yes," Marie said immediately, more in declaration than in question. It was a voice of weary politeness, not a voice of hello. Now here they all were about to swarm in. Marie was as ready as anyone could make themselves for the end of the world.

"Bonjour?" Aramis repeated. It was an exaggerated question, asking as much whether someone was there as asking the faint voice (which he was not sure he had heard) if it existed and if so, might it be willing to speak a bit louder.

Marie raised her shoulders, then her head. "Yes," she said again, with more effort this time. She was no longer afraid. The end had come. There was no more denying. Goodbye to her life.

Aramis pushed the door with one foot. "Oh, hi, bonjour," he said, poking his head in. "May I come in?"

Marie looked at him. She tilted her head and looked at him more. In fact, she stared. Her face shone with fear and bewilderment. (Aramis saw that it shone but thought nothing else.) That was a strange question, Marie thought. Maybe the strangest she'd ever heard. Was he trying to be funny? Perhaps sarcastic? Yet he asked it so simply, so innocently. What? No one, not men, not children, not hens, not mice, not the cat, and certainly not roosters – no one ever asked permission to come into a coop.

"Allô?" asked Aramis again. He saw Marie sitting there in a corner away from the door, away from the nests. She was looking at him, her look frozen and curious.

"Are you ok?" he asked.

With the second question, Marie suddenly realized she was gawking. Oh, he was talking. He asked a question. What was it? Oh. Yes. "Yes, of course, you can come in," Marie responded with a hint of annoyance.

Aramis hesitantly stepped forward. With his coat of black feathers, he looked like a giant, a boulder of flint, moving toward her and blocking the light of the door. He glanced around, confused. The coop was empty. Bare. And there she was, huddled in a corner.

"Bonjour," he said, with a halt in his voice. "Well, this, this . . . is a nice house." It was, in fact, a very nice house, except it had the eerie feel of an abandoned museum, as if all was display, put there as props, stuck behind glass walls, with one moving figure, trapped by mistake.

"Thank you," she said.

"Where is everyone?" Aramis asked.

"Everyone?" Marie asked. "Everyone?" she repeated. "I haven't seen everyone. I mean, I didn't see them. Anyone."

"Oh." Aramis said. He looked to the floor. "Then, perhaps they went out."

"Yes, perhaps in the yard." Marie blankly replied, finding the slightest of hopes that he, too, and soon, might join them outside.

"No," Aramis said as he lifted his eyes to Marie. My goodness, she's pretty. But incredibly shy. "No, they're not in the yard. I would have seen them. Just now. I walked through the yard. In fact, I'm surprised, it's dead around here."

Marie's eyes flashed up to his. There was a long silence that screamed in her ears. She nearly burst into tears. Her exhaustion and pain came back from nowhere and pushed to her eyes the sight of lost housemates playing in the yard. She had not expected the vision and, caught unaware, she was not ready for its return with such emotional force. She froze for a second and let the rush pass by. Then her shoulders dropped slowly, and her expression softened then wilted.

"I'm sorry," she said. "What did you say?"

"The others. I didn't see them in the yard," Aramis said. "I don't know where else they would go. I thought they must be here, maybe asleep."

"No," she said. "Why would they be here?"

"Because . . . " he began.

"They were with you."

"They were with me? Who was with me?" What did she mean? Who was this hen? Aramis wanted to leave.

"The others, of course. The others with you." Why was he making this even more difficult?

Before he could think, Aramis' felt guilty. He was not sure why. Maybe it was the tone of her voice. Or the look on her face. He had the urge to apologize. But apologize for what? For what? He must have done something. But what? He wondered. He was guilty of what?

"No, there are no others with me. I came here myself," he said. "I mean, the farmer brought me. I'm here all alone. And I came by myself. I just stopped by to introduce myself. To you . . . and the others." Then after a pause: "Have I done something to annoy you?"

Marie was about to respond. "Oh," was all she could think of. But not even that sound could escape through the thought that overwhelmed her. One second, she was swept by the vision of those lost, the ones who were buried a long time ago. The next second, she's gripped by a smokehouse of chickens who do not exist. Neither image made sense.

"You're alone?" she asked.

"Yes," he said. "Yes, I'm here alone. My name's Aramis."

"I see," Marie said as if she was still in a dream. "No, no one lives here. I live here. I'm Marie."

And with that, the two were finally introduced. They had learned more about each other in those first few minutes than if they had spoken for hours, though they would know it only later. Because even in silence, there's a message to hear. It might take years to play out, but it's all there from the start. Because the beauty of silence is that betrays what it is, playing richer than the most delicate and complex of chords. Quick, Marie panicked, find a few words to disguise. To cover the silence. Find something to say that will hide all the rest! But the more her mind screamed, the less the words would come out.

"Excuse me," Aramis ventured. "Are you feeling ok?"

With that, Marie suddenly saw how ridiculous she was, still seated in the corner with her dazed look communicating a dazed mind behind it. She had not moved. She had not played hostess. She had not been polite.

"Oh, yes, thank you," Marie said, standing slowly. "Would you like to come in? Oh, you are in. I'm sorry. I'm just a little tired, I guess."

"That's all right," Aramis said, taking another look around. There were at least two dozen nests in this house, in four stepped layers leading up to his right. He could see Marie's. It must have been hers. It was the only one whose edges were not covered in fine dust, and there was a small square of blue and yellow fabric poking over the left side with a few red and green threads that were dangling off the front. There was less straw on the floor than is typical in these houses and in the center sat a wooden box below two dangling perches that looked completely unused.

"Yes, this is a nice house," he repeated.

"Thank you," Marie said. "It stays dry. And, usually it's warm."

Again, there was silence, but this time, less awkward. Aramis took a few steps forward but resisted entering any farther.

While he was looking around, Marie edged about six steps to her left and stood at the base of the descending plateaus of nests. Marie glanced nervously and repeatedly up to her left, in the direction of her nest. Aramis looked toward the back wall. The present silence continued as each of them now, broadening their gaze, furtively looked to the ground, nervously glanced at her nest, then quickly looked left, then to the right, then again to the floor. Only once or twice did their eyes meet as their gaze, randomly shifting, accidently collided.

There was no doubt this was awkward, and it was showing no promise of improvement.

"Yes, this is a nice house," Aramis said again. "Well," he continued, "it was good to meet you. I think I'll go out and walk around for a while."

Aramis waited for a moment expecting some reply. Marie said nothing. He turned to his right and walked out the door. After a few long steps, he stopped, looked at the sky and breathed deeply in.

"Well, that was odd," he thought to himself. "She is definitely an odd one. She barely spoke. She barely moved. But how can there be no one else here? What kind of farmer keeps only one hen? No, I didn't expect that."

Aramis now had many questions. How long had she been here? Why was she alone? Why weren't there others? Had there ever been others? Where did they go? How was the farmer? There were a hundred questions he could have asked. But he could not think of one that had not seemed too personal. "She was not used to having company. That was painfully clear." Marie. That was her name? Marie. Or Maria. Yes. She was so timid, so reticent, so . . . so . . . so brittle, he thought, yes that's the right word, that had she not offered, he doubted he would have asked her name, too strangely private that simple question would have been.

Aramis walked to the broken wire fence that stretched between the end of the house and the side of the shed. It reached up high when attached at the posts. In between, most of it was still doubled over despite the farmer's efforts to overcome the effects of fallen branches and climbing children. One section of the fence remained completely collapsed.

Aramis stopped and peered through. Just beyond was a thicket of oak and ash and juniper, walnut, chestnut and beech. They were a few feet away where the side of the hill sloped down sharply and reached a flat, overgrown field. There was a stream about midway and he could see the top of a church that reached up past the stream. There must be a village. When the time comes, he thought, that's not the direction. Too many people. Too many cars. He turned around. Ah, this was the yard. Not much to see. A typical expanse of scruffy grass, patches of dirt, specked with white stones, some bushes, the walls, and a silent old tree set in the middle.

He walked back the full length. As he passed by the coop, he glanced quickly to his right at the half-closed door. "She was rather pretty," he thought. "Why did she think I was with others? She must have been nervous. I can't really blame her. I was dreading this, too."

"Still," he thought, "I hope she's not crazy."

Marie had not moved. She rested her left wing on a lower nest and shifted her weight to one leg. Her thoughts had gathered in that spot and she did not want them to move.

"He's alone?" She stared at the door, seeing Aramis standing there as he had several minutes earlier. All the impressions that had pushed her to silence came powerfully back. Then she pictured herself. "That was awful. I just stood there . . . staring. Did I even say hello? Did I tell him my name? Oh, how rude. I must have seemed crazy."

"But he's alone?" she repeated. "What is he doing here? Oh, what will I do?"

Marie felt exhausted, drained, but with a lightness that comes from relief. There were no others. No sudden intrusion of a coop-full of hens. "He seemed a bit strange. He was polite, but too much. And rather ugly," she thought. "His comb was all shortened and his wattle was crooked. I wonder if he's sick. But still, he was kind. I should have been nicer. Did I invite him in? Next time, I'll be more polite. Why did he leave? Maybe he's just visiting. Maybe he's not staying. That's ridiculous. He's not here on vacation. Oh, I'm happy that's over."

With that, Marie decided to wait a little while before going outside. She was hungry, but those growling pangs of hunger could not overcome the gnawing pain of embarrassment. She did not want to appear that she was following him or seeking him out. She did not want to undergo the same conversation. She decided to wait, to wait until . . . well, wait until what? . . . just wait for a while.

* * *

Over the next several days, maybe a week, Aramis and Marie saw each other often. It could not be helped. It was, after all, a very small yard. Marie eventually apologized for her lack of graciousness when Aramis first entered the coop. He said he had not noticed. He apologized for knocking so early. Marie nodded and said nothing.

Within those days, Marie explained that she was the only chicken on the farm and she had been alone for more than a year. She said there once were many others, but they were all gone. She did not talk about why they left, and Aramis did not ask.

Mostly, the conversations centered on the farm, the cows, the ducks, the family of the farmer. Marie told Aramis of the farmer's children and grandchildren. Most of his children came to visit once a year, she explained. His daughter visited a few times, at least once during winter and once during summer. Marie remembered because of her clothes. She looked forward to her visits. His daughter was the only one to seek Marie out, to sit down near her, and to talk to her. Marie liked to hear her stories and most enjoyed seeing her dresses.

Aramis asked about the little boys and learned they were grandsons who lived not far. He had met them early. They had come right away after learning from their grandfather that he had brought home a rooster. The boys were disappointed initially that Aramis was locked in the smokehouse. Aramis had heard them outside wanting to enter. But the grandfather said no, they would have to wait.

The boys had returned often and were eager to chase him. Aramis did not mind. He enjoyed the exercise and thought they were fun. Neville moved with the awkward steps of an 8-year-old boy whose legs are too long and muscles too slim. The boy would teeter a bit when he tried to turn quickly, and his longer strides were fast only after the first couple steps. By then, however, he had already crossed the yard so there wasn't much yard remaining to reach full speed.

The 6-year-old, Bellamy, made Aramis laugh. The boy's unremitting certainty that, each time he charged, he would catch "that cockerel" gave Aramis great fun. Bellamy let out a shriek whenever he started, then he'd stare while he ran, and finally he'd loudly voice disappointment as he missed him each time. Aramis enjoyed waiting until the last second, just as the boy thought he would catch him, before flapping up and off in a direction out of reach. The boy, huffing and puffing, would put his hands on his knees to catch his breath, look up quickly and start the chase again with another loud shriek.

Marie, watching from beside a few bushes, thought the whole thing rather foolish, but appreciated Aramis' patience. At times, she even wondered which of the two, rooster or boy, was actually the youngest as they both showed such childish joy on their faces.

But most of the days of Marie and Aramis were quiet and fresh. The two boys were in school and stayed near their house, and within complaining distance from their mother, each afternoon.

Marie liked to watch Aramis, the way he walked, the way he moved. It was so different than being alone. He was so different than the others. There was nothing self-conscious, nothing he did that was done to impress. He would straighten his feathers and clean himself, yes, but it was not like a primp, or the preening that the previous roosters performed. It was for purpose, not show, and when he wasn't looking, she would stare at the white speckle of feathers just under his chest, the way that they faded to soft underneath. His wings had a strength that seemed magnified by their beaten appearance. The long black feathers in his tail, held high and straight but not with pretension. His legs still looked youthful, though sometimes at twilight, his wattle and comb, so distorted and short, made him look old.

Sometimes, Aramis walked aimlessly by himself, Marie noticed, or sat in the yard looking out over the driveway and facing the arch. His eyes would be still, sad, as if remembering a life, whether his or someone else's she was not sure. He sat for hours without moving, except for the slow, methodical play of his wings, which would slide to and fro, the tips softly sweeping the ground, and then he smiled gently, genuinely, suddenly, whenever he caught sight of her from a distance. But he would rarely get up and walk over. She, instead, would go over to him. He never seemed to mind the interruption.

"What are you thinking?" she asked one day as her courage increased and her curiosity overflowed her typical restraints.

"I don't know," he said. "I mostly think of the past – and then I think of the future. Then sometimes, I change it and think of the future then the past."

"That's not much variation," she said.

"Oh, yes, indeed there is," Aramis said smiling. "There's a world of difference. Because it's not what you think. It's the direction you move."

"You don't think of the present?"

"The present is here, it's a vessel emptied of questions. But the past has its facts and the future potential, so my thoughts always tend to go there, to either one or the other."

"Are those thoughts pleasant?" she asked.

Aramis laughed. "Now and again," he said, not moving his eyes from an unfocussed place straight ahead. Then after a pause, he continued, with the same far-off expression as one who has only half-returned. "I'm not trying to be mysterious. It's like anyone's life. There are joys and regrets. Always more of one than the other. It depends how you see things. It depends where you are."

Aramis did not mind discussing the past. And with very little prompting, he described what he'd seen and explained how the pastor had died and how the farmer picked him up in a field near the town. Aramis told the story in a way that made it sound he resisted a bit more than he had, perhaps exaggerating on purpose, or maybe it was how he remembered his struggle. Aramis recounted the week in the smokehouse and how it had been to his liking, that it had let him recover both physically and in thought. He enjoyed living alone but was glad to be out in the air and the sun. Yes, he said, he thought he might die, but it seemed less likely the more days that would pass.

While he spoke, Marie found herself studying his face. Sensitive and kind, it could be placid one moment, then fill without warning with intensity and passion. She tried not to stare in his eyes, which were large and absorbent when he listened, expressive and flashing when he spoke. His face, animated and bright, could sometimes look exaggerated and long, each attribute caricatured and competing with the others. His eyes protruded too much when excited. His mouth could be twisted depending on mood. His cheeks and his forehead were at once wrinkled, then smoothed.

Marie was relieved when he volunteered the story about how he escaped the first time in his life and had set off on his own after his mother had died. It explained his appearance, his comb and his wattle, which were lopsided and short. She would not need to ask. He told how it was the onset of winter and he wandered for days, feeding off whatever he found, dried corn, fallen blackthorn berries, rotting apples and bugs. At night, he hid under tree stumps mostly. He preferred perching on tall branches, but he had to stay warm, and eventually he came to find comfort in the ground. Besides, he explained, he had once broken his wing. Mostly, he talked about what is essential in nature. The life and the joy. The cycles and births. The scamper of red squirrels while they gather their food. And how the buzzards will scavenge. The cuckoos will fight. The deer forage in small groups with their children. The fox prowl at night.

He told how in winter, the forest awoke, mostly at twilight. And except for junipers and cypress, the trees were all bare. While there was much he remembered, it was the light he loved most. Speckled and broken. The sun shattered in pieces. Each of its rays seemed to tell a new story as they broke past the branches and cast shadows on dead leaves. The snow when it fell came down like pieces of cloud and covered everything it found in a frozen white down. It was the first time in life he felt the purity of alone. But, yes, it was hard, he had barely survived. He found little to eat. He grew thin and was cold. It was difficult to sleep as he shivered each night. He was sure he would die when a frigid blast settled in. Yet somehow, he lived through it, despite the frost-bite that caused his misshapen appearance. Yes, it made him self-conscious. Then the spring came back slowly and with it more food. The bugs and the plants. The warmth delivered new life. Then for days, he lay still and soaked in the moments, pulling them in and clinging as tightly as anyone could to those seconds that pass as we watch the next one come by. He knew they would end, those rare instants of peace. They always ended before – the cost to be free. How it then happened, he could not remember, but while sleeping one day, he was suddenly caught. He was in a cloth bag. He was in a new coop.

Marie did not move as she listened intently. She could not imagine what he was describing. It sounded impossible and otherworldly, as if he had just described a trip to the moon. No, even that to Marie would have been easier to picture.

When it was her turn to tell, Marie focused on the present. There were some mentions of the past, but she quickly changed the subject. She preferred to point out flowers or to show a favorite spot or to watch clouds passing over or to comment on the day. "Oh, that doesn't matter," Marie preferred saying if Aramis mentioned her childhood. "That's all in the past." In fact, that was always the answer when he asked about Marie, about anything that happened before he arrived. Soon, very soon, he simply stopped asking.

The only past Marie described, though only very slightly, was the night of the recent storm. She was scared, she admitted, and it was why she was tired when they met. She explained she hated large storms, that they reminded her of times when the others were here. Yes, there had been many others. The coop had been full. But she did not describe more, only that she was glad the storm was over.

Aramis tried to cheer her. "Ah, but what a lucky storm it was! Consider the coincidences. I mean the priest, then the truck, then the storm, then the farmer. Without all that, I would not be here," he said in as light a voice as possible.

Marie did not believe in coincidences. She convinced herself long ago that things must happen for a reason. But she did not say anything. She knew if she did, it would suggest she believed his presence with her, too, had a reason, as if somehow it had meaning, or as if she wanted it to be true. She did not want Aramis to believe she thought he was here in answer to a dream. Because, she thought, she had not had a dream, and if she had, in fact, then he was not in it.

It was late afternoon. The sun was setting slowly over the coop to their right and a quarter-moon was showing, rising quickly to their left. The two of them sat under the old tree watching the clouds slide away.

"You must have missed the others all this time," Aramis said to her calmly when Marie finished her story.

"I miss some," she began, pausing to gather each thought. "Sometimes I miss some. I miss each in a way. I remember some more than others. I suppose I miss them all."

"How about you?" Marie asked, looking to change the topic. "You must have friends you would like to see again."

"Some," he said. "But not too much. I've not had that many friends in my life."

"No? You seem, well, you seem friendly."

"Maybe, but I've never been in one place very long."

"I see," Marie said. "Still, you must miss someone sometimes."

"Not so much anymore. I'm used to being alone."

Marie arched her back to shift her position against the cold tree. What did she hear in his tone even more than the words? A distant echo seeking help or was it weary resignation? Marie wondered what message was hidden, what past was emerging through his all-too-simple words.

"You don't miss anyone?" Marie asked again.

"I'm not sure I do. What do you miss most being here alone?"

"I didn't realize it before," Marie said, "but I suppose I missed talking. I mean talking to someone or something that answers."

"I miss conversation sometimes, but not all that much," Aramis said. "It seldom rings true."

"That's a funny answer. Does everyone lie?"

"No. I didn't mean true in that way. But genuine. Simple. Easy. The fact is I don't understand hens and I don't get along with roosters. They are always trying to prove something, mostly to themselves."

Marie smiled. "Yes, I remember," she said. "Is that why roosters rarely talk to each other?"

"I suppose. We don't know what to say," he replied. "So, we avoid each other."

"I remember some from when I was a child. Those roosters did, however, enjoy talking to hens."

"Yes, that's true," Aramis laughed, "most roosters do." Aramis thought of himself there, talking with her. "Is that bad?"

"No," said Marie. "And do you know why hens listen?" Marie did not wait for an answer. "Because we're waiting for you to say something interesting. We don't, after all, have much else to do."

Marie said this without any hint of humor, though Aramis knew she was teasing. "Ouch," he said softly, smiling. Aramis enjoyed the way Marie would answer her own questions and that often her mind would start in one place and finish in another, with a perspective he never considered, and blend it together in a way that made him smile.

"Why do you think conversation is so hard?" Marie asked. "I mean, why do chickens make it so difficult to have interesting conversations?"

"I don't know. Fear perhaps."

"Fear? Fear of what?" she asked.

"Fear of revealing. Fear of themselves. Fear of sounding silly. No one likes to be regarded as silly."

"Yes, that's true," Marie said, looking to the ground.

"Yet isn't it strange?" Aramis continued. "When chickens act silly, or say something silly, it is the purest and the realest thing they do, because what we think of as silly are just those things that are the most unprotected, unselfconscious, the simplest and the realest aspects of us. Chickens should be sillier, I think."

"But there are things we don't want to show. That's normal, isn't it? Things we don't want to reveal."

"Ah, secrets," he said. "Yes, well, we all have them. It's a shame though."

"Why is that a shame?"

"Because it would be good to confess all. It makes our lives lighter."

"Perhaps. But there are some things that are best not discussed."

Aramis looked at Marie. "Such as what?" he asked with a smile.

Marie shook her head slowly.

"You don't talk about yourself much. You speak of many things, interesting things, but you rarely talk about yourself."

"No, not very often," Marie responded quietly.

"It is said," Aramis remarked, thinking back to a saying that the pastor would quote, "that 'silence is the last joy of the unhappy.' Are you unhappy?"

Marie looked away. She did not want to answer. She did not know the answer. Aramis waited. He was watching her think. It made her face come alive, the twitching of orange-brown flecks above her small mouth, and her sweet eyes moving all about.

"Unhappy? Am I unhappy?" she thought. Marie did not how to answer. But Aramis waited. He would not give in. He would purposefully not help by asking a new question.

"Unhappy," she said thoughtfully. "That's a hard question. I don't know. I'm happy often. I'm not happy often. I don't know where the line is between one and the other. Even if I knew, how do we know which side we live on? It moves with circumstance, don't you think? There can be moments of sadness even in joy." Marie paused.

As Aramis looked at Marie, he noticed how the transparent yellow hue of the sun in decline warmed her back of soft red feathers and shone on the yellow that floated under her wings. How different it was than in the midday bright light, when her white chest-feathers caught the depth of blue sky and hinted at the soft color of lilac. But in this calm, filtered light with the sun's rays cast long, her colors melded into a smooth flow of pastels. Her long and thin feathers cast a magical glow, there but not real, as if his wing could pass right through them if he reached out to touch.

"Even in sadness there can be happy tears," Marie continued. "I suppose we think we're unhappy only when asking. We only ask when we're looking – and we only look when we want to return over that line. And that's what we remember, those moments of searching. And then we cry in that happiness we no longer have."

The way Marie spoke, increasingly quiet, increasingly still, as the sentences flowed, Aramis imagined her eyes starting to tear.

"Our happy times go so quickly without our first knowing," Marie said. "Don't you think that that's true?"

Aramis barely heard the question, overwhelmed as he was and absorbed by her words and the softening sunlight that glowed through her feathers and seemed to lift her from the ground.

"Is it true?" Aramis asked. "I don't know. I don't know if that's true. I don't know what is true anymore. Is there even such a thing?"

Marie suddenly laughed as if a spell had been broken. "You are a philosopher," she said, raising her eyebrows and smiling broadly. "Is there such a thing as truth? That's a good question. How would I know? Is there such a thing as truth? What a question!" she repeated, exposing an animated relief that the topic had changed. "Ah, but maybe your question was only rhetorical. In which case, I would say, yes, I do know the answer. But since you weren't really asking, I won't really tell you."

Aramis laughed and stood up. He was feeling stiff, having sat for too long with his head turned toward Marie. He stretched his neck and legs and asked Marie if she would like to walk. She stood up and joined him and the two turned right around the old tree and began to wander. Aramis looked at her. Marie looked straight ahead. They continued to walk. He continued to look at her.

"You know, when you first came to say hello that morning, I thought you must have come with many others," she said.

"Yes, that was funny," he said. "Well, awkward. But funny. I thought you were living in a coop full of hens."

"Then you left so quickly," she said. "Afterward, I thought you might just be visiting, passing through as it were."

"I thought you wanted to be alone," he said. "It was rather uncomfortable."

Marie did not respond.

"Are you just visiting?" she asked.

"Visiting?" he asked. "I'm not sure I understand. Visiting you or the farm?"

"Do you live here now?"

"I suppose I do. Why?"

"You haven't tried to move into the coop and I was thinking that maybe it's because you were thinking to leave."

"I see," he said. "No, I have no plans. Maybe someday. I don't know."

"Oh," Marie said softly as she watched their feet stepping forward. "Where would you go if you decided to leave?" she asked.

"It wouldn't matter. Anywhere. Out there. Wherever the fields or the trees lead me next."

"That sounds romantic. Unusual though. None of the roosters here before went out there, went out on their own."

"I've never understood why chickens stay in one place," he said. "There is so much to see. There are so many things and places, sights that are indescribable, unlike anything you'll see on a farm. You never know what you'll find. And sometimes you meet other chickens out there. Not often, that's true. But sometimes. And they have experienced so much. They are fascinating to talk to. Of course, some are not kind and some even dangerous, but most are like you, or like me anyway. They understand what it is to be free and a rooster."

Marie gave a slight laugh. "And what is it to be a rooster?" she asked.

Aramis stopped. He knew she was teasing again.

"I don't know," he said with a shrug. "I guess that's why I go out there."

"And what do you discover out there?"

"The world," he said. "I don't know how to explain it. You understand the world is not a small farm. It's not this farm and it's not just this one little yard."

"I've never left here, and I know that already. What good does that do? Going out there to discover what you already know?"

"It's more than that," Aramis said. "It gives you things you never would know."

"Oh, I see. And then what do you do when you have this great knowledge?"

Aramis was not sure how to answer. "It's not what you do," he said, carefully finding his words. "There are some things you cannot understand, can never hope to understand, unless you experience them. You can imagine almost anything, but it can never be real until it is discovered and seen. And the world fills the mind with such a range of what's real. Then by seeing what's different, we discover ourselves."

"It sounds rather distracting," Marie said.

Aramis laughed.

"Maybe seeing all those things," she continued, "just distracts us and delays us from finding what we need. I don't need to see what's different to know what is real in myself. My mind is already too full. And that's why it's so frustrating. I know that everything's here and still I can't find it."

There was a long silence. Aramis was looking at Marie, wondering why she suddenly looked sad, wondering what thought had shifted the topic in her mind.

"Maybe that's why I'm so awkward," Marie added.

Aramis leaned his head forward and looked into her eyes. "What do you mean?" he asked.

"I know that I'm awkward. The others knew it too." Marie looked away. "I know they were right. I was silly. I stayed by myself. We didn't understand each other, and I wasn't pretty like them."

"Oh, Marie," Aramis said, raising his voice to help force away the idea. "That is not true. That is not true. What funny ideas you have sometimes. You are the loveliest hen I've ever met."

And with those words, the two of them froze. The words had leapt from his mouth before he could think, think about how they might pierce through them both. Yes, they were true, but how did they get here? And there they just hung, and hung, repeated in silence, both of them hearing them echo inside.

Aramis quickly considered changing the subject, hiding that thought, covering it over with a flurry of words. But no. He had said them too clearly and the look of Marie said it was safe to go on. He started walking in paces, finding more courage to speak through his steps.

"I like talking with you," he said. "You're kind, and you don't try to impress the way that other hens do. The fact is you don't seem to try at all. I mean, not in a false way. That's good. Other hens seem ridiculous. To me, that is. But you don't seem silly. Although I like silly. And I like watching you. I like the way that you stand. I like how you talk. I like how you move. I like how you run."

"No, you don't," Marie interrupted. "You've never seen me run."

"Yes, I have," Aramis said, smiling.

"Oh, be honest. I never run," Marie said sternly. "You haven't seen me run."

"I am being honest I've always been honest," Aramis said, not knowing what he had said that upset Marie. "You think that's not true? I have. I have seen you run several times, early in the morning, before my crow. I see you look around and when you think no one's watching, you run through the yard. You ran just yesterday. You were by the stairs at the front of the farmer's house and you ran back into the coop very quickly. I saw you the entire time. I didn't mean to spy. I just couldn't sleep. And I like the way you run."

"No, I run like a duck," Marie said quietly.

"What?" Aramis laughed. "First of all, ducks don't run. They waddle. Second of all, you don't waddle."

"Yes, I do. I run – ok, waddle – like a duck and I flap my arms too much."

"No, you don't," he said. Aramis could not stop laughing, wishing he could and hoping Marie did not get even more angry. "You think I'm saying this to be kind? No, I'm not. Oh, forget those others. Maybe they just said those things to be mean."

Aramis stopped walking and leaned toward Marie. She stopped but did not look up.

"Listen to me, Marie," Aramis said. "You run as if you're free. I saw you. The way you run is with unselfconscious joy. You are yourself and you give it no thought. You run free, free of yourself. I've watched you scamper and jump and hop when you run. I see you enjoy it. It flows from within you. It's as if your spirit is running and your body is doing its best to keep up. The body can be a bad interpreter, but your run is beautiful."

"Well," she said. "Thank you. But I don't like the way I run. I think it looks silly."

With that, Marie guided the two back toward the shed, then in front of the coop and along the front driveway. She could smell the start of the linden tree now, its flowers' captivating scent beginning to flow.

"That's too bad," he said. "But as I told you, I like silly. You should not worry this much. I try not to think too much while I do things. That's probably not good. But I love to sing. Now there's an example, I do love to sing. But I know that I'm awful, not because I've been told, though I certainly have, but I can't hear a thing. I know my crow is just fine. But my notes are all scattered. And still I don't care. I enjoy it too much."

"Maybe you should learn to hear yourself better," Marie said, then turned to him, smiling.

Aramis fell silent. Was that a reproach? Or was it meant as nothing more than advice on how to sing.

"Well," he said softly, "Maybe I should."

They had reached the smokehouse. They stopped, and Marie took a deep breath of the intoxicating fragrance of the linden tree nearby. They looked out across the farm, through the arch of the driveway, out over the hills.

"The linden tree's beautiful," Marie said. "I like standing here."

Aramis did not hear her. "What's out there?" he asked, pointing out over the field, past the top of the rise, where the land dropped off to a line of thick trees.

"I don't know," Marie said. "I've never been out there. I've never been past the spot we are now."

Aramis looked at her in surprise. She's never been out there? Not even once past this spot? He did not say anything. He did not want to ask. Marie looked so calm. She was enjoying herself, standing like a flower that could be broken or snapped by just one wrong word. The way he was seeing her now, he wanted to tell her how beautiful she was. But even the gentlest of touches, the slightest of waves, can cause unwelcome disturbance. If the flowering moments of the mind lose half their petals in the speech, then let the bud blossom and be silent in its sight. Standing slightly behind her, Aramis stole several quick glances in Marie's direction as they both looked out over a gentle, young green field.

The remainder of the day passed with no further tension, no laughter either, but plenty of smiles. The two finished their walk, sat under the old tree, then ate their dinner and lingered for the evening. Each went back to their separate houses.

Marie felt more tired than usual that night. She fell asleep quickly and dreamt undisturbed. None of her dreams carried a message to remember.

Aramis, on the contrary, paced most of the night. Agitated. He stared. The smell of the linden tree would not leave him. He had not noticed it before. Did it flower today? Had it always been there? Oh, the way she had stood. Her long and thin feathers. Exotic, he thought. There she was still, sitting in the sun, playing, as she does, mindlessly stroking her yellow, long strands. Or checking for any that might be out of place. How softly she would turn them and align them again. There she was walking. The shape of her tail, so fine, and so straight, like a wedding gown train, held with great care. And their conversations played on, word over word, each expression recalled, the smile in her eyes as he talked much too much. Her few words were soothing, though he wished he could change so much of his own. The words he would use. How clever he would be. Kaleidoscoping thoughts came now as he looked at her face. The blend of colors near her eyes. Oh, those colors, the brilliance, the perfect contour of her neck, the gentle slope of her back, her rounded shape when she stood, the way curves moved when she walked. He heard her voice once more and there again was her smile. She was all radiance and light and it tickled him inside to see her finest of fine silky feathers, their sparkling tips. Something about her still shone.

How many times that evening had Aramis tried to lose this one subject, this subject in his mind that played again and again. He imagined the yard. He imagined the field. He saw the past and the future. But he could not stop returning. No other subject would stay. Only Marie. Again and again. There was something about her. Yes, something different, he thought.

He stood at his door. He sat just inside. He looked out to the right, out through the front arch. Best not to look left. Don't look at the coop. It was too much reminder. He needed to drift. "This is crazy," he thought. "What am I doing?" Finally, finally, he yawned several times, then headed to bed. "What am I doing?" he asked once again. He pushed his feet deep into paper and straw. His eyes wearily shut, and he felt his mind, thankful, quickly close down. "I don't even know," Aramis mumbled. "I don't know where . . . .don't know where I am." Such a small, common phrase he spoke, yet it would be several weeks before he knew what it meant.

Chapter 13

The Old Farmer and the Tree

A long line of black ants in broken formation crossed between the house and a small mound of particulated soil in the center of the yard. The path was narrow, but general, not precise, more like a maze in which all routes lead eventually to the exit. No footprints were left (well, none that could be seen), yet one suspected the travelers knew where the others had walked. Various obstructions lay in the way and the ants, whether going or coming, were forced often to stop. They looked left, looked right, took two steps, then left, then right. Left, then right. Their manner suggested they were little concerned, though there was urgency in their short-legged pace. They chose their alternating way with a confidence that their destination was in reach. Around some white jagged stone or through a green clump of grass. They never stopped moving. If not forward, then in circles they traipsed, turning around and around, before heading back on their way, their antennae performing a sweep of guiding arcs out front. As many made their way to the house, descending into a hole at the outer foundation, as those brethren that returned. They moved as if bound by a schedule. Some marched straight. Others wandered off before reversing course and joining the others en route. Some looked victorious, carrying a small grain of something, maybe a piece of dried bread. Others empty-handed, persevered forward with nothing, walking to walk, serving no purpose except to keep the flow moving, endlessly traversing between two unseen points. The horizon is near. For an ant, it is always quite near. Many, it seemed, stayed near their home, the center of all, dipping down the mound's entrance, disappearing a moment before they, or others, quickly returned. Were they the same? They all looked the same. But which were the foragers, those special few destined to set off, to leave their trail for others to follow, to risk their lives while searching – for something? The solitary ones, whose job it was to keep the other ones nourished, choosing a route through their miniature world, obliged by nature to discover a path.

The old farmer sat and watched. From the small mound to his right, a procession went forth, a procession returned, beyond the reach of his hand, past the heel of his shoe, and on toward the house another four or five feet. It caught his attention while he rested his back to the tree, his eyes swinging left, his eyes swinging right, as he followed the progress of one then another. He felt a small tickle on the back of his hand. He saw a black speck walking across. Was this one lost? Or running away? Maybe it was not from that family at all, but a wandering ant from another small mound.

The old farmer did not move. The ant would crawl off, just wait a few seconds, no need to shift to flick it away or smash it with the slap of a hand. It would be easy to kill, as most ants are, and just as easy not to. The ant would not know. She (for aren't they all female, the farmer thought he was taught) would feel no pain, no sudden recognition that her future was lost. No flashback to her youth in her last dying throes. An ant is not a sparrow so would God really care? It was left to the farmer to unfurl God's plan. The old farmer did not think this, and his body sat still. His mind flowed with the distracted, idle thoughts of an idle old man, his gaze shifting from nature's plenty to the abundance of memories seen by old eyes. There was the yard, the walls, and the barn. There were his children, his wife, and their sounds. There was his car, the driveway, the stones, his brothers, an old tractor, his parents. Then the ants, the grass, and the flowers, with him, himself, his present, his past. He watched the ants. The chickens will find them. He looked to his right as the hen and rooster walked by. Side by side, clucking and bobbing they passed, the hen looking back at the old farmer once, then back again twice.

Seeing them both, the old farmer was pleased. It felt right. He wondered if he should have brought a rooster home sooner. The earlier absence was felt now because it was gone. These, after all, were a set, a pair, one with the other, like two towels near the shower, or two plates on a table. The hen looked less awkward than when she was scampering and jumping and sitting by herself. The rooster was strong, his welcome crows a pleasant and clear reminder of the day. To those who don't know, all chickens are the same, like a forest of redwoods or a field of tall sunflowers. But to one who observes, each bird is unique, like a smile or a thought that won't go away. And with the rooster there now, the yard seemed more full. As did the house. And as did the farm. It was odd, that a small thing can change such a very large picture.

The farmer shifted his weight and stretched out his legs, crossing his right ankle up over the left. He increasingly felt at home in this spot. Comfortable. Soothed. A place with no worries, surrounded by life. The house to his left and the barn and the shed. His farm all around him, miles of sounds coming forth. He was at the center of all as if in the throne of his land.

The sensation had come slowly. For weeks he walked past and circled the tree. He looked at its branches. He examined all sides. It was not just its limbs that convinced him in time. They might be explained, however unlikely, by the impact of the tree that fell in the storm. It was instead a long crevice on one side and the large hole that penetrated all the way through. The deep crack began just inches from the ground and rose nearly three feet high. Its opening pierced deep into the wood, its edges rounded and bulging where it met the grey concentric swirls on the outside of the trunk. This chasm had faced south. It widened at the center, defined by black scales, and sat like a sideways grimace on a motionless face. Then look at the hole. It had been cut through the north side and ran east to west with a tunnel that gaped in the center and narrowed as it left, creating a womb for more life. There, filled with the brown, dank dust of decaying wood, it spawned mushrooms each spring and then held them as they rotted the rest of the year. It was forever home to a spider where small flakes of leaves got caught in its web.

But the hole now faced south; the crevice looked north. It could not be explained. The farmer had known this tree throughout his long life then suddenly it was different, the opposite of its past. He knew it could not happen. But still, there it was. He awakened one day as if to the face a mirror and see image that was no longer his. Why deny what was real because we lack explanation? We do not know all. With luck, we know some. He knew nature played tricks. Whether he would accept it or not, he could not change it back. The tree faced a new way. And what began as a few glimpses to check on the tree had increased to interruptions to walk through the yard, then to spending idle hours seated at its trunk. It was now a location he sought between chores. And so here he was, seated under the tree.

The old farmer lifted his hands from his lap and placed them on the ground. The sun, arcing high in a bright white sky, shone directly down on his dark blue jacket and warmed his old body that sagged within. The limestone blocks, stacked high to his left, the outside wall to his room, magnified the light like a vertical glacier of fresh glistening snow.

He shut his eyes to the brightness. Grey geometrical patterns floated and flashed under his lids. With a slow rhythm and movement, swaths of soft darkness and visual static played in his mind. His shoulders felt heavy and his back sank solidly against the tree's trunk.

The sensation was comforting. The sun warmed his clothes, the air cooled his face, the firmness of earth provided steady assurance beneath. He was nestled in a space that felt all his own. His heartbeat kept time where his back met the tree.

With a deep, slow breath, the old farmer saw where he was. He pictured his farm, its expanse as it rolled up and down out over the fields. The images played quickly, much more rapidly than real, the distances altered, the dimensions his own. He saw the courtyard ahead, the barn on his right, the old building was left, the driveway, the coop, the yard where he sat. He had played in this yard as a boy with his friends. He had sat by this tree. He thought of the tree as it appeared to him then. He climbed on its branches. He hung rope for a swing. He used it as target for slingshot rocks and a ball. He broke the tip of his knife when he tried to carve in its trunk. It was here where he sat when his father had died.

Although his eyes were still closed, the farmer could see the yard now, as an old man seated, the same as he had from the height of a child. His mind drifted pleasantly in the passionless way that some old people dream, where the sight of emotion takes the place of their tears. A sequence of pictures as if painted on gauze, the yard was familiar but different, the way our former home looks when we confront it years later. Of course, it seems small. The bushes are different. The flowers are fresh. A wire fence had been added. But he could see himself now as once he had been, whittling and staring from beneath this old tree.

And then he'd chase chickens, like his grandsons today. A yard full of hens. His mother had at least twenty or more. He had names for his favorites. He talked to them some. Although memory alters, eyes have no age, and the scene was before him as in a boy nearly eighty. He remembered the joy and recalled that lost feeling, the release of himself and how the sounds of his yelps heightened and toughened the strengths of his powers. He felt his legs moving, tramping across with rapidity and ease. He felt himself smiling. The thrill of a chase.

Now here suddenly were friends. Although none could be seen, he sensed them around, all chasing and shouting, flailing arms all directions and kicking their legs. A mass of untamed spirits swirling in and out, up and around. The moves were boy-random, the running so rapid, it was a blur of colors as if swimming in joy. A dust devil of youth and nothing in focus. There was circling and stooping as they all missed the chickens. Then the flutter of feathers and the cackles of hens. Wings flapping upward and frantic and the sounds of their feet. It was like an old song, when you remember the words just a half-beat behind the rest of the chorus. Then the running slowed down, and the shouting softened and stopped. Everyone bent over, legs wobbling and sweating. Some dropped to their knees. They were catching their breath with exaggerated force. Slowly images faded, and the sounds disappeared.

The old farmer stirred lightly. He pulled his knees in and leaned more to his left. His eyes stayed shut and his body went lax, sinking deeper toward the ground, sinking deeper into comfort.

There came a small breeze. The rough barkless wood rubbed into his back. There was the firmness of earth. His weight seemed to lighten as the hard ground pushed up. The beating of his heart, which pushed against the tree, seemed to come from outside, as if pounding against him. The tree's surface sank in, soft as a down pillow. It rhythmically pulsed and was warm on his back. He felt at his stomach as if someone tugged at his belt. It was an odd push and a pull. Then his body melted and lightened and started to rise. There was no emotion. He was not startled. It merely was fact. He floated up with assurance from the strong, unseen hand. His shoulders slumped forward, and his arms hung down, swaying. His legs dangled below with his feet near the ground. It was a comfortable feeling, just to give oneself over. He was weightless, suspended, held there softly without fear.

His sight was a blur. Light flickered through a translucent white gauze. Then faces appeared. Lost faces he knew at indistinct times. He saw them like busts in flashes of pastel, the soft shapes of their mouths, their cheeks, their eyes. He saw them smile. He knew his face was now old, but they did not notice, smiling to him as if he was a boy. His old playmates were eyes and happy, wrinkled noses. Then the picture faded to a hint of some arms that trailed out of sight. Next came indistinct voices saying welcome and hello. He did not know who spoke, but the images were pleasant, and he glided among them, and he watched faces fly. His expression was blank. Except for his eyes, his face did not move. He was cloaked in a cloud of familiar old smiles and he absorbed what he could as they all floated by.

Then the images were gone, and the white cloud dissolved. He stood in the yard. It was a bright summer day. His brothers left for the war. There was his mother. He felt her hand on his forehead as if checking for fever. There came his father, now standing before him. The day his brother was killed, during the war. As a boy, the old farmer was in the field all that morning and had come home to get an axe from the shed. It was the very same moment the news had arrived. The sky was low. It was cloudy. His father was crying. Then he walked up to the boy and gave him a kiss on the right then left cheek. It was the first and the last time he remembered his father had kissed him. For days he worried that it meant he was dying. Then his father was gone and there was his wife. She looked at him with an expressionless face. His children were present. There was a party somewhere and his daughter stood alone. She was talking to something as if to a friend. No words were heard. He had only the sight of her as a child, bent over, arms held behind her, leaning intently above a small hen. She looked up and smiled and started to run. Her small dress to her knees flapped up behind her. Her head tilted slightly. She was flapping her arms and ran as if flying. The old farmer stood frozen as his daughter circled around making sounds like a hen. Although the old man was dreaming, he knew he had seen this, so many times, but never this close. For the first time, he was with her, not watching from afar. She was smiling at him, making faces and flapping and running in circles. The farmer burst out laughing until tears flowed down his face. His daughter stopped running. "I never see you laugh," she said. And the farmer, embarrassed, gave a quick look around. There was his wife, again standing to the left. She was laughing, softly, with the sunlight behind her. Then she too stopped. And her face shone with a smile, her hands on the heads of two little boys. She was smiling. He was staring. Somehow, in that moment, they both knew she was dying. She walked up and kissed him, a soft kiss on his cheek. And there he stood, frozen, seeing her fade, knowing weeks later, with her small hand in his, he did not give her kisses, but watched her eyes close and he squeezed her weak hand.

With a sudden fierce chill, the farmer awoke. And as too often happens, a beautiful warm dream transforms to a beautiful cold nightmare when the images found have no place in the sun. His visions lingered a moment and began to subside. The farmer opened his eyes. They were damp. He, alone, wiped at his cheeks. It was going on dusk, a day sinking to night. The stones of the house, now a dark yellow grey, loomed up to his left. Sounds again filled the air. The farmer twisted in his seat, felt his heart pound from inside, and the tree slide roughly against his stiff back. It felt odd, the contrast of the trunk to its softness in the dream. "The tree," he thought, still in half-awake thinking. "This tree is not as hard as it looks."

He put his hands on the ground and shifted forward to stand up. As he leaned to his left, he felt something drop on his shoulder. A small wet spot appeared at the top of his sleeve. He looked at the sky. There were thin white clouds now, wispy, not moving. There was no sign of rain. He studied the drop. It was not from a bird. Too clear, too small, like a raindrop but firm.

He raised his right hand to the spot on his shirt and brushed it lightly with his fingers. It was thick, and the stickiness pulled at his sleeve. Puzzled, the old farmer sat forward to remove his back from the tree. He looked straight up. There, where the shortest of limbs protruded from the trunk, was a glistening patch where liquid gathered slowly and formed a small drop at the edge of a ridge. The farmer continued to stare as the viscous substance imperceptibly grew to a dangling ball readying to drop.

"That's strange," the farmer thought.

And as he sat there thinking, searching for an answer, another drop fell and landed on his knee. He stood up. Bracing with his left hand on the trunk while rising on his toes and lifting his right arm, the farmer stretched his body and swiped his finger across the wet, gleaming spot.

"How about that," he said out loud. He smelled it, then put a bit on his tongue. He looked up again. He took a step back. There was no hole and no damage. No rain and no dew. Nothing at all to condense or congeal.

But wait. What was that? He did notice something. Just under the glisten that sparkled in the light. Just a few inches down, at the nape of the neck where the shortest of limbs joined the hulking, dark trunk. Whatever it was, it was curved and, yes, spiraled. A strange pattern ran counter to the petrified grain and intersected and diverged with the swirl of the wood.

The farmer took his glasses from his breast pocket and put them on. He leaned forward and raised his head as far as he could. Certainly, there was something. It was easy to see if he looked just askance, to the left or the right, but not straight ahead. It appeared like a circle, with curving lines set inside, swirled and fine, with incisions all worn like the smoothed signs of a scar.

He stepped back again. Now see a glow there. He saw it straight on, wherever he stood. He walked to his left and walked to his right, he tilted his head and then crossed his arms on his chest. He had never seen this before. But how could that be? The wound was too old to have occurred in the storm. The script was too fine to be of natural chance. All those years he spent here, playing on this tree, climbing and swinging from every position. How is it possible, he never noticed it before? Yet look at it now. It was glowing more brightly. It was becoming more clear. It was a very fine G carved into this tree – a fleur de lis placed inside – and the light turned to orange and grew in its brilliance.

The old farmer kept staring with both hands in his pockets. The carving pulsed in, and then it pulsed out, like the beat of a heart. Transfixed by the light, he stood motionless, frozen. A tawny, large spider appeared from the top of the branch. It slowly crawled down on its eight spindle legs, around the throbbing curved shapes, and moved down the dead trunk toward the tree's gaping hole. In the yard, it was twilight. The coldest of cold shudders ran down and back up the old farmer's spine.

Chapter 14

Aramis Brings a Wake-up Call

Marie awoke with a start. Aramis' unmistakable reveille, deep and resonant, came earlier than usual, with not the earliest hint of sun yet to break. The clarion call hung on the still impassive sodden air and reverberated in the coop with prolonged force.

Thrust into an awareness that she was dreamily reliving their previous conversation, Marie fluttered high in her nest. It was not the force of their words that awoke in her a lightness, not his thought that surprised her, just the sheer presence of their thoughts wrapped together. In fact, the whole day just past had felt new and alive, unexpectedly delivering to her a strange parallel world that unveiled itself tenderly as it walked by her side.

Aramis crowed again. This time it was louder as its power echoed through the coop from ceiling to floor as though invisibly announced from within the sagging rafters. It was not so much a sound that arrived through the darkness, but he, Aramis himself, who came to Marie. Before she knew it, she had bounded down to the straw-padded ground and with three quick flaps of her long flowing wings rushed toward the door. With two steps to go, she stopped, though, then slowed her final steps. If Aramis was watching, she did not want her eagerness to be the first thing he saw. As she reached the door, she looked out at the moonlit yard with its pale, false light and obscure black shadows staring and waiting. The sun had not yet hinted; it was too early to crow. Yet, he was out there to be sure. But where? And why? At the last second, she held back from poking her head through the watchful coop door and into the void that lay heavy outside. She listened to the silence. It was louder now in the cool, before-her dark air. She heard herself breathe; she heard nothing in the yard. Marie's heart pounded as she imagined she dreamt his invisible presence, as desire and fear often mix and float in the instant we awake too quickly in the night.

Marie shifted her weight to take a step back when suddenly a third and fast crow, striking from nowhere, filled up around her. The call exploded, then entered her before reaching her ears. Such is sound's power to blot out all else and carry us where it wills. Marie jumped and reflexively inhaled. The reverberations continued through the silence that followed. He was there. She was right. And he filled her night each time that he called. Compelled by the pull, Marie stepped through the door and into the yard where the soft breath of moonlight glistened off the delicate remnants of the dew's morning touch. The yard was still dark, an alien room of black, silver and grey.

Marie did not see Aramis, but heard a sudden, faint flutter above to her left. Marie looked up. There he was, standing at the final tip of the finger-like spire of the highest limb of the silent, looming tree. He was a stark silhouette, a black winged mass against the faintly lightening south-eastern patch of a cirrus-filled sky. The moon, hidden behind Marie and settling toward its night, shone directly on Aramis' front, glistening from his feathers and reflecting off his large deep-set eyes.

"What are you doing?" Marie said sleepily. Her quiet voice betrayed a hint of excitement at seeing him at such an unexpected height.

"But soft, what light? Ah, 'tis Marie! You've arrived! Bonjour!" shouted Aramis, his head snapping down in her direction as he gave a small bow, a large smile on his face.

"Yes," she said. "What are you doing up there?"

"I wanted to surprise you," he said. "It's amazing up here. It's too beautiful to sleep. It's a wonderful morning, crisp and exhilarating. The moonlight is everywhere, and the yard looks so empty. It speaks of peace through its silence. It's like living a dream. I wanted you to see it."

Marie was looking at his face, the soft threads of clouds floating beyond, illumined on the left and fading away as they stretched to the right. It was like a dream. He was right about that. But was it her dream or his? She couldn't decide.

"You scared me, you know. How did you get up there?"

"I flew," Aramis said and held his wings wide. "I stood where you are and just flapped my wings, and, whoosh, here I am."

"Yes, of course," she said. "Or maybe the tree bent down and picked you up."

"Ah, you don't believe me. Ye, who's so little, and has such little faith."

"Really," she said. "I have plenty of faith in the fact you didn't fly up there."

Aramis laughed. "Yes, you're right, your faith is cleaner than mine. I jumped to the branch and walked the rest of the way," he confessed. "But I wanted to wake you with a surprise and here I am. It is wondrous up here. You can see all the rooftops, the entire yard, and into the fields. Stillness all around and a faraway painting below. And you, you look so tiny, like I could scoop you up with one wing. Small and glowing, like a feathery angel, an angel of the earth, who appeared in the night. And now here we are. I'm glad you woke up. You look beautiful."

"You look like a weathervane," Marie replied. It was meant to be funny, but she regretted her words as they were leaving her mouth. He was just having fun. Why did she do that? Why was she always too quick to dismiss the fun of others? He was excited and happy, and in truth, so was she. She had hardly heard his words, so self-conscious she'd become, yet she had heard the word "beautiful" and she would remember it.

"I'm sorry," she said. "Please come down, you're making me nervous."

Without speaking, Aramis slowly, and carefully, retraced his steps down the long incline of the stark smooth branch. The fact was, the climb had indeed worried him also. Halfway up, he feared he was climbing too high. Vertigo and doubt had started to surface. His damaged wing would not hold his weight if he fell. But a challenge is always surmounted more readily when the aim is to impress rather than to conquer, so he had kept his eyes forward and carefully climbed.

When he reached the trunk, he was about halfway down, and leapt from there with flapping wings to slow his fall. Marie walked over. The vision of him silhouetted against the sky and the word "beautiful" remained there before her, and with a self-conscious effort, she displayed a delicate nonchalance.

"Thank you," she said. "But don't do that again. It's frightening to wake up like that in the middle of the night. Then to find you that high, calling from a branch and looking that sinister."

"All right, I promise," Aramis said. "Nevermore, nevermore, my little Lenore." And Aramis resumed his smile, his eyes open wide.

Marie shook her head and could not hold back a slight smile of her own. "What were you thinking?" she repeated more gently.

"I was just playing. I woke up and felt strong and clear-headed. It has been a long time since I felt that. I wanted to fly up high and stretch my wings wide," Aramis said. "I wanted to fly. Haven't you ever wanted to fly? I mean fly, truly fly. Like the other birds? Far and high up, soaring and diving?"

Marie looked at him. She thought of her childhood dreams that so often took her up near the clouds and above this small yard. But she hesitated to speak, to share too easily those early dreams that matched his own, especially now, because they, too, matched his own.

"Not really," she said. "I don't think about that."

Marie looked down, hoping Aramis would continue talking without asking more questions.

"I've always wanted to fly," he said. "To float, to soar, to know no limits, no distance too far, no restrictions on where I could go. To be up there with no walls, no people, no others. Especially no others. Just the clouds and the air. It seems so natural, the way we're supposed to be, not stuck and condemned to live on the ground, chained to one place. I've never understood why we can't do that. We're birds. We were born to fly, skyward we should venture, to far up to the heavens. Yet, but here we stay, bound to the earth, for some unseeable reason, but for a small breath of wind, we, too, could do that. We, too, could soar high."

Aramis looked again at the clouds. The sky's light over the house was a burgeoning violet. Thin sheets of clouds, a textured darkness now sitting as shadows on the sky, were sliding and drifting. Aramis saw himself there like a floating black speck with a vast void around him. The air pushed at his wings. The wind brushed his back. He lost himself there, with his thoughts high above.

Marie wondered what he was seeing. She had been watching him in the pale steel-blue of twilight as he spoke. She saw his enthusiasm and the expression on his face was extreme and singular. She felt pulled by his energy, swept into his thoughts, not to take part, but to watch them and marvel. His intensity played out like a tribal dance from another world, filled with magical passion but impossible to fathom. She tried to compare what he was envisioning with her own imagination. She knew she was failing.

Aramis looked down and then up at Marie. He thought of the way she sat under the tree some days staring at the sky with a strange and distant look.

"I find it hard to believe that you wouldn't like that, too," he said.

"It's hard to believe I wouldn't like what?" she asked.

"To fly. Haven't you thought of it? Even as a child?"

"Sometimes," she said. "I suppose most chickens do. I suppose, when they're young."

"Marie, you're still young," he said. "I thought . . . sometimes now, I see you with a look that suggests . . . you never dream of it now?"

"No," she said. Marie was looking at Aramis. His eyes, naïve in their honesty, open in their query, magnified the guilt in Marie's answer. "Well, sometimes," she confessed.

"I thought so," he said playfully. "You still do, don't you? I can see that in you, especially when you are quiet. I can see you peer off in the distance. I've watched you stare at the sky, at the moon. Your eyes have a look of longing, of sadness even, as if you wish you weren't thinking what you were thinking. But then you also look happy as if you find comfort and safety in your melancholy dreams."

Marie said nothing. It was difficult for her to hear the thoughts she herself tried to deny. It was there, in the clouds, that she saw herself often, floating with images of others from her past. As soon as she thought this, there they were again, springing to her mind with such unexpected ease she knew they had never really left from their recent visitation. She had stopped listening to Aramis, not purposefully, but so powerfully was she in recent days carried off to her memories that his words no longer reached her.

"Where would you go?" Aramis repeated.

"I'm sorry?" she asked.

"Where would you go if you could fly with the wind?"

"I don't know," she said. "There's no place I'd go. There's no place I want to go. I suppose that's our difference. I wouldn't go anywhere."

"How can you say you wouldn't go anywhere?" he asked. "You could fly. You could go wherever you wanted."

Marie looked at Aramis. To her, it was not a real question. It was not possible, so why did it matter? "No, I'd just fly above here, circling around, looking down on the yard, the top of the coop, seeing it all at once like a big, single picture," she said, lifting her wings very slightly. "I don't need to go anywhere. Just the feeling of flying. That would be enough."

"Why don't you then?" Aramis asked.

"Why don't I what?"

"Fly."

"You know I can't."

"Have you tried?"

"What do you mean? That's a funny question," she replied. "Chickens can't fly like that."

"No, not precisely like that," he said. "Yes, I wish I could fly as high as those birds," he said, pointing his wing to the sky. "I wish I could soar up with the clouds. But our greatest wishes are always those we can't have. Those birds up there, I'm sure they wish they could fly even higher than they do. And if they could fly higher, they'd wish to fly faster. It's the way wishes work. You never wish for what you have, and once you have it, you wish something else. It's just that way with wishes. They're never made happy."

"But," he said, suddenly stopping and smiling, "you can fly higher than the dog."

The eastern sky was now a diaphanous blue with hints of red-yellow and, as Aramis grew more excited with his words, Marie realized it was the first time she had seen him like this, talking freely, exuberantly, about his ideas and his desires. She listened to his words but watched him even more intently. His ideas were simple but his gestures and his animated face, which radiated the true meaning of his thoughts, captured her most. His passion redrew the lines in his face, transformed his misshapen comb and waddle from the remnants of wounds to scars he had collected in battles with himself. And at that moment, she remembered one of her mother's expressions: "We all preach best what we most need to hear."

"It's easy to make yourself unhappy by staring at limits," Aramis continued. "We all have them. You know I wish I were a better singer. I'm not. But I can reach the top of that tree. I must let that make me happy. I bet the dog wishes he could do that. Or the cows. Ha! Can you imagine a cow up there?"

Aramis was smiling and looking up at the point of the tree where he had stood just minutes earlier. Marie looked at him. She marveled at his sudden explosion of optimism and gayety, the idealism in his strange way of seeing the world, his grasping at whatever was just out of reach, his repeated, almost obsessive talk about limits, and then his fantasies in which he overcame them all.

Aramis, still looking up with admiration at his achievement, was suddenly aware of the weight of her gaze. He looked at Marie and smiled.

"Yes, you must be happy with whomever you are," he said. "I'm sure you can fly much more than you try. I'm certain you could wish for much more than you do."

Marie thought of the games she created and played to enjoy herself during all that time she was alone. She never once thought to fly. Not really. Not when awake. Nor of wishing for much. Nor of leaving the farm. "And you must make yourself happy wherever you are," she said.

Aramis smiled. Marie was smiling. His expression was of being carefree and forgetting – trying at least to forget where he was. Marie's was of irony, smiling at his ideas and remembering where they stood. Marie stared at Aramis. He dropped his eyes and his smile relaxed. He peered at the ground. A quiet look came to his face as an unexpected realization gripped him.

"It's funny, the idea of being happy somewhere," Aramis said quietly.

"Why is that funny?" Marie asked.

"It's funny because, I suppose, if I could really fly, truly fly, like all those others," and Aramis stopped. He raised his eyes and looked at Marie. "I don't know where I'd go either."

It was such a simple statement. Such a simple thought. A meaningless admission in most conversations. But here, now, it hung. Heavy. Nearly crushing. There was a long silence. The smiles were gone. Aramis kept his eyes fixed on Marie's a heartbeat too long before he lowered his gaze halfway. And the pause endlessly continued, unbroken by either one moving or speaking. Marie had not shifted her eyes off Aramis. Her only reactions had come as he talked, and her mouth tightened to a slight smile or her eyes opened wide or narrowed into a frown of concern. Now these words came, this admission, so honest and so oddly given without prompting. She had not expected this from him – no, not from him, so ready he seemed to leave and head back into the world.

Marie's face signaled nothing. She was absorbing the awakening realizations and unanswered questions this last statement revealed. All that talk of his, all those thoughts, those pictures, those places, they all led nowhere, she thought, not in the world, not even in him. The silence was awkward and the longer it lasted, the tauter the air was, and the silence, unlike substance, became thicker and stronger the more stretched it became. They both understood. Aramis suddenly looked embarrassed at a confession that had not been sought, that he himself had not seen coming. Marie thought to console, to tell him his admission would be kept secret and safe, that she could be trusted, that she had known it already, that she knew how it felt. But she held back. She did not want to deepen the wound by remarking on its presence. Yet, it grew worse with the silence. Both wished to leave or at least change the subject. But either would be an admission that the embarrassment was real.

"Let's eat breakfast," Marie said softly. The farmer had already come down the stairs.

The two ate slowly, masking the lost conversation with the look of half-smiles and the sound of soft eating. The fresh silence was calming, allowing each to pretend the earlier words were forgotten.

* * *

Sheer white clouds of the morning were pushed away quickly by large, pewter bundles filled with foreboding power. There was a breeze gaining in strength to a light and steady wind. It was cool and damp and carried with it a message of rain though none was yet felt. The sky was brighter now but just how far the sun had risen could not be seen through the low-hanging presence of an overcast sky.

Marie and Aramis had walked the yard, sat, and had walked again. Now, they were standing by the arch, each smelling the last lingering fragrance of linden.

"I love these days," Aramis said, finishing his meal. "The cool winds, dark clouds all tumbling, churning, promising a storm. It's one of the things I enjoy most in life. I suppose it's one of the things I'll miss most when I die."

"I don't like this weather," Marie said. "I don't see anything to enjoy."

"Oh, this is thrilling weather," Aramis said as he straightened his back and lifted his wings. "The surge of force, the natural energy, there is a raw vitality, a bit of danger about it. It's passion and power overcoming the complacency of calm. If you stop and listen, you can almost hear the clouds growling and calling."

'Yes," she said. "They're telling you to go indoors."

Aramis laughed. "You can make fun of me. But I think they are saying 'Here we are! And here we come! We will not be stopped! We travel the world and go where we please!'"

"Yes, maybe," she said. "But I think mostly they're saying: 'Don't be stupid. Go inside. You're about to get wet.'"

Aramis' held up his wings and opened his eyes as if in a trance. "I'm a cloud. Beware," he said in a deep gravelly voice, smiling to Marie, and he began to run in circles around her, his wings out to his side as if he was gliding. "I am a cloud, Marie. Beware. Beware. I am dark and wet and you cannot hide. You run into your house and if the roof keeps me out, I'll just come through the side."

Aramis looked. Marie was not smiling. In fact, he saw her shudder, her eyes open wide. He quickly stopped his game, but he could not stop the rising memory of the thrill. The cold blasts that forced shivers down his back or the whipping wind that unwittingly and unyieldingly tore at the feathers, or painfully grabbed and spun them around. He could feel now how adrenaline surged, smothering the discomfort with blood rising for battle against an unseen foe that, life be damned, his spirit would fight. That's what his imagination would shout and what he had wanted to share with Marie – his love of nature when it delivered those moments in which the heart violently pounded, and he was swept inexorably into its unstoppable course.

"You know how most of us face forward, tail back, wings down, then lean ahead, and always confront the wind head on?" he asked, speaking more gently. "Marie, we don't know what we're missing. Turn your back, let your feathers blow up, feel the rush of cold air up your spine as it tosses your feathers up and out. It's like a gift. A gift of living. A gift of chills. Exhilarating. Pounding. The thrill of just being."

Aramis looked at Marie. There was no smile, no shared rush of excitement. On the contrary, Marie was near tears. She had not wanted to interrupt him and repeat the awkwardness of earlier. But she wished he would stop and she was trying her best not to picture what Aramis was describing.

"I don't think I'd enjoy that," she said.

"Seriously? Have you tried?" he asked, sitting next to her. "To be confronted that way, pushed by nature, struggling to hold on as if battling with death?"

"No," Marie said softly. "Please. Why you would do something that threatens your life? What enjoyment is there in scaring yourself?"

"I don't know why I like it. I've always been that way."

"I've never been that way," Marie said quietly.

"Not even as a child?" Aramis asked.

"No," she said.

"I always have been. As far back as I remember. Getting into trouble for walking too close to the moving tractor. Daring myself to jump from tall heights. I suppose it was a way of fighting the boredom."

"I was bored, too, but I never did that. Weren't there others you could play with? I thought you told me there were many in your coop."

"Yes, there were. My mother, my sisters, and many others besides."

"But you say you were bored? Didn't you play with the others?" Marie asked. "You seem like someone the others would like. I mean, didn't they let you play with them?"

"Sure," he said. "There were a lot of children and we all played together."

"Did you have many friends?"

"Friends? I had no choice but to play with others. There were too many of us. But I enjoyed being alone. And the others would let me. They didn't seek me out much if I wasn't there. And I suppose I got used to it. I found it was a more trustworthy way to fight back the boredom. More trustworthy than relying on the distraction of others. As I got older, I stayed mostly by myself. I would sit and think and have conversations in my head. Ones I knew I could never have in real life."

"Yes, I think I know what you mean," Marie said.

Aramis looked at her. The way Marie responded, he knew there was more to the simple phrase than polite agreement. It was said with more thought, with no hesitation brought by reflection. He wanted to ask, but Marie had not moved, had not changed her expression, and she gave no hint that she wanted to explain.

"You were by yourself a lot, too?" he asked.

"Yes," she said. "Most of the time."

"Then you know the enjoyment."

"Enjoyment of what?"

"Of being alone," he said.

Marie did not answer.

"Did you ever play with ideas in your head?" he asked.

"I suppose," Marie answered. "Imagination and games. We all do sometimes. They just come on their own."

"Not exactly like games. More like puzzles."

"Puzzles? Maybe."

"My favorite, when I was a child, I'm not sure how old, I began to wonder and ask myself questions. Most of those questions we forget as we grow older. Either we answer them, or we forget them. One way or another, they go away. But one day, I asked myself a question that I still can't answer," he said, leaning forward, opening his eyes again wide.

"There is an expression you probably know," he said, "when you believe something to be true, but you are not certain. You say, 'I think,' meaning I'm not sure, but I believe, I might believe, I believe a little, if that's possible, or maybe it meant I want to believe. Give me an example and you'll see what I mean."

Marie had a puzzled look on her face.

"Something that might exist but something you can't see," he prompted.

"Like ghosts?" she asked.

"Yes, or God, perhaps. You begin by saying, 'I think there are ghosts.' That's simple enough. But then you doubt yourself. You're not even certain you might believe ghosts. You're no longer certain of the idea that you're uncertain. Then you would say 'I'm not sure. I think that I think there are ghosts." In other words, 'I think I think there are ghosts." So, I started to wonder. Each time you add another 'I think,' you're adding more doubt, another line of protection, another space of separation. I wondered if 'I think I think' makes sense, then so should 'I think I think I think?' And that made sense to me. Then let's do it four times. 'I think I think I think I think I believe in ghosts.' You see how it works? Well, after five times, or maybe it's six, it stops making sense. It has no more meaning. No matter how hard I try. Somewhere in that sentence, in that thought, that I know is true, it stops making sense. Why is that? I know it must make sense. But I lose track. They are too far apart. But why should that matter? Why can't there be an infinite number of 'I thinks' and have it not just be true, but still make sense?"

"I don't know," Marie said. "I think I think I think I don't know. Why?"

Aramis laughed. "I don't know either. That's the question. The unanswerable question. I thought I was too young and I'd figure it out later, that it was one of those answers that comes with the gift of age. But I never have found it, and I've been trying ever since. How, or why, is it that many true things simply never make sense?"

"You started this when you were little?" Marie asked, as surprised by his question as that he was telling her about it. "Excuse me for saying, but it seems a bit silly," she said. "Perhaps not silly. Just a bit odd."

Aramis smiled. "Perhaps. Maybe it is. I don't know. I've never talked about it with anyone before. But it started me thinking. If we are separated from things more than five or six times, perhaps that's too far, too much. We cannot understand. We lose any meaning from the objects we study, from the events as they happen. Perhaps we can know them, watch them, memorize them, color them, describe, detail, analyze, and even draw them. But we can never understand them. Not unless we are there, or perhaps, next to there, or nearly."

Marie tilted her head, her face frozen in question. "Does that matter?" she asked.

"I believe it does," he said. "Think of the implications. We study to know, but mustn't we live to understand? If we are told of a place, of a time, of a picture, and the story is separated from us more than just a few times, then can we ever transform what we know to understanding? Certainly, if we are present, we have the chance – just a chance – to understand. For many who witness, they will never understand. But at least it is possible. And if we are told by someone who was there, we remain close enough to comprehend the event. Almost to its fullness. Even if that person was told by another, I believe there remains a connection, unseen, intangible, but somehow alive, that can be conveyed. And that is the question. Where does it end? If we hear a story from someone who was witness, do we truly understand more than if we are told the exact same story, in precisely the same way, by the great-great-grandchild of that same storyteller? It's not the facts that are lost. Not necessarily. I'm talking about distortion. The distortion of truths. That's what time does. The way we think about thinking about thinking about thinking. And then aren't we destined to repeat all that we don't understand? We never make progress. Never. The most basic questions of life. Why are we alive? How was all created? Does any of it have meaning? The answers are there but the questions die too soon and are reborn too often. We keep sliding back, each of us bound to start over as children, despite all the wisdom the world has created. Each generation is doomed by its youth. And when I realized this, I was convinced that I needed to understand life, to witness, to see, to comprehend as if it were a responsibility I had. Not just to tell a tale that died over too many years. Not to repeat the tired coop rituals that were emptied of meaning. Not just to live in a way that had been stripped through blindness of its most basic foundation. If we could see and touch everything we've been told, we could again make real what has been stripped of its song. We could return to a time when our lives had meaning because we knew what we lived for and then why we die."

Marie tried to keep up with his rapid current of words, to follow his eddies of thought, but it all moved too fast to understand more than the general direction.

"And have you found out?" Marie asked.

"I'm not sure," Aramis said. "Sometimes I think I have, because there is no answer. Not one we can know. In that case, I laugh because I'm done. I laugh because I've found it and yet I never will know. But then I think I'm wrong. There must be an answer. And so I keep looking."

Marie's face brightened and blossomed to a smile.

"A rara avis, indeed," she said, her eyes suddenly shining.

"A what?" Aramis asked.

"A rara avis you are."

"What is that?" he asked, though he knew by her tone that he should be pleased by her words.

"It's not every day you meet a romantic rooster," Marie said lightly, skipping past the question. "But no, Aramis, no. I never thought about that. I never really thought about any of those things. I don't want to offend you, but isn't it all rather a waste of time? Why would you do that? We just are. That's all. And then we are not. That's what I think."

"What do you mean why?" Aramis replied, surprised by her question. "It's important," he said. "It's, well, it's . . . " Then, Aramis laughed, a sudden, pure and cleansing laugh. "Actually, I don't know why I do it. I never asked myself why. It's just interesting. But I don't know. I don't know why."

"Anyway," Marie teased. "At least you're not alone. I've heard many French roosters waste their time like that."

"That's true," he said still smiling. "It's in our nature, I suppose. Or in our language, which is worse. That is harder to change."

"How did that teach you to love storms?" Marie asked. (That was, she remembered, the original topic.)

"Storms. Storms were exciting," Aramis said. "Little else changed on the farm from one day to the next. But the storms. That was change. Beyond all imagination. There were fantastic storms that would blow through. They would come, and all the others would run to cower from the thunder. They would worry about the winds. They would cry and complain. But I found them different. To me, those winds, those storms, were filled with an unknown force. There is such power in them. As they rolled in, it was like they were talking to me, looking at me, piercing right through me. I didn't understand why the others were scared. I would dream of learning where they came from and where they were headed. I wanted to go to wherever they started and ride them to the end. I pictured other lands, where the fields were all sand, or where mountains and thick forests bent and broke under the weight of heavy rains and powerful winds. After the storm passed, I would watch the clouds leave and wish I were among them, floating with them and travelling the world, seated above and looking down over wherever the wind went."

Aramis paused. He had erupted into monologue, like his own storm blowing through. He was bombarding Marie with the scores of dreams he had about clouds. His mind was caught in picturing that late afternoon years earlier when a storm had churned and rolled and sped across the sky like no other time, not before, not since, its greys and silvers and yellows and blues and whites mixing with a terrifying brown and green and turning the air like a field tilled with a single violent plow. Aramis could feel again the delicious smell and sensation of impending rain, just seconds away, as it approached and asserted its ability and right to overwhelm all. There they were, the recurring tests of wind, hurling themselves forward before the storm arrived fully armed, or the sight of others finding shelter too soon to feel the brunt and the demands of nature unstoppable. Aramis could feel these inside himself now. He wanted to talk of his love of those moments, how alive he'd felt in the face of its threats. How he would clench his wings and hold fast, stare into its face, this unseen power, and defy it to frighten or dare to deter. Then with a deep breath through his nose and a force of will down his spine, he would turn his back, and invite it to course, wait for it to course, upward against the flow of his feathers.

But Aramis said none of this. He was awkwardly aware, aware of her gaze. He waited for a word, a look, a gesture, anything that might invite him to continue living in those moments. Instead, he sat motionless, incapable of plunging into his second pool of churning words.

Marie was quiet. And as Marie kept silent, Aramis also kept silent. Marie regretted reminding him of storms. He enjoyed listening to him talk but wished he would talk of other things. For Aramis, he suffered from that common affliction of those who spend too much time in dialogue with themselves. When speaking to another (oh, to have someone listen!) a soliloquy explodes. And just as quickly as it erupts, it burns itself out. Only a sign, or word, is all they need to reignite. Then, how sad they become when met with pure silence, a stare, or a gentle change of subject. The listener, unaware, assumes the thought is finished, and the speaker, collapsing inward, assumes there is no interest.

The wind was blowing more steadily now. A rain was felt lightly tapping their backs and heard flicking the bushes. Small swirls of dust rose in the corner where the coop met the barn and two grasshoppers jumped clumsily toward the house.

"You seem worried," Aramis said.

"I don't like storms," Marie replied softly.

"Oh, that's nonsense," he said.

Marie raised her eyes at the comment, heard as reproach, not casual reassurance.

"I only meant," he said, "that there's no reason to worry."

Marie was worn down, not by his words, but by her own thoughts. The past, which lived inside her, had threatened to break through so many times. It would not let her be. It would not recede. It was spilling over her uppermost barriers, drip by drip, incessantly, unstoppable. She could no longer, she wanted no longer, to hold it all back.

"Aramis, you don't know about this, but you asked me why I was alone. You asked me when we met where the others were." Marie's voice was flat and thin.

"You know, I've mentioned, I've not always been alone. More than a year ago, this farm was full of others. Some were friends, most were just here. I didn't like them. They didn't like me. But my mother was here, too. Until a day when a storm came this way."

Aramis froze. The cold tone, the look on her face, he knew he had suddenly entered a chamber without knocking and was listening to her read her private diary to herself. Yet Marie was volunteering these words, talking to him, speaking for him to listen. She spoke in a way that came not from her thoughts, but from inside her chest. The words escaped as if spoken through her by a ghost – passionless, expressionless, calm, disembodied. Conveyed with passion, words live and expand beyond their thin meanings. But when stripped bare as dry dust, they can impart such a hollowness that one dares even breathe.

"I did not appreciate them," she continued. "I thought I didn't need them. I didn't like them. I wanted them to leave. So many times. And then one day they did. They left. And they took my mother with them. The wind took our coop. Suddenly, there was no one. No one to talk to. No one to smile to. No one to listen to. No one to hug. No one to avoid. No one. No one even to hate. All there was was silence. Silence. Nothing but silence. A scream of silence. Overwhelming and loud. Yet still I heard my breathing. In fact, it was all that I heard. As if I was the one who had been buried. And the past disappeared. Nothing was left. It had never existed. Except for the ghosts. The ghosts of all memories. The feathers of others still floated in the yard. Like a cruel joke. Random. And constant. Like someone teasing you to remember. Punishing. Laughing. And I discovered, when the past leaves, the future does leave, too. There is no future, when all the past goes away."

Marie's eyes filled with tears and she dropped to her knees. Her words were exhaled back to herself. "It was because of a storm. A stupid, horrible storm. Cruel. For no reason. And everyone gone."

As Marie spoke, Aramis felt the crush of his own words, spoken before, of the wind, of the rain, of the wonder of storms. I didn't know, he wanted to shout. I'm sorry! Truly! I just didn't know!

"I'm sorry," Aramis said as softly as possible. "I only . . . "

"I don't understand why these things happen," Marie interrupted, a fury, but no images, returning with force. "Life ends too soon. I don't understand. There is never conclusion. It's either a storm, or the farmer at night, or something else we never do see. It doesn't matter. It just ends. Then everything ends."

Tears fell effortlessly from Marie's eyes. Aramis was paralyzed. He wanted to soothe her, to wipe away his words and all of her thoughts. But now, he felt hollow. His thinking was useless. Marie was too clever, and she would recognize his pitiful and paltry, thin attempt at consoling. If only his heart could speak with no sound, without the trite filter of words in his over-practiced mind. That's what he wanted. To convey all within him without any words.

"I know," Aramis said. "I'm sorry. I know."

"But why?" Marie sobbed. "Why is the end never really an end? Life just stops and then it's all over. That's not an end. An end has a reason."

"Marie, I know. But it is also a beginning."

She looked at him blankly.

"I know it makes no sense," he said gently. "It's awful when it comes. Terrible. The end. It's not a conclusion. That's what makes it so painful. If only the end would come as conclusion. If only life concluded and then the end would arrive. But it doesn't. They're the same. Life's last interruption and the one that everyone must notice."

Marie hung her head forward. She was still crying. She heard Aramis' words, but she gave them no thought, too filled with her pain to consider his reason. Yet the tone of his voice, a blanket of empathy that was spread out before her, provided that comfort only another can bring.

Marie took in a few haltering breaths, then exhaled deeply. She inhaled once more and let it out slowly. Her tears had stopped, and she wiped them away. "They all died too soon," Marie said, the words barely escaping. "They were all too young. And my mother was, too. She was older than most . . . but she was also too young."

Opening her eyes wide, Marie looked at Aramis and tried to bury the past with the sight of him there.

"My mother was beautiful," Marie continued. "She was so gentle and pretty. I really loved her. I didn't know how much. I don't think I showed her. I don't think I ever showed her."

"I'm sure she knew," he said. "Love shows itself even if we don't. Sometimes, it shows especially when we don't."

Marie was silent. Aramis saw by the way she was staring that she was seeing her mother. It could not be stopped. When a ghost comes to visit, we must keep the door open. They never leave until ready and will not be ignored.

"What did the two of you do?" he asked.

"My mother with me? We didn't do much," she said. "She was just here. She would stay with the hens most of the day and I would play with the chicks or be off by myself. Sometimes we would talk, especially in the afternoons. She would take me to that old tree in the yard and we'd sit under it when I felt sad or scared. And she would tell me stories."

"Stories?" he asked.

"I remember one," Marie said. "There was a tale, my mother said, about this old tree. It was a children's story. A little sad, but I loved it. She said the tree was a spirit, warm with old memories and heavy with wishes. It had left its old home, looking for life, or looking for love. I remember some of the children said it was haunted, but my mother told me it was here to protect. That it needed a place to cry amid smiles. It needed a place to sleep amid dreams. It needed to sit in silence amid laughter. It's funny, I know. It didn't make sense. But it was nice listening to her, and I believed it back then. Today, I'm not sure I ever knew what she meant. I wish I had paid more attention to her."

Aramis listened lightly, absorbed less by Marie's words than by the look on her face, that look of innocence and grace that comes after cries, after the tears of love wash away false protections. He wanted Marie to keep talking. She rarely spoke freely, and her words and her face combined at the moment to a beguiling perfection.

"What else did she tell you," Aramis asked.

"She would point out the branches," Marie continued. "She would show me the long thin ridges in the branches and I would think I could see things carved under them, designs or letters, like when you look up at the clouds and see funny shapes and make them into animals and things. She would show me the scars where nature pushed through and where man had tried to destroy its old strength. She would show me the roots that poke out of the ground. She would show me the holes that opened up in its trunk, how they split its cold flesh and burrowed all the way through. She said those were openings where the spirits enter and leave. I remember one time she walked around it and counted her steps, and then told me it's was more than a thousand chickens old."

Marie laughed. "I always found that funny," she said. "I was little, and I would try to picture a thousand chickens. Can you imagine a thousand chickens all in this tree? What a noise! What a mess! All of them hanging on, some hugging the branches, some the trunk, with wings held out trying to balance and many others falling off?"

Marie was smiling, broadly and freely, not at Aramis, but at her own thoughts. Yet Aramis welcomed it as a treasure all his own. Inside her imagination, she was mimicking the chickens, and she began swinging her wings out and around and upside down, tottering as if losing her balance. Aramis watched while her head tilted down slightly to her right, and her eyes bounced up to her left as she smiled, and she spoke. What a sweet smile! How delightful she was! What contrasts played within heartbeats of each other!

"Can you see that?" she asked with a small, quick laugh. "All of them, hanging on with their feet as they lose their balance, swinging upside down for a second before dropping on their heads. Others hanging on for dear life. It's silly but it wasn't until I grew up that I knew what she meant. Not a thousand chickens at the same time, but one after another. Generation after generation. That's how old the tree is."

Aramis could not stop smiling. He was imagining her then, as a thin little chick, the last remnants of baby down dropping away, awkwardly stuck to her new yellow feathers. What images she had then, so many pictures that didn't make sense. Yes, children see so much that does not exist, the reality of which they come to miss only later.

"What else did you do?" Aramis asked. He wanted to hear more — to hear her voice happy.

"Not too much," she said. "She was simply my mother. There was nothing more we should do."

"And how about your friends?" he asked. "What did they do?"

With the word "friends," Marie unexpectedly felt caught. She looked directly, very briefly, at Aramis. Very, very briefly. "Oh, that's enough about this," she said. Her voice was soft, not angry, tired, not sad. "That's enough of the past. I have thought about it too much these past few days. I was young, and I guess I imagined my life with my mother forever. Even the others, who I did not like, I always imagined them here."

"I only meant . . . " Aramis said.

"Aramis," Marie interrupted again, "then the farmer would come, and I never understood. He would come and friends. My mother's friends. Then my friends. The few that I had. And they never came back. They forever were gone. Forever. Just gone. It was awful. It was awful. Aramis, is it like that on every farm? Is it true everywhere? Is the whole world that cruel?"

Aramis pictured briefly the life he had known — an image of friends, of family, of twisted necks and dead eyes open. "Sometimes," he said.

"And Aramis," she said, "they never came back. None of them ever came back. Eventually, I found out. We all felt so helpless. These friends, these others, would one day be gone. I cried so much as a child. My mother . . . my mother . . . she would tell me stories and say it was all part of life . . . that sorrow, that fear, that loneliness we have when someone leaves and never comes back . . . it was all part of life, she said. She would tell me, though all this was true, still we had life, and for that, she said, we must always be thankful. She explained it would end . . . someday for us all. But before it all ended, we should be grateful we had it. Because happiness is one of the finest gifts we receive. It is simultaneously warm as we become one with another. Yet it is also our rejoicing in the solitude we find. For no one can see the fullness of joy that's within us. And it's this loneliness that's our temple. The true temple within us. It was our place to go. It was there we'd be thankful, and it was there we'll retreat, every day and again, to refind our lost strength. It was where we remember our love. She would tell me one story she loved most of all. There is a secret place inside us, she said. We should go there when we need, and we should be happy when we visit. But we must not stay there, she would say, in that loneliness, that place. It was only there for us to visit. A secret place, Marie said, a far land of tears. We can all go there to live, but never to linger."

Aramis looked down and slid his right heel out to the side oh so slightly. He did not look up. He did not know what to say and his silence, brought by an impotence in the face of all this pain, left him hollow and weak. He had nothing to say.

"It was from her favorite book," Marie said, barely above a whisper.

Aramis folded his wings in front of him slowly, pulling his shoulders down. Marie arched her back and raised her head. Looking forward, her eyes began to tear again as she again saw the past.

"One day, a storm came. And it took my mother," Marie said. "And now I try not to remember the past and I don't want to think about the future. It is filled with nothing but worry."

"Yes," Aramis said. "But Marie, there is no future without worry. There can be no future without worry," Aramis said. "But there are no dreams in the now."

Marie looked at Aramis, then turned her gaze to the ground. Aramis did not move but continued to look at Marie. He watched the dance of fine feathers above her eyes, the gentle shimmer of her cheeks, the way she held her mouth firm when she was deep in sad thought. He remembered how he saw her, early that first morning, when the sun began singing in the light of her eyes.

"And if you think only of what is lost to the past," Aramis continued, "you will find that your dreams are the true and only victims, for they are all that is lost for the future."

"But we are not our dreams," Marie said. "Maybe we try, but they are just wishes, and sometimes they're fears. Whatever they are, I know they're not real."

"Yes, but where there is fear, there is hope. It's the hope in our dreams that let us explore," he said.

"I have no need to explore. I only want to live for the present," Marie said quietly. "I don't think of the past and the future is not here."

"Marie, if you live in the now," he said softly, "you are forever alone. The now always is and is always alone. That is its sadness. There is no room in the now for anything else. It is the true pain of love. That sense we cannot lose that the other is not here, even when they are lying or standing beside us. Our lives are as words. We only have meaning when our lives are with others. And others are the future. It is the context of our lives, and it can never be found when left to itself. It is only from the past and only exists from the future."

"If what you say is true," Marie said, "then we are doomed in our loneliness for the only real is what we have now."

"Is that what you want?" Aramis asked.

"Yes," Marie said, "because I do not want my past and when the past becomes now, I know there is no future."

Aramis paused. The torture in her voice was beyond a mere sadness. It was the expression of a hollow, a bleeding void that would not heal.

"Marie, that is not true. The past always is but cannot be without future. They cannot be separate, or they cannot exist at all. They are not black or white, where one is not conceived by seeing the other. Seeing white shows not black. And seeing black can't teach white. There are no opposites in time. The past, present and future. Like shadow and light, they are not without each other. The past joins the present and, in our dreams, makes the future. The future becomes now, and the present remains only as a line that divides. We must know they are fiction. Because in those very rare moments when we finally see clear, we know that time's trinity becomes one in an instant and the past, present and future meld into all that we are and ever will be. That, Marie, is the pure magic of time."

"Maybe," Marie said. "But what good is that magic when it is not what we want? It brings us things we did not ask for and reminds us of life that is gone?"

"Because in that magic," Aramis said, "in that magic is our future. And thanks to our future, we have dreams in the now. And then thanks to our dreams, we again exist in the future. They never are separate. So, we must have our dreams or else we're alone. For it is our dreams that open our lives to another. Dreams want to be one. Like the sun and the earth. Like shadow and light. They are meant to touch others. And when they converge, they fill up together, and when they match, they expand, and with them, the future."

"No," Marie said, "the future only brings pain and the dreams of today will fade or be . . . " Marie hesitated. Why couldn't she say it? It was just a word, after all. Not saying it will not change it. Not confessing cannot make the deed any less real.

"The dreams," she repeated, "they will fade . . . or be . . . killed. What then, Aramis? What happens then? What's left after our dreams . . . all our dreams . . . when they die? Yes, they die. They are killed, our dreams die. Like those whom we love."

Aramis watched Marie. She seemed to him to be floating just then, almost translucent, a sparkling round fullness swimming in pain. His face warmed. "They don't die," he said gently. "They are dreams. They change. They must change. Dreams always must change. Whether we sleep, or we wake. Dreams are created to change. Marie, that is their nature and that is their gift."

With that, the two fell silent. The circles they had spun collapsed into themselves. They sat there, unmoving, but in every way not unmoved. The two knew, at that moment, there was no place they'd rather be.

Chapter 15

Music
and the Forgotten Room

There are some days in this strange life of wakefulness when all seems strikingly bright and lightly scented. They are days that best arrive unforetold and they bring joy unforeseen. There is no expectation of rare pleasures to come. No presents to gather, no parties to attend, no circus in town, no journey to commence, nothing to anticipate excitedly upon awakening. They are, simply put, days that announce themselves exquisite at dawn, and they are glorious to receive.

It's not certain, of course, but the old farmer seemed lately to have noticed that many of his days fit this description. Because after Aramis' repeated dawn declarations and the whistle of a morning, hot kettle, the farmer introduced a new chore to his day: turning on the radio (in fact, given a slight and welcome loss of hearing, turning *up* the radio describes the chore best). And with a flick of a button (how simple it was), music joined the rooster, the whistle and the cows in morning singing. Indeed, like a lost friend who announces their return, music embraced this farm all the more vigorously because of its long and obstinate absence. The vibrations now affected even the light, casting it brighter and clearing the air for the sun's piercing rays. These new voices and old melodies quickly became as much of the farm's patois as the moos, twills, and chirps that bid the dark sky adieu or the red sun bonsoir. There were trilling pianos, coos of bass strings, the lowing of horns, a machinery of drums. Sonatas and dirges, symphonies and ballads, men and women warbling of newfound or lost loves. The tune did not matter. Each playful strain, each raucous blare, each soothing refrain amplified the history that resonated inside the timeless white stones of this rundown French chateau. From outside, one would think the buildings themselves were singing and stringing, so natural were the sounds that bounced through and around.

Just listen awhile. Here comes original Lully, violinist Leclair, romantic Berlioz, melodic Fauré, harmonic Debussy, playful Ravel, prolific Offenbach, resister Poulenc. Not enough time to hear them all prance. Just a few in the morning to get the day started. Then in the evening, wait for Aznavour, Chevalier, Piaf, Cabrel, Trenet, Montand, and Brel. Words of love, of loss, of dreams, of pain, of joy, of hope, and of loss once more. Wait a little bit more and hear the tickling of fiddles, the whine of accordions, the frenetic, loud horns and the dancing, fast polkas, singing out loud in bold celebration. At dawn, at night, at dawn, at night. A metronome for weeks, set to the day's bookends, played a rhythm for the hours that came in between.

The precise moment that inspired the farmer to play music cannot be determined. A man may indeed change overnight, but at what time in the darkness it occurs is impossible to say. For the farmer, it occurred at some moment before he flipped the radio on, but after he returned to his house with a wet, sticky spot on his upper left sleeve. Somehow, the lingering mist of a fog-bound past had dissolved around him. In its place stretched a landscape of small shards from his past laid out before him like a field of browning, dry flowers that has just begun to seed. The resignation of lost petals was present in the farmer, but so was belief in a burgeoning green come the rains and the warmth that would be delivered in time.

Although the old farmer's step had lightened, his routine remained. The morning toilet, a breakfast, the food for the cat, dog,

Marie, and now Aramis, then quiet resting at the table while he chewed slowly and drifted lengthily, imaginatively counting through his many spent years. With the lyrics and music and a luminescence to his mornings, the series of past journeys now felt inevitable and more rewarding. There was a landscape of context, a remembrance of reasons, a catalogue of decisions that combined to fill out a natural progression that comforted by answering the unasked questions of how, if not why.

For Marie, waking to music was like a holiday morning when the sun came shining through a freshly washed window. It was a bright, happy friend calling good day. It was leaving a solitary night and entering a world that was glad to be there. Why shouldn't music to birds be what their trilling song is to humans? If the calls of a robin and the whistles of a sparrow can bring nature to us, why should opera and ballads not bring our world to these friends? Yes, it seems, divas and fowl sing the other's aspirations.

That first morning of music caught Aramis by surprise. At the first sound, he reacted as if competition had arrived. His back straightened, and he turned his attention to the house. But with the next few notes, he recognized the tune. The priest had played a similar song. And soon Aramis, too, felt lighter, more one with the farm. The music pushed. It wrapped. It pulled the yard's creatures as one, like an audience brought together, the way a street-performer unifies suspicious strangers on a sidewalk. Suddenly, in a city, serious people on their way to many serious places, slow their steps to listen and perhaps nod to each other, as if they belonged where they were, at least for a moment. Just so Aramis felt as the music played on. He even waited for pauses, or the end of a tune, before announcing his call, exerting great strength to hold back his crow. No need to interrupt, he thought, a kindred spirit in song.

Curiously, at about the same time the music began, or perhaps at a moment while it was playing, there came a strange occurrence. The whole farm began suffering a remarkable change. Marie was the first to notice one night. She saw it in the moon. See how its phases were jumping. A new moon one evening, the next night a half. Then the weather was confused. Did it rain late yesterday, or was that last week? Then with no warning at all, flowers appeared. When did they blossom?

Days later, Aramis felt it. It started with the sun. Its path in the sky, though climbing in height, grew faster and shorter. Shadows on one side, in the blink of an eye, had bounced to the other. Then his crows grew more crowded. A few in the morning and then more for the night. There was hardly time for rest in between. And for the old farmer, his discovery came when he rushed to make dinner. There was a lively walk through the morning, then a chore back at home. Afternoon came and went. No time for a nap. Day in and week out. The time passed so quickly though. It was the same all around. Breakfast then a wander. Then a sit and a stroll. A few precious words. The last chore was done. Dinner was late. Then it was dark. Another day gone.

By now, for Marie and Aramis, the morning after that day of inadvertent admissions was just a shared fragment of memory. Immediately after, they had smiled, but self-consciously and forced. Each looked at the other shyly. Each would have happily stared if the other had not seen. Their gaze was given but how heavily it fell. Look, they thought, but avoid those eyes. Yes, they each thought, those beautiful eyes, that look from the other. But it was worse because the other was known and they, for their part, now knew too much. Yet, the night had marked an important end and as it happened, an ever more fateful beginning. There was no going back, not after that day. How much they enjoyed it! Still, those confessions of the past. How much they had opened! But tears for the future. How much they had learned! Yet, that guilt in the present. They had opened their doors, and like any stuck door that is shut for too long, when pushed, it tends to swing open too far.

In their own ways, Marie and Aramis each tried to retreat but the door would not shut. So, they peered at each other, as it were, through the crack near the hinges. Each felt the other peaking. They knew, in the sunlight, shining full and warm over their days, what the other was thinking. It was what they thought themselves. And finally, as we all do when our emotions start dancing, they each took turns leading, first one then the other, admitting that look they both had in their eyes that drew them together. There was no stopping. They had set their rhythms and heartbeats in time to each other. And as the melody of music brings an openness of heart, so the melody of hearts brings a courage to life. Now when one spoke, the other would listen. Now when one paused, the other would wait. Now when one sighed, the other took note. Now when one smiled, the other was happy. Back and forth it went, like a pendulum arm, increasing its arc with each new sweep, swinging incessantly between the two hearts. And as it is known, in these situations, that each new word is a drop of warm rain, each new sentence paints a landscape of beauty, and each new laugh feels more joyous than the first.

Of course, being on a farm, there was not much to discuss day in and day out. But that did not matter. Long periods of silence were neither uncomfortable nor tense. Marie and Aramis would walk away from each other and explore on their own. One would shout out a thought or return with a trinket. One would sit and watch the other who never wandered so far that they could not be seen.

Marie enjoyed this routine. It combined what she knew, being alone, with the sight of a welcome companion, another heart beating. She was at home, and if ever there was something she missed, she reached in her thinking box and brought it along. When she thought no one was looking, or forgot that he was, Marie often walked, then stopped, and talked to the flowers. Then she'd talk to the grass, then talk to the sun, say hello to the clouds, bid adieu to the trees, or wander the yard, smiling and skipping, conversing and laughing. Aramis would sit there. He could only imagine. It was many days later when Aramis finally asked, in a talk of the present, what was it the flowers said to her in return. Marie shrugged and smiled and said mostly they giggle. He said the clouds must shout loudly for them to be heard. No, no, no, Marie replied laughing, the clouds of all the things just whisper and sigh. It's the trees! she exclaimed. It's the trees! Oh, those trees! I keep telling them, she said, to lower their voices. And then they ignore me! Imagine! They ignore me! "The trees are too haughty, just because

they are tall. They won't be so proud when they're naked come fall."
And the two of them laughed, Aramis the loudest.

Mostly, Marie enjoyed watching Aramis. He would stare at the
ground or stare straight ahead. He would lean his head back; his gaze
would follow the clouds. He moved his face in odd little ways, his eyes
open wide, making expressions that showed he was thinking, even
talking, but never aloud. Marie was convinced that the look on his face
was a thousand years old. His travels and worries and loves and his
losses flowed through generations and he experienced them all.

The way that he walked showed he had been off a farm, she
thought. Unlike the others from her past, he rarely looked to the
ground as he strolled through the yard. Sometimes, his legs marched
forward as if determined and destined to reach distant lands before
night. Typically, he only went from one side of the yard to the other,
but there was a confidence, a sturdiness, in the way that he moved.
He'd stop and look at her, then make some remark, most often a small
observation. Then the sound of his voice. There was the sound of his
voice. It made everything feel important, so sure, so known. It could
resonate and soothe unlike any other she had heard. Then later, he'd
grow silent. If only she knew what pulled him inside. She wanted to
ask. But he never smiled, not once, in those moments of quiet. He
was imposingly serious, she found no right to intrude. How could she
ask when he ventured alone? Should she wait or plead to go along on
his journey? Why, she lamented, does my little brave heart arrive only
when not needed?

Marie was right. It was true at those moments, Aramis' thoughts
took him far from the farm. To places of his past. First one, then
another. Varying lengths of very disparate journeys. Or he wandered
ahead to places unseen formed by a strange mix of fields through
which he had traveled. And he was alone, yet never by himself. He was
forever accompanied by that nagging ache we all know, the pull on our
hearts that compels us to write those paper-thin notes: "Here I am
somewhere, and wish you were here." How libraries are filled, by
poetry and prose, in our feeble attempts to convey what that means.
Wish you were here. It means in the present, right here, touching

hands. Feel what I feel and see what I see. These grand miracles are shallow. Time comes, then is gone. It's the irony of love. The sadness of happy. Only by sharing can we magnify. The farther our loved one, the more thinly we see. Yet have them beside us and we still ache all alone. No matter how close, they still are too far. How sad to discover this great weakness of life, that distance and pain are wholly inside.

For Aramis, these days, this distance inside grew smaller and smaller. All he need do was turn and start talking. Marie was right there. Wherever he wandered, those past years off the farm, she remained in the yard with a face like a flower, her smile at the center of long yellow petals. Yet however he tried, he could not bring her with him. As when describing a dream, the thickest of words stumbled futile and thin. Distance condensed. Time reduced to a flash. And how to explain those past conversations? He wanted to tell her, paint her a picture, lay it before her. But how to a child describe the pain of old age and regrets of lost youth? How to a beloved explain they alone are all when your world is over-filled with too many others. No, he could not take Marie. Not to the places his mind travelled. Best to be quiet because somewhere between the black memories of sorrow and the grey ghosts of the future, you, Aramis, are still feeling lost.

* * *

Another day starting, Marie and Aramis walked past the barn. The sun shone fiercely and was drying the yard. Light clouds had sprinkled their rain overnight. The sound had been pleasant, like small bird footsteps on the roof. Now, the ground glistened early and was happy to be clean.

Aramis stopped and peered in at the shackled cows. There were nine being fed. Two lay on their sides while a younger one, who was closest, pulled at her chain as she tried to reach the threads of scattered loose hay that her nose had pushed away. The sound of the conveyor, behind where they stood, filled the barn with a low-pitched rumble.

Aramis looked at the cows. Marie looked the other way.

"Do you like living here?" he asked.

"Why?" Marie replied.

"Well," he said, "you seem to find comfort in it. But sometimes I see you don't like it."

"It's pleasant enough," she said. "It has all I need."

"But do you like it?"

"There are things I don't like. These cows," she said, glancing inside the barn. "They're sad. They can't move. The chains and shackles they did nothing to deserve." Aramis noticed a strange look in her eyes. "But out here," Marie said more brightly and with some cheer, "the yard's not large but it's big enough. The ducks can be mean. The cat's a bit strange. The dog limps. But the food is good. And there are plants and bugs and rocks that keep me company."

"That's good," he said, "but that's not much."

"Maybe not. But it's home."

"But that doesn't mean you are forced to enjoy it."

"It's all that I know," Marie said in defense not so much of the yard but of her position in it. "And if I don't like that, there is nothing left to do."

"You like it because it's all you know?" Aramis asked. "That's not a good reason."

"Maybe it's not, but it is a good answer," Marie said smiling and she began to walk to her right with Aramis at her side.

"What if you had a choice? Haven't you ever wanted to go someplace else?" Aramis asked.

"Aramis, you asked me that before. And what I told you remains true. There is no place I want to go."

"I remember. But all this time sitting here. You must imagine things you would someday like to see."

"No, I think that's you," Marie said. "You're the one who does that. Besides, what other things would I see? Another yard? Another farm?"

"No," Aramis said. "Those are pretty much the same. Someplace different. Someplace new.

Someplace, maybe, you've never imagined."

"How can I want to go someplace I've never imagined?"

"To see what's there."

"But if I don't know what's there, why would I want to go?"

"You would want to go to see what's there."

"Yes, but if I don't know what's there, why would I want to go?"

"To see what's there," Aramis laughed. "Are you trying to confuse me?"

Marie smiled. "Don't be silly. You do that on your own without any help."

Aramis laughed. This was his delight in talking with Marie. His serious questions met with play, with challenge, and with unexpected diversion. He increasingly laughed now in a way he had long since forgotten, an unconscious laugh we all have as children when playing with our friends a spontaneous game.

"You think so?" he said smiling. "If I'm that confused then why are you the one not answering the question?"

"You want to know where I would imagine I want to go if I didn't want to go anywhere I cannot imagine? That's what you want me to imagine?"

Aramis smiled. "Not exactly, but yes."

"I don't know," Marie said. "What do you imagine? I'll go there with you."

"No, that's not fun."

"Ok, I actually do have an answer for you this time. I've been thinking of this since you asked me before."

"And what did you think?"

"The Cape of Good Hope," Marie said firmly. "Yes, the Cape of Good Hope."

"The Cape of . . . " Aramis started to say.

"Not the Canary Islands!" Marie said, interrupting. "No! Not there. Canaries are too annoying. And messy. And loud! Not the Canary Islands. Definitely not the Canary Islands."

"Ok," Aramis laughed. "Why the Cape of Good Hope?"

"I don't know. I heard the name once and I decided I liked it. Does there have to be a reason?"

"No," Aramis said. "Do you know where it is?"

"I have no idea. I don't know where the Canary Islands are either. Come to think of it, I hope I don't go to the wrong place by mistake."

"I don't think there's much chance of that."

"Why, do you know where they are?"

"No. But I'm sure they're too far. And since we don't fly, and I don't think we can walk there, we don't have to worry about going to the wrong one."

"That's a shame," Marie said.

"Why?"

"Well, it must be very beautiful, the Cape of Good Hope. Like here in the spring after a rain. All the flowers. All the grass. Plenty of food. Everyone happy. Everyone smiling, cheerful every day. It must be something like that. A place filled with good hope. I would like to go."

"Yes," Aramis said.

"Or maybe it's not," Marie said, suddenly changing character. "Maybe it's cold and raining and terrible all the time with nothing but spiky bushes, wind, mud, and rocks and . . . and . . . wild hungry animals and awful people."

"And loud and annoying giant canaries," Aramis added, his eyes widening. Marie looked at him. She liked the joke, especially that he was playing along, but she was too intent in her thoughts and imagination to smile.

"Yes," she said. "Maybe they have nothing to enjoy and life is miserable and it's hard to stay alive and no one smiles even just once a week. So, everyone can only exist by relying on nothing but hope. That's why they call it the Cape of Good Hope because that's all they have."

"I hadn't thought of that," Aramis said in mock seriousness. "Perhaps we should go somewhere else."

"Yes, perhaps someplace else I can't imagine. Wait, let me picture it," Marie said. This time she was laughing.

"Very funny," he said.

Throughout the conversation, the two continued walking, stopping intermittently as they playfully answered, and starting again as new questions arose. Now, though, Marie made a point to stop. She looked at Aramis. Her eyes wide, her head slightly tilted, she nodded her head with each word in that manner one adopts when making a definitive, undeniable, and absolutely final, concluding statement.

"Aramis, what difference would it make where I went?" Marie asked. "I could go a million places out there. And then, one day, when I'm not looking, I'd find myself right back here in this yard. All that effort. All that struggle. All that time. And when I got back here and I looked in a mirror, I'd still be myself. All that travel. All those places. All that thinking. And none of those things would change who I am. Marie. A small, farmyard hen."

"Perhaps," he said. "But new experience is like food. Whether or not we can feel it, it becomes part of us. We don't notice at first, but after a while, we realize we're different. The experiences shape us. Maybe not now, but it changes who we become."

"Who I become? I am already who I became."

"I mean who you become in the future."

"Oh that," Marie said.

"Yes, that."

"The future will come whether I stay here or not."

"That's true. But your place in that future, that could be changed."

"Aramis, you're a strange one," Marie said in a light, but serious, tone. "I don't mind your questions, but you ask them like you're trying to tell me something, not ask me something. Do you think I should leave? Do you want me to leave? Are you trying to . . . ah, I know," she said with a crooked smile, "you want the yard to yourself. That's it, isn't it? You want me to leave because you think it's not big enough for us both. You want it all for yourself!"

Aramis laughed. "Ah, you found me out!" he said. "You discovered my secret! My plot has been foiled!" The two smiled at each other and continued walking, past the driveway, past the house, past the tree.

"No seriously, Marie, I'm not suggesting you leave. I want to understand why you stay."

"I don't know," she said. "I'm not sure I can explain. But I know you'll figure it out, and then, when you do, you let me know."

And with that, and with each smile still lingering, each slipped back into their separate thoughts. They circled past the shed where the iris and the periwinkles were showing more buds amid the weeds that had reached the height of the plants. Marie looked down at the place where Aramis liked to sit when he was thinking alone. The two came back around the tree and walked along the side of the house.

"Let me ask you a question," Marie said as they neared the corner of the yard. "Where do you go when you sit and are quiet?"

"What do you mean?" he asked.

"Sometimes you're so serious," Marie said softly, not looking at him. "I've seen you and you seem so dark at times."

"Me?"

"Yes, you. You sit, and you stare. Your face is blank, yet it sends a message you are gone. Sometimes it looks animated. Then it looks lost. And always it looks serious. I don't know how to explain. It's dark somehow. I look at you and all your black feathers. They're usually brilliant and so much alive. But at these moments, they no longer have color. They seem to lose substance, as if you're a shadow. You look almost like you no longer exist."

"It's not that serious," Aramis said. "I can assure you I'm still here. But where do I go? I don't know if I can explain. Mostly I drift. Through many things, or many places. It's rather vague, I suppose."

The answer, though it sounded sincere, frustrated Marie, like being told of a secret that no one will share. What was vague? What was drifting? What did that mean? It was difficult enough for her to ask the question. The answer made it worse.

"I don't understand," Marie said. "In a funny way, you sit there, yet you leave. I don't know where you are. I don't want to interrupt but I'd like to know where you go."

"I don't go anywhere in particular. I go to the past, sometimes the future," and Aramis looked at Marie with a small smile. "Yes, seeing places I cannot imagine. I'd like you to come. I mean, I'd like to be able to take you. To explain it to you. But the truth is I don't know how to bring you along. I've wanted to. But I've never tried before and it all seems so, well, vague."

Again, there was quiet, and again, there was that word. Vague. Marie was relieved that Aramis wanted to take her along. But why hadn't he tried? Why hadn't she asked him? That childhood feeling of being left out was surfacing again. Marie was determined not to let it take hold.

"Do you miss being out there?" she asked and then immediately wished she had not. It had been the first thought she had and out it came as a question. She wanted it back.

"Sometimes," he said. "Sometimes, I do."

"Sometimes?" Marie said. "Why?" she asked softly.

"There are some things I miss," he said. "I enjoy being out there, by myself, without a coop, without a smokehouse, without a farmer. To have no one around. There's a freedom unlike anything on a farm. No other faces. No voices to hear. No food to be shared. No schedule to keep. There's a unique quiet that arrives when there's no one around to remind you of yourself."

"That sounds lonely," she said.

"Sometimes," he said. "Sometimes, it is."

"When you feel lonely, what do you miss?"

"Do you remember you asked me about conversation. Whether I miss conversation? It doesn't happen often, but I miss those rare moments when a discussion with someone comes as easily as it comes inside our own brains. I have conversations in my head when I'm alone. It's pleasant. It's easy. It's comfortable. There is no competition. Cleverness is understood with a smile or a nod. Questions are genuine and not filled with silent meaning. But then after a while, it all feels transparent. It's not rich. It's not full. No matter how I try, or how many people I imagine, after a while I can't escape the fact that it's just my own words, it's just all myself."

"I have those all the time," she said. "It's been good to have another voice answer back."

Aramis smiled at Marie. Her voice sounded childlike as if confessing some secret. It felt good to him also. He had wondered how it became easy to say what he wanted. No reproaches or raised eyebrows. She listened, and she answered, and she said what she thought, never tossing out the words that others wanted to hear.

"If that's the only thing you miss, then it doesn't seem too bad," she said.

Aramis was silent. He knew that was not all. He often thought it himself. He had told himself many times he did not need conversation. He was better living alone. He knew that was not true. How could it be true? And still there was more he wanted to say. It was more difficult than silence, more painful than solitude. I miss the touch of another, he failed to confess. The inadvertent quick brush of a wing. An enduring embrace. With that, no conversation is needed. It's that touch I miss, he wanted to say.

"Yes," Aramis answered. "That is all that I miss."

Marie looked at him. There was something in the pause that preceded his words. His look told her he was thinking of thoughts not yet shared. It was not hard to read, that face lined with sadness.

"Oh" she said. "I thought there'd be more."

"I suppose there might be," Aramis said quietly, then paused again. "But they are things I don't understand. Sometimes I'll miss something simple, like corn or a nest. Mostly, though, the desires are like the clouds, always shifting and moving. If I were to tell you what they are, what I think they are right now, it might change tomorrow. I wish I was more like other roosters. But what I hate today I might adore tomorrow. And then vice versa. And what I said today would not be true tomorrow. In the end, I'd be lying. Of course, not with intention, but through mistake and omission, and that's the worst type of lie because it's told to ourselves."

Aramis stopped. Marie had a quizzical look. Her eyes were frowning. Her mouth was pursed shut. Had he confused her, or did she not believe him?

"You said to me once that I was not being honest," Aramis continued. "I don't know why you said that. It's difficult sometimes, but I never have lied to you."

"When?" Marie asked.

"When I said I liked the way you run. I was not lying. I do like the way you run," he said.

"Yes, well, maybe," Marie said, lowering her head and looking at the ground. She wanted to change the subject. Suddenly, a different thought welled up inside her, unexpected and urgent. It came from nowhere and swelled with such speed and rushed to her head. Her mind, overtaken, was struck with such force she was sure it would burst. There was no holding back.

"No, not maybe," Aramis was saying, seriously but gently. "It's true. I do like the way you run, because you . . . "

"Are you going to leave?" Marie suddenly interrupted, still looking at the ground. "Are you planning to leave?" And with that, she looked up, straight in his eyes, her face a frozen intensity showing an innocent fear illumined by a bright flash of anger.

"I . . . I don't know," Aramis stammered. His strength left his legs, and he felt the blood drain from his face. For a moment, he thought he might actually fall over.

"Why haven't you moved into the coop?" Marie said abruptly and rapidly, shooting the question as if an arrow at Aramis.

"I . . . I . . . I don't know," he replied, stuttering again. "I thought about it. In the beginning. But then. At first, I was going to. But then. Well, we talked. I didn't. I don't know. I thought it might be," and he searched for the word. Marie looked at the ground. "I thought it might be . . . I'm not sure . . . .intrusive," Aramis continued. "It was your home. It is your home. I didn't want to intrude. And then, more time passed, there never came a day. I mean, I had no reason."

"Right. It's ok," Marie said, suddenly and ashamedly realizing the scene. "It doesn't matter. You're right. You shouldn't. I'm sorry I asked." And though her words were true, Marie knew they were wrong.

Aramis did not move. His mind reeling, he tried to think back to the topics just discussed. Had he said something to prompt this? All that talk about leaving. Going someplace. But they were talking so calmly. It was just conversation. Was she angry? She seems angry. But at what? I saw her running?

Marie, too embarrassed, was unable to look up. She took a step to her right and with Aramis following her lead, the two began walking. Marie was confused. Aramis was very confused. The silence between the two lengthened and tightened.

Marie walked along looking straight ahead at the ground. Why did I do that? What was I thinking? What have I done? What was so wrong? We were talking and then . . . then . . . I should say something. Now. He probably wonders what happened. Oh, why did I do that?

Aramis searched all around. He could see Marie from the corner of his eye, but he dared not look over. She was offended that I didn't move in? That was it. That must be it. But why get that angry? He thought about asking permission to move now. But that wouldn't be good. She would think it was only because she raised the idea. She would be right. I should be quiet.

The two walked silently.

But why hasn't he? she asked herself.

Why haven't I? he wondered.

And with that one simple question, unexpected and, let it be said, downright serious and disturbing questions took root inside Aramis.

* * *

While Marie and Aramis played their own melodies of contrapuntal thoughts, the farmer worked through another day in his increasingly bright and light motif. A walk through fields accomplished, he returned home for lunch and to seek out a task.

Weeks had passed since his right slipper had gone missing. He thought of it as he pulled his boots off. And as he rubbed out the sand that had blown in his eyes, he suddenly remembered the night of the storm. Was it there? he wondered. From that night the wind howled? It was the only place he had not yet searched, a room long discarded as forgotten in his life and left silent at the end of the long hall to the left. Except for that night, he had not entered for years. There had been no need. Today, however, he found no other chore and he went to explore within his own house what he might have misplaced, what he might have forgotten.

What precisely, he wondered, was in those corners he'd not seen? What were those dark boxes in the shadows that night? There were small figures on the bed. This had been the room of two children until they were grown, and then his wife used the room mostly for sewing. He had no memory of the room's contents, the color of the walls, whether there were curtains, or even a carpet. He knew there were two beds and at least one old table. He assumed there was a chair. Perhaps there were objects he needed in there. It did not occur to him that he could spend the entire day straightening and cleaning the room, and then brick it up for all he had used it or would need it again.

The old farmer opened the door as one opens a mystery. One had to start somewhere, and the rest would unfold. He stood in the doorway. A scatter of clothing, hanging from nails, strewn over chairs, overflowing from boxes untidily stacked, gave the impression of a hastened departure from many years past. It had the careless arrangement of a teenager's things having been stored and tossed and then searched and left with a faith that the room was a vault in which all would remain.

The large bed in the center lay still beneath two large windows hidden by sheets of yellowing chintz. The bare blue mattress stretched out, asleep. Rolls upon rolls of many colored cottons and two boxes marked "photos" sat where pillows once played. The room had the cozy smell of old calico dresses hung for years in a forgotten closet. The old farmer moved cautiously between the scratched rough-pine footboard and a child's simple desk set against the right wall. He looked repeatedly down to ensure a clear step. Under his feet a carpet lay wary, a brown and yellow pattern of either small flowers or interlocked circles, too worn to distinguish with his soft failing eyes. From under the bed poked out books and some papers and along the long wall were six shelves and a dresser. Other walls were bare except for a football team poster and a picture of flowers. The floor at the edges was home to stacks of old boxes where the top ones hung open. One tall pile tilted left with a corner sinking into the crushed box below. On a few of the boxes were the names of his children while others were scribbled as books, clothes, or "things." Some of the boxes showed nothing, except jagged shapes of dried water stains.

The old farmer walked to the shelves avoiding still more clutter. On the top were some ribbons and trophies for sports, but he could not remember who won them or why. Textbooks of science, fiction by authors he did not recognize, and books about history were lined up below. Volumes of children's books, light green and pink, took turns on the shelf with Asterix comics. Farther down was *L'Auberge de l'Ange Gardien* next to *Le Général Dourakine* and then Cécile Aubry. On the bottom shelf were records, mostly old 78s with no jackets, some albums from his children. He examined them all. Then he moved onto boxes, picking lightly through each. Most were filled with books and loose papers, and there was knitting half-finished, a receipt for some clothing, and two spools of thread. An old phonograph sat inside a broken banana box. He went to the shelf and pulled three of the records he recognized from the past. Another box was half-filled with old letters and a saucer but no cup. There were two small dolls, clothes ripped and arms missing, and an airplane and boat and seven pencils, four pens. Every so often, when he found something of interest (a photo, a notebook, a small jewelry box), he would take it and sit on the large bed. Unlike the small bed on the side, which sat forgotten and barren, the large center bed was covered with long rolls of cloth of mostly white, green and blue. They were the remnants of fabric his wife had collected to make dresses for his daughter or shirts for the boys, though they outgrew them too fast.

The farmer spent hours, sitting and opening, standing and looking, down on his knees and wandering the shelves. It can take surprisingly long to review what accumulates in the randomness of life. And by late afternoon, the searching was finished. He either could not find what he wanted, or perhaps found too much. All he collected was a stack of small pieces of fabric to send to his daughter and a football he discovered flattened under the bed.

Closing the door tightly, he walked down the hall and directly out the front door. He looked to his left and stopped, lingering for a moment with the site of the field a shining yellow-green horizon through the open front arch. He thought he saw something move. Then he turned to his right and sat on the steps. With the swatches of fabric placed by his foot, he squeezed the flat leather sphere, first one way, then the other, pulling at the surface, trying to force it to find its intended full structure. He looked up as Marie and Aramis were just walking past.

The sun, just above his forehead and staring straight at him, was warm and silent and the wind, feeling fresh, was made all the more welcome after the hours he spent in the back, closed room. As a third clear breeze caressed his straight back, a realization occurred as if someone had spoken. Still holding the ball, the farmer stood up slowly and walked to the kitchen. The small pieces of fabric began to scatter down the steps.

"Dorothee? Allô, it's me," the old farmer said on the phone. "I know it's not Sunday, but perhaps the children want to come over for a minute. I found something they might like."

Dorothee, with a damp dish towel slung over her shoulder, could barely speak but managed a short "merci" before putting the phone down. She stared at nothing and pushed her wavy brown hair back over her shoulder. What could it be? She wondered what the farmer could have possibly found that would lead him to call and ask for the boys. The last time this happened (it had been more than a year), it was because he was angry when he found several tools in a scatter and a pile of rocks in a circle. Dorothee decided she would go with them.

The news that their grand-pere had called to request them sent the two boys scrambling. No, they had done nothing wrong, they both assured their mother, then they raced through the yard, with their mother behind, and they ran past the shed, around the thick old dead tree, and to the farmer's front stairs.

"Grand-pere, grand-pere!" the expectant boys shouted as they pushed through the door.

Walking out of the kitchen, the farmer held the ball out in front of him and gave it to Neville.

"Take this," he said. "It might have been your father's. But you have it now, it just needs some new air. Go look in the cellar. There's a pump down there. Turn left and go into the first room on your right."

The smiling boys grabbed at the ball without saying a word and ran to the cellar to search for the pump. Dorothee looked at the farmer. He seemed to be fine. He had not smiled, nor had he said anything more, so he was not acting strangely. Still, his eyebrows were raised a bit more than normal and calling her house and asking for her children was an occurrence different enough.

The pump was not found, but the boys took the ball home with their mother's assurance that their father would fix it. (It had not been his, but it did not matter anymore.)

The rest of the day passed uneventfully and, as every day does, it eventually grew dark. The farmer ate dinner with the radio playing and though it was late, he had one last chore. Finding a pad of paper and a broken, black pen, the farmer placed them on the table. He walked back down the hall and found the phonograph and three old records he discovered that day. Then back to the kitchen, where he put on the first and turned it up loud. He sat, listening to the words of one sad song then another and another. His daughter's letter swirled through him. He had read it many times. He knew what she was feeling, and it was time to respond. Words from his years flowed out through his fingers and formed a weak script that hid the strength of his hands. They were words he could not speak, but words that were there, that had always been there, waiting for release like the last drop of nectar when it falls unseen from a forgotten, brown flower.

To My Daughter Charisse,

Do not worry. I am well. Nothing was destroyed though the marigolds suffered. A dead tree fell in the yard, but nothing was broken. Now the old tree looks strange. You will see when you come.

I hear you spoke with Dorothee recently, so you have any news. Your brothers live their lives. Do not worry for them. They are cutting their paths. My thoughts, however, turn to you. Especially as I read your letter. I will not say, I must not say, you are my favorite. That is not something a parent can say. Each child is different and our feelings for each are different as well. But I give you more thought than I do your brothers because they are more like each other and when I think of one, I can think of them all. But I need different thoughts for you. Your spirit is evasive. It is not easy, not easy for me and not easy for others. And I fear very often, not easy for yourself. You are not a person who can look in the mirror and see who others see. Because no matter where they look, they only see themselves. To them, and to you, I fear, your reflection is blurred.

I knew when you were a little girl that you wanted much from this world. Too much. I cannot help you get it. I cannot help you find it. But I can tell you as an old man, you never find what you seek by expanding your search. There are always more choices and the more desperate your search, the bigger the maze. Instead, live your decisions. The path always leads forward. And just because you run does not mean you get there any faster. You remember your uncle. You were young when he died but you remember him here. He was not always like that. He had been happy and funny when we were still boys. But after the war, he started to look, and he didn't know why. There was no aim to his search, or if there was, he did not know it. And though he came back to die, he never returned.

I've tried to live a good life. That's all I could do. I never moved from this farm. But when I reread your letter, the questions you have were familiar to me. I too had a desire to leave here and travel. I wanted to explore. Every day I was young, the farm seemed to grow smaller, the boundaries closed in and there was no room to walk. But then with the war, I was the only boy left and I had no choice but to stay. Time barely arrived before it was gone and then many years later, when you were all children, I realized suddenly the farm was not small. Somehow it expanded. To an immeasurable size. To the size of the world. I knew that most of the world was out there, but it no longer mattered. It and the farm had become the same size. The only difference was that one was my home and the other was not.

And now it's your turn to discover the world. You are my youngest. You were your mother's youngest. You are her final creation. It is not a responsibility you have, but a duty to yourself. Because your duty is last. As the final harvest decides whether planting was fruitful so in a way is the final child's wishes. You are both sunset and sunrise – the last efforts in a passing day, the last moments of an ending night. And in front lies a gateway, closed to me but open to you. And you must go through it, and I will watch while I can, for it is the beginning of the future. I only ask you not to run. The reflection will be blurred. And you will miss all the beauty and God's simple truth that life, as we live, becomes what it is.

We hope to see you soon,

Papa

The old farmer, with the letter complete, put away the pen and rose from the large kitchen table. He turned off the phonograph and the light, and walked slowly to his bedroom, where his left slipper remained without its companion.

A week and three days later, the farmer's daughter would be silenced by the words of this letter. She would sit in her chair, disbelieving these thoughts, these compassionate words, came from the man who never hugged her nor kissed her – not at moments of love, not at moments of sorrow. She reread it many times, searching for her father. She could not find him. Two days later, she called to tell the old man she would visit.

* * *

While the music played from the kitchen, Marie and Aramis were alone and quiet in their separate homes.

Aramis was more puzzled than ever. Why haven't I? he wondered. Why didn't I? he asked. She's right . . . but still . . . .just moving in . . . there was never a reason . . . I would if I lived here . . . do I live here? . . . does she think I want to leave? . . . what have I said? . . . maybe I should . . . the yard feels so small . . . it's all too familiar . . . how nothing ever changes . . . but she did look so pretty . . . oh, now, now, let's not do that. Such were the random thoughts and questions that kept Aramis pacing. In the smokehouse, around the iron bars and the bucket and rusted pots and large rocks. He did not need the light. He knew where they were. Maybe she was right. Maybe I won't stay. That's why I haven't moved in. I thought I was polite. But maybe there's more. Still, why was she angry? What did I say?

Luckily for Aramis, Marie was not there to ask. In fact, Marie had been asking herself many of the same things, mostly repeating: "Why am I angry?" Marie slowly sank down just inside her front door and thought through the day. The words. His looks. The smiles. His laugh. Her outburst. Her fears. And once again, his smile. She was barely aware of the ballads and sad songs that swayed through the air from inside the kitchen. Why do I care at all what he says? It doesn't matter if he leaves. Nothing will happen. The yard is the same. I'll be the same.

Like the male and the female of any one species, hens and roosters understand the other best when they do not compare thoughts. Because for a rooster, when he puzzles, a question tends to be little more than a question. It has an answer, usually simple, waiting to be found, and a conversation has trajectory where the destination is foreseen even if forever undiscovered. In other words, his mind is more checkers than chess with each step taken in reaction to the last. It's so simple, in fact, that when explained to a hen, she couldn't stop laughing. Because for a hen, indeed, that's all wasted effort. It is the question itself that is already the answer. There's no need to go on. That the thought merely is says all that is needed. No matter the game, just set down the pieces, sit back and enjoy. The sheer existence of the board is the point of the game, not the outcome because, well, what's in a game?

This is not to suggest that roosters and hens should not play together. They do complement each other, after all, with one's thoughts flowing while the other is ebbing, one's question asking while the other is answering, one's idea shining while the other is hiding. It is simply that, at moments like these, with Aramis pacing and Marie sitting quiet, their individual thoughts would clash, not meld, if they attempted to share. So while Aramis asks: "What did she look like?" and "What did I say?", Marie instead wonders: "What did he say?" and

"What did I look like?" The problem, of course, is there's no one to answer.

For Marie, this separation was particularly acute. After the discussion that day, she wanted to apologize, or at least see his face. "What is he thinking, right now, right now while not here?" she wondered, and she knew she would know with just one simple glance. There are too many things I will never understand, she thought. So much that he thinks that I will never follow nor fathom. I wonder what he's doing, what he's thinking, right now. Is he pacing or sitting? Looking out at the field or facing the coop?

"If only I could see him," Marie thought as she sat by her door. "His smile and black feathers. His large eyes expressing. His small mouth showing what he tries to ignore. I would understand it all. I would. I would. If only I could see him and know he was smiling." Yes, how gentle he would be, her thoughts, gliding and curving, continued to say. How thoughtfully, how softly, how beautifully he would talk. And she would understand it all and listen while watching his soft distorted comb announce his hard, embattled life, and she would hear what he said in the full context of him, not as before with the pressing of time.

Slowly, Marie had the feeling that time was creeping to a stop. All around her rose and fell like the coop was slowly, sleepily breathing. What was *he* doing? It was the first time since childhood – no, perhaps the first time in her life – that another sprang to mind so real and so close. There were two on this farm. How are there two? "Two," she repeated. The night had stopped moving. She no longer felt just the beauty of night. She felt quiet. So quiet. She was alone with her calm. Yet, she wasn't alone. It was solitary replaced by a placid serene. "Where did this come from? How did all stop? Like when I played as a child and it was suddenly late. Too happy to stop. Time stops for the happy. It's only the world that gets older. Is that what I am? Am I happy right now? Is that what I feel? Is this how that feels? But somehow there's nothing. I expected happiness to be, to be something to touch. Yet, yes, here it is. Maybe it's the absence of all. It's nothing, just warmth. Yes, happiness is warm." And with that sudden awareness and with her mind still racing, Marie became unexpectedly aware of warm thoughts of tomorrow. That was it. Marie smiled. That's what is different. Because happiness is knowing the joy of tomorrow. It's a desire for days, many days, yet to come.

Suddenly, the music stopped in the kitchen. Both Aramis and Marie turned their heads toward the house. They had grown accustomed to music and were disappointed each night when it came to an end. Aramis enjoyed drifting away with the words. Marie enjoyed the notes as companion. Both were startled that it ended so abruptly this night, stopping as it did in the middle of song. The farmer always waited for the singing to end. Now a sudden quiet filled in the yard. Crickets and buzzing, a car down the hill, some scratching and moos returned to the farm.

Unknown to Aramis and Marie, inside the house, the farmer fumbled with the phonograph he had pulled from the room. He had unplugged the radio to make room on the kitchen's side table. The Columbia label started to turn, the needle scratched loudly, and the volume was raised with the turn of a dial.

The voice of Edith Piaf appeared as if she was perched up high in the kitchen. The song started to play. This must have been a present, the farmer thought. Too much Paris for him. He never would have bought it. It was "Le P'tite Marie." And the farm held its breath. Aramis, in the smokehouse, swirled his head toward the house and saw there before him, in transparent illusion, Marie's smile and the play of delicate feathers that sparkled just under her vulnerable eyes. In the kitchen, the farmer raised his right hand and began to conduct the sad strains and the words he'd forgotten he knew. "Alors là, j'ai pensé à nous . . . "[1] And in the coop, very simply, Marie arose slowly. Marie started to dance.

Without thinking, she could not resist. A song with her name. A song about her. Marie, in the first moment, thought she was deep in a dream. But she knew it was real. Somehow more real than she ever had known. To her, it was a lullaby, though the words were so sad, and

---

[1] "And then I thought about us . . . "

Marie lived in slow motion and moved with the tune. "Eh oui, voilà . . .
Tout est fini"[2], she heard. And it moved her near tears. Was the song
about her? No. But it was. In some strange way, she knew the words
were for her. And she imagined his face, so soft and so strong.

With her first few steps, Marie felt she was falling, falling past her
body, falling through time. She had not danced since, well, she could
not remember when – since the others were gone, since before her
mother last cried. And tonight, for the first time since those long
hidden days, Marie's weightlessness returned. And she danced. And
she danced. Yet it was more than a dance. Marie flowed. Then she
twisted. She reached. Then she bowed. She curtsied. She kneeled. She
became and transformed. She lifted and she arched and on one leg,
she balanced, and she reached and she leaned until she would almost
fall over. Still, she never did. A soft sweep of her left wing with her
right wing held upward, she pirouetted and tossed her head strangely
forward. It was an odd type of dance. Unbalanced. Yet smooth. She
swayed to one side until again she might tumble. Then suddenly, on
one leg, she spun, and she turned, and then she finally leaned over.
Again, one wing raised, she twirled twice around, and all through the
motions, she never left her feet. Then she spun and she dove and she
curled and she arched and was serious and frowned and then she
smiled and then laughed. That was the most beautiful thing to hear.
She giggled to herself as a child would giggle, happily inside, not caring
about others, what they thought or would say, not caring if they
watched.

"Qu'on s'en aille chacun de son cote,"[3] came the lyrics, and with
"R'garde un peu ce qui peut t'arriver . . . "[4] Marie, down on one knee,
her right leg forward, wings spread wide, curtsied a slow, deep and
graceful homage to the beauty. Her head, lowered to the left and nearly
touching the ground, held its position, waiting, waiting, waiting, for

---

[2] "Well, yes . . . everything is over"

[3] "Then each of us goes his way,"

[4] "Just look what can happen to you . . . "

the entrance again of the sadly, playful, resurgent music and the oh-so-sad-sad words: "Alors là, moi, je pense à nous"[5] and with that, she arose and again began subtle sweeping as if in slow motion she were soaring unencumbered through a bright, cloudless, blue sky.

Aramis, seated with his back to the hinges of his door, watched without moving. Indeed, without breathing. He sat still, transfixed. Marie's front door, though not fully open, allowed him to view almost half of her room. Aramis watched her appear, dance past the front door, before she again was swept out of view. Over and over, he saw her glide and her twirl and then disappear. "Je la revois, la p'tite Marie. Mon Dieu, comme elle etait jolie."[6]

And Marie danced.

"Mais lui qui reste, ça c'est affreux. Qu'est-ce qu'il va faire de ses journées et de toutes ses nuits, et de ses années?"[7]

And she danced.

"Aux p'tites histoires de rien du tout, aux choses qui prennent des proportions rien que dans notre imagination."[8]

And she danced. Her eyes grew heavy and her throat tightened as she thought again of the words. It might be true, of course, inevitable, soon. "Hier encore . . . et aujourd'hui."[9] But the future, she thought. Oh, yes, there's the future! And she pictured her Aramis, smiling and watching. "Leur belle histoire, elle est finie."[10]

---

[5] "And then I thought about us"

[6] "It's like seeing her right now, little Marie, my God, how beautiful she was."

[7] "But the most unfortunate is the one who is left behind. What will he do with his days and all his nights, and all his years?"

[8] "About the little stupid stories, about things that grow extremely important only in our imagination."

[9] "Yesterday still . . . and today . . . "

[10] "Their wonderful story is over."

And she danced to the end, where there could be no more doubt that dancing with herself was her sweetest conversation. And Aramis, from afar, could not help but try to listen.

"Mon Dieu, ayez pitié de moi. Demandez-moi n'importe quoi, . . ."[11]

---

[11] "My God, have mercy on me. Require from me whatever you want, . . ."

Chapter 16

 When Marie and Aramis
Share a Moon Bath

Some days later, a dream awakened Marie and then it was gone. Her eyes opened. Inside the coop, she saw the silvery blue streaks of moonlight shine its stripes through gaps in the slats of the east-facing wall.

Marie sat up quickly. She did not need to find her energy, it was there, laying at the surface, jumping out from her breast. Marie leapt from her nest. She propelled herself to the door and ran outside, looking up to her right to confer with the moon as she scampered, smiling, to the smokehouse.

"Aramis, Aramis, wake up, wake up!" she shouted as she neared his door. "Wake up, wake up, I can't let you miss, the moon is full, you have to see this!" she called, slipping back into her rhymes as she did when excited. She knocked, then banged, then banged again on his heavy wooden, front door.

"What? What is it?" came a rough, sleepy voice. "Wait. Marie, is that you?"

"Yes, yes, yes. Who else? Wake up!" she called again. "Come. Come quickly. I want to show you something."

"Ok, wait . . . wait," he said. "Ouch! Ok. Ouch!" he repeated. "Wait, here I come."

Aramis pushed open the door. Looking tired and rubbing the side of his leg, he slid a wing over his eyes and yawned broadly, not at all politely, but forgivably, as he was barely awake.

"I want to show you something," said Marie hurriedly. Her eyes were open wide, and her face had such a delightful smile that Aramis quickly was absorbed into the spirit of the moment, though he had no idea what that moment was. He came outside and looked around, confused now even more that his suspicion proved correct – it was, most certainly, the middle of night.

"Marie, what is it?" he asked. "Are you ok?"

"Yes," she said. "Follow me. You have to see this."

Marie led him past the front of the house and into the edge of the yard. She looked up to her left and slightly behind. She backed up, directing Aramis to follow, then to stop, to wait, to back up, to stop, to back up, to stop, and then, finally, to sit. Marie kept looking up . . . up . . . up.

"Do you see?" she asked. "It's a full moon. It's a perfect full moon. And it's a clear sky. And it's calm. There is no wind. Sit here and look up. It's a full moon, Aramis, and tonight is perfect for a moon bath. I wanted you to see."

Marie's face was absorbedly open and blank with joy. She leaned all the way back and was watching the moon beam through the two upraised limbs of the tree whose trunk silently stood just past her head. Lying on her back, she slowly moved her wings up and down along the ground, as if trying to make angels in the grass and the dirt.

Aramis sat next to her, watching her watch the moon's glow. A moon bath? he wondered. He had never heard of one and he tried to guess what she meant. What was so important? And what should he feel?

"What is a moon bath?" he asked with some hesitation and then followed her example and laid on his back, staring up through the limbs at the flat face of the moon.

"You don't know?" she said. "It's when the moon cleans us with light. It is saying hello and tossing us a smile and sharing its energy. And if you're still and you're quiet, you can hear it whisper a clean wish."

"Hmmm," Aramis responded, as he tried to stay awake. He was feeling his energy flow, but he felt it flow toward the moon, not coming his way.

Marie held her breath and continued her stare back through the rays, trying to meet them up there halfway. Her wings moved up and back in tiny repetition, the tips curling in, while she swayed her feet from side to side with a rhythm set by opposite clocks. "Can you feel it?" she asked. "It's taking a bath without getting wet, without using the ground, without being touched by anything but light. Like a spirit, a friend. The moon seems to sing."

Marie said these words with such clarity and certainty that it was if she were speaking to herself in a crisp, light voice. Aramis was surprised by her tone. She sounded sure and confident and plain, without the soft uncertainties that typically choked at her thoughts.

"You say you feel the sun. But I feel this. You can stare at the light. You can feel its cold warmth. The sun shines too brightly. The moon hugs you with coolness and it brings you clean peace. And when it's done singing wishes, it asks for your story."

"What story is that?" Aramis asked.

"Whatever story you tell it. It just likes to listen."

"Do you do this every month?" Aramis asked. "You never mentioned it before."

"No, I rarely find such a night," Marie said. "It is either too cloudy or too windy or too cold. Or I sleep all the way through and miss the right time. But I love these nights when the moon is like this. My moon is your clouds. Except it always comes back."

Aramis liked that Marie sounded happy, and though he enjoyed the moment, he was not feeling cleansed. Not in the least. He wondered what was missing. To him, the sun and the moon were not magic or alive, just random spheres that found their way near, and rose and then fell, in regular order. It was true that Aramis said he spoke to the sun and the sun spoke to him. But he knew he was the one who did all the talking. It was but a simple expression – and an excuse, he knew, to let himself listen.

With Marie next to him, Aramis was trying to understand, attentively watching for that something beyond, to see the world's objects as she saw them, mysterious yet friendly, alien yet familiar. It was a beautiful night, the air was fresh, and to have a companion lying near can indeed magnify a moment and fill a strange void. Yes, he thought, comfort can be found, even on a farm, where it does not belong.

"The full moon lets me live in a place where nothing ever changes," Marie said. "I like that. I know it will leave and a smaller one return, but I also know that in a few weeks, it will come back to me once more. That's the way things are. Everything leaves, but I like to think that everything comes back. And that all is connected, sitting and talking and understanding each other."

"What did you mean that it was the same as my clouds?" he asked.

"It is the way you talk of the clouds," Marie said without moving her head, her eyes fixed on grey contours on the moon's glowing white surface. "The way you describe floating, of riding the clouds from the place they begin to where they arrive. Your clouds are my moon. I look at it and think about drifting and riding. I don't want to live there but just bathe in its light. It is cleansing, the light, all clear and silver and yellow and grey. I look at it and for a moment, my life feels so small that I feel part of a world that extends out forever. It's a comfort somehow to know we may be nothing but we're part of something big. We may be here for no reason, but even so small, we might be important. At least to the moon."

Marie paused. She heard insects jumping in the grass to their right. Crickets thrummed along the stone walls. There still was no breeze, but branches far behind them could be heard gently moving. Aramis thought he saw something fall near his head.

"You are important," he said. "I don't know if we're important to the world . . . " and he stopped for a moment. It seemed a long moment. "But I know you're important. You must be important."

Marie's thoughts shifted to Aramis and quickly back to the moon. The position Marie had chosen placed the moon well above and to the left of the barn. The two arms of the tree pointed out above them, each to one side, as if holding the moon between its dark grasp.

"I like these moments," Marie said, "when all is the same, just the moon slowly moving, and everything remains. Wouldn't it be nice if nothing ever changed?"

"Yes, it would," Aramis said. "If we could keep our best moments preserved and unending."

"And nothing ever leaves," Marie said. "Or if it does go away, then it always comes back. Like the flowers each spring. Or the sun every day. Or the full moon each month. It might go away, but unlike your clouds, it always comes back. I like that thought. That everything stays. And what doesn't stay, will someday return. That's the world I enjoy."

"That would be good, a good way to live," Aramis said.

"I've been thinking about what you said, about dreams, about change. About the past and the future," Marie said. "It is the way things seem. But I don't know if it's true. I don't know if you're right. I think instead we're all connected together. Everything, I mean. I can feel it at times like this. An energy flows around us and we are bound up inside and we're such a small part, but still we are in it. Nature placed us here and sometimes I think everything here is the same. The rocks, the flowers, the people, and us. Even the past and the present. And maybe the future. It all exists now. We just imagine they're different. That's our mistake."

"Or we imagine they're the same," Aramis said. "That's what makes some moments feel special. We create the connections."

"But from where would we get the idea to do that? It's from something that binds us. That's what gives us the thought."

"Or maybe it's nothing. And when we confront it, and can't lose it, we imagine it's something."

"Well, that doesn't mean that things aren't connected."

"Marie, I don't know. Just how are they connected, if everything moves?" Aramis asked. "Everything moves, and everything changes.

Even those things we think are the same. As snowflakes, we're different, and each is alone."

"Maybe that's what we think, but that is not real. It's our small mind that divides things. What if we were different? And see everything is one. The trees and the rocks and the coop and ourselves."

Aramis lay there in amazement. Were these thoughts and questions new in Marie? Did they all occur since the discussion they had? Or had she always thought this and only now brought it up? He still looked at the moon and the moon's glow made him smile.

"What makes you say this?" Aramis asked. "Because of the moon?"

"Because it seems to me that if something created everything, then how can there be nothing?" Marie said. "I think it's we who make nothing and, in fact, all of nothing is something. The something that is us."

Aramis did not know what to say.

"You must think I'm silly," Marie said. "I don't know anything about this. They're just questions I've thought of. They don't make any sense."

"Oh, you're wrong. They're very good questions. As good as they get. As the priest used to say: 'What is seen is temporary; what is unseen, eternal.'"

"What does that mean?" she asked.

"It means all you just said."

"You don't sound like you agree."

"I hope that you're right. That we all are one and time is all now. But I don't know," Aramis said. "If it's true, then it's here. Yet I search and can't find it."

"If it's true," Marie said, "then searching won't help."

Aramis knew she was right. If. If all was connected. But it wasn't that simple. All the kernels of corn in a bucket connect, but that doesn't mean you don't search for the best.

In an unforeseen way, this discussion of connections, this longing for connections, this absence of connections weighed on Aramis and shifted his mood in an unexpected direction. It reminded him that, in the midst of this warmth, even with her, he still was alone. Isolated. Singular. The fact the moon gave him nothing. And that sense of nothing grew strong and took hold. He felt something for Marie, but a unity? No. A tenuous connection of his own, feeble making. It had happened before, before he was destined to leave. It could never be trusted. It would leave without warning. So it was that this intimate talk in a special, moonlit moment, suddenly spun and got shredded and Aramis plummeted with an unwelcome thud, a surprising and sudden melancholic thud.

The two fell quiet. The moon, unblinking, held a steady gaze upon them, each by themselves listening to their thoughts. For Aramis, his reaction made the moment uneasy. He worried Marie would sense this, as she had that small knack, and he moved to cover his doubts with words.

"Have you always been spiritual?" he asked.

Marie turned her head and looked at him.

"I don't think I'm spiritual," she said. "It's not like that."

"It's not like what?"

"The way others believe. There was an old hen here who used to hold meetings and she would read fallen feathers that were left in the nest. Or the feathers that stuck to the eggs while they hatched. She'd tell the future with them and lead prayers to the sun or the ground or the corn. Everyone agreed, she was in touch with the spirits. I'm not anything like that."

"You can be spiritual without believing those things," Aramis said.

"Perhaps," Marie said. "But can you be spiritual when you believe that nothing is something and nothing is nothing?"

Aramis laughed. "Of course," he said and turned to look at Marie. "Especially if you know that something is something even when something is nothing."

Marie smiled back to him. "My moon is much simpler. I think I'll go back to that." And she turned her head and the two resumed their attempt to be cleansed.

"You lived with a priest," Marie said after several minutes. "You lived near a church. Didn't that help you find answers?"

"The truth is," Aramis said, "it just created more questions. I would listen to the priest when he practiced his talks and he would say that god created all and all that is not. Which, it seems, was what you were saying. I suppose the priest would agree with you. It was very convincing. It sounded so real."

"So were you? Were you convinced by what the priest said?"

"I don't know. I thought so at first. But my friends being taken. The sadness and death. And the church near our yard. We were never let in. And I wondered if God created us, then how can this be? I continued to listen, but I stopped being convinced."

Marie looked at Aramis. He was looking at the moon but seeing rows of pews and dead friends. A chill ran through him.

"Now, I don't know what I believe," he said. "Maybe the moon. Maybe from now on, I'll worship the moon."

Marie looked back up at the sky. "I've never been to a church," she said. "What is it like?"

"I don't know really, not from inside," Aramis said. "From what I've seen, they're all made of stone with colorful windows and big wooden doors. They have bells in a tower, like that bell we hear sometimes. And they fill with many people, all dressed up and fancy, who go in and out together, and usually they smile."

"I'd like to see that someday," Marie said. "I've heard so much about them from stories and tales. They must be very special."

"I don't know if they're special, but there is something different. The people look different. Little children with flowers. Old people with canes. Some people are sad, dressed mostly in black. Some people are happy, all yellow and white. When people don't die, then weddings occur. And when the two people come out, they smile in a way that says they've never been here before. I don't know if it's true, but it's a good dream to have."

"What's a good dream to have?"

"That they became someone else and they'll be happy forever."

"You are a romantic," Marie said, laughing. "I told you that before."

And Aramis smiled. "I don't think so," he said. "That they will always be happy. That flowers always bloom. That the sun always shines."

"Not like that," Marie said. "In the way that you wish things were so. That you imagine a life believing it could be."

"I'm romantic, in that case, the way we all are. Everyone sees life in the way they create."

"But," Marie said, "we don't create what happens."

"In some ways, we do. Look at the old hen reading those feathers. Or the moment of twilight, cloaked in a blur of half-existing soft edges. It's a mystical time of fear and dark magic. It's the sun disappearing, its flame extinguished forever. Or it's just the earth moving. At least that's what we're told. We don't create that it happens. We create what it is."

"You think we create all the sadness and pain? Why would anyone create all that terror and pain?" Marie asked.

"As much as we create all the happiness and joy," Aramis said. "We're all romantic in the same way. We create our own world and then live as if it exists. Most of us see a life of harshness and fear. Yet we mourn when we leave it. If life is so hated, then why cry when it's over? It's because we know that we love it but are afraid to admit it. That's the irony that makes life so hard and keeps us alone. We should just be glad we're alive and hope there's tomorrow."

Aramis again noticed something pass near his head. He stopped talking. This time, he heard the sound of the drop hit near his left ear. He moved his eyes and stared above with the moonlight's bright glow.

"Marie," he said, "is this tree alive?"

"What do you mean?" she asked. "Alive, in what way?"

"Alive, like a tree. Are there leaves, are there flowers, are there berries that come?"

"No," Marie said. "I've never seen that. I talk to it. It listens. But it never shows any signs that it's living, not like that."

Aramis stared and focused hard. "Something is dripping from the branch up above. Look to your left. You see that dark spot? A drop just came down and fell by my head."

Aramis sat up and pointed. Marie sat up as well, and the two stayed still looking, watching and waiting for the next something to fall. They could see the spot growing larger, hanging just under the lowest reach of one branch.

"That's strange," she said. "That's the second strange thing that's happened with this tree."

"What do you mean?"

"Before you got here, the night of the storm, I was in the coop, scared by the storm. I heard a huge crack and the sound of terrible crashing. A tree had fallen from the other side of the fence. It was terrifyingly loud. The next day I came out and that tree had been stopped by these branches above us. I would have been killed if they had not been in the way."

"That was lucky," he said. "You were lucky the tree was here."

"Yes, but that's just it. The tree was not here. I mean, it was here, but not here the way it is now. It pointed in a different direction. You won't believe this, I barely believe it, but before that night, this tree faced the other way. Those branches faced back. If this tree had not moved, I would have been crushed."

Indeed, Aramis did find this difficult to believe. Marie imagined so many wild and impossible things. Was Marie telling a story as when she talked to the flowers? Or did she really believe the tree spun around?

Aramis looked back up at the tree. It must have been pushed by the weight of the fall, he concluded. The spot of liquid continued to grow. The moon had slid and was now behind the large branch.

"Are you certain?" Aramis asked.

"No, I'm certain of nothing," Marie said. "I don't know if the tree moved. But I imagine it would if somehow it could."

"Why?" he asked. "Why would it move?"

"I don't know," Marie said. "Maybe to tell us its story."

"What story?" Aramis asked.

"I don't know what story, but everything has one. The air. The house. Even the rocks. They all have a story. They're so old, you know, they must have a story."

"And what would they say? Or what do they tell you?"

"They say 'Here I am. I'm here. Pick me up, stop and listen.'"

"Like what the moon does with us," Aramis said. "The way you said that it wants to hear our stories."

"Yes." Marie smiled. "The moon wants to listen. It wants to listen to us both."

Chapter 17

Night of Echoes, Days of Silence

Us. "Us." The word would not leave him. Aramis had not thought of that word. Us. Not that way. Not here. Not now. Then "both." What does that mean? Both? Us? The words repeated over and over. Us. Both. "Us both." Through nearly a cycle of moons, the words lingered, waning at first, then waxing again. "The moon wants to listen. It wants to listen to us both." The words clanged in his mind like bells beaten by the wind, with no rhythm or sense, no tune and no meaning. It was deafening. The sound of it. Suddenly, the clouds were too close. A fogbank rolled in. And it was real, every day, every time he looked at Marie. Every time she sat close. Every night when he thought of her sitting in her coop, thinking of him. Especially then, whenever, he thought, she was thinking of him.

It had been beautiful, the night he was with her, looking at the moon. He was grateful for the time because she let him believe, at least for a moment, he was part of something more, that there was, indeed, something inside that might be connected to what is unseen. He had been shown a new place and he remembered the details and the long conversation. He could put words to the feelings he remembered he had. He could describe them like a painting or a past journey he lived.

But now there were too many weeks that got in the way, too many weeks of always the same, every dawn creeping, every morning dragging, every afternoon lingering, every evening hovering, every sun forgetting, every sky-filled night returning and everyday sitting until it all began again. The emptiness arrived slowly as a boredom that gnaws and names itself only when it grows. Then boredom is frustration, and irritation becomes anger, not toward the object but toward those things that surround it.

So now that one lovely night, that night of closeness and ease, was but a few dreary hours stripped, empty and cold. Memory had sanitized as it swallowed the joy and left but the stark, hollow vision of crystallized thoughts. Those ideas, once soft, were now plain and pointed, splinters of remembrances that irritated and poked.

Aramis recalled that this was how it happened, no matter where he would go, it always happened the same. It was always the same. He was always the same. He was fooling himself to think his world could be changed. No matter how often, every time he moved, every single time he thought to start over, dedicating himself to begin a new life, his old life returned – the same thoughts, the same memories, the same hopes, the same outcome.

It was no coincidence, then, that since that very same night, the night of the moon, the night of the words, the farm's walls became thicker. The yard inside shrank. The world outside grew. He was tense with Marie. He could not deny it. He was annoyed whenever she came to sit near him. He was distracted by birds, the fence, the arch, so many doors, too many walls, the old black dog (who never left the driveway), all the indistinct thoughts that signified nothing. He could not make himself listen. Everything around him demanded his attention, yet nothing around him could interest him long.

Marie, for her part, had noticed Aramis was quiet, more quiet than usual. How could she not? His silence was startling. She had asked him about his stare. "Nothing's wrong," he would say. She asked him again what he was thinking. "I'm not sure," he replied. She inquired, timorously, if he was feeling all right. "I'm ok," he responded. Aramis grew bothered. No one likes repeating an answer when the first time suffices. "I don't know," he would say, and the more times he said it, the farther he slid from discovering the truth and the more frustrated he got that he still didn't know.

Finally, it happened. Just a few days before, Marie softly asked if Aramis would join her for a walk. "Marie," he snapped back. And as his gaze swung to hers, he saw her sadness and hurt, and his face quickly softened to no expression at all. "No, no thank you," he said quietly. "I'm fine sitting here." Marie silently stood and slowly walked off, and from that moment on, she asked no more questions, nor said much of anything at all.

So tonight, here was Aramis, inside the dank smokehouse, and the night sat heavy. It was a weight that kept coming with each evening's arrival and the darkening of sky. Then, the stars and the moon (especially the moon) would show as reminders. Blinking, staring, screaming, mocking and disclosing, unyielding in the face of his attempts at distraction. The day's final hours were always the same. He would walk to his smokehouse and sit for long hours, agitated and tense, cursing himself for what he'd created.

Aramis lifted his wings and tried to stretch. But the room had become, like that very first night, a mausoleum of thick air and of walls much too close to permit a full reach. He felt his motions had slowed and his muse of clear dreams had long since departed. He was having more visions of the world looking blurred and he was convinced more and more Marie was to blame. She could not understand. Not his past, not his thoughts, not the feared loss of himself. She could never catch up and if she did, once there, she could never keep up. Not to the pace of his questions, nor to the depth of his doubts. There was no one to listen. He had only himself. There was no other choice. At least when held captive, when there is nothing to be done, frustration can be conquered through resignation and release. Now with no walls, no locked doors and no bars, there was just himself sitting, not running or floating, just here, by himself, thinking of her. Her. That's right. She was the reason. She was the blame. The jailed as the jailer. The other that steals. The beautiful eyes that froze all his thoughts.

How odd it is about echoes that they always sound best with just one voice bouncing back. And in bouncing, it grows louder as it goes out again. As it goes out again. But it's a fool who finds comfort in these words that he hears. So it was that Aramis, a willing fool at the moment, was decidedly deaf to any voice but his own.

Yes, if not for those eyes, he might think clearly again. But was it really that simple? (Oh, if not for her eyes.) Was anything simple? If so, from where did it come, this sting of remorse and the pain of a guilt that overwhelmed and eroded his newfound conviction? Why was it so painful to look into those eyes? (Wasn't it her fault he was feeling this way?) Why should he feel guilty? He did nothing wrong. He studied himself as a million times before. If guilt was there, then how was there trust? The truth of remorse tells the lie of a thought. Or is it best to ignore it when it gets in the way?

Aramis paced deep into the night. He tried several times, but he could not sit still. In the darkness, he saw the sights of clear fields and an open blue sky. As he walked back and forth, his feathers lightly fluttered in an imagined cool breeze that swept under his wings in a field of tall grass. Distant sounds in the night were heard as calls from afar. It was his twin, freedom, from whom he was separated the day he got caught, pleading and calling to have him back at his side. Yes, potential was out there, not of any one wish, just the rawness of possible, and a ground, firm and cool, that compels feet to move and a mind to be silent. There, I hear it again. A mind to be silent. And hear the echo once more. And a mind to be silent. Oh, please, for a moment, for the mind to be silent.

All his best days were out there. (See how memory lies.) The purity of life never comes on a farm. Clarity and vision arrive when alone. Only singular thought finds the real that is here. Stripped of all others, only truth will remain. Aramis was talking. And he heard his past answer.

He had known many hens. (Was Marie truly so different?) There were many he liked. Some he thought pretty, and a few became friends. But they all wanted days filled with safety and waiting, long days of chicks and of nests and of food and of other delusions as if nothing would change. If those things could be had, they thought nothing would change. Oh, what made them think that nothing would change? What makes him think that those things can be had? Can those truly be had? With them, nothing will change. Nothing will change? Oh, here comes that echo. Tell the echo to change. Please, someone, please, tell the echo to change.

Once, it was true, Aramis thought himself in love. She was a young white hen, all bright eyes and laughter, with an easy, wide smile and a coquettish walk. Aramis was smitten and lived for her look. But an elder rooster knew better and pulled him aside. "Woman was created for our destruction," the old one advised, "and it is from her we inherit all our miseries." But Aramis scoffed and lived in his dream – until the hen changed her mind, and without a word, it was over. Never would he miss her, just how she made him feel. Never would he miss her. How did she make him feel? How did she make him feel? Try to remember. Try to remember. There again is that echo. How did he feel? Where to find quiet? Oh, where is the quiet?

Aramis looked at his door. How happy we are unaware as we are of our cold, empty depths. Then the moon comes along and its alluring warm light shines on accursed dark corners and we are suddenly aware that we will never be filled. Never be whole. Never be filled. Never be . . . never. He lowered his eyes and he looked to his left. There were the tips of her feathers unawaredly sweeping the fine specks of soil, oh-so-delicately brushing the tops of white stones and flittering back as she walked through the yard. There was her spirit', its aural glow shining upon her small feathers. The sound of her breath as it pushed and it pulled the air that gladly and noisily passed through her smile. Again, he looked at the black expanse of his door. His large eyes were tired. They were foggy and sore. Did he keep himself moving because he was unhappy and restless? Or was he restless and unhappy . . . oh, what does it matter?

His childhood was there. Nevermind many friends, or that it seemed happy. Now, it was lonely and long. His mother had loved him, but she didn't know better. His sisters were there but their bond was not chosen. And the youngest among them – the poor smallest and sweet one. He ran, and he left her. How could he have left her? Did he really just leave her? By now, she was dead. Her sudden last moments from the coop to the block. No time for goodbye, just the shaking and shrieks until her blood poured out thick and her eyes remained open. Did he really just leave her? How could he have left her? He really did leave her. It's that echo again. Oh, no, not that echo. He really did leave her. Tell that echo to leave! Please, someone, please, force that echo to leave.

Then the next farm he lived on. How happy he was when the barn had burned down. The fences were trampled. He could finally escape – to the worst days of his life. There was no place to hide, few fields and no forest. For months without food. How did he survive? He barely remembered. There were train tracks and trash. The stench of dead animals. The bells of a church. Dogs barking at night. The branch that crushed his left wing. The close escapes and the terror. Was that his true freedom? The putrid around him. That was a pure life? All those sounds and the fear? He wants that again? That's where he found peace? Yes, just wipe clean the picture. And silence the echo. That death and the stench. That the freedom he wants. Bring back the stench and the terror. Give him back his lost freedom. But first silence this echo. Someone silence the echo!

Yes, salvation arrived. Or so he had thought. To the priest and a church. Could life be a blessing? Just wait a few days. Then with innocent look, both cheerful and calm, the priest got his knife. And slaughtered some friends. In front of them all. A twist of their heads with that look in their eyes, and the sharp slit that emptied their bodies of blood. They were hung upside down, their legs going limp, their heads frozen in place, wings fallen outstretched, dead feet bound up together. Don't look, they all cried. But it couldn't be helped. Three hanged at a time. Not even the priest could see that his prayers could be shared by the others so different than he. No, the priest did not know. Three hanged at a time. With others so different. The priest did not know. Three hanged at a time. The others so different. The echo is there. The priest should have known . . . there's no end to the echo. It will never be silent. The echo is there.

These thoughts were too much. Aramis needed to run. "Why live among this and bow down to the horror?" he angrily asked himself out loud. "I'll take the cruelty of nature. Better to keep moving and trust the unknown than succumb to the numbness of living under those hands I can see." To hell with the priest, he thought. To hell with his anticipation and acts. To hell with the reflective black vapors of anticipation that always outshine the flat dismal grey of reality. "Give me the grey. At least there's dimension." He walked to the door and gave it a violent shove. Out of the smokehouse, he looked to his left at the silent white coop past the edge of the yard. Inside was Marie. Inside was a smile and a heartbeat and eyes and her face began forming . . . and with a half-step delay, he abruptly turned right and walked under the arch and out to the field. Aramis disappeared quickly among somnolent tall grass. And as he wandered in the emptiness of the world's open darkness, he took in a deep breath and opened his wings and embraced the night's gift of a welcoming silence.

* * *

As the sun rose through the yawning arch, Marie awoke with a laugh as bright and as clear as the light filling the coop. Chicks. There were dozens of chicks still swirling and dancing in her head as she opened her eyes. She let out a laugh, then another, and then another once more. Yellow spots of small fluffy chicks, all chirping and turning, still covered her sight. What were they doing? How many were there? She could not stop giggling at the indistinct faces and the legs that were twisting and jumping in air. Her mind calmed for a moment and then she saw two or three more bounding around at the edge of her eyes. She smiled again, and the dream disappeared.

Marie sat up. She saw the hour was later than usual with the sun's warming rays breaking into the coop with great strength. Yet the dream pulled more strongly, and she hurriedly settled back down, trying to recall the story that accompanied the chicks and find the memory of her lighthearted thoughts. Alas, none could be found. They had appeared and were gone.

The idea that she had somehow slept through Aramis' crows surprised her and Marie skittered down and walked outside to find her breakfast and stretch her wings. It was that promising hour when the warmth increases with each tick of the sun and the mind seems to float higher with each passing breath. It was a very good morning.

Besides, Marie was feeling lucky. Over the past few days, she was surprised and delighted as small squares of fabric had appeared in the yard. She found several of these after the night of the moon. But this morning was extraordinary. There, behind the second-to-last step, was another small pile, maybe five, maybe six, of these small square cuttings. Red and orange and purple and blue, white in patterns of flowers and checks and squares and circles and tiny round dots and interwoven plaids. Such fine cottons with threads poking out. There were more than she had ever seen, and they weren't just little specks or single strands of thread but entire sheets of cloth. Marie was breathless and giddy. She scooped them up and held them fast in her mouth as she ran to hide them deep in her nest. She marveled at how gifts in life can appear with no reason. "Thank you," she said as she scooted inside. "Where did you come from? How nice you are here. Let's go to my nest. You have nothing to fear."

Skipping back out of the coop, she ran to find Aramis and tell him the news. Hoping, as so many of us do, that the world still sleeps when we wake up late, Marie ran to the smokehouse and knocked lightly on the door, smiling at the thought he, too, had overslept.

"Aramis," she shouted, and she knocked again and waited. "Aramis, oh Aramis," she lightheartedly called.

There was no answer. "Aramis?" she questioned, and this time, she poked her head in.

Marie stepped back for a moment and looked to her left. She turned back to the yard and wondered if he was wandering the edge or sitting by the tree. She had passed by so quickly she had not even looked. Still filled with excitement, Marie quickened her pace. She might have missed him when she first came out. But she had gone back to the coop and surely she would have seen him, or he would have called her name.

"Aramis!" she cried more loudly as she turned past the house. She began flapping her wings to speed through her search.

"Aramis!" she called again, this time running to the trees near the hill before turning back past the coop, past the barn, past the cows, as she circled again left and flew toward the arch. "Aramis, Aramis!" she called several times.

A sense of dread rose in her stomach and began to tighten her brain. She raced back to the yard, looking left, then right. She quickly glanced into the tree, hoping for an instant he had climbed back up there. But no. "Aramis, Aramis," she shouted again. The fear rose to panic when she received no answer and her wings began shaking inside erratic up-and-down flaps.

She ran back again toward the smokehouse. Her eyes wide now and her breath coming hard, she stopped in the driveway and felt her mind spin. Where could he be? she wondered. She turned right and stared at his room. She looked down. Several feathers from his tail were lying about. A chill ran through her that was cold and malicious. It sucked at her heart and pulled down on her legs.

The worst of all thoughts appeared in her mind. Where was the farmer? Where was the farmer?! What had he done? Oh no, that was not possible. Not that. Not that! These thoughts screamed in her brain. No, that just can't be! He wouldn't take him now, not after so many weeks! He wouldn't do that! No, he couldn't do that!

Marie could not move. She stood looking out through the arch, holding her breath and waiting for Aramis to call. Her chest began heaving and her eyes filled fast. She stood frozen, seeing Aramis before her. Nothing made sense. Nothing was real. He couldn't be gone. Just like that. Disappear.

Suddenly, behind her, Marie heard a door.

"Bonjour," came a voice.

Marie swung her head.

"Where's your friend?" the farmer asked as he smiled, then looked away and walked down his steps.

And with that, Marie collapsed. She sank to the ground, unable to move, except for her sobs, the shuddering sobs that pounded forth tears, tears of relief, of terrifying relief. "The farmer did not take him. Oh, no, he did not take him. Then where is he? Where did he go? Oh, Aramis, where are you?" Marie cried, shivering with cold. Slumped on the ground, Marie's wings fell listless and her head hung forward, bobbing involuntarily slowly up and down. Her legs lost their feeling. Her thinking box collapsed. She could not think. She could not move. Numbed, emptied, and now shivering, Marie hunched over and barely breathed. Every snippet of memory came back to her clearly, like the details of life said to come at the end. His arrival, his smile, his voice, and his presence. "Oh, Aramis, Aramis, what have you done?"

* * *

The farmer, unaware as he was of the drama unfolding on his farm, stepped lightly and cheerily under the sunshine air. After addressing Marie, he attended to small chores in the barn and the shed. He walked through the yard and plucked, dying yellow leaves from the plants. He shifted tools for the tractor from one shed to another and threw out a stack of wet, moldy papers. Next, he emptied and refilled the dog's drinking water and searched in the cellar for plum jam and some wire.

With his morning nearly finished, the old farmer (who had resumed his lost habit of walking the farm) turned toward the fields. He noticed Marie had not moved and as he walked past her, he stopped and bent down and placed a hand on her back. Marie, startled, stood up and jumped a few steps. The old farmer continued and walked out through the arch.

A mid-summer noontime is a book fully open. All of nature shows itself, and each living thing is vibrant and calling. Without words from another and no clear thoughts from within, pure sensation is strongest, and to a man without thoughts, it overwhelms and is welcome. So it was with the farmer on his daily walks now, through his land of butterflies and grass and beetles and wind and rocks and trees and rain and leaves, and through soft sounds of close insects and of far-away neighbors and the sky is four-fifths of the world all around and the land sits there steady and it gives and it gives and it welcomes each traveler and holds them all tight while the sun warms the neck and reflects off the green and the yellow and brown and white pebbles and flowers and time remains frozen and lingers and is marked only by clouds that float like loose hands past the clock of the sun. This, to the old farmer, was what his fields had become.

Once in the open, he now avoided the paths, preferring to fight across bumpy, straight rows through the thick and tall corn. He would lose his direction, but it did not matter where he walked. He felt hidden among the tall stalks of corn and somehow as one, one with green leaves, one with brown earth, one with blue sky that watched from above. The old farmer stopped with hands in his pockets and his chest expanded and his chin pushed out high. He felt the sun on his shoulders and the cool air on his legs. He took in a deep breath. The fragrance of nature, a lavender field off to his west, the smell of wild garlic, rosehip and poppies, the air replete with its message filled him strangely as well with an assurance that his final destination would be wherever he walked.

* * *

Even among the faithless there is no denial of faith. It cannot be otherwise for we are walking creatures. Our steps require an absurd belief that life's next step will lead us somewhere, somewhere among the three spatial axes or somewhere into the next dying moment. We have no choice. We are the playthings both of time and of space and, unforgiving and relentless, they cast us along. Our journey is theirs, yet we do the walking. They do not care where we go, because there is no place among them that matters more than others. They watch, and they laugh as they see we are lost. Yet. still we believe. That each step leads to somewhere. That each moment moves us forward. If only we lived without the illusion, the false faith in the next, as if everything was waiting and our steps had a purpose.

Such were the thoughts that accompanied Aramis as he had walked through the night. Although he preceded the old farmer by

only a few hours and was met by the very same presence of the same
blooming flowers and by the identical fragrance of the abundance of
nature, Aramis was met with no message or assurance. Indeed, rather
than suspect that his steps led him forward, with each new step he
took, Aramis had the feeling he was walking in circles, not because he
veered one way or the other, but because no matter the direction, he
had no place to go. He reasoned, quite rightly, that this did not matter.
He sought no destination, merely the negation of one. He was not in
a hurry, and no fear drove him forward. He wanted only to be far, not
there in the small, shrinking yard when the light rose in the morning.

The first part of his walk had led him toward the far row of trees.
His moon shadow trailing followed him closely. Aramis avoided
looking up at the accusing full moon. No need to look up. He did not
need to see it. He did not want to see it. His trailing shadow was
enough, jumping as it did from one dark stick to another, taunting
him, daring him to leave it behind. Around the first turn to the right
he walked blindly, tilting his head and averting his face from the tips
of the grass. His gait slowed to a wander as he sank further in thought
and then he strengthened his pace when the present returned. "She
never talks of the future," he was thinking just then. "The past is too
painful and the present's too empty." Aramis curved along the edge of
the field, then followed the patches of low grass beyond the tall corn,
walking mindlessly whichever way seemed to beckon. "She just sits
there, content. Content to be what? Content to be what? Content to
be what?" he asked himself, repeating each sentence until the next
thought was formed. "As if waiting for something. As if waiting for
something. But nothing will come. To sit and to wait. For nothing.
Nothing. That's no way to live. Yet that's all that we do. All that we do.
Sitting or walking. But sitting is walking. And seeing is dreaming. It
adds up to the same. There's no difference. Not really. Not really. No
difference. But still, just to sit. There was nothing to do. Each day.
Each day. It all is the same."

Confronting now a patch of tall grass, Aramis suddenly noticed
his shadow was in front. The moon was behind him. He had lost his
direction. When had he turned? Which way had he walked? He

stopped and looked out, trying to decide if it was the path of the moon, or his own twisted path, that caused his shadow to move. It was longer than before. In fact, it seemed to stretch out forever, past the slope of the hill, past the far grove of tall trees, to the unfocused stars sat unconcernedly winking. He stared at the stars, slyly laughing they were, at the tops of the trees, staying just out of reach. See the stark tentacles grasping from the tops of black branches. Why do they do it? Why do they bother?

Aramis stood there and watched until the first red-with-orange clouds began to slither past. He was contented to know he accomplished his task of avoiding the sunrise that he would have seen that same morning out the same smokehouse door through the very same arch. He felt new in the world. His thoughts had no echo. The voices had stopped. His breath came more easily. Nestling between two large stones, he sat down to rest. But rest would not come. The sun delivered its warmth, and to Aramis, it seemed, it brought something more. The sun's message was blurred, but sharply arrived with the light. It was a sense that someone was watching him do the wrong thing.

By the time evening had come, Aramis was grateful for the darkness and the silence that returned. The day had been long. He had been forced to stay hidden and to listen cautiously for any sounds that came too close. He was surprised and alarmed when during the day, he saw the old farmer walk near. Why was he here? What path had he taken? Aramis assumed, that in his trek through the night, he had walked far off the farm. He was momentarily confused (and strangely, disturbingly, somehow relieved) to know he had not.

With the sun leaving once more, a full moon again rose. This time, Aramis could not take his eyes from it. He stared to the east at the cold light through the trees. Look how the moon breaks, sliced and broken in white slivers, each piece sliding slowly and separate between trees. There is nothing between. But we know it's illusion. Now watch how those bright fragments rise ever higher and expand and emerge and are again one when they meld back together, released by the trees that brood in the night. See the branches stretch up and still reach for the moon. Why do they bother? The dead and the living, together their thin fingers desperately clutch at the sky. Then look at the stars, from the bright and the steady, to those that twinkle and glimmer, on to others that come and go as mirage. Do they live with the moon? Is that a cloud floating by?

Aramis stood with wings crossed before him. His eyes stayed fixed on the trees, while the moon's silver light shone off his iridescent black feathers. He was a stone of black granite. He was tired and weak, and he wanted to grasp at the stars or lower his body and sink in the earth. Neither was possible. Neither was real. For hours, he stood, the time vanishing in bursts of substanceless minutes. His thoughts drifted, aimless, from haunting long memories, to snippets of present, to rolling new visions of a variable future – a future of walking, a future alone, a future of hope, a future of tears, a future of search, a future with others, and a future of more and more-tenuous futures. Aramis gave up. Oh, how he wished to stop trying when he was infinitely resigned.

"This doesn't seem real," he said to himself. "But yet, here I am. And still, it's not real. How can that be? Nothing is real. Look at the trees. This is not real. All this will change."

Aramis finally sat down. He closed his eyes slowly, shutting out the full moon, the tops of the trees the last image he saw. "All this will change. That's why they're made," he mumbled in whisper. His wings collapsed at his sides. A flickering light showed brightly behind his heavy, closed lids. Grey clouds with no texture filled, then floated through, the dark sky in his head.

"Why should it be different?" he heard himself think. "All this will change . . . while we're awake . . . it's all made to change . . . all made to change . . . change . . . to us both."

Chapter 18

A Long Night's Walk to Awakening

Marie's day had been blank – a brutal dark screen of agonizing questions, of sudden tears, of surging anger, of convulsing sobs, of desperate periods of empty sadness, each sweeping over her in random repetition, ending, finally, with a biting cold exhaustion. Her day was, in short, a long single moment in a hollow of deadly stillness.

Marie returned to her nest after the farmer's light touch and she did not move, holding her wings to her chest and gripping what hopes might arrive against her permanent fears.

With each noise outside, she anxiously listened for a sound Aramis might make – a flutter of feathers, light footsteps on the driveway, a husky cough, a simple word, a knock on her door, or, of course, a strong, defiant crow. She sat, trying to breathe as silently as possible. She had never heard so many sounds during long hours of no noise. She sat and she listened. The sounds kept coming: the dog limped in the driveway, the cat stretched with a yawn, ducks quacked over nothing, sparrows played in the eaves, cows shifted their weight, grasshoppers jumped willy-nilly, flies struck the top window, crickets rubbed their front legs, boards crackled in the heat, a horn honked far away, a crow cawed in a field.

Each sound heightened the loneliness inside her, as if each passing noise purposefully mocked her waiting, calling out with disdain "That's not him!" in a tone from her childhood, with the teasing and ridicule she had felt many times. She remembered now why she hated her days as a child, why she had wanted to run away, why she had retreated into herself, growing the world inside her, expanding her internal universe of reality and conversation in an attempt to need the world no longer and to convince herself that the world no longer needed her. She believed she succeeded after her mother had died, wanting nothing and seeking nothing but small episodes of self-inflicted smiles or random diversions to persevere through her present. She wondered what life would become, now that she experienced the interruption from a companion, the fleeting linden fragrance of joy, an unreal dream of living in love.

Marie sat through the day, watching the shadows of the tree's arms lengthen and slide over the yard until they passed from the top of the coop to the side of the house. To Marie, the shadow's spikes of darkness were like the hands of a clock, a clock counting zeros, a clock that meant nothing. Once, in late afternoon, Marie started and raised her head quickly. She was inside her coop and heard the stones of the driveway. But she knew it was not Aramis. Just the farmer returning. His heavy rhythmic boots crunched the pebbles as he walked. His footsteps ended after the first three steps, and Marie heard the smokehouse door open. There was a silent pause, and then the farmer crossed the driveway, walked up the stairs and into his house.

Although the shadows foretold the coming of night, it seemed sudden to Marie when the sun began to set. It had been a bright day, light all around, shining strongly on the yard, reflecting, permeating, and warming all. The glow had lessened, imperceptibly to Marie, who from her nest could not see an orange and crimson glow at the horizon in the west covered by the ripple of dying yellow under a light and cheerful blue that led to a deepening peaceful darkness. She noticed only the coop grew more grey with everything inside sliding in the spectrum to the flattest color of uniform shadow.

Indeed, the darkening abyss that grew in her coop matched the deepening emptiness of her spiteful resignation. The obvious question, the question of why, crushed down upon her. Why did he leave? Why was he happy? Why was he gone? Why was he here? And just as we do when we don't know the answer, we pick several to joust until one of them wins. Aramis lied about staying. He was captured and taken. He lived a deception. He'll come back and explain. He planned this forever. He'll be back any minute. He left here for good. He'll be back any minute. He will never come back. He'll be back any minute!

With a numbness of present and her emotions played out, Marie slowly climbed down from her nest and sat by the door. She considered waiting in the yard, but she liked the closeness of her room, the familiarity of its walls, and its distance from the field. She found comfort in knowing there was but one direction to watch. From her seat near the door, there could be no surprises, no sudden appearance – just in case she was right. Or maybe she was wrong. Because he will come back. Or he'll never come back. No, soon he'll be back. Yes, he will never come back.

For hours, Marie sat. Her face, her limbs, her eyes became lifeless. The arrival of tears slowed and then stopped as they emptied Marie of the energy needed to summon her hopes or make sense of her fears. Several times, she thought she heard her name whispered. But each time was illusion, the creak of a hinge, the fine hushes of leaves. She knew, after all, it was her thinking box talking. Or whispering. Or calling. Or sighing. Or wishing. And finally, Marie emptied, and slept where she was, her head on her heart, her heart by the door.

* * *

The night was humid, and the moon was straight up. The yard's soft buzzing sent the same empty message as other summer nights. Crickets filled the air with percussive mating calls while fireflies' tails did their own lighted dance. The damp grass twitched randomly as insects migrated through the yard. And aimless gnats in large swarms flitted about in small circles.

Marie's chest heaved as she breathed deeply in her sleep. Small twitches surfaced on the tips of her wings and at the edge of her neck. Under closed lids, her eyes were aflutter and the small feathers above them rapidly twitched. If she was dreaming, her dreams were too opaque or transparent to be caught by her memory. Her head, sunk to the right, and her wings drooped by her sides, her long coat of feathers wrapped all around as a quilt of bright colors might surround a small and sickly child.

Marie's rhythmic breathing moved the warm air that everywhere hung as if clinging to her in fear. In her sleep, time stopped moving. In the darkness, hours fled. And the night stilly lingered. A sequence of moments did no longer exist. Minutes stripped of their seconds; seconds stripped of their meaning.

It was sometime past midnight, after the moon crossed the yard, that a light sensation appeared in the center of Marie's back. Her mind raced to the surface – but the touch was soon gone. She curled down to her left and plunged again back to sleep. Then there again, a light touch on her back. But again, it was gone. And, as earlier that day she had heard many times, "Marie," came a voice from somewhere inside. Again, Marie stirred. And once more, a light touch. Not real. It was there. It was there and was gone. Her soft breathing continued. Then her name in a whisper. Her name in a breeze. "Marie" it had called. What's that gentle stroke on her neck? Again, the wind called. And in that moment between shadows and a light from inside, she opened her eyes without looking up. There before her stood Aramis, without motion and silent. He was outside the coop, except for his wing, which was shyly outstretched and stroking her back.

"Marie," he said softly. "Marie, I am here." He gently touched her fine feathers. He felt her back rise and fall.

Marie raised her eyes. Her emptiness sat with her. He looked thin, Marie thought, somehow empty and plain, not at all the same rooster who surrounded and swept her thoughts off the farm. Somehow, he looked stripped of all the energy he had. His eyes had no strength. His mouth and shoulders looked small. Marie arched her back quickly against his lingering touch and Aramis, understanding, pulled back quickly and returned his wing to his side.

Marie did not know whether to ignore Aramis or smile, to be angry or laugh, to be silent or cry. Her body did not move. In the stillness was safety. In the silence was calm. Let the world make a sound. Let something first move.

Aramis crouched down, his shadow straight at his feet, the moon straight above. He looked at Marie. He saw her eyes glisten. They had a sparkle, he thought, like the small, fine salt cubes in the light of the sun after a warm summer rain. He knew she'd been crying. And suddenly he felt a terrible crush – the weight of a lie he now carried alone.

"I'm sorry," he said. "I'm sorry, Marie."

Marie was awake, but her mind, her emotions, her body, her eyes, none were connected, one to the other. She was on the edge of a cliff in the middle of dreaming.

"Why?" she asked. "What did you do?"

"I came back," Aramis said. "I'm sorry I left."

Marie said nothing. She looked into his eyes, blinked, and said nothing.

"I want to talk to you," he said. "I came back to explain."

Marie looked at him. Yes, she wanted an answer. She wanted a hundred explanations. Why had he left? Where did he go? How could he do this? But mostly, why was he here?

"I'd like to show you something," he said. "I want you to see. I want to explain."

"Show me what?" Marie asked. "Explain to me what?"

"Explain why I left, and why I came back. Why I am back. I think if I show you, you might understand."

Marie stood with no answer. Her dream would not leave. "Which way do we go?" she asked as she took a step forward. Aramis led their way across the small yard. They passed under the old tree's long shadows of its two outstretched arms, along the driveway, past the smokehouse, until they reached the white stones of the silent, gaping arch. Marie suddenly stopped. They had reached the fine line that divided for Marie the world of her home and the world of all others.

"Where are we going?" Marie asked. "I'm not going out there." And she turned to look at Aramis. "Why can't you tell me without going . . . out there?"

"We won't go too far," Aramis tried to assure. "Marie, you won't understand unless you see it out there."

Marie looked out over the field, at the million silvery flashes of dark leaves in the moonlight. It was a sea of flickering white caps that swayed and sparkled with their own piece of the moon. And beyond was full darkness, the black wall of a forest that waited and crouched out over the hill. It was solid at night, but Marie knew it was illusion and she imagined open edges, the hiding creatures awake and waiting unseen.

"But Aramis, where are we going? It's night . . . and it's dark," she said tensely. "I don't know if I want to. You run away . . . and come back. And after such fear, I should walk into the darkness?"

"I know it seems strange," he said. "But it will make sense when we're there. I won't take you too far. Just up past that hill."

"Is it safe?" Marie asked with an innocent softness.

"Safe?" he responded. In the sound of her words, he had heard the voice of a child. "Together we're safe. I promise we are." Aramis knew it was a promise he had no power to keep. But still, existence is deliberate – it's living that's random. No need to explain there was no place to hide.

"Why can't you tell me and explain it right here?" Marie asked.

"Because every moment of life, every now that we find, arrives at us new," Aramis said. "And everything new is what threatens the most. If I don't show you what I found, you might never understand."

Marie stared straight ahead. She imagined the yard as it lay there behind her. Her coop. Her nest. The old, silent tree. The comfort of here. The protection of here. Then, in a flash, she saw her memories come. A glimpse of red bodies. Inaudible screams. Death finds you no matter, whether here or out there. Now Aramis was here, inviting, entreating. She had the chance to go someplace she had never imagined. She struggled to go. She did not want to go.

Finally, Marie exhaled deeply and took the first step. Aramis turned quickly, and the two, side-by-side, crossed the turn in the driveway and entered the path that led through the field. Marie had seen the tall grass but had never gone near, and she struggled to move as it repeatedly slapped against her wings as she walked. With each step she took, she had the sense she was falling. She was fully exposed, the air on her back was unknown and it threatened. The farther they went, the more she felt swallowed, into the vast of unknown, engulfed in an ocean of infinite depths. The air around her grew heavy. There was no distance before her and her legs went atremble. The ocean of grass on both sides began closing in. She felt claustrophobic and dizzy. She became suddenly aware she had entered a picture, a living green landscape that only before ever had two dimensions. Now here it was, terrifyingly real, living, moving past her, to her left and her right. Disappearing behind her. Marie turned and looked back. The box tree was missing. The linden was gone. The house, it looked small. The coop wasn't there. "Look around!" something told her. "Look around! You are lost!" There was nowhere to run. No cover to find. Marie's breath came in fast starts and she felt her heart pound. Her wings rose up slightly. Her legs moved without feeling.

Marie looked at Aramis. He was her guide and her trust in him was her only protection. Had he known the faith she bestowed, he might at least have walked slower. But the excitement he felt propelled him ahead. How sad it is we often ignore the presence of others when we're busily intending to show them our love. So it was that Aramis, eager, remained always two steps ahead.

Strangely, as the two walked silently, Marie noticed, as they moved through the field, the same sounds and airy movements so familiar in the yard: the buzzing, the flapping, the ticking, the flitting. It was odd that those sounds should be out here too – all the same sounds that calmed her and pleased her at home. Were the field's hidden creatures the same ones in the yard? How can life be familiar where it never existed? This was all unexpected. She could not have described what she thought or expected to be here, except that it all would be different, and all would be new. Yet this was eerily familiar, as if nothing had changed. All she saw was the green grass before her and Aramis ahead. And that never-changing view, the sounds, out of place, yet intimate and known, soothed her and spoke, and she thought for a moment, were calling her name and saying hello.

As they reached a small hill, Marie stopped and looked back. Suddenly, unexpectedly, she started to tremble. Her legs felt weak and the tips of her wings began to nervously flutter.

"I can't see the yard," Marie said in a panic. Her heart quickened, and her breathing became erratic. "I can't see the house. I can't see the farm. Aramis, where are we? Are we lost? I feel lost. Aramis, seriously, I'm terribly scared."

"Marie," he said, turning back and walking to her side, "we're still on the farm. The house is still there. It's simply hidden from view. But everything is there, and we'll return to it soon. Where we're going is not much farther. Just on top of that hill."

Aramis stood by her side as Marie took several deep breaths and stared at him. Aramis looked at her in the moonlit dark, at the purity that comes in a face filled with fear, at the beauty of a child in the face of a hen. He wanted to hold her and stop her from shaking. He thought of returning her home to the yard. But they had come this far, too far, and he knew if they stopped, if they went back now, it would not be repeated. He would get no more chances, not at night in this field, not with her by his side.

"Marie, we'll go back soon, but I need you to see this. I could have tried to explain this for years, and for years you could not have fathomed. You asked me what I find when I find myself here. You wanted to know what it is that I've seen. I did not choose to get lost the first time I ran, and I felt the same fear you must be feeling now. I promise it will pass. I know it will pass."

As Aramis spoke, the edges of Marie's eyes softened, though her look of empty fear continued. She was thinking of nothing but his words, and of the power and the care his voice calmly conveyed. And in her look, Aramis knew, he might, if he tried, show her a path and a reason to forgive.

"It's that feeling of climbing, or of flying up high. Each time you come out here, it's as if you reach a new height. There is always some fear. But you come to know it will pass. And you move beyond the familiar, past the gates that feel safe. Beyond all that you've named. Beyond all that you know. And each time you move higher, you see new fields or new trees. There is no one around you and all shelter is gone. And with it goes safety. And when the world is unknown, then the gates disappear. And the higher you climb, the more the sky you become."

"I don't understand," Marie said. "You're speaking in riddles. What gates disappear? What sky do you become?"

"I can't describe it precisely. Like at night when you're forced to look slightly away to see what's in front. What happens out here is a tale that makes sense only when told in dark colors and words posed as dense riddles. To understand, you must savor those dreams when you fly through those boundaries that are of your own careful making. That's what happens each time we go out in the world. We float higher, through gates, but only if we're open to leaving the ground."

Marie was transfixed, more by his look than the flood of his words, most of which, it was true, she did not understand. "Aramis, you're a strange one," she said, but her look told him she was listening and content to be near. "These gates you describe. Are they something you see?"

"You see them only after, after they're gone, and then you think they're the last. But you always find others because there's more that's unknown. Then over time, the unknown is familiar, and what is known is unclear. As I said, it remains all a riddle, until you have only one choice: you find comfort in not knowing; only there you believe."

This last thought, so passionate, so confusing, it seemed to Marie, that she almost began laughing. She didn't, however. Instead, she watched how the feathers above Aramis's eyes were raised higher than she thought possible, and instead, she smiled, a warm, thanking smile.

"You find comfort in that?" she asked. "You find comfort in not knowing?"

"Yes," Aramis said. "You have to find comfort. There's no other way. Of course, you never stop trying and maybe someday, you hope, the knowing will come. But in the meantime, it doesn't. You must create it yourself."

"After you fly through the gates, then when do you stop?" Marie asked.

"I suppose," Aramis said, "when you've seen all that there is. And by the time you know that, you have reached to the clouds, where inside there is nothing and all looks as one. Because by the time that you reach there, there is no more to see."

"Is that where you found comfort? Is that what you brought me here to see?"

"No, I haven't reached there. I'm still a long way away. I once thought we went through the gates by making the world more familiar. By getting to know. By running around. By throwing ourselves in it. But you eventually discover that by knowing the world, if you're not very careful, you can lose yourself in it. By distraction. By avoidance. By living through others. I did that at first, with the chickens I met. The strange roosters. The hens. Especially the hens. I lost myself in them. I adopted their interests and, eventually, their lives. And I came to resent them. I thought maybe that old rooster, the one that I hated, that maybe, somehow, that rooster was right. Hens were here for destruction. That's why they're created. To destroy who I am, and worse, who I'd be."

A sickening feeling began to overcome Marie. Aramis was talking of the evil of hens, unnamed and unseen, as if she weren't there. She was filled with a sensation as alien, an emotion as treacherous, as the dark field around her. That was his life? Unknowable. Unknown. And how many others? What did they look like? Marie's stomach tightened, and she forced her attention to turn herself back to his words.

"That's what I thought, and I decided to run. And again, I was wrong, this time with the world. I wanted to see as much as I could. To see everything in it. To see all the angles. To see every small place and meet everyone. I thought by seeing it all was the way to fly higher. But then the faster I went, the more I lost myself in it. The world opened its arms. It let me fall in. And I found no more gates, just the illusion of some. And the more that I spun, the deeper I went. Until the fiction revealed there was no place to go."

"But Aramis, I thought if you see all there is, you get to the clouds. So you must see all the world and everything in it."

"Yes, that's what I thought," Aramis said with a smile. "Until last night, from a hill, when I was shown something more." He put a wing on her shoulder and leaned close to her face. "So please, it's not far. Let's walk a bit more."

Marie had stopped shaking. She was soothed and diverted by the sound of his voice, the look on his face, determined and sure. And this mystery he brought. What did he mean? The only mystery she knew was the mystery of loss. It is not sought but delivered. To search a new mystery was a now-welcome sensation. The two began walking, a bit quicker than before. For the first time that night, they were sharing a mission. Down a slanted path they both hurried and then up to the right.

At the top of the hill, Aramis lifted his wings. He looked and smiled at Marie and took in a deep breath.

"Are we here?" Marie asked. "Is this the place we were coming?"

"Yes," Aramis said. "Now, stop and look there. See the trees straight ahead. Watch the trees straight out there."

Marie glanced at Aramis to see what he saw. She followed his gaze. "What do you mean, watch . . . ," she started to ask.

"See the trees and the sky," Aramis interrupted. "The field is in front, the trees in the middle, the sky far away. Those are like gates. You go through one then the other. The first one is here, the next is not far, and the third is out there. Each, in itself, is the mystery and answer. Each is both, if we see, they are one and the same."

Aramis paused. Marie remained silent. She did not understand but waited quietly to hear what this mystery contained.

"Now see the trees that are standing with no leaves on their limbs," Aramis said. "It seems every third tree is standing there barren, just dried sticks for their arms, and waiting to fall. They are dead. There's no life. There's no flow in their bodies and their spirits have left for wherever they go. But they once were alive. And when I reached this spot late last night, I did not know where I was going. There was no place to go. I thought I was leaving. And I stumbled in the dark and I somehow turned around and walked my way here. I don't know why I came here. And as I looked in the moonlight, I saw all these trees. I looked carefully at each and then saw them together. And the more that I looked, the more my life made no sense. I tried to think of my life, but I could not stop thinking of you. How you talk to the grass, how you talk to stone walls, how you talk to the nests, how you talk to the moon. And how, if you were here, you would talk to these trees. And the more that I saw you, the more I tried to understand . . . to see how you see . . . to know how you are."

Aramis' words, spoken swiftly, were strong in the cool damp of night. Marie, excited and warm, forgot where she was. The scene was a dream to her, alive yet unreal, the place, the time, so far from experience, so far from her past.

"All these trees were small seeds when they started," Aramis continued, "and they later had leaves, beautiful and soft and green, and inside flowed with their sticky clear blood. And now some are dead, but through all their lives, they remained where they were and now they sit among others that are still young and strong. Maybe those next to them grew from their seeds. But see where they are? They never did leave. Not one of them left. They lived all their lives there and grew and matured and felt the same wind each day and watched the same clouds float past. They were made wet by the rain and made white by the snow. And they experienced it all, all from one place. The dead ones were beautiful as the others are now. And they lived a full life and they learned what they learned. Without ever moving. They accepted the fact that here they were born and here they will live and here they will die. Standing and being with others around them. I realized last night that I'll never know what they thought, but somehow they knew they belonged to be here. And you can see just by looking it is right they are here. They tower over elders who have fallen where they lie, flat and broken as they seep back to the earth. Yes, the centuries are before us and there's the balance and justice in death as in life. Those trees did not move to find they were home. That's what they were saying. I never heard it before. I didn't know it existed."

Marie began to speak, but hesitated. "You . . . you didn't know what existed?" she asked.

"Oh, it all seems so simple. To make sense of what's here, I knew you must see it. The more that I chased, the more I thought I became. It's true to a point. But just to a point. It's not the task of the world . . . it's not there to be counted or arranged for our comfort. It can reveal what is hidden no matter where you are, in whichever directly you stand, and as you glimpse what is there out of the corner of your eye, you know the more that's revealed, the farther it flees."

Aramis stopped. Marie was silent. They both stared at the trees while the sounds of small life, in a field, in the country, cloaked their night in unmistakable shared comfort.

"I had to admit it. I had no place to go. My wings had no purpose. My legs were both numb. I knew my eyes must be open and I looked but saw nothing. There was nothing to see. Except your face in the trees. And all I heard was an echo, the same echo I've heard since my days as a child. I knew I was lost. I had to admit I was lost. Completely, and finally, irrefutably lost. And that's when it happened. The strangest feeling occurred, from the center of my body, to the wings and my legs. My body dissolved. And I no longer existed. Like never before, I said to myself, I no longer am. I have no body and no feelings and no past and no future. I am, in fact, nothing. It was like being under the spell of a dream while awake. I don't know how to explain. There are no words, or rather, not enough words can exist. I was lost . . . and empty. And I stood. And I stood. It lasted most of the night. My eyes did not move. I stared straight ahead with no strength to go on. Insects were buzzing, and trees remained still. The moon crossed the sky and my shadow moved forward. And slowly . . . it was strange . . . Marie, it was so strange. I just stood with no thoughts. I can't remember one thought. I saw the trees, then the forest. It was the same as the field. It was part of the sky. It stood there alone, no longer separate, just one. There was no more to be sought. No more time. No more space. Just effect, no more cause. And instead of a fear, I suddenly and strangely felt it was good. There was no longer distinction. We were all the same thing. And I did not exist. Marie, I didn't exist. I know that sounds crazy. But I felt free and more real. Nothing was separate. Nothing was real. Not nothing. But no thing. No thing was real. And there was no separation. Space was one whole. Time disappeared. Because without pieces of space, there can be no more time. That's why our dreams find the real. They exist in one space. They neither live nor can die. That's how the fiction of life is disclosed in our dreams. For what is real is between us. That transparent warm cloud we only feel when we see. And I did not exist, and I knew if that was true, then anything was possible. It must have always been true. It must have always been so. Then without thinking, I was beginning to smile. And that surprised me. I was happy. And I started to think, it would always be true . . . it was always true . . . even awake. All the hens I have known and the places I've seen, those horrible moments of pain and of death, the warm summer days of freedom and light, were equal somehow. Without existence or judgment, they simply just were. And the world didn't sit there. It doesn't care to be counted. It's created somehow. It's created between us and that is the way it discloses our dreams. I think there cannot be nothing, only what we deny."

Aramis turned his gaze away from the trees and looked at Marie. She turned to look at him halfway. Aramis strangely felt closer to Marie at that moment than he did to himself. More trusting, more accepting, more forgiving. For her part, Marie tried to grasp the meaning of his words, so convoluted and odd, and relate it to something she knew. To the moonlight, she thought. Or the yard. Or to Aramis, right then, the way that he looked, the sound of his voice, the feelings she had.

"Yet even at the time, in the midst of these thoughts, when all seemed so separate even from myself, I knew even then that sometime later, this dream, this dream would be over, and all would again be illusion. All the things that we go through. All the separateness we feel."

Aramis looked back at the trees. "What I believe today, I might not tomorrow. But I'll always know that inside that dream it was real. Not like a dream when you're sleeping. Or a daydream awake. But the dream of just being. Nothing more. Nothing less."

All at once, Marie felt tears suddenly choke at her throat. Something had changed. She inhaled with a stutter. Her face became warm and her eyes widened large. Suddenly, she knew, there would be no more teasing. There was no one to taunt her. No one would laugh. She could run, she could talk, she could dance with the stars. He'd make certain of that, and he would smile the whole time. And as long as he watched, she'd be safe to go on.

"And Marie," Aramis continued, "I want you to know I'm sorry I left. I know I should have told you, but I didn't know how. It would have been simple if I had known what I wanted. If there was someplace I'd go. You remember that morning, I was up in that tree? I was there a long time. I stood a long time there just thinking. About what I would do if I truly could fly. And I was surprised to discover I didn't know where to go. It was hard to admit. I didn't think it was true."

"Yes," Marie said, "you seemed surprised when you told me."

"I surprised myself when I said it. The fact is, it was not just that I did not know where to go. I did not want to go. That's what I'm saying. There's nothing for me out here. And I don't want to leave. I want to stay in that yard. I want to stay there with you."

Marie felt her head pull back quickly. Her eyes opened wide, suddenly, involuntarily. She wanted to swallow but her throat was frozen. What was he saying? She suppressed a small laugh, then she suppressed a small tear.

"The last few days," Aramis continued, "life itself became too real and too present. It was pressing around me, squeezing me, crushing me. I know we must find our comfort inside, but I don't understand why I must find it alone. It's only in silence that I know how to breathe. And sometimes, I can only find silence out here."

"Then if you need to be out here," Marie said, "I'll go with you. I'll go with you out here."

"I won't ask you to do that," Aramis said. "That's not something you want."

"Aramis, you don't know the pain or my fear when you left. Walking these fields at night all alone could never equal the emptiness of the solitude that came. I don't need to live back there on the farm, in the coop. There is nothing there for me but memories and my days without future or hope."

"No," Aramis said. "That's what I want to explain. These hours alone are important to me. They let me remember why I choose to stay here. But in being alone, I found something else. I also discovered why the sun doesn't help, not the way that it did before I came to this farm. Because the sun, I have found, is no longer mine. It stopped talking these days because the message it brings now exists to be shared. Just as my life makes no sense. It is no longer mine. The sun is still there to show us its strength. The clouds are still there because life always changes. And now I see the full moon, and I know we might hope to be cleansed. And underneath these we are like two small branches on a tree. And that tree just stands still though we think we run far."

"But Aramis, I know, you don't want that life on the farm. And I don't want you at a home you don't want. I want you, instead, to find the home you have sought."

"Marie, don't you see, I have found that home. Not here, but there. Or maybe nowhere. But the only home I'll know is with you back in that yard, in that coop, next to you." Aramis smiled. "Besides," he continued, "I can always go out in the evening for walks."

Marie looked at him and matched his smile, only broader. "Yes," she said, "but not for all night. And not without telling me."

Aramis lifted his right wing and gently stroked Marie's soft cheek. She took two small steps towards him.

"Not at least without telling you. I won't do that again."

And there the two stood, both feeling larger for being understood.

"What is the rest of the world like?" Marie asked.

"It's very busy," Aramis said plainly after a moment of hesitation.

"How do you mean?"

"Well, many things happen. Many chickens, many people, they all rush around. They go many places. They meet many others. They have many conversations. They do many things. They return home if they have one. And eventually they die."

"Is that all?"

"That's quite a lot. They fill their hours and their minutes and then even their years the best way they know. The only way they know. The funny thing is," Aramis said, "at the end of it all, I suppose they wonder if they did too much, or maybe if they should have done even more."

"It does sound busy," Marie said.

"I don't think you'd like it. However, they do, through those years, build more memories than you."

"More?" Marie said with a laugh. "I have too many already. I don't need any more."

Aramis smiled and nodded his head. "Sometimes I think we're born with too many."

"But I don't see the world you describe here," Marie said. "To me, it looks beautiful, quiet. Not at all what I expected."

"What did you think you'd find?"

"I never thought I'd be out here, but I suppose I had images from stories – castles, dragons, lakes, and tall mountains. I did not truly think they were here, but I didn't know what to expect. Except to be surprised. And now I'm surprised that there are no surprises."

"Disappointed?" Aramis asked.

"No," Marie said, "I'm relieved, in a way. In fact, I like it. Does all the world have such quiet fields and dark trees? Is it all so still in the world when no one is busy?"

"It has the appearance of still at moments like this. All in harmony and calm. Because the world can be wondrous, filled with miracle and grace. But beneath what you see and in places you don't, there is also sadness and death. Just like you've seen."

"Can't you live and avoid it?" Marie asked. "The sadness and pain? The world looks so big, there must be someplace to hide."

"Ah, if we could live by ourselves. That's the world of our dreams. To live outside and run free, unburdened and light. Just on our own. No one else. But there is no such world. We don't live all alone. And the world lived with others is one of ignorance and anger. Tricks and illusion. It can be worse than deception because it is unwitting and hungry. There's but small understanding and little desire for more."

"That sounds awful and cruel," Marie said. "I don't see that out here. But I know that you do. You understand the world well."

"I don't understand it at all. That much I know. I've never felt part of it. It happens around me –and I watch it go by. I see – and I'm surrounded. But I have a feeling I'm not in it. And nothing, before last night, before now, felt connected. Everything external. Attached, maybe touching, but far, far away."

"I remember feeling like that. After everyone went. After everyone . . . died. It was maybe the same. And it was lonely. Very lonely."

Aramis stared at Marie. He thought he saw something, somewhere through her eyes, into the depths of her past, to a dark, frozen pool, and a little girl crying at the edge on a rock.

"It can be lonely," he said. "It can indeed be very lonely."

Just then, suddenly, the two of them heard low grunts and footsteps nearby. Marie jumped, spun her head toward the noise and then back toward Aramis. Dozens of footsteps crunched the dried leaves as they moved. No longer did they stand in a safe nest of their creation. They returned to where they were, in a vicious dark world in the middle of night.

"What is that?" Marie asked. "Something is out there."

"It's just the sanglier," Aramis said with a light voice to reassure. "It's their time of night. There's no reason to be worried. They're not interested in chickens." He knew it was a lie.

"Are you sure? They're very big, aren't they?" Marie asked.

"Yes, it's just the mother with children. They'll stay together and leave soon."

"I'd like to go home," Marie said. "I'm tired and I've learned enough for one night."

Aramis knew she was right. He had had the same thought. "Yes, we should return home," he said.

With this last sentence, Aramis stretched, spread his wings and held them high, reaching his head upward and raising his face to the sky. Marie, for the first time that night, saw him as she had before he disappeared – full, strong, with an energy that exceeded his size and a passion that exceeded his awareness.

The two began walking, back along the overgrown path that had guided them away from the yard. For Marie, the grass no longer bothered. She welcomed its role in taking them home and gladly walked, this time, two steps in front of Aramis.

Aramis walked slowly. In fact, strangely so, until they reached the final turn in the path. "Marie," he said suddenly and just as abruptly stopped walking. He looked at the ground. Marie stopped and saw him hesitating – not just to walk, but also to speak or even to look at her. Aramis gazed up to his left. The moon was there behind broken clouds. He looked down and kicked at the ground. Then he raised his head again and looked at Marie.

"Marie, before we leave, before we leave this spot, this field, this . . . outside, I want you to know something." Aramis looked again at the ground, and peering at her quickly, blurted, "I love you." The words came so abruptly and intensely, the statement sounded almost a command. Marie's eyes opened wide. "I do. I love you," he said. And with that, just that, Aramis suddenly felt, like the relief of confession, two nights of heaviness – maybe a lifetime, he did not know – suddenly melt far away. His breath became easy. He thought he was floating. "I tried not to be," he continued, staring in her eyes. "Honestly, I did. I didn't want to be. In fact, when I realized, I tried to convince myself I wasn't. But I cannot. I'm sorry. I tried, but I cannot. I discovered these past days, these past terrible days, that I love you. I do. And now that I know it, I don't want to stop."

Marie, as you might imagine, did not say a word. She did not move. She barely could think. She was too busy seeing every move of his face and hearing his voice, the sound disconnected from the meaning of words, a pale presentation of the idea he was sharing. It all seemed in pieces, his face, his thoughts, the night, the field, her standing there in the middle of ocean. And yet as he spoke, she slowly felt covered, enveloped in something she could not describe. It pressed against her from all sides, but it did not feel heavy. It extended inches beyond her, but it was not something separate. It was familiar, and close, and welcome, and strange. And she felt all the pieces meld together and exist there as one. Then a warmth spread throughout her and a smile arose on her face.

"I'm glad you are smiling," Aramis said. "I did not expect this. I truly did not. I never expected to fall in love. I was resigned myself convinced I was happiest without it. In fact, I was certain, I could only be happy without its encumbrance."

Marie was still smiling and still only half-listening. "Why are you sorry?" she asked.

"Sorry?" Aramis asked.

"You said you were sorry."

"Oh, I . . . I was sorry for all that time I tried hard not to love you. I thought it was better. But then I started to think. Last night, I remembered a question I once asked you. It was some time ago. I asked you if you were happy. I remember wondering, because some chickens in this world will never be happy. You can't make them happy. They will never be happy. No matter what they do. No matter what they have. But with you, I could not tell. There was something inside you that was impossible to see."

"Actually, you asked if I was unhappy," Marie said, with her smile growing broader.

"Yes, yes, you're right!" Aramis said. "I remember that now. I asked if you were unhappy. So, I asked you that question and I remember you never really answered. It was almost as if the question made no sense. Not to you. And I remember the way you looked. It looked to me as if it was the first time you had ever heard the question. And for hours last night, I thought about you. I thought about that question, well, the way I remembered it, and I pictured your look. And then by myself, we had a conversation, most of the night, out here. And I realized, you were right. You might not have said it, but you were absolutely right. It does make no sense. It *is* the wrong question. And we do that too often. We ask the wrong question. It's why we bicker and fight and live miserable lives. Because if you ask us that way, of course. we're not happy. Look what we live with. We have to say no."

Aramis paused. Marie was still smiling.

"What is the right question?" Marie asked, gently prodding, if not teasing.

"Yes!" Aramis blurted out, and he started to laugh. "That's it! That's the right question! What *is* the right question? And what does it mean? And the more times we ask, the farther we go, until we run out of room. Because the first question is wordless. Before all else begins. Somehow, the most basic question in us is the one we can't ask."

Marie tilted her head, silently asking her own sort of question.

"That's exactly what you do," Aramis smiled and said softly. "That bend of your head, or the shrug of your shoulders. The way that you answer your shrug with a smile or a second small shrug. Or sometimes you sigh. And sometimes you laugh. At sad times you cry. They are how you always ask questions without saying a word. I think that somehow you know this. We discussed it last night. You know that words are like colors, broken specks of a whole that we piece back together to see our view of the world. We trust that it's right, those combinations of specks or our small words of thought. We put them together and when we run out of colors, or words for our questions, somehow only then can we know that we've found the right answer."

"That's the conversation we had here when I wasn't here last night?" she asked. "Did I do this much talking?"

"No, not really," Aramis said, and he laughed. Aramis then began to look nervous, his eyes darting left, then up to the right, then down at the ground, and over again. "But when we were done, one more question remained."

Aramis paused, and Marie felt the weight of the silence she carried. She turned and started walking.

"I'm sure that you do. If there's one thing I know, you'll always have more."

Aramis did not answer, and the two headed home.

"Why did you not talk to me about all this before?" Marie asked.

"All this?" Aramis said.

"Yes, everything you've told me. You must have been thinking about much of this before."

"Why?" Aramis asked. And his eyes made a frown while his mouth smiled sadly. "Why?" he repeated. "Did you ever want to be with someone you could tell anything to? Tell everything to? To have an endless conversation holding nothing in reserve? To have the faith and a trust that after saying it all, somehow there'd always be more to discuss? And know that the other would stay after hearing it all? To have that kind of friendship? To have that perfect partner? To have a perfect life?"

Marie looked down as the two of them walked side-by-side. Her eyes searched left, then right, and she paused a long and curious pause. "I don't need to," she said quietly.

"Ah, but that's not what I asked," Aramis replied.

"I don't know," she said. "I don't have that much to say."

"Of course, you do. I can see it in your eyes and in the way that you act. I can see your brain working and the conversations you have. Marie, you talk to yourself all day, just not to me. I don't know why you do that. I'm there. And I'll listen."

"I don't know," Marie said.

"Do you think I don't care? Do you think that you're boring?"

Marie did not answer.

"That's it," Aramis said, with a playful little shout. He leaned in close to Marie and did a little shuffle, almost like a dance – but honestly, more like an itch. "Ha! My dear, you think you're too boring" he said, "but if you're so boring, then wouldn't I be bored? And do I look bored? If I was so bored, I . . . I . . . I don't know . . . I wouldn't be talking so much, would I?"

Marie's face softened to an innocent smile. "You do talk a lot sometimes," she said.

Aramis let out a guffaw, and if you know nothing else about roosters, know a guffaw is rarely heard.

"Ok," Marie said, "yes, of course, I've wanted someone I could talk to."

"And tell everything? Anything?"

"I don't know. Maybe not that much."

"Do you think it's possible?"

"I hope not," Marie said slowly.

Aramis looked at her.

"Why do you hope not?" he asked.

"Because if it's possible, I've a missed a perfect life."

Aramis laughed once more. She was poking fun at him again. It was an admission, of course, and one they both knew to be true. Even through his smile, Aramis could not help but feel guilty. He had coerced Marie into this sad assessment of her life. But at least there was humor. He admired the way she could absorb all the pain and salve it with humor. No matter the subject, she could always bring that. He looked at Marie, ever so slightly, then he looked down again. He kept his gaze fixed, near hers, but not at hers. He avoided her eyes.

"For me," Aramis said, "I've always dreamt of that. And then, out of nowhere, for the first time in my life, I came to know you. And I thought it was possible. But then I was worried. What if it's not? Even with you? Then it would never be true. And what happens then? We harden inside when there's no one to listen. Then we learn to stop trying, and inside we are cold, and our skin becomes rock. It's true for us all. In fact, as you say, is there anything around us that has no need to be heard?"

"Aramis, I will listen. I want to listen. And I will try to talk more. But you, you tell me so much, yet even with that, I know there are still many things you don't say."

"Despite my desire, I worry if some things should never be said," Aramis paused. "You told me once I needed to hear myself better. I don't think I know how. And I was thinking last night, about all I might say. I realized I am afraid, because if I describe the many things for which I should never be loved . . . it's a risk I don't take . . . the risk of saying too much and losing your love."

"But if you love me as you say, you must tell me all. If you do not, you do not trust me enough to let me fully know you. You do not love me enough to let me fully love you."

"But what if I start and tell you too much? The respect you have, then, would soon disappear. Our friendship, too, might soon disappear. And without those two, the love could not hold."

"How can one lose respect when someone shows them the same? And what greater respect than to tell someone all?" Marie said, and she lit her own special smile. "Now I'm sounding like you. But you know the alternative is worse. To hide your true self and live secrets all your life."

"I would forever live in secrets to ensure I had your love," Aramis said.

"But you'll have only part. My love could never be full, not unless it knows all," Marie said. "That's not what I want, but that's what you'll have."

Aramis was silent. He admired Marie. The way she responded was so simple and true. Without confrontation or turning his words, she could touch that single note he played a symphony to find. And what was that sentence about sounding like him? Aramis smiled.

Marie and Aramis slipped back into silence, and continued their walk, his wing repeatedly reaching out to brush against hers. When they climbed the last hill and Marie saw the full moon directly in front, over the yard, over the coop, she knew it had waited to guide their way home. It illumined the path that led through the stone arch. It shone on the house and the looming, stone barn that dwarfed her small coop. It showed the old tree's branches that stuck out from the yard. All around was home, she knew it so well, yet somehow it now seemed she'd only seen it in dreams.

As they entered the yard, unknown to each other, the two felt the same welcome sense of release. The crickets still chatted. The fireflies still danced in the small grove of trees and two bats swooped between the house and the barn. Grasshoppers wandered through the grass to nowhere. The marigolds sat, wilted, in a row by the shed. The old tree sat silent, glistening in spots where the moonlight reflected.

As they approached the silent coop, Aramis stopped. "Let's wait to go in," he said. "Just for a moment."

"Please not too long," Marie quietly said. "I'm tired right now. I just need to sleep."

"I promise not long," Aramis said. "But this night begs not to end."

"I understand, and I agree. But I won't agree long, so just a few minutes."

"I have one more question. I know that you're tired. But it's a question that only comes after all others. And it makes sense that I ask it and to ask it right here."

Aramis paused. Then he looked intensely at Marie. "I want us to marry." And he stopped for a breath. "Marie, will you marry me?"

At that moment, Marie's face dropped into a look so indescribably blank that one would have thought she had either frozen to stone or entirely stopped being – or somehow, if it's possible, a combination of both.

"What?! What!?" her thinking box screamed, drowning all else, all sight, all feeling, all awareness of all. "That was the question?" the thinking box shouted. "That's the one question this has all been about?"

The words, like those Aramis spoke that night from up high on the tree, continued to resound with a resonance that echoed in Marie's ears. How many questions can there be in one night? How many surprises? How many tears? How many smiles? How many words? And how many flashes to life past and present? Marie's mind did a swirl, a tumble, and a jump. Her eyes showed a smile, trepidation gripped her heart. It was no longer the present that reached out before her, but a path to the future that never existed, a path all too real, too suddenly placed, that had come with no warning, not even in dreams.

It took no more than a moment for all this to pass, so few, in fact, Aramis saw her freeze but an instant. To Marie, however, it was a lifetime that changed.

The past all condensed. Just the future remained. Marie's eyes quickly glistened with small tears of love, each like a fine note of grace as her past smiled upon her – and then disappeared.

"I don't know," she said slowly, then she laughed her small laugh, both nervous and soft. "That really *is* a question. You talk about questions. I don't know. I don't know. I love you, I do, but I don't know about marriage. I don't know what that means. Marriage? I don't know if I see . . . how can I see . . . something that far?"

Marie looked to the ground. A strange sensation overcame her. The air around her turned still. She felt in a warm bath. Or was it the touch of her mother? Or the moon had just smiled? No, everything smiled. They were smiling and happy. It all felt so odd, like the whole world was playing with the beats of her heart.

"Oh, Aramis," Marie said, slowly shaking her head. "I don't know. I don't know. I look to the past and you've experienced so much. I'm a silly little hen who knows nothing of the world. I don't have your past and I don't know the present. Then you throw me a future. How can I know? You ask me this question. I don't know the future. Aramis, I'm sorry. I don't have an answer."

"I don't ask you the future," Aramis said in almost a whisper. "It is always unknown. All we can trust is that some future is real. And if it is not, we've lost nothing but dreams."

Marie stared at Aramis. Although she said nothing, her look said she would listen.

"Marie, you cannot add more time to your life by worrying about it. It may feel very long, but it never will be. Instead, you and I have a future, maybe not the future you dream of. In fact, that might not exist. But the future will come both for you and for me whether we dream it or not. We must allow ourselves to accept new dreams. Mine began yesterday in a way I never saw. You're right. I don't know which dreams are imagined and which ones are real. I don't know whether any will come true. But I do know all my dreams now exist only with you and only with you I know they might become real."

Marie remained quiet. She had not moved, except to look at Aramis each time he spoke and then to look away again each time he finished.

"Are you frightened?" Aramis asked.

"Of what? You or the world?" Marie said smiling.

"Me? Of course," he joked, "but I meant of the world, of the future that's here."

"There are so many things," she said, "I don't yet understand. The worst of it is, I don't know . . . truly know . . . what you want me to say. I fear whatever I say, I won't make you happy. And should I fail to do that, I would know that I failed you."

"Failed me?" Aramis said. "How can you fail?"

"By not giving you want you want. What you expect me to give."

"That could only be true if my expectations did not love you," Aramis said. "But they do, because they know you. They expect nothing you won't bring, and they want nothing but your contentment. Marie, you cannot be happy unless you are wholly yourself, genuinely, unhesitatingly, and unreservedly yourself. Like when you run. That's all that I want. That's all I expect. And if you are all those things, you can never fail me. But if you are not, then you'll fail us both."

"That is a lot to ask," Marie said. "The reality of opening myself fully is not a simple promise. Aramis, I love you. I do. And I know that now. That's not the question. I suspected I did before last night, then when you left, I knew for certain. But Aramis, that's also what frightens. I felt so alone. And separate, from everything, like never before . . . at least since that night. There was no connection. Nothing would speak. Nothing was close. And I thought once again, oh, why must things change? It's so difficult to find any comfort in life. Then suddenly it changes and it all starts all again."

"But life does not change suddenly," he said. "It changes all the time. What is sudden are interruptions, when we realize things are different. When that happens – and it will always happen – it only means, for a while, we stopped paying attention."

"Yes," Marie said, suppressing a yawn. "That happens a lot."

Aramis looked down. "Don't you want to live your dreams?" he asked.

"I don't know if I'm ready," Marie said softly.

"Ready?" he asked. "What does it take to be ready for dreams?"

Marie, shrugging slightly, barely noticeably, looked, watched, waited, and hoped for him to continue. But Aramis was silent.

"I'm not sure I can change. I'm not sure I believe enough to let any dreams to become real," she said.

"But that's the way it must be. Are you not yet done living a life you don't want?"

"Aramis, you're so sure dreams are real. I'm not yet certain those dreams can exist."

"That's why you must talk," he said. "You must say what they are, to me or yourself or the grass or the stones. You must speak of your dreams because dreams are created to be outside of this world and to let them be true, we must put them in words. We must make them alive. Or they forever are closed and remain without purpose – because until they are spoken, they remain without meaning."

"And what if I believe what you tell me and I trust in my dreams and then I am wrong?," Marie asked. "What if I speak them aloud and they don't become real? Or I reject what I get when I've been given my dreams? Or I lose them? They die? Then what do I have? More confusion and fear?"

"Maybe that's true," Aramis said. "But what are you left with now?"

Marie had no answer. And the two remained quiet, each of them waiting for something to say. Marie thought of her answers and let them play and cascade, one over the other, replacing and sliding while they battled for position. Some answers were easy. The hard ones could wait. What indeed was she left with? All was the same. She was fine. She was happy. No, that wouldn't do. She had nothing, or something, but whatever it was, it was all that she had – and it came with no risk. No, that wasn't right. She couldn't say that. Now nothing was right, and the silence was growing.

"I don't deserve you," Marie said softly.

Aramis picked up his head and looked down at her soft face, her eyes shut, her tired mouth closed. He imagined it smiling. Instead, the faintest hint of sadness sat in her eyes.

"Don't say that," Aramis said. "You should never say that. You receive love from everything around you and you accept what you can. Marie, I love the way that you are. There is no other reason. There is no deserve in that."

"Aramis," Marie said. "Please, let's talk in the morning. Our life tomorrow must wait."

Aramis pushed open the coop's door and let Marie enter first. Both of them flew gently up to the top row of nests, Marie settling in hers while Aramis sat in the nest to her left. She put her head down, resting it on the front of the padded edge. Aramis lay his right wing on her head, while Marie shut her eyes.

Aramis slowly placed the left side of his head on the edge of the nest with his face toward Marie. Minutes passed with the breaths of each dancing through the tips of their down. Aramis' eyes followed the contours of Marie's quiet face, the speckled yellow feathers lying perfectly on her cheeks, cheeks that caressed her now-sleepy eyes.

"Thank you," Aramis said.

"For what?" Marie asked.

"For letting me love you," he said, and he stroked her head twice, letting the tips of his feathers glide gently against hers.

Marie shut her eyes. "I'm so happy," she said, then yawned a large yawn. "And I'm so tired. So tired. Why does this happen?"

Aramis asked Marie what did she mean. Marie, however, was already asleep.

Chapter 19

When the Dream Meets Marie

As Marie slipped to sleep, she felt Aramis' soft breath, gentle and rhythmic on her cheek. His body radiated a warmth and closeness that meant more than he was near, and Marie knew through closed eyes that he was watching her, inviting her to snuggle under his gaze and strengthen the trust she placed in him during their long walk that evening.

It was under this shared blanket, then, that Marie heard his last question while her sensations receded, her thoughts dissolved, scattered images took flight, and vaporous crystals of pictures appeared.

She was suddenly warm, in her yard. A bright yellow day with green all around. Small puffs of air, a slow wafting of freshness permeated the yard. It was the softest of breezes and it carried a message from afar that it brought just to her. With a fragrance of lavender and linden, it came in low and deliberate from out over the field and through the white arch. Its path was visible, sweeping past the smokehouse, gliding over the steps, turning at the yard, then circling the tree before sliding out past the shed. The air was clear, but it rippled as if watching heat waves playing and dancing on top of tin roofs.

Marie heard light joyful sounds of many young chickens playing and laughing. They sounded distant and muffled, as if in a faraway room, though she knew they were near yet refused to be seen. They were friends, to be sure, yet no one she knew, and there were many, all laughing, chasing and dancing and giggling around her. She looked at her feet and saw the smiling brown earth, large patches of brilliant green grass, and soft specks of tiny white rocks. Marie was back in her childhood though she knew she was old. There was no one in sight. Somehow, her mother was near; Marie was certain of that. She felt protected in a cocoon of innocence and light. She was secure in the way that children know without knowing, which will someday betray them but only much later.

Marie started running. Circling the tree and darting through the yard. Still unseen children were shouting and laughing as Marie, giddy, scampered with her arms flailing and waving. But this time, there was no teasing, just the sounds of encouragement as she awkwardly flapped – turning left, running faster, turning left, running faster, turning left, running faster, with incredible speed.

As she rounded the tree for the eighth or ninth time, she stopped and bent over. She tried catching her breath. Suddenly, she felt a strange pull from behind and Marie was drawn back and placed on the ground. At the base of the tree, she sat down with legs forward. The yard continued to spin from her dizzying circles and she smiled as the colors spun somersaults before her.

Through her smile, Marie panted. The spinning slowed down. In front was the barn, then the coop and the shed, there's the driveway, the house, and the grass and the flowers. All was the same, except the marigolds were gone. There were lavender and freesias and daffodils and iris. How beautiful they were. How fragrant and calm. In perfect alignment in full bloom by the shed. Then Marie looked up. The tree's cold, bony arms reached up high toward the stars, where the clouds, floating white, played on the placid blue veil of a bright summer sky.

Marie pushed her head back and felt the stone-hard trunk of wood holding firm. Her gaze followed up along the sweep of a branch as it pointed to the clouds. Those white bundles of message slid ever so slowly. Incandescent in the brilliance of this clean summer day, the changing billows of white were forming shapes that she knew. There was the face of a friend she could not quite remember. There was a cow with a head whose ears were too big, then a frog with a leg that was not long enough, then a round house with a chimney that leaned to one side, then a tree on its side, or maybe a spoon. A funny face passed by next with its mouth hanging open, then a dress full and flowing, which became a fat chicken that dissolved into two . . . two what, she wasn't sure . . . two big feathers, or rocks, that floated together.

Then came a breeze that distracted, a breeze that circled the tree and tightened its grip as it increased its speed. She felt it around her like a gentle, firm hug. The pressure moved down to the small of her back and it started to tug until it lifted her up. The old tree pressed against her, its barkless skin to her back, and upward she slid, and with dangling feet and her wings tucked in fast, a sense of wonderment filled her. She was weightless and floating.

Farther up the hard trunk and under the tree's curving arm she slid. The ground receded beneath her and she began to tilt forward. Clumps of grass passed her eyes, strangely moving top to bottom, as she glided up the branch, her legs still hanging straight down and her mouth gaping wide. She spread her wings open. The tree's touch reassured, and Marie felt safe but hesitant about how far she could go. And just as she reached the very end of the branch, she felt a gentle quick push, like almost a kiss, and Marie was set free, alone in the air.

At first, panic ran through her. Certainly, she'd drop. She was ready to fall. But wait. She did not. She stayed where she was. She was floating. In air. Marie hung weightless in space, bobbing up, bobbing down on tiny, clear waves. This makes no sense, she thought. How could this be? How does this happen? It was a marvelous feeling. It was miraculous, for sure, yet somehow she felt she might have known all along. Of course, I can fly. Yes, I know I can do this. I forgot I knew how. Why have I not tried? It was here all the time!

Marie raised her head very slightly and began to glide forward. She swung her wings back and her body soared upward. She discovered with just a slight tilt of her head, she controlled all her movements, and with the flutter of wings, she could soar front and back. All she need do is decide a direction, and the sky would respond without question of why.

Marie floated and flapped herself higher and higher. She looked back at the tree. Its branches were full of green needles, its sap glistened and sparkled. Then the ground moved away, and the tops of buildings passed quickly. The fields opened before her with nothing but flowers, all colors, all shapes, that covered the land. An expanse of red poppies. Clover and daisies, then violets and periwinkle, chicory and mallow. The light was sunflower-yellow between her and the fields and the hills clunkily rolled past as she soared through the sky.

The size of the land, so vast, overwhelmed. Never had she seen, or imagined, the infinite distance such expanse could deliver. And everything was there on the ground where it stood. All was at home. All was connected. So, this is the world she did not understand. Look at the fields, all the life it embraced. She marveled that everything there, both the living and dead, were contained down below. Even the birds had their nests there. That's where the clouds came to call.

And she pushed herself forward to find the horizon, to see what was out there, to see where it ended. But the horizon kept moving, pushing away, no matter how far she flew. And as fast as she flew, that's as fast as it moved. More fields kept appearing, more trees, and new houses. Curious, she thought, and she flew on and on, passing forests and hills and valleys and farms.

When she reached the next hill, she spun to her left and turned back around. Her yard was so far, an unknowable distance, it could barely be seen. But as only dreams can provide, there appeared the shape of her yard, rising from the horizon, the one that remained no matter how far she flew.

She swept her wings once and rode the breeze back toward home. The sensation was strong. Cool air underneath. Her tail pushed down firmly by the air coursing above. The feathers on her head laid flat and her ears filled with the whoosh of a rushing of air. Her wings felt so powerful, straight out, barely flapping, they bent, and they curved to move her left then the right.

Marie coasted on her side and looked up to the clouds. There was the moon, full and white during day, against the bright sky. There were its holes in the center, the same color of blue. She lifted her head and flapped her wings to a cloud. Up to the biggest she saw, the fluffiest cloud. She brushed her back on it. It felt buoyant but rough, cool and damp, spongy soft. She was tempted to enter but it seemed rude without knocking, so she played with its edges as she moved her wings through. Small trails of white fluff shifted from its sides, like small and fine down that floats away in a breeze. The more that she pushed, the more white billows flowed outward, and one by one, up ahead, they formed arches around her and they swirled and then closed and melted to nothing behind her.

Suddenly, Marie began to hear music through the soft hush of air that flowed through her feathers. "Alors la, moi, je pense a nous," a voice was singing. "Rien que dans notre imagination." And the more Marie heard, the more that she soared, and she danced in the air: "Je la revois, la p'tite Marie. Mon Dieu, comme elle était jolie." And again, Marie flowed. She twisted. She reached. She bowed. She curtsied. And she kneeled, with one wing raised over her head. Then she twirled twice around. She spun and she dove and she curled and she arched. A slow weightless spin, a tumble and roll, and a prolonged curtsy brought the song to an end.

She smiled and said "thank you" and then Marie, without effort, continued toward home. She looked down to her right and knew that was the hill where she and Aramis stood on that miraculous night. And the more that she looked and remembered their words, the more the ground started to undulate and roll. Again and again, the fields rose and they fell. And the flowers, standing straight, remained pointed to the sky as the landscape waved beneath them and the trees remained upright as their roots were exposed, then buried, then exposed, as all played on the surface of the rolling motion of the ground.

Marie flapped her wings once more and unexpectedly discovered she had arrived at her farm. She began to curve downward, and she passed the top of the barn and circled the road that led into town. She saw the farmer in his tractor, sowing fields of bright sunflowers. From the distance above, brown smoke from the engine was the only thing that moved, except her shadow, which followed and flickered and jumped among the grass and the flowers. Her shadow was an odd little friend, one she learned to control, and it laughed as it bounced to a roof or a tree but it never did mind and it never stopped moving. She looked again at her coop. The old tree. And her yard. There were small specks all over. They were running and pointing. She heard some of them shout. And now they were laughing. She heard laughing again. Yet something was different. These chicks were familiar. Marie suddenly gasped. They were babies, and she knew them. And they were calling her back. To the earth. To the farm. Back to them all.

Marie felt a flush of confusion. Overwhelming confusion. Utterly. Painfully. How could this be? How did I leave them? Why am I flying? Laughing and playing, they were calling her back.

Marie lowered her head and flapped her wings twice. Downward she spiraled in a quickening motion. And as she circled and circled, she felt a small emptiness open. It was a curious, brief sense that she was leaving somewhere she never quite knew but somehow she loved and was sad to depart.

But with the sight of these children, the sensation was gone. Down below, there was joy. The warmth of the ground rose up to greet. And she neared the old tree, then her feet touched the ground amid a blur of dusty colors. In less than a moment, the noises had stopped. The children were gone. The tree stood alone, and its branches were bare. Its green needles were missing, and red berries were gone. The tree, as before, reached up toward the sky, and it was silent and solid with no signs of life.

Marie opened her eyes. All was the same. It was all as before. But what . . . what was that? A flickering bright glint blinded her momentarily and she quickly looked away. She carefully glanced up again. Something twinkled above. Up under the curve. Was that a small carving, she wondered. She blinked trough the brightness until she could focus on the spot. Was that a cross? No, a letter. It was inside two circles . . . the two circles had points. And the circles are glowing. That's a large T in the center. It's pulsing and beating. It's all glowing gold. Of course, it was there! Marie remembered it now. It had always been there. She had seen it as a child. Her mother had shown her. And wait! There were others. She must have forgotten. Yes, now she remembers! The tree had three letters. Oh, where is Aramis!? I see them! I see them! Come stand beside me! Look up at the tree!

Then Marie finally awoke. She was back in the coop, deep in her nest. She picked up her head and looked at the door. There was her shadow. She knew she was home. But what was that journey? It lasted forever. Or was it one moment? It was impossible to say, as to count time while dreaming is to measure the ocean with a spoon while you swim. But no matter how long, Marie welcomed the day and the coop's dim blue light that happily wafted its way through the ramshackle wall. She looked to her left. Aramis was gone. But with the loss of his presence, there came no hollowness this time, no fear and no emptiness, no presence of nothing. Because now, Marie knew, that an absence was a presence that for but a moment had departed.

And as Marie relaxed in her nest, her dreamt images slowly left her. She heard noises outside. The call of Aramis came and soared through the welcoming yard. She was again certain that her mother was near, and she smiled and looked up and slowly started to cry. Marie knew where she went and from where she just came. She had reached that small place, that hidden secret small place of which her mother had told, that place filled with tears that need no longer be shed.

Chapter 20

The Farm Sees the Past and Discovers the Present

The old farmer was already in the kitchen. He had awakened early, his blanket twisted, the sheet turned in half, a pillow that normally resided an arm's reach away tucked under his head. He had looked at the clock past the foot of his bed through the grey-blue streaks of a still-sleeping day. The clock was not moving. It was time to get up.

This, for the farmer, was increasingly the way he started his day. He would open his eyes, see the clock with a face of static approval, and decide it was time to arise and begin. Indeed, if the farmer had cared, which he did not, he might even have noticed that not one of the clocks in the house was now moving. They all had stopped. Even the electric ones. This was not because of some mystical occurrence where all of existence suddenly stands still. It was, as we mentioned, because the old farmer did not care. That's all it took. Indeed, it had been some time (and given the circumstances, just how much was undeterminable) since he had raised the weights in his time-telling sentinel that stood in his room or placed a new battery in the one in the hall. As for those that plugged in (which run whether one cares to mind them or not), the clock in an old bedroom had been broken forever and the one in the kitchen just sat there unplugged. Because, as the farmer observed, correctly enough, there's no reason to pay to keep this one moving when the mechanical ones do the same thing for free – redundant as they are, that being a clock's nature.

As he drank his coffee, the old farmer listed his chores. His daughter was coming and there was too much to do. There were tools to move, jams to be brought, animals to feed, and shopping to sort. And one other thing. He had laid out an old dress that was made by his wife, his favorite of all she had sewn through the years. Thin white cotton with a fine pattern of blue flowers and a curl of lace at its hem, it was fitted at the waist and flowed in its length. He remembered how the dress wrapped his wife in a flouncy light billow that looked like the sky, with its sleeves, loose and airy, that buttoned near the elbows, and a wide belt that tied with a bow in the back. His wife had made it soon after they married, and she wore it to church and some parties in the village and put it aside when she soon became pregnant. After four hurried childbirths, it never fit her again, but it might be the size of his daughter, he thought, so he had taken it that day from the room in the back that he rarely went in.

The dress now lay across the back of a kitchen chair. The farmer would iron it, and though not a skill he had mastered, how hard could it be to flatten some wrinkles? With the last wistful sip of his tepid black coffee, he heard a rooster crow outside his front door. The old farmer was pleased. He wanted his daughter to see the two chickens. She might be happier to be there if she saw the farm full with a new friend she could make. The farmer stood up, went to the steps and served the animals their breakfast.

With Aramis' call, Marie also arose. She lifted her head and flew to the door. Aramis was eating in front of the house. He looked up and back and smiled at Marie. The remnants of twilight still hung in the sky and in the shadowless blue, Marie appeared both a child and a ghost. Aramis stared. Marie's long yellow and red feathers, without the color of sun, stood grey in relief against the dark coop inside. Like a fresco, she stood, still with a smile as if painted, yet warm.

"Bonjour, Aramis," she said after a pause.

"Bonjour to you," he said, and he began walking towards her. "How do you feel? How did you sleep?"

"I slept very well," she said, "though I feel strangely strange."

"Whatever that means," Aramis said with a smile, "it suits you quite well. You look beautiful this morning."

"Thank you," Marie said, blinking and stretching. "That's the second time you've said so. Both times in the morning. I'm beginning to think your eyes like to sleep late."

"No, my eyes are very much awake," Aramis said. "They like this time of day. I think they see you more clearly before the sun has a chance to get in the way."

Marie looked at him quizzically. "I like it when you and the sun are still half-asleep," he explained. "It's the two of you in twilight. Like two twins in a room, in separate beds to be sure, yawning and stretching and rubbing their eyes."

"That's a beautiful thought," Marie said. "I think from now on, I'll appear only in mornings."

"If you do that," Aramis said, "I'll wake you up earlier."

Then each of them tossed the other a smile, the smile of a loved one, a smile that says I have no message but this. And together they shared a breakfast side-by-side. Glancing up between bites, Marie looked at Aramis as if she were holding a secret. Aramis watched her, never moving his eyes, even as he reached to the ground for more food.

"You keep staring at me," Marie said. "Is there something wrong?"

"I don't know," he said. "I can't describe it, but you do look different this morning. Strangely strange, as you said. Even more beautiful. Radiant. I'm not sure what it is."

"Perhaps it's what happens when dreams survive the first light," Marie said.

"That's an odd little answer," he said.

"It's an odd life we live," Marie said. "That's what I've learned. That's what you say. We dream when asleep. We dream when awake. When one meets the other, a lesson they make."

Aramis laughed. "Very good," he said. "It appears Mademoiselle Poétesse has returned." And he offered a slight bow as he swept open his right wing in front of him. "I'm glad you could come."

"It is very good to be here," Marie said with a laugh. "Thank you for attending." Then Marie's face turned soft with a look of reflection. "But honestly, Aramis, I wish I could describe to you the dreams that I've had. They meant nothing at first. Now they seem to be building. And I don't know if they're new or if I now understand them. But somehow I find that it's only in dreams that possibility begins. And without them, we discover our lives much too late."

"I believe that is true," Aramis said. "Dreams never tell lies even if they're not true. So maybe these dreams are making you see. Possibility. Discovery. What you should do."

Marie smiled. She had not intended to introduce *that* topic, that one topic she knew remained ready to burst forth from Aramis, that unanswered question, that lingering possibility. But here they were, each staring at the yes and staring at the no, which were waiting for Marie, especially for Marie, to select one or the other. Marie looked closely at Aramis.

"Aramis, you know I want you here. I want us to be together. But it's not all a dream. It's real. If we are to be married, you must promise to include me and not dream dreams alone. You have shown me what they are, but I must know that you know what they never can be."

"I will try," he said. "For you, I will try."

"It's not for me that I want this. It's for you . . . but also me."

Aramis thought back to that night, that night in the field, that night he was gone, that night he was one. That night was a dream – as real as the nightmares that echoed before. In fact, it all was a dream. And everything in it. "But Marie, I worry. If I stop all my dreams, I'm not sure what I have," he said.

"And with too many dreams, what have you then?" Marie asked. "I don't want you to stop. I want us to share them and to keep them together."

"I promise to try," he said. "If you promise to show me if I ever forget."

Smiling, Marie gently nodded her head as she watched how the smallest movement of air played with the fine feathers on his strong and round forehead. She saw muscles twitch near his eyes, the shifting smile of his mouth, the inquiring moves of his head. She took a deep breath, leaned forward, and gave Aramis a kiss. Tears swelled in his eyes.

"Then yes," she said quietly. "I will marry you with joy."

Aramis had not yet heard the last word when his mind suddenly stopped moving. The smile dropped from his face, and just as quickly his eyes opened wide, and his smile reappeared, not just at his mouth, but his whole body transformed into a show of delight. His entire face broadened, and his wings lifted from his sides. Then he turned to his left and let out a crow that shook the whole farm, and with both wings upraised, he scraped at the ground as if marking the spot, the place where it happened, the place of his love.

Marie looked at him and she, too, of course, broke into a smile. A softer, gentler smile filled with grace and relief. Here was the Aramis that Marie so much loved. Here was the Aramis who gave her a life. Here was the Aramis who brought her the world. She watched his whole presence. She saw how he moved. She felt all their joy. What bound them together existed before, but somehow these words they had spoken made the possible real. And as she looked at his face and saw the small tears in his eyes, a flicker of light made her glance past his wings, at the old silent tree, which stood just behind him, with its two outstretched arms reaching up to the sky. There were no shining letters, as she had seen in her dream, yet all at once Marie felt her fears and her worries and all her past moments disintegrate and scatter as if she had just been reborn from the moon's cleansing rays.

"Now, I have something to ask," Marie said gently, and her smile slowly softened. "Actually, it's more a demand," she continued. "You must go for the day and leave me alone. I have something to do. Don't ask me what. Please. We can be married tomorrow out here by the tree. I will come out to find you and we can say our vows then. Until then, please, please, you must leave me alone."

With great relief and no argument, Aramis looked puzzled but happy. "I don't understand," he said, "but if that's what you want, I'll leave you alone. But know that I'll be here waiting for you whenever you're ready."

"I know," Marie said. "I'll be ready tomorrow. Now leave and I promise, I will always be here."

Aramis looked at Marie for one last prolonged moment and then walked away, not sure at all where to go. And before he could even turn to see her once more, Marie started humming and skipped into the coop. Then she closed the door tightly. Within seconds, she moved things, sat in the nest next to hers, smiled to herself, and set down to work.

* * *

The farmer was busy through the morning with his tasks. Tools were moved. Front chairs were wiped. Jars of jam were found. Stairs were swept, and the driveway was raked, the sound of stones chattering filled the small yard. The rabbit, who had woken up happy just a few days ago, was now ready for dinner. The sun reached noon, and the farmer sat on his steps and awaited his neighbor. He had asked her to bring him some bread and a cake, three cheeses and grapes, a jar of foie gras, her famed garlic soup, and bacon and radishes from the stores in the town.

But the neighbor, who was undoubtedly stuck leading her own conversation, was nowhere in sight. So in her place, it seemed, the postman arrived, delivering his own first-class package of boredom and gossip.

"Bonjour, Mort," said the cornstalk with ears, which, has been noted, looked ready to seed.

"Bonjour, Monsieur Ricoeur," the farmer replied. "What brings you up here? Something important?"

"That depends how you see things," the postman responded, bounding and bouncing ahead in his steps. "That's not all there is to it. No, there's always more to it. Don't you think so?"

"I suppose," said the farmer.

"I came to tell you that no one's lost an old rooster. Not that I found. And I've been asking around, everywhere I go."

"Thank you. I appreciate your trouble."

"No trouble at all. No. Not at all. Not at all. I was happy to check. Just part of the service, you might say. Happy to do it. I asked all around. No one knew of a rooster. Not that they knew."

"Thank you again. I appreciate you tried."

The postman nodded, and before his head returned upright, he opened his mouth. "By the way, did you hear what just happened?" And without waiting for an answer, correctly predicting that none was forthcoming, "a cow gave birth to a calf with two heads," he continued. "Yes, incredible, isn't it?" He then pleasantly described in detail what the family had done, not just with the calf but also sometime prior, when their middle child went missing and the father, upset, drank too much cheap wine, of course, which led the wife to hit him and then her family came over and the boy was in the barn. But that wasn't all. Another family in a neighboring town, the name's not important, had gone on vacation and when they got back, their fence had been broken. They think a neighbor man did it, but certainly, he said, as the man's a good friend, it couldn't be him. He wouldn't have done that. And that was not all. There was that outbreak of fungus, that ugly divorce, and that policeman was killed. Well, yes, he crashed alone on the weekend and it was down in Toulouse, but it all goes to show you that everything happens. And some many minutes later (it was still after noon), the postman bounced and talked his way back to his truck. He was in a hurry, just then, with all the mail to deliver.

By now, it was clear, the old neighbor was late. Oh, I shouldn't have asked her, the old farmer thought, as he went to his kitchen to make himself lunch. With bread on the table and some butter and fish, the farmer sat down with a fork in his hand.

"Allô?" he suddenly heard from the driveway out front. The brittle screech of the voice sounded like a knife scraping his plate. The farmer groaned as he stood from his chair, hoping the visit would be short and as silent as possible. It was, as most wishes go, made all the more insistent as it was all the more unlikely.

"Bonjour?" the voice cackled, with the second syllable rising to an impossible pitch, as thin as a line and with the point of a pin.

"Bonjour," the farmer said, as he walked to the door. "Bonjour, Myra," and the farmer shook his head. Myra, indeed.

"I have your groceries," she said. Her round face and cracked red cheeks glowed like fresh bricks, their color set off distinctively by a grey and pink headscarf blending in fine contrast to her bright orange sweater. Her yellow cotton dress with blue and green stripes fell loosely to her knees, except where it caught at the bulge in her waist.

"The grocer tried to cheat us, but I set him straight. 'Special grapes,' he said. Five euros, he said, for special grapes. I told him, the only thing special was the ridiculous price. Who does he think I am? The queen of Monaco? I told him I could go steal grapes that taste better than these, then those would be special. They would be free. These are nothing special. Just grapes," she continued, looking at the farmer and roughly pulling out items, one by one, each providing a reason to find something more to say. As she lifted the grapes from the bag, six perfect round ones fell to the rust-colored floor. The farmer bent down to pick them up. "And the bread," she clucked, "they make it smaller every day, and yet the price goes up like they're baking in gold. It's the same everywhere." Then she grabbed the flimsy white box with her thick stubby fingers, and without noticing, pushed the top down with her thumb and into the cake.

"So, your daughter is coming?" she asked, shuffling her beaten leather shoes across the linoleum floor. She placed the cheese in the refrigerator and returned to the table to pick up the bacon.

The farmer, seated at the table, was trying to stay out of her way and out of her conversation. How did she know? he wondered. He had purposefully not told her why he wanted these groceries. But it was futile to try to keep secrets in a village this small no matter how big the farm.

"Yes," he said. "She should be here soon."

"Good luck to you," she said. "Is she still living in that city, still all alone?" And without waiting for an answer, Myra happily continued. The farmer, who knew better, had not attempted to speak.

"She should be here with you. You need a woman here and she has nothing to do and no business far away. I don't understand why we let these children just run and go searching for ideas that mean nothing. And worse. They should be here with family and take care of their home. Unless, of course, she marries, and the man takes her away. That's tragic, of course, but beyond her control. No, Mortimer, you should tell her. You are her father and she must learn what is right."

The farmer's mind began to drift, and his hearing was diverted from the scratching sound of this woman's voice to his own softer thoughts, which were thankfully growing louder.

"She must find her own way," he said.

"Her own way? Even when it leads nowhere? Seriously, now, she's getting too old to marry and what then?" she said. "She will thank you some day for forcing her home now."

"It's not right to keep someone who does not want to stay," the farmer said quietly. "She will find her own home, maybe back here. Seeds blow in the wind and replant where they land."

Myra might have been listening, but except for the fact they were four feet apart, there was no evidence she heard a word.

"Yes, she will thank you someday. Otherwise, we just die and then that's it. We live and what do we leave behind? Children who have left us, who have no home. They forget where they come from and don't remember how they got here. It's all disposable to them. Just throw it away. Throw it away and with it their lives. Give it away and with it goes hope. There is no hope for the future the way they behave. Even my grandchildren, they're still young so they don't know. They deserve a life with a home, not some rented flat in a city where no one knows the other. Is this what we worked for? Oh, by the grace of god, I despair for our future. My son called last week and there again, he . . . "

"Myra," the farmer very wearily interrupted. "How much do I owe you?"

The woman stopped talking. For a moment. She shrugged, reached in her pocket, and gave him the receipts. "Here, you see what life comes to? This is the price of living. The cheaters, they rob us blind."

The farmer stood and counted the money from his pocket, then moved to the door to show her the way.

Myra did not leave. Instead, she sat down.

"So, your daughter will visit long?" she asked, sitting at the table, a cheese knife twirling slowly in her hand. She was staring at the farmer. It was clear that this was – for her – the start of the conversation. The farmer sat down, resigned to this incessant woman who had married his neighbor more than fifty years before. That neighbor, of course, was dead now. The farmer began fumbling with the table bottom, sliding his hands out and in with his fingers pressing up underneath, tapping at random intervals a small drumbeat with no rhythm.

And just then, as if salvation can arrive in a rented yellow car, the farmer's daughter pulled into the driveway, beeped the horn lightly, and loudly shouted "Bonjour!"

Her dark brown hair, falling just past her waist, had a red bow at the end of its long simple braid. While that might have looked odd on someone else of her age, Charisse still had the look of a small shy farm girl who had not quite grown up over her thirty-four-and-a-half years.

The farmer appeared at the door and smiled. Myra followed close behind. "Bonjour," Myra said to Charisse. "Your father's been expecting you." And with that, Myra turned away and walked out through the arch with her much-practiced look of disapproval, purposefully flavored with extra disdain.

Making his way slowly down the steps, the farmer walked to his daughter to help her with her bags. Charisse had also stopped for cake and bread and the two types of cheese she most preferred.

"How was your trip?" the farmer asked as they stepped inside.

"It was fine, papa. It's never too long," she said. "And how are you? You look well. Are you feeling better now?"

The two walked into the kitchen discussing trifles and politely conversing about their respective healths, which each remarked to the other was "fine." They then turned to topics less personal and more relaxing, about the farm, about family, and about whatever soft gossip they could comfortably share. It was the start of a visit that happened each time, small conversation about nothing important and certainly nothing revealing that might bridge the distance of four decades or so.

After Charisse washed the grapes and the two finished their lunch, the farmer went to his room for an afternoon nap. Left alone, Charisse felt the chill that always accompanied her as she walked through the house. It was a chill of recognition, of both memories known and memories forgotten. It was as if she was followed, not just by spirits, but generations of worry, of unhappy lives, of a weight that comes from centuries gone, generations of lives lived under one roof. Her smile now came heavy and all her motions felt worn as if she followed a maze made of deep, muddy trenches. And though she dreaded her visits, she could not deny that her home made her happy – the way that pictures of lost loved ones make us smile when we cry.

"Bonjour?" she suddenly heard as the front door swung open. "Allô!," she replied. "Dorothee?"

"Yes, bonjour." Dorothee entered the kitchen in her typical quick steps, carrying two heavy bags with her long dress flowing back. "Oh, I'm so happy to see you. Did you just now arrive?"

"Not long ago. Papa's taking a nap and I was straightening up."

"That's perfect," Dorothee said. "You can help me with dinner."

And the two young women stood side-by-side, pulling the various items from the two twin bags and talking of their lives that had become so different. There had been a brief time some years prior when they were both on the farm, in their separate houses, spending their days in unseen tandem, both cleaning and walking and cooking then cleaning at similar hours for similar men. Then, every Sunday, they would do as they did now, help each other perform their unspoken duty of preparing the dinner. Now, standing together with their backs toward the door, they still shared the same upbringings that placed them in plain cotton dresses with their long brown hair pulled back, Dorothee with simple ponytail, Charisse with a braid. Yet they had become decidedly different, from two different worlds, despite their like dress, one still firmly planted in the dark soil of the farm while the other tried to root near to sidewalks and busses.

As they prepared the vegetables and lamb (store-bought, not fresh), they talked of small things and updated each other about people they knew. Once during discussion, they both started laughing as they remembered a friend who had red hair, two older sisters, a small struggling farm, and eight growing children, and one husband (at least for now, they agreed).

"Oh, yes, Pepin and I are fine. I think." Dorothee said as the conversation turned to family. "We have all the regular static that comes from many years married and two small children. Some days the silence is so heavy, and the hours are so long. But then the weeks go by and then a year and another. I'm not sure how to change that. I'm not sure I can. Not now. Not soon. For now, it appears, my boys are my meaning and Pepin's my life."

Charisse picked up the carrots and corgettes, walked from the table to the sink and turned on the water. The conversation quickly turned from Dorothee and her family to most of the others: Charisse's aunts and brothers, a few cousins and nephews. Each had an event, and some even several, that had defined recent months.

"I don't want you to worry," Dorothee began when Charisse asked about her father, "but your father is different, a bit stranger these days."

"How do you mean? Do you think he's sick?" Charisse asked. "I worry so often that he'll fall ill and be here alone."

"It's not illness," Dorothee said. "At least, I don't think that's the case. He is just different, somehow. In many ways, of course, he is perfectly the same. But now, well, now he sometimes looks lost . . . and then odd as it sounds, sometimes he seems happy."

Charisse brought the vegetables back to the table, coarsely scraped and coarsely chopped. "I wondered if something had happened," she said. "He wrote me a letter a little while back and he said some things that made me quite worried."

"Oh, dear. Really? Did he say he was sick?"

"No," Charisse said. "At first, I thought he might be confused. The letter was to me, but somehow it seemed, in one or two places, that he must have thought he was writing to somebody else. Or even to himself. I don't know how many times I reread that letter. It was so . . . well, so . . . so new . . . so open."

"That's funny," Dorothee said, rubbing with both hands fresh herbs on the lamb. "'Open' is precisely the word that kept coming to my mind. I said to Pepin the other day that, with your father so different, even the farm feels more open. Like the way he invites the boys, during the day, after their school, to come help him with chores. The way he talks to them. And he smiles. He even pats them on the head. Pepin says he's just getting old. 'A bit rattled,' he says. 'A little bit loose.' But I don't know. I've seen others get old. They didn't change like this. If anything, they became more . . . solidified somehow. They didn't loosen and ease. Not like this. I mean, I know your father is older, but I don't know if that's all."

As the two finished preparing, Dorothee shrugged her shoulders and they both agreed Charisse could do nothing but wait to see for herself. There was nothing else to do. They would sit down to dinner and she could decide on her own. And about three hours later, with all six of them seated, the dinner was served. The two young boys, as usual, sat on either side of their mother, Neville to her left, Bellamy to her right, while Dorothee sat with her back to the stove. On the opposite side of the long wooden table, the old farmer took his place across from those three, with his son to his left and now Charisse to his right.

The light conversation, the same with each dinner, began with Dorothee's questions. Charisse, how was your trip? How's your house and the city? Did you know that Neville won a school prize for spelling? The eyes of the old farmer and those of his son kept darting about, resting mostly on their bowls and their spoons as they rose. Bellamy, by now, was again swinging his feet. The talk moved slowly from Charisse to her brother, who was explaining new prices and the health of his cows, plans for the barn, a machine he had seen, how the tractor was dying, the weather that year, the need for more rain, the welcome hard winter that kept down the pests, and all the consequential problems that were taken in stride. With the soft clangs and tings of spoons on six bowls, the slurping of soup and the smacking of lips, the loud chewing of bread by the two little boys, and the monotonous droning of familiar, light talk, the old farmer sat there, forgetting to chew a piece of bread in his mouth. He began to feel his two legs swaying forward and back as if they were swinging under his chair, like the chair where he sat when he was a boy. Back then, he sat where his grandsons sat now, his own mother to his right and the older men straight across. His grandfather was here at this very same table, in the very same chair, in the very same way, very likely forgetting to chew a mouthful of bread. Yes, the place was the same. The space was the same. The voices, and looks, and conversation were the same. The only difference was time, and when that happens, as we know, fickle time likes to vanish. There was no question of yesterday or the passage of years, the span had no meaning, just more or less instants in a sequence of motions. And suddenly, with no effort, this old man was his grandfather, seated at this table. Yet he was also a boy watching his father there sitting next to his father, taking him back in a meaningless moment. Without the blink of a thought, the centuries condensed into nothing and there, all in and around him, was the past and the present, one finite and gone, the other more real as it swallowed him whole. And there in the shadows was his nonexistent future that had yet to be born, born of the sequence that someday would come to this unyielding space.

"So grand-pere, grand-pere!" the old farmer suddenly heard. "What do you think?"

The old farmer returned. "What?" he asked.

"What do you think?" Neville repeated, his voice in excitement rising in pitch and also in volume. "What do you think? You saw the old tree?"

"Yes," the old man said. "Yes, I saw it. I did."

"I was right, then, wasn't I? It's different. It moved."

"Well," the old farmer said. "Well, yes, I will say, it does appear that way, doesn't it?"

"See, I told you," Neville said, leaning his face toward his brother, flashing the taunt of an open-mouthed smile.

"I was the first one to say it!" Bellamy shouted. "You didn't say it! Mom, I said it. I said it first!"

And in just a flash of that moment, the old farmer heard his brother, one of many who sat at this table back then. The teasing and shouting and then stern admonitions, harsh looks from his father, a fist slamming down. This was the future, the one he imagined in the eyes of a child as he watched those old men.

"Ssssh!" Dorothee said quickly as she gently pushed Neville to sit straight in his chair. "Don't shout at the table," she said turning to Bellamy. "Now, sit up correctly. It doesn't matter who said it. Calm down and don't shout."

"Ah, let the boy shout," the old farmer said. "If you can't shout at six, then when can you shout? Let the boy speak if he has something to say. Now what was that, Bellamy? Go ahead and tell us."

The entire table went quiet. Hands froze in the air, on their way to their mouths or descending to bowls. Dorothee glanced at Charisse and then quickly looked down. Charisse did not move. She had been watching her father obliquely yet closely all during dinner and when he said these few words, her eyes opened wide. Pepin, mid-bite, stayed for a moment with his fork in the air. The boys looked at their mother. And with a nod of her head, Bellamy launched in, struggling with excitement and the disorder that comes with a 6-year-old's thoughts to describe how he (and his brother) had seen the old tree, after the storm, (remember the storm?), sometime the next morning, a tree had crashed down, it was after the storm, (the really bad storm), and the old tree, when they saw it, the one in the yard, was turned back to front, and now faced the wrong way. Some of them nodded, and some of them shrugged, and Dorothee thanked her young son for the story.

After dinner, after dessert and after a thousand furtive glances, the kitchen was cleaned, and the young family was leaving. Dorothee gave a quick kiss to Charisse then looked in her eyes and said "I'll talk to you soon," and they both knew what that meant and what the topic would be.

Charisse excused herself from her father and went outside and down the steps to the cellar to unpack her things in her old room to the right. The sun was just setting and after hanging or folding the clothes from her bag, she headed outside to visit the dusk and what remained of her youth. She looked up at the house. With each visit, she thought, the house was much older. Did she just see more defects or can houses truly age and wrinkle that quickly? Cracks gave birth and stains deepened and spread. The rooms grew smaller and pipes made more noise. The house reminded Charisse of those strangers who recurred in her dreams. She knew she had seen them, having become, as they were, almost reassuringly familiar, but there was a quality about them that lurked with intentions of kidnap and chase. The memory upon awakening was of a lingering relic of past travels and people that haunted in ways that were gone but too real.

Now, she wondered, what would she do there for all her five days? There was her land, and some neighbors, the woods, and a brother. She could drive to the town on top of the hill. She could read and sort boxes and walk the fields once again, searching for truffles and bleuet, or medlar and pomegranate, if already ripe. Mostly, she would search for what lingered within her new life and compare the present to memories and so many ghosts. And there were those letters, the ones she and her father had written each other, and the thousands of topics she thought to explore. How to discover that man – a father, a husband, and son wrapped as one, the one who still lived somewhere beneath, whose surface had aged like the stones of the house, yet who suddenly showed a glimpse of warm spirit?

As she aimlessly wandered away from the house, a soft lavender breeze billowed her dress and outlined her small frame. She stepped into the barn and kicked through the straw to raise the reliable smell of unmistakable farm. The one that is sweet, of molasses and waste, another organic, of grass and dried straw, and the third one of must and of mold and decay. No city can bring that fragrance to life. But the cows tugged at their chains, struggling to reach just a little more food, and Charisse spun around and turned left out the door. Across the driveway she walked, where the dog was asleep, and into the yard, where the ducks had just left, and the cat closed its day. And there it still sat, the quiet old tree. The one that he mentioned. "Something strange" he had written. Then Bellamy's tale, so complete with belief.

Yet now, to Charisse, it appeared the same tree, the one she and her brothers had branded as target, or foe, or friend, or castle. It was whatever they decided their imaginations could see. No, Charisse thought, it still looked the same. The same tree. Undamaged. Still in its place. Still lurking. Still grey. Still sleeping. Still present. There's the trunk. And the branches. The ridges. The holes. The . . . well, that is strange . . . wait . . . yes, that's odd. Strange. It's the same. But it's not. Charisse stopped. Just steps past the driveway. It was the same tree. All the tree was the same. But the scene did look different. It almost appeared it was the yard that had changed. And the shed. And the fence. And even the house. The picture was right, but the brush strokes were off. Or it was seen in a mirror with some of it backwards. It was like dreaming of the room you're sleeping within. You open your eyes, it's the same you imagined, but the distance is off, or the door has changed walls, or the windows have shrunk. That's the branch. She remembered. Her swing swung over there. It never worked well, always hitting the trunk. She looked up to the left. There are those two. Not as high as she thought but that's what childhood will do. Still, that didn't explain why they looked out of place.

Charisse looked around. "This whole place is haunted." Then she laughed a small laugh. Maybe the tree has stayed still and the whole farm spun around. That makes more sense. And she looked again at the yard as if seeking a clue. Nothing else was misplaced. It all was the same. The marigolds were dead amid weeds by the coop. The fence had been crushed but the house was still there. The barn was behind her. The ducks still annoyed and the cat was still sleeping. And the chickens. That's funny, she thought. Where were the chickens?

She looked at the coop. Now how can this be? She had not seen them nor heard them the whole time she was there. Her father had said that now there were two. Even the chickens were hiding. But they always make noise. A playful fantasy of fear crept into her imagination. She slowly walked to the coop. Where am I? she wondered. Where did they go? And when she pushed the door open, Marie jumped so suddenly that the loud and violent fluttering of feathers sent Charisse in the air as well. Her head hit the ceiling and she let out a small cry.

"Pardon!" said Charisse as she and Marie both recovered. "I didn't mean to scare you. You scared me right back. How are you, little hen?"

Marie had seen Charisse a few times before, but the way that she stared was as if a spirit appeared. Charisse's long hair like feathers. Her smile full of love. Her voice soft and soothing. But it was her dress that enraptured. A blend of colors and of shapes, as if a kaleidoscope of magic had just burst through the door.

"What's that you're doing?" Charisse asked Marie. And with no answer forthcoming, the two stood for a moment, neither saying a word. How beautiful, they thought, and they wore their own smile. How beautiful, how simple, that other appears.

* * *

Aramis stood with his back to the coop. After leaving Marie, his direction was gone. He stopped for a moment after considering the fact he had no place to go – though certainly to a less grand degree than in the previous days. This time, it was nothing more than he found himself, very unexpectedly, and suddenly, alone. He did not want to stay near the coop and be teased by a place that announced he was not welcome. He could go into the barn and watch unhappy cows, which he decided was not worth the gamble as watching them struggle was sure to either make him feel better but probably worse. No, the barn was depressing, the smokehouse too small, and the arch and the field, now filled with their memories, would only magnify his solitude and make it seem long.

So, without any planning, Aramis had a new direction to walk. Turning left past the shed, past the end of the broken-down fence, he ventured along the thick grove of trees that fell off toward the stream and down to a church. Ahead a small distance, he could see the son's house. It was not far away, so he slowed his pace to a wander and examined whatever he found along his new route. Mostly, he kept to the edge of the small woods to his right, where the mass of old trees rose amid a ground covered in branches with twigs and rough bushes and piles of dead leaves. With its brambles and nettles and overgrown brush, it was an impenetrable barrier to anyone his size.

Aramis varied his pace, such as it was, between stopping and thinking, then stepping slowly and peering deep into the woods. It was a day, suddenly granted, when one feels (as the expression goes) that they have nothing but time on their, well, in this case, wings. So taking advantage, Aramis thought of his recent long night when he ventured out on his own, of the long walk with Marie, of the past several days, and of what they discussed. He tried to find again that belief, or at least a small memory, of feeling invisible, of being connected somehow with all that surrounds, with all that there is. He found the memory close, but not the sensation, which maybe stayed in the field or had gone into hiding.

Mostly, though, he thought of Marie. He saw her that morning before fully awake, the sun played from her feathers, the moon glowed from her eyes. See her slight movements. Hear her soft voice. Watch her smile disappear when her eyes open wide. Aramis stood at the edge of the grass and stared into the trees. But it was more than just the sight of her face, the sound of her voice, the shape of her smile. How to describe what cannot be drawn? How to reach out for what cannot be touched? What cannot be held? What cannot be kept? It was there though and real. It was his companion that night. It was unseen and loved. Still, he wondered, had it been fair to take her? So far into night? Had he explained anything at all? Had his words any meaning? He questioned his future had she said no. No doubt he would leave. Then he repeatedly questioned what she would think of this tree. Or that plant. Or this flower. Yes, look how those butterflies chase one another.

And so the day passed. Slowly. Alone. Except the restlessness stayed. He walked farther along to where a small clearing appeared near the edge of the woods. His thoughts remained far but his sights focused near. The larger branches were gone, the area filled only by sticks and dead and dry leaves. He went a bit closer. A small wooden board poked out of the ground, its perfect flat front in stark contrast to the round, jagged nature of a nearby chestnut tree's roots. Aramis took another step forward. A second piece of flat wood was nailed to the first. That wasn't from nature. Some man put it there. Aramis suddenly saw it was a small wooden cross. It was mostly covered with leaves. He kicked them away, and on the crosspiece, he saw the faint writing of a child. There were letters at the top that were faded with some missing. He peered in closer and now he saw words. He stepped lightly aside to move his shadow away. The shades began to form letters. Areas obscured began to stand out. "Rest in peace," it was written. And there was more to the right. He kicked again at the leaves. More letters appeared. "Little chickens," it said. "Rest in peace, little chickens."

"Rest in peace, little chickens." The coldest of chills shot down Aramis' back. He shook and fell backwards, recoiling so quickly without lifting his feet. He flapped his wings once and jumped out from the leaves. With his feet on the grass, he kneeled down on the ground. A feeling of nausea gripped his insides. Oh no, Aramis thought. Oh no, this is it. This is the place. The place where they took them. The place where they came. Marie's full story of that terrible night – it suddenly rushed back. The destruction. The cries. Aramis had listened, overwhelmed by her pain, hearing of the horror but too concerned for Marie to picture the scene. Now he saw all. All the images of horror overwhelmed with a rush. Now it was real, and just inches away. All the carnage and blood and limp bodies appeared. He could see it at once, the way they were carried and dumped in the ground. And here they were left, right there, barely hidden. Yes, death remained close, residing no farther than behind the old shed.

Aramis' heart pounded. Oh, what of Marie? The pain she would feel! She had no idea it was here. She did not know of this place except in nightmares and fears. Oh, what would she feel? It would bring it all back. The destruction and pain. The loss and the tears. If she knew this was here. If she knew they were here. Her mother, the others, all were this close. Aramis leaned back and sat down. He clutched his wings to his chest. He did not want to see, but he could not stop staring. There's no need to see to know it is there. Yet how to stop looking? It demands to be seen. Like the complaisant balance that's offered by a grave in the serenity of prairie. What is and what was set in harmony and peace.

Aramis tried to keep his eyes lowered. He desperately wanted to leave and turn his back and forget. To ignore this adventure. To negate what he found. But knowledge has a way of not wanting to forget, and the sacred, when it's seen, is not so simple to dismiss. For this was sacred, in a sense, at least to some in this world. Not hallowed yet holy. There lay her mother, deep beneath trees, marked by a child who could not understand.

For the rest of the day, Aramis drifted. Time would stop and then suddenly pass quickly. He was no longer there, riding, instead, along death's bloodless message, the cold one that ends in a borderless void. He sat with his sisters when he was a boy. He embraced a silent image of the smile of his mother. He smelled the fragrant large yard where he played as a child. How sweet and how pleasant to feel innocent and free. We long for its end and then lament its fleet passage. Why? Aramis wondered. Because we stand in its midst, but life does not care. It is and is not. That's the game that it plays. It leaves connection to us, like this grave in the woods. There's no hiding the truth; we're the way it unfolds.

Yes, Marie deserved to be told. She would want to be told. And he would tell her someday. And with the two of them here, when she cried, he would comfort, and together they would listen to the silent way graves place us deep in the present – surrounded by dead who lived in the past without whom we live in precarious future. Yes, he would show her someday – someday, but not now. Not on this day, their last day alone.

For now, Aramis knew, it was time to focus on living. And with the sun to his left and a warm breeze blowing through, Aramis watched nonchalant clouds parade past and he searched for a smile about his days yet to come. He believed, for the first time, that the world was indeed small, and Aramis, finally, believed he was home.

Chapter 21

A Special Day

Chickens don't have many weddings. They are not opposed to the idea. It's just that the occasion seldom arises. So today was a special day.

To anyone who might have wandered here unaware, all would have seemed a typical morning on this picturesque farm surviving the past. Animals scrounged for food or made noises for more. Insects pushed ahead on their journeys. Sounds of distant people echoed from their lives. The sun brightened in a sky with bundles of thick and white clouds, and the light warmth of the air made all bodies feel brighter.

For each of those living on this farm, however, the day felt even lighter. Perhaps the sounds sounded crisper. Or the birds sang songs louder or the leaves shone green brighter. Or the grasshoppers jumped a bit higher. Or the flies' wings fluttered stronger. As for the dog, no surprise there, it was contented as usual. The cat, however, seemed inordinately pleased. And had they all come together and collected and discussed their respective starts of the day, they might have reasonably concluded it was the farm as a whole, and not each separate experience, that partook of this light. But there were no conversations, and no one shared notes. For all that they knew, they each were alone.

The first signal, of sorts, that the start was not normal was the first call of the morning from Aramis. Aramis was happy but restless all night and his first crow was so weak that Charisse was not certain if she heard him or not. Then the sun came up, and Marie had not left the coop for her breakfast. The farmer awoke as usual and, suddenly he realized, his clock was not moving. He had forgotten to wind it. He still did not care. Charisse woke up spritely, stopped for a moment to remember where she was, and was pleased to encounter the day set before her.

True to his word, Aramis had not disturbed Marie since he left her the morning before. He walked out of the smokehouse and wandered the yard after eating his breakfast among several morning calls. He was determined to wait for as long as she needed, for as long as he promised.

Aramis' early hours passed quickly while he repeatedly thought of his vows, then of her mother and the place he had found, of the past several days, of the past many months, of his life before here, and again of his vows. By afternoon, he still wandered the breadth of the yard, growing more and more eager each time he circled and passed under the tree. He had seen many weddings and heard parts of their vows. But none of them applied. Not today. Not to him. He worried that Marie would be disappointed in the sparseness of their ceremony. He knew she had never seen a traditional wedding, but still he grieved a lover's grieve for what she would miss. No, there was no one to speak. They could not exchange rings. There would be no album of photos and no flowers offered by those distant relations who might sweetly weep for her joy. There was no man in black cloth. There would be no signs of a blessing and no children of innocence twitching in clothes filled straight through with starched boredom.

But Aramis was happy. He knew these things did not matter. A witness of chickens would not make this holy. Vows would be spoken, and they would reach where they needed. The meaning of church, whatever it was, would somehow arrive and would see them and hear them, no matter how far. Cannot a covenant be made as strongly in silence as when shouted and showered with the structure of others?

So, Aramis paced on, slowly repeating his path, around and around the yard and the tree, glancing at the coop each time he turned left.

Then he'd circle once more, for the five-hundredth time, walk to the house, then back under the tree.

Suddenly, behind him, he heard the door of the coop. His heart did a leap and he spun with excitement.

Marie came out slowly. The bright midday sun glowed off her shimmering soft feathers with a twinkling, golden, almost blinding, brilliance. She was smiling, standing, with timid expectation. Aramis began to smile at Marie's small, delicate face. Then, in that instant before he knew what he was seeing, Aramis froze. This was not possible. He thought how could this be?

"What?" Aramis stammered. "I . . . I mean . . . how?" he said as he began to step forward.

"Do you like it?" Marie asked with an embarrassed, shy smile.

Aramis could not answer, absorbed as he was by the glowing kaleidoscope before him. Pieces of fabric delicately woven together with small threads of straw covered Marie loosely from the top of her head past her long, upturned tail. She was wrapped in a gown as if in a dream made of whimsy, reds, soft blues and dark greens, all bordered by yellow with patterns of flowers. Sheer blue patches of heaven dangled under her wings. A breeze ruffled her dress and the pink checks cascaded into the thinnest black squares then to purple small circles and an assortment of plaids. Marie took a small step toward Aramis and her motion lifted the shimmering white field of the sheerest of fabric that draped over her head, a field that he saw as a translucent white cloud caressing her face under small light blue flowers.

Aramis stood, unable to move, with no desire to move. His smile remained fixed. He raised his wings without thinking in silent exclamation. Marie walked towards him as her dress lightly floated each time she stepped forward. She stopped just before him, the two of them standing between the tree's two outstretched arms.

"I cannot believe it," Aramis finally said. "I've never seen anything like it. I could not have imagined. You are amazing. And this dress. Your dress is amazing." Aramis again stopped. His eyes were fixed on Marie's, then darted to her left wing, then to her face, to her right wing, to her feet, and back to her eyes. "Marie, beauty cannot capture what you've done, how you look. You are making it jealous with its own dream to pursue."

Marie smiled and said nothing. She looked at Aramis and tilted her head slightly, admiring his face, which she saw had permanently transformed from a mixture of mystery and a dark confusion of passions to a blend of familiar, even comforting, warmth. Even his damaged comb and his waddle, so strange and misshapen, had become indelibly him, so endearing and unique she was glad it had happened.

"Oh, how I wish others were here to see you," Aramis said. "You look so magical, miraculous. Marie, you are beautiful. Under this tree, with this fragranced warm air, and you standing there, so radiant and so happy . . . I see . . . I believe . . . I know now . . . " and he stopped. He had ex-hausted his words. Except those in his eyes And the yard remained silent.

What movement there was only came from a breeze, a breeze that wafted in slowly and curled round the tree. And it, too, made no sound and it could not be seen, but they accepted its message and both of them knew it was time to begin.

Aramis looked at Marie and Marie lightly nodded. "Yes, please, Aramis. Please say your words first."

Aramis smiled. He took one step forward and a deep shaky breath.

"I love you, Marie. And I have fought to find words. I have struggled to think just how to express, to find the right thoughts, to show you my love. I do not know if I can. Because my words come from love and, from what it begets, we can never explain. Not the whole as it is. Not that which is derived. Words are never enough. We need the world to help show us. Perhaps years from now, you must watch for the moon's glow next to Venus. Or the stars as they shine through a cloud of fine mist. Or you'll hear of my love in the thrumming of crickets. In a rustle of trees. The distant cry of a child. Yes, then you might know, all the truer when wordless, just what my love means.

"For you have brought me true love, the love of the present. The most powerful love. Not the lingering soughing of the remnants of past. Nor a love in the future, like a false siren's lure. But the real love of now, the all of our nows, the ones that are gone and the ones yet to come. And you brought this to me, and showed me the world, for it remained my chrysalis until my butterfly was you.

"Now, here we are. I seek to give you my vows. The vows said in church, I don't know what they are. Yet I know what they mean. They all say the same. They say what I feel, and I will try to find words to blossom before you so you might share my joy and breathe for a moment the fragrance you placed so deep in my heart. If we are lucky enough, our words of love are like magic. Like the magic you bring me. The magic of one. The one that must come, but only when we marry the unspoken and spoken. For marriage needs both. It must bring them together – the silence of love as well as long conversation. For marriage is both. And like magic they'll live and float for an instant and then they'll be gone. Yet in the oneness of now, they cannot disappear.

"Yes, Marie, my world is now one. It is like the feathers that surround you, it is bountiful and long. But its meaning is granted only as one, as you are but one, as your voice and your wings and your smile and your eyes, your thoughts and your fears and your dreams are but one. I could count all your feathers as I could count all the grass. Or they might be as stars. Or they might be as trees. But only as one, as a field, as a sky, as a single thick forest, can their beauty have meaning, and can their meaning be true. Thanks to you, they are one, and for me, you're the center of all the world is, and all I can be.

"So, Marie, from this day, I live with you as one. With the two of us as one. And if that can be true, I live as one with myself. For that is the gift you give me today by becoming my wife. And if you promise to have me, I will forever be yours."

Marie's smile appeared slowly, her mouth twitched with emotion, she subtly blushed and her eyes slowly glistened. Marie's eyes had not moved. She had studied him closely, how he looked at the ground to compose his next thought, how he stared straight at her to make a fine point. Aramis' eyes were quiet and still, expectant, and waiting. And the sides of her dress swayed and then floated as the wind blew through the arch and filled the small yard.

"Yes," Marie said. "I do gladly promise. I take you as my husband."

Aramis smiled and hesitated, then he took a step back. Now was Marie's turn to look down at the ground, up at the sky, into his eyes. It was her turn to find the right words, to summon them, to show them, to expose them to light. Her smile turned more serious and her chest rose and fell lightly in a broken forced rhythm. She raised her head high, took in a deep breath, and stepped a tiny step forward.

"Aramis, you say that words are like magic. I now believe that is so. They are how I lived for so long. They kept me alive. Thanks to their magic, I had a world full of friends and we all were connected. Not by touch, or by smell, but only through words. The words that I spoke. Or the words that I heard.

"Then one day you arrived like an unwanted gift. Unexpected, unsought for, you destroyed all my words. And interrupted my world. For you showed it was built on silent words for myself. They were thin and went nowhere. Echoes from past were hollow when spoken. Words of the future died before thought. Only words of the present survived for a moment, but even those emptied as silence returned.

"I discovered from you that words and dreams are the same. They need to be heard. They need to be shared. And they must live as one. For words must have dreams – dreams give our words life. And dreams must have words – words give our dreams breath. And when said, they expand, and sometimes explode, as feather balls will when tossed to a wind. They fly into the world and they make the world real. And they meet dreams of others and fly back again.

"Yet until you arrived, my dreams had no words and my words had no dreams. And I had no way to know that the world was right here. That here was the world. And it waited for me. It waited for words. It awaited my dreams. The dreams you delivered and then this world was my own.

"Then as soon as you showed me, you found a new world. The world of that night. The night of the field. The night that you left. And I'm happy for you. It is good what you found. Yet I wonder how many worlds there can be. And I know you still search for what I don't see. You float on the clouds in faraway skies. You drift in your mind and though you give me your heart, when I seek it for warmth, it is already gone.

"You know in all of my time, my time spent alone, I never asked clouds from there they had come. I watched them. We spoke. Yet I never did ask about their past home. And now that I know you, I know where they're from. You're from the same place. That place in the world from which miracles come. A world beyond words, but where all words are born.

"I also know where they're headed. For they could be going no place as wondrous as where my life will be floating in the future with you. This is why I beseech you. I want to go too. That is all that I want. To join you wherever. To be on that journey.

"Aramis, my love, I do want to be with you. But please understand, not with you as one. I lived that too long. Too long by myself. I'm most happy as two. A world made of us. The two of us always. Held together by dreams, side-by-side for all time.

"So, if you promise to have me, I will live in each moment, the rest of my life, forever and ever, as your loving wife."

Aramis could not stop himself. He did not try. Tears fell from both of his eyes as he stepped forward toward Marie and gave her a kiss on her speckled, soft cheeks. That she ended with a rhyme transformed for him suddenly all of her words to a single bright crystal of multifaceted thoughts. His right wing on her left, they stood there a moment. They saw in each other a life lived for this time, and as with all revelation, the depth of the joy came from the journey past traveled.

"Marie, I will have you, and I promise to take you wherever I go," Aramis said. Then he moved his face close, and in a serious tone, continued: "And now that we're married, I have my own favor to ask."

"Oh, really," she said smiling. "And what would that be?"

"Well," he said, "if you wouldn't mind." And Aramis stopped, and showed a sly smile, and to Marie, it appeared, the world was reborn, and all that it was became happy and new. "May I move into the coop?" Aramis asked. "Honestly," he chuckled, "the smokehouse is awful."

And Marie joined his laugh. Hers was a hard, quick laugh that mixed the warm sobs of joy with expressions of love. "Yes, please," she said. "That's a very good idea." And as her laughter subsided, her tears began flowing.

"And now," Marie said, as she swallowed back tears, "it's my turn for a favor."

"Yes," Aramis said, "whatever I can give."

"I want you to tell me know what you want, what you need, to be happy in this yard, to stay with me forever."

Aramis stared at Marie and he thought for a moment. Then his eyes opened wide, and he smiled a great smile. "You want me to tell you what I want, what I need? Then I will. But I warn you, if I tell you, Marie, you must make me a promise, you will never again ask, but merely continue what I tell you, for as long as we live."

"That sounds big," said Marie. "But yes, I will promise. I want to know what it is."

"I want you to dance," Aramis said. "For the rest of your life. To be happy and dance. Dance today, and tomorrow, and I want you to never, to never stop dancing."

Marie lifted her head. Then she remembered. She remembered that night. That night with the music. That night with her song. Yes, he must have been watching. Watching and smiling, the way she imagined. And so, Marie rose, peering down serenely before backing away. She shut her eyes for a moment and Marie started to hum. The song filled her again and she swayed left to right, her dress flowing smoothly. It played from her wings as it rode the soft breeze and lifted the air. "Alors là, moi, je pensé à nous" played the song. "Le p'tite Marie. Mon Dieu, comme elle etait jolie."

Marie started dancing. She danced and she danced, with a glow and a grace, for hours she danced, until the moon cleared the arch and stars escaped from their dreams. Marie felt herself floating with the past, present, and future, and for the first time in her life, she could welcome this partner, for though time might destroy all the beauty she knew, by dancing she would open what now always becomes.

Then, Marie stopped for a moment and she held out a wing. "Aramis," she said, "as my husband, please join me, and now show me the difference between music and tears."

Aramis stepped forward. And as he walked toward Marie, he saw over her shoulder, at the base of the branch he had climbed months before, an intricate letter carved into wood. Bordered by swirls, like the shells of a snail, a bright B was pulsing as if the beat of a heart. The tree looked to be smiling and for Aramis, just then, he felt no surprise. For it all seemed to be, as if all was just one. Then Marie touched his wings and together they moved, and they soared uninterrupted, their feet firm on the earth.

* * *

There is no telling what the farmer and his daughter, or anyone for that matter, would have thought of this sight, a hen covered in fabric and a large, black rooster dancing as one. But no one was home, and no one would see.

Both the farmer and Charisse awoke early and moved with acceptance into this warm summer day. They ate the breakfast that Charisse prepared and they agreed to go for a walk after driving to town. There was nothing they needed. The act of journey was enough.

Charisse was wearing her mother's white and blue dress. To the farmer, it fit as he hoped. For Charisse, it fit in a way she hoped she could fix. But for today, it would do. For her father. And her mother. Her vanity could wait and stay at home for the day, during her brief visit to town, during her walk through the fields. What she could not adjust was how she felt in the dress. After fastening the last button, she suddenly felt she was smothered in fabric, a fabric of worries, of burdens, of hopes, of sadness, of fears, of longing, and of new and lost love. Her mother's hands had touched it, had cut it, had smoothed it. Her thoughts designed the pattern and directed the stitches. She had chosen the buttons and fastened them on. It would never only be a simple dress for Charisse just as the flower of a linden tree never only was a flower wherever she moved. It was the scent of her home. It was the tree by the arch. It was the fragrance of youth.

After returning from town, the old farmer and Charisse knew it was time for a walk. Out through the arch, the two wordlessly turned left, stepping briskly along the driveway that wound down the hill toward the village. Neither discussed destination, though each one assumed the other had reason for choosing this path, past the berries maturing, past the sign to the farm, turning left at the bend that led down to church.

The two walked in silence. Charisse looked at her father repeatedly and slowly summoned the courage to ask the question she had repeated silently to herself the past several weeks.

"I received your letter," she said. "Thank you."

"I received yours, too," he said. "I was pleased to read it."

"It started me thinking about things," Charisse said.

"Did it?"

"Why did you write that my spirit is evasive?"

"I thought you should know," he said.

"Yes," she said. "But why?"

"In your letter to me, you sounded lost. It made me think of myself, and of some things I should tell you."

"It made you think of yourself?"

"Yes, in some ways it did," he said as he kicked at a stone. "But not anymore."

"I don't understand," she said.

"We all become lost at times in our life. As if our spirit has wandered. Or maybe it's hiding. If we're lucky, we find it. Nature has a way of bringing it home. But then again, sometimes we don't."

"Maybe," she said, "we're not meant to know."

"We always know," he said. "But we don't always discover."

Charisse said nothing. What did that mean? We know but can't find it. She was ready to speak but unable to choose among her dozens of thoughts, most of them questions, some of them simple, but none of them ready to volunteer next. Indeed, at one moment, overwhelming impressions of her father, this path, taken so many times, crowded out words. At the next moment, it was a torrent of doubts, of questions, of fears that flooded her mind. The two continued walking, down toward the creek, between the rows of thick trees.

Finally, one surfaced. "Do you think it's possible that we find it in dreams?" Charisse asked timidly, hoping this question might include all the others.

"It depends what you dream," the farmer said.

"I don't know," Charisse said. "I don't remember my dreams."

Again, in silence they walked on. For seven decades, he had walked this way. And though his steps remained steady, they were now weary and uninterested for all the years that had passed, it seemed little had changed. Charisse walked by his side, their steps out of pace but equal in length. Separate generations drawn into unison, sharing the same course of a narrow long road, walking as one within an envelope of time. In profile, the two had the appearance of belonging, the contours of each amplifying the other. Her aquiline nose a softer version of his. Both faces of tradition with broad and high brows and two matching chins, one gentle and both pointed. His face of hard years, course and well-weathered, thin with small cheekbones and tired hazel eyes. Her face made delicate by youth and smooth skin, her shining eyes nestled above a woman's gentle cheeks.

Immediately after Charisse spoke, the guilt of her answer lay heavily within her. Of course, that's not true. She remembered her dreams. No, not all. Does anyone do that? But enough to discuss, enough that it mattered. Charisse tried to forget, but the pathway refused and dared a confession.

"Sometimes, I dream. I dream of the farm," Charisse finally said. "I dream of mother and of being held and of people I know. And sometimes I dream of flying and of looking down and making everyone happy with only my smile."

"Those are good dreams," the farmer replied. He watched his feet step into the ruts of the rocky dirt road. "They are the types of dreams that make sense at your age."

"What do you dream?" Charisse asked quietly, afraid she had no right and then especially afraid of what he might say.

"Me?" he asked, and he gave a small laugh. "Well, I dream of the past," he said. "That's what old people do. I dream of lost friends, of the farm, and my children."

"Do you ever dream of mother?"

"Not as often as before."

"No?" she asked lightly.

"No, the older I get," he said, "the more she's with me when awake."

"You mean you dream of her during the day?"

"If it's really a dream. Or is it remembrance and thought? Or is she still here? The older you get, the less difference it makes."

"It makes a difference to me."

"Because you're still young."

"What did you dream when you were my age?"

"When I was younger? I dreamt many things you dream as a child. I dreamt about friends, about school, about leaving the farm. But those dreams have long past. They stopped years ago."

"Leaving?" Charisse asked. "Leaving to where?"

The farmer thought for a moment. He had not known where to go, he said. He had thought, of course, to move north to Paris. But Paris was not a city of mystery to be explored by those seeking to discover the world – not if first nurtured by this part of France. Paris was elite, filled with the wealthy's pretensions of France. It was not, for farmers, filled with the qualities immutably French, the alloy of cultures that had swept through these fields. No, it was true, he had nowhere to go. But he believed at the time he could not stay on the farm. Then, the second war came. He was barely a teenager and his brothers were gone. His father remained, but the work was too much. And within a few years, his father fell ill. That's what life brings. By then, he was grown and the only one left. He liked the radio and its music, and he found the newsreels exciting with black and white images of jungles and ships.

Charisse could not imagine her father as a boy, or as even a young man, or the age she was now. She wondered if he had ever been passionate and spry, jumping and laughing as some men will do when mortality remains beyond the horizon and the sun of their life has yet to crest in the sky. Charisse only saw her father as old, taciturn, deliberate in his shrouded set ways. He had always been father, but her mother had dominated the ways of the house. He was mostly a presence, at home, on the farm, a man, a figure, a stone, a dry twig.

Charisse listened intently. She knew some of these stories but not all that he told. Now, here she was, walking next to an old man, who still was her father, listening to his youth, his questions, his dreams. She was eavesdropping on thoughts. And she wondered if her brothers knew of these things. Perhaps they'd heard them before. Maybe she'd heard them, too, when she was too small. Perhaps everyone knew, yet no one had said. Or maybe nobody knew, as he talked to himself.

When they approached the stone church and walked left off the road, the two quickly grew silent. The farmer slowed his steps and let Charisse enter first onto a narrow, fresh path through a small field of tall grass. He walked a few steps behind, watching her back. The sway of her hair, the bounce of her dress, the way that her hands played out to the side as her thin arms swung awkwardly forward and back. He pictured her face, the face of a child, the face of a child who was now an adult.

Reaching the fence to the left of the church, the two stopped and Charisse reached out to open the gate. It was there, inside, the small cemetery sat, where his wife and her mother had been laid down to rest. After some minutes of silence, the farmer lifted his head. "Look at the stone," he said with soft surprise. "Isn't that today, the date on the stone?"

"Yes, papa," she said. "Today is that day."

'I like that coincidence. We're both here today."

"Yes," Charisse said. And she thought for a moment. It had been ten years already. There was no reason to tell him that it was why she had come.

"I'm glad you are here," he said quietly. "Do you enjoy being here?"

"I don't know," Charisse said. "When I'm not here, I miss it. Then when I'm here, I'm not sure."

"You don't like your old home."

"That's not it," Charisse said.

"It's too empty out here."

"No, not at all. In fact, whenever I'm here, I feel there are too many spirits. They follow me around."

"Yes, well," he said, "that happens in old houses, especially when the spirits are those of your family. Your imagination can make things real that are not."

"They feel real to me," she said.

"Then maybe they are. What you believe becomes real, and what you dream, you become."

"What do you mean?" Charisse asked.

"It's just an old saying," he said.

"I've never heard it before," she said, still looking at the gravestone. They stood again in long silence, natural in feel with the minutes uncounted.

"Do you think that old saying is right?" she asked.

"Probably not at your age," he said. "But the older you get, the truer words are."

"I enjoy old sayings," she said. "I write them down sometimes. So, I'll remember them. And the old stories as well. When you wrote to me about the storm and you mentioned the tree, I thought of that story also."

"Which story?" he asked.

"About the old tree in our yard. And when I visited it yesterday, I remembered it again. You said a strange thing happened. You'll laugh, but I thought for a moment that the tree was not damaged. It moved all the way round. I don't know. That couldn't be true. But something has changed. The yard feels so different. It makes the whole farm feel strange."

"Yes," he said. "Changes will do that."

"And then I thought back to that story. I'm not sure when I heard it. I must have been a child, but I've forgotten most of it now. There was some story about it."

"There used to be one," he said. "Many years ago. But no one tells it anymore."

"I think mother used to tell it," she said.

"Yes, your mother liked that story."

"Then you know it too?"

"It was one of her favorites."

"I never heard you mention it."

"She heard it from a neighbor," the old man said, "an old woman who once lived on the farm to the east."

"Wasn't the story about our tree and how it was planted at this church and . . . and then one day . . . ?" Charisse stopped. She suddenly felt like a child, recounting a child's story to her father out here. She was an adult now, too old for such tales. That was what she had wanted her father to know. Each time she visited, each time she wrote, even if she admitted some doubts, she wanted him to know they were doubts from a grown-up, not a silly, small child.

"It's a funny little story," she said. "I suppose, long ago, some thought it was true."

"I suppose people did," he said.

"That's a funny thought, though. A tree that moves."

"Yes, maybe it is."

Charisse was not sure what to say. She thought of the tree, the odd way it now stood.

"It's a funny thought, though. I wonder, if it could, what it would do if it moved."

"You've seen the old tree," her father said.

"Yes," Charisse said.

"Then you might have the answer."

"The answer to what?"

"To what it would do."

"Papa, I don't know what you mean. You think the tree moved?"

"I'm very certain I don't know. But I do know, sometimes, we don't know what we see."

"So, you believe it might be?"

"Charisse, I am sure I don't know. But the world is what it is. And we'll never understand about all that can be."

Charisse reflexively turned her head to the left to look at her father, then stopped.

"But," she began.

"There's as much real that is hidden than in the silence we hear. Don't you think that is true?" the old farmer asked. "Because we don't see, does that mean it is not?"

Charisse suddenly felt dizzy. What did that mean? This was her father. What has happened to him? First his letter, and now this. She was standing with a stranger. Has he gotten so old? Or was it she who'd grown up?

She would not ask again, and he said nothing more. The two stood without words, each watching the site where their woman was laid, each hearing emotions for the spirit they missed. Charisse stepped forward and picked up the branch of a linden tree that had been tossed by the wind, and she held it in her right hand as she walked back to her father.

The old farmer remained still with clasped hands hanging heavy. He shifted his weight and pushed the tips of his thumbs together, then slowly circled the right around the left thumb that stayed still. His old quiet eyes, with lids slightly lowered as if waiting to sleep, focused on nothing but stared straight ahead, somewhere between the second and third letters of his wife's silent name. His thoughts, as if they too had lids halfway lowered, floated elsewhere, also unfocussed, sometime and somewhere among his collection of years. His thumb circled once more. Then he unwound the fingers of his two beaten hands. His impassive left hand he slid into his pocket and, with his eyes still fixed forward, his right hand reached out, slowly out to the side, then forward it floated, unobserved as it went. There, without seeing, it found a small hand – the small hand of a woman who had more questions to ask. And with uncertain fingers, the hand gently went

beckoning and tightened its clasp, and the thumb began sliding over
the warm flesh of his child.

Charisse did not move. Her breath suddenly froze. She could feel
her heart pounding and it seemed everything stopped, except for the
quiver, which deepened to shiver, then ran with a shudder down the
length of her back, before moving deeper, then into her heart. Her
hand remained still – and then slowly her fingers curled gently around
his. And there the two stood, without saying a word. Neither thought
of the future. Neither thought of the place. Only the land was heard
speaking and everything in it, the stones underneath, the trees all
around, and the small clump of grass under the farmer's left foot.

That small clump of grass. Just a few inches round. If only they
knew. That small clump of grass, with blades wilted and brown, that
clung onto life and pushed roots through the earth. Into the same dark
brown earth, once turned and once blessed by a middle-aged priest,
where, held silent and deep by the centuries of all that can change,
buried far in the ground, was placed a white block of clean limestone,
polished and smooth, and carved with great care. That block that had
been once carefully laid in the yard by a tree and was left with a blessing
for those who would come. Still and unyielding, here it remained,
holding the message, the etched words on its face, a simple "Gari Tés
Blaessure," which the priest had once written, not with church words,
but of the land and its people. "Heal thy wounds," he'd repeated, in
self-admonition, as he then slowly rose, with his knife in firm hand,
and inscribed the three letters, three initials of words that carried this
message, under the sapling's soft branches to marry these two, the tree
and the plaque, the wood and the stone, his beloved and he, her grave
and this land, in the place they had shared. And there they were left,
the stone and the tree, bound together by message, his final prayer and
his gift, to guide his small village and those who would live, and those
who died in its care.

At that very same moment, yes, at that very same time, with the
plaque in the ground and the old farmer and Charisse united by held
hands, up to their right, beyond a small stream, through a thick grove
of trees, on top of a hill, in a quiet small yard between stone house

and a coop, two small chickens were dancing, one covered in cloth and both of them smiling. To their right was a shed, to their front was a barn. A sullen cat wandered and blue butterflies flitted. A black dog was sleeping and green grasshoppers jumped. In the yard's quiet center was an old silent tree with skin turned rock hard and three clumsy bare branches. No, the tree did not move. There was no reason for that. Instead, up on one branch, the one that faced north, inside a deep crevice between two hardened crests, a small breach was born, imperceptible to all, except to those who might witness a slow-pooling tear ooze languidly down. It was there, deep within, that this tale finds conclusion – not yet a true end. The world had not stopped. But it was there, yes, right there, that a new dream appeared of a nascent green bud, resurrected again, that broke through the surface and saw the hello of a brightly smiling, blue sky.

Finis

Lightning Source UK Ltd.
Milton Keynes UK
UKHW05n0011251018
331074UK00005BB/221/P